REFLECTIONAL LEADERSHIP:
A Leadership Principle Found in Every Chapter of The New Testament

By Allan Thompson, Ph.D.

Copyright © 2023 – Allan Thompson.

All rights reserved. This book or any portion thereof may not be reproduced or used in any manner whatsoever without the express written permission of the publisher except for the use of brief quotations in a book review.

ISBN: 978-1-960116-44-4

Scripture quotations taken from the (NASB®) New American Standard Bible®, Copyright © 1960, 1971, 1977, 1995, 2020 by The Lockman Foundation. Used by permission. All rights reserved. www.lockman.org.

Scriptures marked ESV are taken from THE HOLY BIBLE, ENGLISH STANDARD VERSION (ESV): Scriptures taken from THE HOLY BIBLE, ENGLISH STANDARD VERSION ® Copyright© 2001 by Crossway, a publishing ministry of Good News Publishers. Used by permission.

Scripture quotations marked CSB have been taken from the Christian Standard Bible®, Copyright © 2017 by Holman Bible Publishers. Used by permission. Christian Standard Bible® and CSB® are federally registered trademarks of Holman Bible Publishers.

INTRODUCTION AND EXPLANATION

How to Use this Book: This book is a collection of essayistic writings on leadership principles found in every chapter of the New Testament. It is drawn from teachings, readings, meditations, training, experiences, sermons, and lessons gleaned from over fifty years of ministry and leadership. It contains mini-glimpses into the servant leadership heart of God from His Word. I have tried to write for people of all faiths and no faith, to show life and leadership principles from a day-to-day perspective. I believe anyone who has led, aspires to lead, or just needs some help in leading their own lives to glorify God, will benefit from these pages. The Bible has been my guide, my comfort, and my foundation for the last five+ decades; I commend it to you as a prime source for your leadership development. While the subject matter of each chapter will have unapologetically Christian overtones or relate to a biblical topic, I attempted to show its worth to leaders from all avenues of life. It would be profitable for the individual and for a church or company staff to pursue and discuss the chapter together.

Reflectional leadership is not a complicated theory or brand of leadership. It is simply an approach to leadership born of the spiritual discipline of reflection, a lost art in the hypersonic pace of change currently in charge of our daily lives. Decision-making should not be informed solely by charts and reams of data, nor are one's "gut instincts" an infallible source. Purposeful, habitual reflection involves rumination; evaluation; consideration of multiple perspectives; letting ideas mature and ferment; association of past, present, and future; learning to find the best among the good; pondering possible outcomes; and decisions born of conviction and deliberation rather than deference to the last voice heard, the last article read, or the last budget report from accounting.

Format: The format for each of the 260 chapters will be 1-2 pages of material related to a specific Bible chapter, an application entitled *Lines on Leadership*, and a few blank lines designed for your reflections or intentions. Due to the book's length, I quote sparingly from the Word but constantly refer to it. <u>The greatest benefit will come if this book is accompanied by an open New Testament</u>. A few minutes taken to read the respective chapter of God's Word <u>before</u> you read its companion entry in this book is strongly advised. What He has to say is infinitely more important than anything I can say. It is why our Lord gave us two ears and one mouth; we should use them in that same ratio. Most Bible quotations are from the New American Standard Bible (NASB), English Standard Version (ESV), or Christian Standard Bible (CSB) unless noted.

This book will not have a grand scheme or diagram designed to become a marketable franchise. Leadership is best learned in the context of life lessons that defy classification. Some insights come from the classroom; most arrive unannounced as indelible moments with the Master in the course of everyday living. I pray a biblical theology of leadership organically comes together through your reading of the separate entries. The book does not pretend to be exhaustive or systematic in scope. It is a quasi-devotional approach, letting a portion of each NT chapter speak to us, through a lens of leadership. It is not a commentary and does not claim to be comprehensive. There will usually be one main leadership idea emphasized per chapter. To look, for example, at the Sermon on the Mount in Matt. 5, 6, 7 and mention but one principle per chapter is laughable. Consider this an invitation to add to this work. If it finds resonance in your life, I invite feedback for future

THE AUTHOR

I wrote this book in my latter sixties after a career that spanned five decades and several continents. I have three degrees that revolve around ministry (bachelor's in music ed., master's in religious ed., and a Ph.D. in Leadership Studies). The ministry venues have ranged from local church to college campus to different countries and cultures. I logged many of those life experiences in 80+ journal volumes totaling 20,000+ pages. This book comes largely from those journal entries, sermons, teachings, course material from leadership classes I have taught at the bachelor's and master's level at college and seminary, and personal reflection. My driving life purpose has been to prepare the next generation of servant leaders for the Kingdom of God.

The richest blessing of my life has been my partner in it for forty-eight years and counting; we have a 'bi-cultural' marriage (I grew up in the swamps of SW Louisiana and she is a Texas Panhandle gal). We have two grown sons. At the time of writing, we lived in the heart of Appalachia in southern WV; previously, we lived in TX and, before that, overseas in Europe on career assignment with our denomination's International Mission Board. I have led 80+ mission trips on four continents and many countries. I count it a joy and privilege to have been a Paul to hundreds of Timothy's, both male and female, as discipleship is teaching others to teach others to teach others. Most of my time in the last ten years has been spent listening to church and business leaders and helping inform their decisions. I try to be a practitioner of servant, adaptive, and transformational leadership.

My hobbies in such a beautiful environment as the Mountain State gravitate toward hiking, canoeing, fishing, golfing, and playing whatever musical instrument is nearby, which most days is the soprano recorder that stays with my editions, and especially your additional insights from the chapters. My email for this dialogue is: reflectionalleadershipat@gmail.com.

Cross references according to principles taught will be offered in this manner (i.e., see Titus 3 entry). If verses are referenced without a chapter (i.e., vs. 8-10), that means they are from the chapter currently being addressed. I tried as much as possible to practice good hermeneutics, a theologian's word for Biblical interpretation. One should extract the principle (*exegesis*) from the chapter instead of reading into the chapter a personal thought or principle (ei*segesis*). With 260 chapters, I am sure I bent that guideline at times.

There will be obvious truths and important passages I did not address; that was done not out of ignorance or avoidance but simply for the sake of the book's length and to stay true to describing just one principle per chapter. It will lend itself to a charge of what is politely called "cherry picking," being selective about which verses/principles to include. I ask for patience and mercy on that count. You can start wherever you wish and use it however you like, a devotional supplement, a reference, or a companion to Bible study. Understand I did not strive to come up with 260 unique lessons; considering the subject matter of the NT there was bound to be repeated applications among the chapters. I have tried to cross-reference common themes to a degree. Again, I invite the reader who finds interest in the subject of reflectional leadership to write me about your additional insights and discoveries within the pages of God's Word. *Soli Deo Gloria*.

journal and Bible in my backpack---or a guitar. The murky lines of demarcation between hobby and addiction could easily be the subject for a future book, one I am not qualified to write since I have trouble distinguishing the two. The pieces of evidence are strewn across my man cave and are named Martin, Aleyas, Yamaha, Sigma, and Gruene, with several handmade by luthiers in Peru, TX, and WV. When my wife repeatedly asks, "How many guitars is enough?" my reply is usually, "just one more."

    I want two things on my tombstone: he shared the joy of life in Christ Jesus, and every point on this earth is equidistant from the heart of God.

DEDICATION

I dedicate this book to my dear wife, Jana, who has encouraged me over the decades to pursue God's call on my life and to prepare the next generation of servant leaders for His Kingdom, and to those who allowed me to invest in their lives so we may all better serve Christ and our fellow man (Mt. 22.37-40).

GLOSSARY OF TERMS AND ABBREVIATIONS

CSB---Christian Study Bible
ESV---English Standard Version
ISV---International Standard Version
KJV---King James Version
LEB---Lexham English Bible
LUT---Luther Bibel
MSG---The Message
NASB---New American Standard Bible (multiple editions)
NEB---New English Bible
NET---New English Translation
NIV---New International Version
Vs. or vs.---verses
v.----verse

Table of Contents

INTRODUCTION AND EXPLANATION i
THE AUTHOR iv
DEDICATION vi
GLOSSARY OF TERMS AND ABBREVIATIONS vii
MATTHEW'S GOSPEL 1
MARK'S GOSPEL 59
LUKE'S GOSPEL 88
JOHN'S GOSPEL 136
BOOK OF ACTS 180
LETTER TO THE ROMANS 245
1ST LETTER TO THE CORINTHIANS 275
2ND LETTER TO THE CORINTHIANS 306
LETTER TO THE GALATIANS 333
LETTER TO THE EPHESIANS 346
LETTER TO THE PHILIPPIANS 358
LETTER TO THE COLOSSIANS 367
1ST LETTER TO THE THESSALONIANS 377
2ND LETTER TO THE THESSALONIANS 388
1ST LETTER TO TIMOTHY 394
2ND LETTER TO TIMOTHY 409
LETTER TO TITUS 422
LETTER TO PHILEMON 429

LETTER TO THE HEBREWS	433
LETTER FROM JAMES	457
1ST LETTER FROM PETER	466
2ND LETTER FROM PETER	476
1ST LETTER FROM JOHN	483
JOHN'S 2ND LETTER	494
JOHN'S 3RD LETTER	496
LETTER FROM JUDE	499
JOHN'S REVELATION	501
FINAL THOUGHTS	540
FOOTNOTES	541
BIBLIOGRAPHY	554

MATTHEW'S GOSPEL

Intro: Matthew's gospel is the first of four different accounts of the life and teachings of Jesus. The word 'gospel' means there is good news, that God offers us eternal life because of the death, burial, and resurrection of His Son, Jesus Christ. Each gospel will tell that story from a different perspective.

Matthew's audience was decidedly Jewish. He used a great deal of Old Testament (OT) references in his writings. His is one of two gospels written by members of Jesus' companions (called apostles) during His public ministry (the other is John).

++

Matthew 1— Highlights: Genealogy of Jesus, Conception, Birth, and Naming of Jesus

The first chapter of the New Testament begins with the lineage of Jesus, the famous "begats" which trace the birth-line from Abraham to Joseph, Jesus' earthly "foster" father. Abraham is considered the *Urvater* of the Jews (Matthew's primary audience). In v.21, an angel announces to Joseph, in a dream, that his son would bear a specific name, <u>Jesus</u>, and that it would mean "He who will save His people from their sins." Assigning a name to individuals is a universal human experience; everyone born eventually acquires one. It can denote family or clan (My last name is Thompson), or that one has an additional connection to a prior generation (my first name is Allan, as it was for my father and grandfather).

The names and titles we assign to people can be restrictive or liberating, a prophecy or a curse. Growing into the fullness of a name or trying to live up to it (how many fathers have admonished their children to 'make me proud and honor our family's name'?) can be a satisfying accomplishment or terrifying burden. In the 1999 US film *Matrix,* the protagonist becomes aware of what the crew of his ship calls him: the One. In a discourse with a crew member, the question arises, 'how do you live with that "mind job?"' The film centers around the development of this character from a minor employee in a firm (inside the Matrix) to someone expected to save the 'real' world outside the Matrix. He acquires a new name, he was no longer Mr. Anderson, but Neo. Jesus is told from birth on His name denotes He is God, come to live among men (see John 1.14) and to be their deliverer. He spends most of His public ministry describing His true identity (see Gospel of John), His Kingdom (Matthew 5-7), and what He is NOT (a political, military, or social Messiah). In v. 23, the quote from Isaiah identifies Him as *Immanuel*, God with us. So, in this first chapter, He is introduced as a son of man (the lineage) and the *Son of God* (vs.18, 21); what an amazing assignment of name and mission. 'Jesus' was a common name in His day; He could have remained anonymous as one of countless Jesus/Joshua's, but He chose to live up to and fulfill His name and His ascribed titles (v. 1, Messiah).

When people reach a new station in life, they often change their names to either signal a new chapter or to provide closure to a previous life segment. Popes take on new names once installed; freshmen at college often shed a high school identity or nickname by referring to themselves with another name. In the OT, Abram becomes Abraham as he enters a covenant relationship with God (Genesis 17), and Jacob becomes Israel after wrestling with Him (Genesis 32). Post resurrection we see Jesus acquiring additional titles such as Lord of Lords (1 Tim. 6.15), Great Shepherd (Heb. 13.20), and Alpha and Omega (Rev. 1.8).

In our adult life, we have numerous opportunities as leaders/parents/educators/mentors to empower or enervate those whom we lead simply by the names we use to identify them. Jesus called one of His lead disciples Peter (a rock) at a time he was anything but a firm foundation (see Matthew 16 entry). Philemon has a servant named Onesimus (useful), who proves to be in Paul's letter to Philemon anything but, yet Paul pleads for the opportunity to grow into that name. (see Philemon and Acts 13 entries)

Lines on Leadership
Nicknames can denote endearment (the German word *Schätzen*, meaning little treasure), or a significant event (Champ), a physical trait (Ol' Blue Eyes), or a characteristic (Shifty, Squeaky). What are the motives and reasons behind the names you call your associates/family/friends? By what name are you known by your associates?

_____
_____

++

Matthew 2---Highlights: The Magi visit Herod, then Jesus; infant slaughter; Jesus' family in Egypt

Good and bad leadership examples abound in the verses of this nativity narrative. The magi[1] are travelers in a foreign land, and by their inquiries in Jerusalem about a coming Christ, word gets to the political and religious leaders that something is afoot (vs. 1-7). Herod assembles his research assistants to determine if these rumors have any basis. When he learns Bethlehem (v. 6) is the birthplace of a future ruler, which is almost a stone's throw from his throne, his eyes likely widen, and his skin pales. The Micah 5.2 passage does not specify the when. However, strangers asking questions like this put Herod on red alert; what if this is the time, right now, during my reign?

Written accounts last (compared to other media) for which we are grateful, but mostly lack inflection, which we must speculate or infer. Herod, as a master politician, feigns solidarity with the wise men's desires, and expresses a mutual desire to know the whereabouts of this future Messiah, so Herod may also worship him (v.8). Locating a future Messiah holds promise for one group, peril for the other. Herod is following an ancient tradition of eliminating potential rivals to one's power but cannot be excused or exonerated for his broad stroke slaughter of infants (vs. 16-18).

Stars and dreams play an outsized role in the ensuing events. The magi follow a star (v. 2, 9, & 10) from a faraway land to one particular grotto among the hundreds that dot the hillsides of Bethlehem that protected shepherds and their flocks every night. In four dreams, 1) the magi are warned not to share this information with Herod (v. 12); 2) Joseph is warned to leave for Egypt to avoid the coming infanticide (v.13); 3) Joseph is informed of Herod's death and that he is free to bring his family back to more familiar lands (v.19); and 4) because of a subsequent dream (v. 22) he shows prudence in avoiding Herod's successor, Archelaus, by settling in Nazareth instead of anywhere near Jerusalem. Luke 2 describes Nazareth as Joseph and Mary's village before Jesus was born in Bethlehem; perhaps with all the extraordinary revelations, angelic pronouncements, and travels, Joseph had become uncertain where they should call home and raise their unique son.

Three avenues to gain knowledge are utilized in this chapter:

1. <u>Inquiry</u>: Well-placed questions will garner attention and gain you both an audience and notoriety

2. <u>Investigation</u>: when possible, always use prime sources (see Luke 1 entry). Researching the OT prophets pinpointed the location of the coming Messiah's birthplace.

3. <u>Intuition</u>: in Western society, logical, reasoned thinking is often prized above dreams and promptings from a spiritual source such as angels (this chapter) or the Holy Spirit (Acts references). While it can be argued that the arrival of Messiah was a special circumstance warranting dreams and heavenly beings as messengers, dreams and Spirit promptings continue to play an important role in millions of lives today (as can be seen by multiple accounts of Jesus revealing Himself in countless Muslims' dreams, especially during the month of Ramadan[2]).

<u>Lines on Leadership</u>
The proper balance of these three (inquiry, investigation, intuition) can facilitate good decision-making. What is your "go-to" or default of these three? Are you open to including the other two as counters to and influencers of your decision-making process?

_____

_____
++

Matthew 3---Highlights: preaching of John the Baptist; baptism of Jesus

John is one of the more fascinating characters in the NT. Born in *Ein Karem* (a lovely hillside village a short distance from Jerusalem), John has a clear understanding of his place in the Kingdom of God. He is related to Jesus (Luke 1), and even before the birth of John and Jesus, John's mother, Elizabeth, knew Mary's son would far exceed her own (Luke 1.42-43). The description of John's appearance (eating off the land and wearing garments made of camel hair, v.4) suggests to the modern eye and ear someone creating his own brand and who would have been a countercultural hit on social media. He began preaching in the Judean wilderness, a desolate area between Jerusalem and where the Jordan River empties into the Dead Sea. For people to make the long journey from the Holy City to the desert near the lowest open point on the globe (the Dead Sea) indicates John's preaching was striking a deep chord resonating far beyond the region. It was a region near the Essene community of Qumran, which many scholars feel was a place of study for John prior to his public ministry.

He minces no words and looks the religious leaders of the day square in the eyes as he excoriates them for their curiosity masquerading as contrition (vs. 7-12). His sermons emphasize repentance and shine the spotlight on the Kingdom and the coming King, not on himself (vs. 2-3). When Jesus comes to him for baptism (to announce the beginning of His public ministry) John knows he is standing in the presence of One who will surpass him in terms of message and stature (v. 14).

The faith of John wavers and wobbles at times (Luke 7.19ff) but never becomes bitter or envious. He is the forerunner prophesied by Isaiah (v.3, "the voice crying in the wilderness"), and he knows he is the setup man, not the main act. He sets the stage for the grand entrance of the main player. Some people are content to play this role temporarily as a training ground for when they will one day ascend to the top position of their organization, to use the subordinate role as a learning period or springboard to greater things. This is not the case for John. There will be one Messiah, one King in this Kingdom about which he preaches, there is not room for two (John 3.26ff).

Lines on Leadership

John the Baptist's loyalty and willingness to fulfill this "lesser" role and stay in Jesus' shadow are lauded by Christ when He calls John the greatest born among men (Mt. 11.11). Textbooks and parades highlight generals but few colonels, majors, captains, or lieutenants. Can you find joy in the accomplishments of others who may bask in more of the spotlight than you? One of the toughest assignments in an organization is when someone is hired for you to train with the knowledge that new hire will one day (sooner than desired) replace you or leapfrog you within the organizational leadership structure. If this ever happens to you, how will you handle it?

_____

_____

+++

Matthew 4---Highlights: Temptations of Jesus, onset of His public ministry, calling of the first disciples.

To have and articulate a grand vision for one's ministry/organization can be compelling, intimidating, or a mixture of both. Many leadership books talk about possessing a great vision that can be recounted over and over with joy and passion in the form of a strong narrative that others pick up quickly, something that resonates with their desires. Fresh from His temptation in the desert (vs. 1-11) Jesus selects Capernaum, a town on the north shore of the Sea of Galilee, as His public ministry's headquarters. The first two pronouncements from the Nazarene are:

1) "Repent, for the kingdom of heaven is at hand" (v.17), and

2) "Follow Me, and I will make you fishers of men." (v. 19)

The term "kingdom of heaven" is often found in the book of Matthew (30+ times) and is a connection to the prophet Daniel who mentions it most in the OT. The phrase 'repent, for the kingdom of God is at hand' hearkens back to John the Baptist's sermons noted in the previous chapter (Mt. 3.2). The Baptizer has just been taken into custody (v. 12), and now it seems like Jesus, known to be John's cousin, is taking up John's message. John had disciples just like any other itinerant rabbi, and Jesus begins to gather His own disciples unto Himself.

The first followers were fishermen, so Jesus relates His appeal to their profession (become fishers for Me) and, with a turn of a phrase, intrigues them to quit fishing as a profession and make it a higher calling (become fishers of men). The appeal is at once familiar and new. This is likely not the first time they have heard Jesus teach (see Luke 5, John 1.35-42), but it is a step beyond just listening to and liking His teachings. Itinerant rabbis came through villages often and taught for considerable periods of time; it was customary to sit at their feet and learn from them, perhaps to walk alongside them for a few days at a time. It was the ancient version of a short retreat or workshop where someone with new ideas, a new approach, or a new outlook came through town; some spent casual time with them, some listened intently, and some became devotees, but they eventually returned to their livelihoods.

If Jesus had revealed the true and full gospel of His new Kingdom all at once, most would not have comprehended it. Even if they had and had realized the extent and scope of His call on their life, most would have high-tailed it, most would have declared Him a power-hungry maniac or a deluded fool. He took their curiosity and waited three years to mold it into commitment. The ability to clearly present a vision without overwhelming the group is a precious skill. It will be on full display in the next three chapters as the Sermon on the Mount unfolds.

Lines on Leadership
What we do not say is usually as or more important than what we do say. Room for imagination and interpretation should be included in one's appeal to cleave to a vision. What phrases crop up repeatedly in your day-to-day conversations that convey both the content of a vision and your appeal to commit to it?
_____
_____
++

Matthew 5---Highlights: Beatitudes; first chapter of Sermon on the Mount

Chapters 5-7 (Sermon on the Mount) constitute arguably the greatest sermon in history. Whether it was an actual oration in one sitting (approx. 18 min. read aloud) or a compilation of Jesus' teachings, it is His magnum opus of instruction regardless of the source, situation, or composition. To select one leadership principle from each chapter is difficult; I suggest you study Matt. 5-7 thoroughly on your own to see how rich and transforming they are on a day-to-day basis as well as an overall life direction. The first twelve verses are often called the Beatitudes. Some people recall them as a grandmother's framed cross-stitching, quaint proverbial sayings on the wall. They are the distilled essence of the Christian life, and every teaching and action of Jesus can be traced back to them almost as scientists aim to trace all origins of matter back to their beloved Big Bang theory. This is not about reducing your life's philosophy down to bumper sticker size or slogan-steering your life. They serve not only as a preamble; rather they are like an operatic overture, containing all the themes to follow in the main body of the work, or an abstract at the beginning of a dissertation that describes the research question, the methods, and the conclusion.

Every leader should be able to articulate his/her life's direction, goals, rationale, and purpose in a concise set of statements to share at any time. They should refer to it daily to remain on point/on mission/on target. It should be prominently displayed; pervasively well known among your followers, church members, or employees; and the guiding point of reference for your personal inner life. I often preach and teach Matt. 5.1-12 because it is foundational and a brilliant beginning to this extraordinary, unparalleled sermon.

Jesus introduces and describes life in His new Kingdom, and from the first "blessed are" it is clear it will look nothing like the present world order (Roman), and it will also turn society on its head. Success and greatness are not achieved here by acquiring and exercising power, wealth, or authority, but by understanding and living the sequence outlined here. In simplified and cursory fashion, here is the synopsis of the synopsis:

I have nothing to claim as worthy ("poor in spirit," v. 3) and never will. This leads me to mourn my dilemma ("mourn", v. 4). Since I will never achieve it on my own, I humbly bow my knee and spirit to the King ("meek or gentle," v. 5, a motion difficult for those accustomed to the American mantra of 'I can achieve whatever I can dream up, and on my own efforts, and we have never had a king'). When I see what He offers, I hunger and thirst after it ("righteousness," v. 6) and in His grace and mercy He grants it to me (evangelicals would term this the point of salvation). After I receive His mercy, I want others to receive it also. Instead of preaching it to them, I show mercy in my daily walk as He showed mercy in His daily walk ("merciful," v. 7). The more I walk, act, and think as He does, the process of sanctification occurs and the clearer I see God for Who He is and what He's doing ("pure in heart," v. 8). I want others to experience this true inner peace of the indwelling rule of Christ's Spirit, and I try to bring it into their lives ("peacemakers," v. 9). When I do the inevitable happens when a person tells another person their life will have to take a different path than they're currently on ("persecuted," v. 10). To make sure they understand this will surely happen, He mentions it a second time more forcefully (v. 11). If this is a new kingdom, it will have a new King, and asking others to renounce their citizenship in the world and bow their hearts and minds to a new King in Christ Jesus will result in persecution. He mentions this a third time in v. 12. It will place you in a long line of those who were so persecuted before you.

    The gospel as outlined in the Beatitudes is also a gauntlet, a threshold to step over into a new dimension, a new reality. It is by definition subversive as it upends the world's power and societal structure with ramifications for government, economies, and culture. Bend the spirit, follow a Person willing to sacrifice His life for mankind, draw my life from His, learn to walk as He does, and take the consequences.

    He segues into the rest of the Sermon on the Mount by saying He has not come to abolish the Law but to supersede it by fulfilling it (v.17). Starting in v. 21 and repeating it often as a literary device Jesus says, "You have heard it said . . . but I say unto you . . ." and then expounds further on how this new Kingdom will be unveiled, establishing a new order.

Lines on Leadership
Whether it is a new company policy, a new vision, or a new gospel, the word new implies it will replace or supplant

something "old." Change will bring resistance and that is sometimes costly both to the group and to the individuals who make it up, be it a local congregation or a multinational corporation. Do you have a defining set of statements that tell everyone including yourself where you (singular and plural) are headed, and are you prepared to pay the price for implementing it?

_____

_____

++

Matthew 6---Highlights: alms, fasting, and prayer; priorities; the Model Prayer

Verse 33 is the fulcrum for this chapter: "seek first His kingdom and His righteousness, and all these things will be added to you." It is one of the rare ultimate verses in the NT where if one thing is done everything else falls into place (see Matt. 22.37-40, Philippians 3.13). The other admonitions in the chapter are not extracurricular or optional; they all flow from the one overarching statement of seeking first the Kingdom. Alms giving, fasting, and prayer are not introduced with "if" you do them, but "when" you do them (vs. 2, 5, 16), indicating they are non-negotiable. They are not given as sacraments, something necessary for salvation, but as vehicles for becoming "pure in heart" and thereby seeing God more clearly (Mt. 5.8). In today's world of euphemistic expressions we would talk about donating to those in need, discipline to forego pleasures or gratification, and my spirit communicating with the Spirit of God. Space dictates a look at one of the three signs (giving, fasting, or prayer) of a changed life, all of which are to be practiced in secret and not for show among men (vs. 4, 6, 8).

Perhaps some of the most famous verses in the entire NT form what has often been called the Lord's Prayer, vs. 9-13. No speech or instruction session covers everything there is to learn about a given subject, and the Model Prayer is no different concerning prayer: it does not touch on intercession, global outreach, and is short on specifics. But it is a peerless example of a prayer that can be often repeated, meditated on, and used as a diagnostic to show what is out of balance about my relationship with God and man.

It begins with worship, recognizing the person of God, the power of God, and the position of God (v.9); and it ends with worship, acknowledging the same (v. 13b does not appear in most early manuscripts but we will include it as a traditional ending to the Model Prayer as found in many older translations). The requests of vs. 11-13 (sustenance, forgiveness, protection from temptation) are preceded by a subjugation of my will to the Father's will (v. 10). This is not about just thinking the thoughts of God (meditating on His Word, for instance) but fulfilling the express will of God. Too often we concentrate on understanding a concept instead of obeying its obvious command.

Prayer is not about bending God's ear and will to ours but aligning our will with His. He gave us two ears and one mouth, and we should use them in that ratio. All other admonitions in the chapter (i.e., where the treasure is, there is where your heart is, v. 21; serve one master or the other, but not both, v. 24) are outgrowths of this alignment.

<u>Lines on Leadership</u>
Concepts can be discussed till the sun goes down and the discussion picked up where it left off as the sun rises on the next day. <u>Commitment is an outward manifestation of trust</u>. What

person or set of principles do you trust so much you are willing to commit to following him/it?

_____

_____

+++

Matthew 7---Highlights: judging others, the Golden Rule, true fruit, two foundations

    I have been privileged to visit some of the great world class art galleries or museums (Art Institute of Chicago, the Louvre, the National Gallery in Washington, DC, the Smithsonian, the British Museum). The first strong emotional response a casual stroll through one of them usually produces is being overwhelmed. The color, the information, the displays, and the wonderment wash over the senses. By the time one reaches the third chapter of the Sermon on the Mount (Matt. 5-7), the reader is almost numb from so many deep truths and conditions of the new Kingdom life. To make it easier, here are a few to ponder in chapter 7:

    vs. 1-5. Judgment begins with one's own motives and actions.

    v. 6. Don't waste precious truth or time on those who cannot appreciate its worth.

    vs. 7-11. Most translations do not convey the continuing action of the verbs here, to keep asking, seeking, knocking; we mistakenly put the attention on our imploring of God when the real emphasis is on how merciful and loving He is to us.

    v. 12. Matthew's version of the Golden Rule is to treat others as I would have them treat me, and to take the first step to do so, not waiting on the other person to signal their intent.

    vs. 13-14. If the path to salvation/success was easy, everyone would be able to access it. This has little to do with ability or persistence and everything to do with recognition of the path Jesus outlined in Mt. 5-7 as the true one.

vs. 15-23. It's not what is on the bottle label; it is what's on the inside, the nature of the contents that matters.

vs. 24-27. When adversity strikes (and it surely will), it will expose the surety or folly of the foundation one has built for his life/organization.

v.28-29. Jesus did not speak from trends, charts, and citations of others' ideas, but from a direct authority. The new King had just finished outlining what life in His Kingdom looks like.

Lines on Leadership
Which of these leadership directives is the easiest for you to accept? Which is the hardest?

_____
_____
++

Matthew 8---Highlights: various healings, invitation to follow Him, calming of the stormy sea

One of the most tried and true ways to learn how to lead is to follow and learn the art of "followship" (see Mt. 11 and 1 John 3 entries). This passage involves two basic aspects of followship: 1) recognition of authority and 2) willingness to go in the same direction as the leader.

1) Recognition of authority: Every person is my superior in at least one way (see Titus 3 entry). That would mean no matter what my position is in life or in an organization, I can always learn from and follow another person. The centurion assigned to Jesus' adopted ministry center (Capernaum, vs. 5-13), had no doubt observed Jesus' comings and goings and had heard Him teach on several occasions. As one accustomed to

giving orders and having them obeyed, he recognized that same authority in Jesus' actions and teachings. It is a mistake for those accustomed to leading to forget they should retain a sense of "followship." This pagan centurion recognized in Jesus not only His ability to heal but His supreme authority and showed humility towards it (v.8, "I am not worthy for You to come under my roof, but just say the word, and my servant will be healed"). When someone comes in my presence who has authority in an area of my need, I need to be humbled and follow his lead, regardless of my degrees, accomplishments, or positions. The key is why he wields his authority; is it for my good and the good of society? The trustworthiness of a leader has as much to do with his moral character as well as his power over anything as shown in the next aspect of followship.

2) <u>Willingness to go in the same direction as the leader</u>: Many who wanted to follow Jesus did so out of curiosity about or fascination with His teachings and His miracles, and as a passing interest, not a life-long commitment. In vs. 18-22 Jesus' replies to two people seem harsh and uncompassionate. To one He says I'm on the move, and many times it is without comfort or honor; can you handle that? To the other He says there is no priority higher than following Him, will you forego any and all things to do that, including things dear to you (such as bury your own father, vs. 21-22).

There is a sense of trajectory in both statements. I often end my emails or letters to former students with 'ever onward, ever upward,' a version of tried and true encouragements (i.e., *ad astra*, to the stars; *excelsior*, ever higher). James Lovell in his poem "The Present Crisis" uses similar language ("they must upward still, and onward, who would keep abreast of Truth[1]"). Lovell may have meant truth was ever evolving or developing; Jesus is the Truth, and rather than evolving or developing He is constantly on the move; Leonard Sweet describes it this way in *Rings of Fire*: "Jesus taught us to live *out* of the past, to live *in* the present (not in the past), and to live *into* the future[2]." Ever onward, ever upward.

Lines on Leadership

If you are in a leadership position, who has entered your life as authoritative or knowledgeable in an area where you have a need? Did you not only acknowledge it but follow him/her in this instance? What personal priorities are you willing to release in order to follow this person more closely or for longer periods of time? Have you determined the person has a moral anchor, and if so, what is it? How do you determine if the leader is living out of the past, in the present, and into the future?

_____

_____

++

Matthew 9---Highlights: a paralytic's cure, Matthew's call to follow Jesus, a miraculous healing

This passage is best known for Matthews' call to follow Christ and the old/new wineskins verses (see Mk. 2 entry's version of those stories). Verses 18-32 are accounts of various healings by Jesus. But the focus for today will be vs. 35-38, a poignant portrait of Jesus either surveying or reminiscing about all the villages where He has healed. I imagine Him standing at some vantage point like the corner of the Temple or the Mount of Olives, viewing the entirety of old Jerusalem and the surrounding villages at its feet. "He felt compassion for them, because they were distressed and downcast like sheep without a shepherd" (v. 36).

During our mission work in then West Germany, we lived in Trier near its western border with France. The regional grouping of German Baptist churches desired to conduct what were called *Evangelizationen* (evangelistic efforts over a period of ten days). Three locales were selected where our church in Trier already had some level of outreach: Bitburg, Prüm, and Gerolstein. Bitburg already had a fledgling congregation with potential to become its own self-sufficient church. Prüm and Gerolstein were smaller cities/villages where a local Bible Study met regularly; we desired something more permanent. An English-speaking congregation (Trinity Baptist Church) in the village of Metterich outside of Bitburg related mainly to the then active USAF base nearby. The large group of folks who came to assist with the Evangelizationen camped on the Trinity grounds and used their church facilities for showering, feeding, and meeting. They fanned out to the three localities to conduct tent revivals, sing, preach, and do dramas on street corners, canvas neighborhoods, and to share their faith with anyone who would listen. It was one of the most physically demanding ten days of my life; I remember well sleeping 17 hours straight when I returned home to Trier.

Much preplanning took place before these multiple engagements, foremost being able to secure permits and sites to erect the three revival tents. After several consultations with city fathers and local religious leaders of the state churches (Catholic and Lutheran; German Baptists were considered *Freikirchen*, free churches) in Gerolstein, we discovered there were three locations allowed for such public events. We were given permission by the city officials to use the grounds next to the Gerolsteiner Sprüdel factory (see John 7 entry). Here is where the "rest of the story" relates to this Bible chapter.

Unbeknownst to us one of the participants in the Bible studies there in Gerolstein had prayed for years for God to provide an evangelical witness in this town. His name was Horst Strohschein. He had been a schoolteacher but retired early due to fragile nerves and occasional nervous breakdowns. He was a frail, quiet gentleman who had prayed Matthew 9.37-38 over Gerolstein many times ("The harvest is plentiful, but the workers are few. Therefore, beseech the Lord of the harvest to send out workers into His harvest."). He often prayed on long walks in the region. One high point overlooking Gerolstein was a lovely promontory named the Kalkenstein (chalk stone). On one prayer stroll Horst walked to its precipice and gazed at the valley below to Gerolstein's 7,000 inhabitants. A distant tent and the faint noise of revelry caught his eye and ear. Noting a local festival that day, he knew it was a *Bierzelt* (beer tent). He prayed words to this effect: "Lord, would it be possible that one day on that very spot instead of people being filled with spirits to celebrate being filled with Your Spirit?" We both teared up as he told me that story, because the tent he had seen was on the exact same spot the city officials later chose for the tent revival. God hears and answers in His time, in His way, and with uncanny precision. After the tent revival, sufficient interest was generated for times of worship to continue so that a local German Baptist church was begun; it meets to this day in more permanent structures near the Kalkenstein. The years I and other *Mitarbeiter* (fellow workers) from the church in Trier spent driving and traveling by train in the Eifel mountain range to Gerolstein to help birth this church were some of the most formative of my ministry. To be one of the "workers in His harvest" prayed for by Horst and others and to be a literal fulfillment of these verses were some of the deepest joys of my life. I thought I was one of the leaders in this effort; the real leader had been Horst whose vision and prayer for a new work according to Matthew 9.35-38 was heard by Heaven. I was simply one of the obedient harvesters.

Lines on Leadership
Who paved the way for your success? Have you honored them or thanked them for their contributions? Who plowed so that you could harvest?
_____
_____
++

Matthew 10---Highlights: The twelve sent on a mission; warnings about the cost of discipleship

      The twelve had traveled with Jesus long enough, heard enough, and had become familiar enough with their Master's teachings to be sent out on a preaching tour of their own. Jesus proceeds to speak during the entire chapter on how to conduct themselves (vs. 5-15), what to expect (vs. 16-23), and the ramifications for their sermons and stances (vs. 24-42). Some have been with Him from the beginning of His public ministry, have heard the groundbreaking 'Sermon on the Mount" (chaps. 5-7), seen healings (chap. 9), and experienced His control over nature (chap. 8). They are beginning to sense He was an extraordinary man but no one has yet dared to offer the possibility that this rabbi might be the Messiah (that comes later, see Mt.16 entry). Some have just joined like Matthew himself (chapter 9).

      It is difficult within the four gospels to create a timeline with any degree of exactness as to when this or that event took place since their sequencing is different, as are the audiences for each gospel. Did the apostles have sufficient time to establish trust with and in each other? Had they found some sort of truce about their political affinities? We can only assume they traveled as a group, since no mention is made of subdividing them in this passage (see Luke 10 where a larger number is sent on a similar preaching mission in pairs). The only implied directive as to any group structure was naming Peter first, signifying he was likely the spokesperson or leader.

A seminal statement for leaders is "the first duty of a leader is to define reality[1]" (see Jn. 3 entry). One of Peter Drucker's most famous adages (attributed to him and many others) is "the best way to predict the future is to create it.[2]" Jesus as leader does both for His disciples in this passage as He instructs them about the parameters and the purpose of this preaching trip.

He defines reality by honest depictions of what will happen when they enter a city, preach, and the types of reactions they will encounter. He creates reality when He says now they can do the things they have seen only Him do, up to this point: heal the sick, raise the dead, cleanse the lepers, and cast out demons.

He defines reality by listing precisely what they can and cannot take on the trip: do not take money for your services, don't even take a bag in which to deposit money for your services, pack extremely lightly, basically live off the land as the "worker is worthy of his support." (vs. 9-10). He tells them to create reality by preaching, "The kingdom of heaven is at hand." (v. 7) Defining and creating reality are not in tension with one another, they are mainly complementary and from time to time synonymous. The effective leader learns to blend both as they shed light on the present and share a vision of the future.

I often work with church search committees and transition teams as they seek a new pastor. The first of five major areas we always tackle is "heritage:" how did the church start, what ups, downs, and detours through the church's history have led to its present position, and how did they get from the point of inception to the point we call "now"? The last of the five major areas we cover is the future, the vision of where the church wants to head (our denomination practices congregational polity, where the church members make the decisions). When the church has agreed on that direction, then it is ready to find a pastor who will help them get from where they are to where they have articulated they want to be. They must <u>define</u> what the reality is, which reality they desire, and which future they want to <u>create</u>.

<u>Lines on Leadership</u>
When I lead any group into a new area or new level of endeavor, I need to <u>define</u> and <u>create</u> the reality in which they will operate, to identify the present boundaries and help them see which ones need to honored, which ones need to be tested, expanded, obliterated, ignored, or redrawn. Which areas of your work need a reality defined and/or created? Which boundaries need to be tested, expanded, obliterated, ignored, or redrawn?

_____

_____

++

<u>Matthew 11</u>—Highlights: John the Baptist questions Jesus' identity; unrepentant cities; take my yoke

(See Luke 7 entry concerning John the Baptist's doubts about Jesus being the Messiah) Most with little to no familiarity to the NT have likely heard vs. 28-30: "Come unto Me, all who are weary and heavy laden, and I will give you rest. Take my yoke upon you, and learn from Me, for I am gentle and humble in heart; and you shall find rest for your souls. For my yoke is easy, and my load is light." To a population of urban dwellers, who have probably not seen a yoke except in farm photos, the idea (to take a yoke of Christ upon themselves) seems burdensome and akin to punishment; the mental image resembles languishing in a stockade on some public square ridiculed by the crowd. Nothing could be further from the truth.

When Jesus' teachings are weighed against the hundreds of commands contained in the teaching of the rabbis, His yoke really does become light in comparison.[1] Why else would he preface the command to yoke up with Him with a promise of comfort and rest? How could He alleviate my burdens by my being yoked to Him?

For years I have had a miniature replica of a double yoke that leans against books on the shelf (along with many other small metal sculptures, and items I use as object lessons). I have always imagined this verse speaking about a double yoke. I mean no irreverence to say in this instance Jesus would be the senior ox, and I would be the junior ox. Instead of me grunting and swaying as I pull the plow behind me alone. He allows me to be yoked together with Him, and we work in tandem, doing far beyond all I could possibly do by myself (Eph. 3.20). Compared to what I labored under alone, it feels like rest; I don't have to think about staying on a straight path, He as the senior partner in this endeavor called life knows which way to go. He knows when to work hard, and when to slow the pace, and when to call a halt. As a type A personality who scores a high 'D' in the DISC leadership assessment (Dominance, Influence, Steadiness, Conscientiousness) I admit this grates against my constant desire to push, strive, and always go, go, go. For a Timothy, who Paul gently chides for being timid and reticent (2 Tim. 1.7), being yoked to Christ means ready or not, you are on the move.

This is more than some idyllic, pastoral scene with birds chirping and clouds floating lazily across azure skies. In Matthew 11 Jesus behaves outside the societal norms more than anyone expects (vs. 18-19), speaks more directly than most of us would dare (vs. 20-24) in public, and makes bold claims as to His identity (v. 27). Jesus does not call us to take on His yoke in order to obtain a pass on our responsibilities or hard work. He calls us to walk alongside Him, learn from Him (v. 29b), and get in sync with His purpose and His direction. He says it more graphically when the mental image changes from a yoke to a cross (Luke 9.23); the terminology changes but the meaning remains the same when the writer of Hebrews tells us "for the joy set before Him He endured the cross, despising the shame, and sat down at the right hand of God." (Heb. 12.2) The rest doesn't come when I put on the yoke; the assurance I am His and we will get through this together is there, but the rest comes when the purpose has been fulfilled (Hebrews 4). Yoked to Christ means His fate will be our fate, His reward will be our reward. It is frightening, but not burdensome; David foreshadowed this when he wrote the immortal words of Ps. 23. 4, "Yea, though I walk through the valley of the shadow of death, I will fear no evil, for Thou art with me." (KJV) Leadership seems like a solitary pursuit, and that it is from a human standpoint, but I don't have to lead alone if I take upon my shoulders the yoke of my Lord and follow His lead (John 12.26).

Lines on Leadership
'Followship' precedes and instructs good leadership (see Matthew 8 and 1 John 3 entries). To whom or to what am I honestly yoked? Upon what or whom do I totally rely on in a true partnership of trust and effort?

++

Matthew 12---Highlights: various encounters with the Pharisees

Jesus uses a word image in vs. 43-45 not found in the other three gospels, only in Matthew. In it an "unclean spirit" either leaves a man's house (a euphemism for his life) of its own accord or is driven out. After wandering around it decides to go back to see what shape that house is in, and finds out it is "<u>unoccupied, swept, and put in order</u> (v.44)." Upon discovering this it goes and recruits seven other entities more wicked than the original "unclean spirit" and they all decide to live in that house, which is in worse shape than it was at the beginning.

This is not a treatise on demon possession, a theology of evil spirits, or a warning about losing one's salvation, which is subject matter for a biblical commentary. The leadership application is simple but it is ignored time and time again. When a new leader comes on the scene, be it a political candidate, a reformer, a new pastor, or a new CEO, the inclination is to point out everything that is not working, inefficient, deferred maintenance, encrusted, out of date, or antiquated and take it out, haul it to the nearest literal or figurative landfill, and "clean house" as the saying goes. No doubt much of what is there upon the transition is neither workable nor worthy and needed to disappear, physical, psychologically, and personnel-wise included.

But when the effort is considerable to get everything cleaned out and cleaned up, the temptation is to relax and think the battle is over. It all looks nice and neat, might even have new carpet, curtains, and lighting. But if it has not been repurposed and occupied with new life, new vision, new people dedicated to the direction of the new leadership, just as nature abhors a vacuum surely that empty space will once again be filled with less than desirable elements or purposes, or become unusable simply through neglect, since we live in a fallen world that tends toward entropy.

Yes, get rid of that which is unproductive or undesirable, but be sure you have a plan to fill that cleared out space in your company or your life with something better. On a level of personal thoughts, whether you want to consider self-image or sinful thoughts, trying to rid one's mind by NOT thinking about something undesirable is rarely as successful as replacing it with positive thoughts. This is why Christian meditation is not about emptying the mind, but saturating it with the thoughts of God, and why regular Bible reading and memorization is essential to conquering the thought life of a believer.

Lines on Leadership

As a leader, what person/program/thought/piece of furniture/company division needs to disappear? What will you put in its place?

_____

_____

++

Matthew 13---Highlights: Parables of the Sower, tares among wheat, pearl of great price, the dragnet

The Sermon on the Mount (chapters 5-7) is rich in truth about life in the Kingdom of God. Matthew 13 uses a series of parables to continue describing Kingdom life. Most of the illustrations deal with what starts out small (a mustard seed, v.31; seed strewn on different soils, vs. 3-23 (see Mark 4 entry); a grain of sand that becomes a pearl, v. 45; leaven, v. 33 (see Luke 13 entry)) growing large; something of value to seek (a pearl, v.

46; a treasure, v. 44); or a sifting of that which is kept or discarded (the wheat and tares, vs. 24-30; fish in the dragnet, vs. 47-50)).

The parable of the wheat and the tares (a type of rye grass found in Syria and Palestine the seeds of which are poisonous[1]) has a primary lesson for leaders in patience, and in that respect, is connected to the pearl and the mustard seed parables. Patience has never been my foremost attribute. I would prefer to draw lines in the sand, force an issue, and have everyone declare which side they are on. At the beginning of the two crops' growth they look similar and dividing them would be difficult if not impossible. The parable cautions to wait until the wheat is ripe; the difference in the two crops, one beneficial and one harmful, will be made apparent upon maturation of both crops. The harvest can commence along with the disposal of the unwanted intruders sown by the enemy (v.25). The theme of patience repeats in that it takes time to grow a pearl in the oyster and time for the tiny mustard seed to become one of the larger plants in the garden.

Lines on Leadership

In terms of salvation believers and unbelievers can look similar as far as church activity and use of the same vocabulary; it is when the fruit is produced that the difference is noticed, something to which Jesus referred often (Mt. 7.16, 20). How would this principle play out in your organization? Where do you need to exercise patience in sorting out the players and the pretenders?

_____

_____

++

Matthew 14---Highlights: Death of John the Baptist; feeding of the 5000; Jesus walking on the water

v. 25 "And in the fourth watch of the night (3-6am) He came to them, walking on the sea." As a conservative evangelical, I believe Christ as the sovereign Deity in charge of every atom and empty space in the universe could walk on whatever He wishes (vs.22-33). The leadership emphasis lies not in the fact or fiction of walking on water but rather in the exchange between Peter and Jesus (vs.27-31).

Someone walking on water has never occurred before or since this incident; the disciples' reaction of fear and wonderment is natural and the reason why Jesus said 'don't be afraid' twice, (v. 27). Once He was identified, Peter spoke. He had a habit of speaking first and thinking later (see Mt. 17 entry) and this was totally in character. Jesus knew what would happen, and could have easily said, "no, Peter, this will end badly, no need to attempt it," and saved Peter the embarrassment. Jesus also knew Peter needed to learn by practice rather than learn by precept, so He simply said, "Come!" (v. 29) He knew each disciple and tailored His responses to their learning styles and their spiritual needs. Yes, Peter only made it a few steps and then, either taking his eyes off Jesus, or concentrating more on the wind and waves than the Master, he began to sink and required a Master's rescue (vs. 30-31).

Lines on Leadership

When everyone was back in the boat, the wind stopped (vs. 24, 32). Perhaps it blew merely to assist with the lesson to Peter and the disciples (see Mt. 8.26). As a leader among the disciples, Peter often overstepped, tripped, blurted, and misfired. But every time he did, he grew and learned; a reading of Acts and 1 & 2 Peter shows his prominent position in the early church and his wisdom had grown to match his courage. If the situation allows, some people learn quicker and surer when allowed to make mistakes. I often say to future leaders, <u>if you're going to make a mistake, make it glorious</u>. Make it confidently. Make it without hesitation, fall down, evaluate, and do it again.

It takes a secure leader to create a culture where organizational members are given freedom to fail. Jesus was nearby and provided a safety net in this instance. How have you created a culture where your colleagues have freedom to verbally or volitionally launch out---and fail? How have you built in parameters of safety and cushion? Does your relationship to that member give you the reciprocal freedom to admonish and instruct in a way that affirms (v.31)?

Another facet of this incident is the disciples' response of worship and calling Jesus God's Son (v. 33). Two chapters later in Mt. 16 is Peter's confession of Jesus being "the Christ, the Son of the living God." They progressed in their understanding of Who their itinerant rabbi was. How patient are you with your team/church as they slowly adopt your vision for them?

_____

_____

++

Matthew 15---Highlights: disagreement with Pharisees; true defilement; Syrophoenician woman; healing of the crowds; feeding of the 4000.

A mark of a good leader is his ability to distinguish between that which is substantial and that which is superfluous, what is surface and what is core. In vs. 1-2 the Pharisees complain that Jesus and His followers do not wash their hands before eating. Note carefully that they refer to this as "the tradition of the elders." This may refer to the *Mishnah*, a set of interpretations of the Law of Moses that some felt as authoritative as Scripture[1] or simply an oral tradition based on but not accurately following Mosaic admonitions meant for priests (Exodus 30.19) or general rules after touching that which was declared unclean (Leviticus 15).

Jesus counters (vs. 3-6) with a clear comparison of traditions of men and commands of God and declares that men conveniently use their own traditions to ignore or circumvent God's commands. They use their law as a loophole to keep what should rightfully be given to honor their parents. Therefore, tradition trumps command for the Pharisees when Jesus declares it is vice versa. He continues to rail at the Pharisees (vs. 10-20) about making such a big deal about what is clean and unclean to eat, yet ignore the nature of the inner man. Christ insisted that everything we eat is "eliminated" from the body and does not defile a person, but the corrupt sinful nature of man is what defiles him (a recurrent NT theme: Acts 10, Galatians 2, Colossians 2). He brings them back to what is truly important.

Have you ever seen a church/organization sidetracked, stagnated, or stalled out, not collectively able to <u>transition</u> in a forward direction because of a <u>tradition</u>? Most traditions have humble, real origins that somehow rose from a desirable action or attitude to sacrosanct status way beyond its true importance. Being able to distinguish between what needs to be kept as sacred and what can be discarded for a better way to do something is a hallmark of a good leader. As said in other chapters, the message is the main thing and should be kept intact, but the method used to convey the message is subject to change; it is always subordinate to the message.

<u>Lines on Leadership</u>
Too many church business meetings and corporate boardroom conferrals end in discord and tension because something inferior came to the fore and overshadowed the superior. The message

was lost in the arguments over methodology. Debates in churches about the proverbial color of the carpet or where to place the organ have overshadowed greater truths and split congregations. In some companies retention of a product line or loyal advertising firm became more important than a company's values.

What is a deeply held conviction you operate out of that might be a tradition instead of a direct command of God, a long held assumption that in truth is not derived from your company values?

_____

_____

++

Matthew 16---Highlights: conflict with Pharisees; Peter's Confession; Jesus foretells His death.

Location enhances revelation. A wedding, a proposal, the reveal of a future baby's gender, the unveiling of a statue, the curtains pull back to reveal the opening scene of an opera—their impact is largely influenced by the physical setting, the background details, the lighting, and the audience's perspective when the revelation is shared or experienced.

Caesarea Philippi lies in northern Israel and is a "must see" stop for all Christian pilgrims. Jesus deliberately chose it for the disclosure of His true identity to His disciples. It is a dramatic backdrop because of where Jesus has them seated. Behind them is the main source of the Jordan River with lush plants alongside its waters. In front of them is a formidable cliff in which temple after temple to pagan gods has been carved out; together they attract hundreds of worshippers and curious onlookers daily. As they gaze upon this scene, Jesus steps between them and the pagan temples and asks, "Who do men say that I am?" After some good-natured bantering, Jesus asks, "Who do <u>you</u> say I am?" (vs. 13-20) With numerous gods to choose from as he sees Jesus in front of the panoply of temples Peter blurts out, "You are the Christ, the Son of the living God." It is the moment of separation: Jesus to this point was an extraordinary teacher, a rabbi worth listening to, and a miracle worker. This one statement by Peter declares Jesus to be worthy not only of admiration but worship.

To this point Peter has been known as Simon son of Jonah (v. 17). Now Jesus calls him Peter (*petros*, a rock). Peter was more a flounder than a foundation for most of his training with Jesus, yet He called him a rock. Sometimes we need to allow folks time to grow into their names or titles (see Matthew 1 entry; Philemon entry).

Jesus calling Peter a rock has caused considerable theological consternation over the centuries: He said He would build His church upon this rock (*petra*). Catholics interpret it as building His church upon Peter himself; Protestants point to the confession of Peter; some (including this author) believe Jesus pointed to Himself as the Rock upon which He would build His church. Whether the true interpretation is the person of Peter, or his profession, or the Person of Christ, the present-day existence of the church 2000+ years later is an enduring testament to the Incarnation being more important than the infrastructure.

Lines on Leadership
What important pronouncement of yours is coming up that would be enhanced by an appropriate setting and coming aside from the day-to-day routine? Have you chosen carefully the terms you will use that will become part of the organizational vocabulary from then on?

++

Matthew 17---Highlights: transfiguration of Jesus; healing of young boy; fishing for tribute money

Most champions in major sports are determined by tournaments or rounds of elimination. The excitement of spectators reaches a fever pitch as fewer and fewer teams or individuals are left in the competition. When the last out of the World Series is logged, or the buzzer of the deciding NBA Finals game goes off, the sportscaster usually goes silent and lets the joyous celebration of the players and the raucous cheers of the fans provide all the excitement needed. The silence of the broadcasters at that point lets the fans and team/player rightly take the center stage after achieving that sport's pinnacle. Whatever the commentator might say has a good chance of being perceived as trivializing the moment, turning the spotlight on himself, or hackneyed.

The presence of greatness elicits various responses. In the previous chapter Peter gives a correct response to Jesus' question because the Father in heaven gave it to him (Mt. 16.16). He correctly singled out Jesus from all other deities as the Son of the living God. In chapter 17.1-8, Jesus leads Peter, James, and John to a nearby peak (traditionally Mt. Tabor 12 miles west; other scholars (and your author after visits there) favor Mt. Hermon to the north, the tallest peak in the entire region). He allows them to witness two remarkable sights reserved for just three sets of eyes out of all humanity: 1) Jesus' *shekinah* glory is visible to them (v.2); and 2) as the glorified Son of God he converses with Moses and Elijah, two of the most revered figures in Jewish history who represent the Law and the Prophets (v.3). In Matt. 16, Jesus declared His Deity; in Matt. 17, He demonstrated it. Peter would have honored the moment best by remaining silent; instead, he acts like the student in class who feels compelled to say something, anything, regardless of its awkwardness. His comment about building three memorials (v.4) prompts a rare direct response from God the Father to focus on Jesus and nothing else.

Peter, James, and John were privileged to witness such a scene. They were leading figures within the circles of Jesus' followers, and Peter had scored with them all by having the courage to speak out in chapter 16 concerning whether or not Jesus was THE Messiah, or just another pretender to the prophecies. When we are designated as leaders in ongoing situations, it often feels like we should speak to each situation in which we find ourselves. As one who thinks and speaks quickly, I have had to learn from experience this is not always appropriate or appreciated. A good leader learns to acknowledge a great leader by becoming in that moment the great leader's learner. It does not take away my status as a leader, it means I recognize when I'm in the presence of one who is light years beyond my ability or accomplishments and am content to learn or simply observe greatness.

Lines on Leadership
When was the last time you blurted out a response, sent a social media post, text message, or email that was honestly meant to impress more than instruct?
The person who is defensive in his thinking and tries hard not to make a mistake will never become proficient in another language, get better at a skill, or learn to perform vocally, instrumentally, or keep an audience engaged. Peter is to be both admonished and admired in this instance. Because he exposes his faulty thinking, it can more easily be corrected. What gaffes

and faux pas in your past have been helpful in forging your effectiveness as a leader?

_____

_____

++

Matthew 18---Highlights: various teachings of Jesus
Most chapters in this book focus on one leadership principle to the detriment of others in the same Biblical chapter for brevity's sake; otherwise, this book would be enormous. Some focus on interrelated principles found within one chapter; a few chapters have one principle with multiple iterations. In Matthew 18, Jesus begins with extolling the virtues of childlikeness in the Kingdom, what to do when someone acts childish instead, and how to restore people to that childlike state.

When Jesus said in v. 4, "Whoever humbles himself as this child, he is the greatest in the kingdom of heaven," He was not endorsing childish behavior but rather childlike purity of wonder and singular devotion that has an endless capacity to learn. C.S. Lewis said it best in Mere Christianity:

> He wants a child's heart, but a grown-up's head. He wants us to be simple, single-minded, affectionate, and teachable, as good children are; but He also wants every bit of intelligence we have to be alert at its job, and in first-class fighting trim[1]."

He then gives severe advice to discard whatever hinders a person from singular devotion to Christ, up to and including one's very own limbs and organs. Even as He is compassionate towards children, He is uncompromising when it comes to the warnings in vs. 7-13. This combination of compassion for the childlike and consequences for the childish continues in vs. 12-20 as Jesus emphasizes the individual as important (leave the group of 99 being obedient and productive and go seek the one gone astray) but also that in doing so, individual discipline is necessary to achieve harmony within that group. The chapter ends with a proper way and improper way to restore the group's unity by seeking the restoration of the solitary transgressor. It spells out what happens to those who want everything on their terms regardless of how it affects others; these are classic behaviors of childish people.

A corollary of the discipline described in Matt. 19.15-20 is the concept of sphere of influence. If there has been a transgression or indiscretion, it should be treated within the sphere of those aware or affected by the transgression. If it is a private matter between two, that is where both the counsel and consequences should remain; for a leader to allow something done and dealt with in private to expand throughout the whole group till all are aware, is likewise acting childish. Current social media expose, ruin, and leave little room to apply restorative forgiveness to an individual's life.

Lines on Leadership

In business as well as church life it is difficult for leaders to balance affirmation and admonishment. Do you see that balance in how you treat your followers or team?

_____
_____

++

Matthew 19 ---Highlights: teachings on marriage & divorce; children; wealth & power in the Kingdom

Divorce lawyers, a chirping crowd of children, a person who owns half the town, and several perplexed disciples all step into the room. It sounds like the setup for a bad joke, but in chapter 19 all characters appear on the scene for seemingly disparate reasons. The divorce lawyers try to trip up Jesus on legal technicalities (vs. 3-12), the children are shooed away as bothersome (vs. 13-15), the rich <u>young</u> (term used 2x) man inquired about how to obtain salvation (vs. 16-22), and the disciples try to make sense of it all (v. 23-30). Jesus, the consummate leader/teacher, deflects all of the intents and questions to show the true values of the Kingdom.

Kingdom marriage is about love, not loopholes. To be sure, Jesus lays down some clear principles about marriage and divorce; He does not speak in vagaries or ambiguities (v.9). But He takes them back to the original purposes of marriage (vs. 5, 8, "in the beginning it was not so"). In my years of campus ministry, I met some students who chose their classes by skills needed <u>when</u> they divorced, and this was <u>before</u> they were even married!

Kingdom subjects are not rated according to age; Jesus was quite content to allow children to surround Him. Recently I visited the home of a former student I had not seen in years. I had never seen their four lively offspring, all under the age of eight. It took approximately 30 seconds after I sat down in their living room before children were crawling in my lap, asking me questions, showing me their favorite videos or laptop games. The parents gave the customary apologies while I told them how this shows me the love in this house, that all who enter under its roof are friends to be loved and trusted; let them love in their unique crawling fashion. I could contact the parents anytime on social media or call and talk, but to have these loving eyes and laughing, giggling smiles bouncing in my lap was precious; I was more than content to let them interrupt the conversation.

Material wealth is not condemned by Jesus, just less important in the Kingdom than most would expect. In the time of

Jesus, there was no such concept of a middle class; there were haves and have nots. 'To have' was seen as better than to have not, pure and simple. And to have wealth meant to be not only well off but favored. The disciples were confused when Jesus uses hyperbolic humor to show riches are of little consequence in the Kingdom. They thought it meant, if rich people don't get in, no one has a chance. He meant the opposite, wealth doesn't get you in the gate, anyone gets in if they follow Him (vs. 21, 28). We often talk about the streets of heaven as paved with gold (Rev. 21.21) because on earth gold is precious; in heaven it is used for paving materials on par with gravel and asphalt.

He brings it all together in the last verse which appears often in the gospels (v. 30, "But many who are first will be last, and the last first.").

Lines on Leadership

Jesus displays consistency, creativity, and patience in repeatedly showing Kingdom values are not the same as those of the world. How many times in the last week have you had a similar conversation with a church member or employee to consistently, creatively, and patiently show them how their actions or comments are not in line with Kingdom values/company policy?

_____

_____

++

Matthew 20---Highlights: parable of vineyard laborers; disputing disciples; servant Savior; two blind men.

v. 28, "the Son of Man did not come to be served, but to serve, and to give His life a ransom for many." This verse is at the heart of servant leadership and is not isolated from the narrative of the chapter but is rather a culmination of its teachings and actions.

1) Jesus tells a tale of day laborers signed on to work in a vineyard at various times of the day. They each agree with the vineyard owner to work for either a denarius (v. 2), or whatever is right (v.4). The owner does this five times, hiring folks throughout the workday (which was normally divided into four three-hour segments[1]) at the 1st, 3rd, 6th, 9th, and 11th hours. At the end of the day the paymaster is instructed to issue each day laborer a denarius, which was normally given for a full day's work. It would appear to be an unequal distribution of wages <u>if the work output of each laborer had been the issue</u>. Jesus shows <u>everyone got what they contracted for or more, making the issue the vineyard owner's generosity and mercy</u>. It is one more example of Kingdom economics and Kingdom living according to the spiritual Magna Carta known as the Sermon on the Mount (Mt. 5-7). Fair does not mean equal, rather a concept of fairness emerges from the character of the Kingdom's Ruler.

2) The quintessential maternal advocate enters the scene in v. 20 and lobbies for her two sons (James and John) to get preferential treatment in the soon to be Kingdom of God. Her actions, while understandable from a familial sense of loyalty, betray a rather marked ignorance of both the Kingdom and the qualifications of those who would rule it. Rather than an open rebuke (see Mk. 10 entry) Jesus defers to whatever the Father wishes to grant and chooses not to elaborate on what He meant by drinking from a similar cup as His (a cryptic reference to His impending arrest, trial, agony, and crucifixion). He ties the two incidents of the laborers and the would-be co-regents into the single profound statement of v. 28. It reiterated that greatness in His Kingdom does not consist of achieving a pinnacle of power or wealth, but rather it is obedience to the Father and trusting Him

with one's life. The goal is sacrifice for and not supremacy in the Kingdom (see 1 Peter 5 entry).

Belhaven University is a small Presbyterian college in Jackson, MS. It is a lovely campus complete with typical Southern trees and architecture. A person entering the campus is greeted by a large attractive brick wall emblazoned with the following in large letters: "For the Son of Man came not to be served, but to serve, and to give His life a ransom for many. Mt. 20.28" I spent several days on that campus conducting interviews of staff, faculty, and students for a writing project. I discovered that this verse had been the campus motto for over a hundred years. The more I spoke with them the more I realized this was more than a motto or a byline; it was a lifestyle for everyone affiliated with the campus.

Lines on Leadership
Would your members/employees describe you as fair? Would that be based more on a sense of equality or your personal character? How would they likely describe your treatment of members/employees to those outside your organization? Would their depiction of your leadership include the word 'servant?'

_____
_____

++

Matthew 21---Highlights: triumphal entry to Jerusalem, cleansing of the temple, barren fig tree; parables of two sons and the landowner's son.

The parable of the two sons is unique to Matthew[1]. It is brief and simple but contains an important leadership principle. The father says he has a task to be performed. The first son says, 'I'll do it,' but in the end does not engage. The second son was asked about the task and says basically, 'no way,' yet later regretted it and performed the task. Jesus asked the priests and elders gathered around Him who had done the will of the father. They correctly answered, "the latter."

There is *that* person, the one who grouses and mutters every time a task is offered him. He finds multiple excuses as to why he shouldn't do it, defers the attention to someone else, and acts like the task is beneath him. You would love to dismiss him outright but he either has seniority or the executive's ear. Yet when the deadlines near, you discover the task is sometimes completed by those who complained the most.

Although the task is now completed, it feels---incomplete. You had to wait to see who would step up, and sometimes it feels as if it takes on a sense of brinkmanship, which one will blink or blow his stack first. Ideally someone should offer willingly to do the task and then be counted on to perform it as a mature son or member of the group. Life happens outside the realm of the subjunctive (shoulda, woulda, coulda). Saying "I will do it" and then not even attempting to do the task is to remain in the land of the subjunctive (I truly meant to, I really wanted to, I had every intention, if I had only known . . .).

In the parable, the task requested was a normal, daily one, to go tend the vineyard. It was an important task not only for a crop of grapes to produce income but perhaps to provide for the survival of the family unit. It is a father asking his sons in the sequence of birthright. We can only speculate that perhaps the sons had become of age to the point where they were expected to be in the vineyard instead of playing in the neighborhood, and this is the first time they have both been asked to complete the task. The father did not put it up for bid, did not offer incentives, did not pit one against the other, and did not spell out any punishment. The key here is that the second son regretted his reticence and obeyed. It was a delayed obedience but obedience nonetheless. Jesus is spelling out to the priests and elders that being the first born or the person with first rights doesn't guarantee anything, rather that obedience is more important than ordinal standing in the family. The following parable (vs. 33-44) confirms it.

Lines on Leadership
In your church staff or corporate setting, which is more important to the rank and file; obedience or pecking order? If the latter, what created that culture, and how can you conform it more to this parable?
_____
_____
++

Matthew 22---Highlights: parable of the wedding feast, new guests; tribute to Caesar; marriage in the resurrected life y/n; the Great Commandment.

Jesus: "You shall love the Lord your God with all your heart, and with all your soul, and with all your mind. This is the great and foremost commandment. The second is like it, you shall love your neighbor as yourself. On these two commandments depend the whole Law and the Prophets."

Many refer to Matt. 22.37-40 as the Great Commandment. It is the quintessential bumper sticker/encapsulation of the OT (Jesus says as much in v.40). Jesus quotes twice from the Law of Moses (Deut. 6.5 and Lev. 19.18) and gives us the simplest yet most solid life framework possible. It loosely parallels the Ten Commandments (see Ex. 20.1-17): the first part is a "vertical" relationship to God and the latter part is a "horizontal" relationship to self and society. The common denominator for both passages is to love.

If I have just a short time with one church or group of people, I usually teach what is called the Disciple's Cross, a diagram derived from a book of the same name[1]. In the diagram of a simple cross, I draw a circle in the middle to represent *Abiding in Christ* (John 15.5); vertically downwards the section is labeled the Word (Jn. 8.31-32); and vertically upwards the section is labeled Prayer (Jn. 15.7). To love God in a purely "vertical" sense is to *abide in His Word* (the Bible) and *abide in His presence* in worship.

In addition to the vertical relationship with God, we love Him by loving His faithful (His children) and those not yet of the family of faith (His creation). I label the right side of the horizontal beam *'Fellowship'* to denote loving those in a covenant bond in Christ (John 13.34-35). I label the left side of the horizontal beam *'Witness'* as we love on those not yet of the family of faith (John 15.8).

The Disciple's Cross helps me as a diagnostic tool as I lead my respective ministry in light of the Great Commandment. Periodically I examine my life to see if I am "in balance" and not out of kilter, emphasizing some things to the neglect of the other. In leadership of oneself, a church, or an organization it is easy to go overboard in one area of need and ignore other areas that soon create an unbalanced and unproductive leader.

Lines on Leadership
What are some areas of your leadership that are out of balance due to obsession or neglect? Jesus says earlier in Mt. 6 we should seek God and His righteousness, and everything else falls into place (6.33). When there are deadlines, headlines, lines in the sand, and shifting lines of demarcation, the Great

Commandment helps us to remember what and where our priorities are. Love God, love His people, love those not yet His people, and love myself, and keep it in proper perspective. It may look like a DIY project and all my initiative (love God, then love others) but in reality, we love because He first loved us (see 1 John 4 entry). How does this speak to your need for a "balanced" leadership?

_____
_____
++

Matthew 23—Highlights: Pharisees hypocrisy exposed; Seven Woes, Christ's lament over Jerusalem.

This passage contains what is normally labeled "the seven woes," which are aimed at the local leaders. Jesus takes off the gloves and comes out swinging with direct, bold statements at the entrenched religious establishment. This is recommended only if you want a short career. Jesus should not be seen as the poster boy for activism railing against "The Man." The woes are focused on the insidious substitution of manufactured or manipulated truth for God's truth.

A closed system tends to rapidly reinforce its chosen values, and a false sense of normalcy quickly solidifies into orthodoxy, regardless of whether it is rooted in biblical truth (or in the case of an organization, company policy). Repetition of an act or catch phrase can take on an aura of quasi-credibility simply because it becomes, at first, the <u>accepted</u> and then the <u>expected</u> way of saying or doing things. We have practiced it so long we have become inured to how others react when they experience our church/org. for the first time. When was the last time anyone challenged you to give a rationale for the way your church conducts itself? What would happen if your church leadership undertook a thorough review of not only your constitution and bylaws, but the times you have services, the order of worship, the literature used to disciple, the ministries you deem important and why you never undertook others, all in light of Scripture, not "that's the way we've always done it as long as anyone can remember?"

Traditions are habits that acquire a pseudo-sanctity and are often elevated to parity with Scripture. If you don't think so, try introducing new hymnals, a new pulpit, new carpet. One time I did pulpit supply for a small country church. The pastor had warned me ahead of time how the members were contentious, but he didn't mention what the offending issue was. When I arrived that Sunday, the issue became apparent quickly as I could not make my way through the deacons who were in the middle of the foyer. They were arguing loudly about how many inches to expand its entrance into the worship area. The line of reasoning revolved around whether to restore the original dimensions of the church or change it entirely to serve future needs.

Traditions can have several positive aspects: 1. Stability---everyone knows what is expected; 2. Certainty---stability's first cousin, the known outweighs the unknown; 3. Trajectory---the sequence of events will unfold in a predictable direction and pace; 4. Identity---a church (or organization, a family) is known by its signature traits or style of worship, its set of traditions sets the church apart from others of their kind; 5. Theme/Standard---it's hard to introduce a variation or innovation if you can't recognize what is the standard; 6. Longevity---since traditions need time to coalesce and harden, traditions denote the institution has been around for a long time.

Traditions can also have negative aspects: 1. Triteness---that which is predictable often becomes ritualistic and loses its depth of meaning; 2. Lack of Dynamic Nature---we begin to worship a system more than a Savior who is alive and dynamic; He's steady but not static; 3. <u>Non-changing Trajectory</u>---sometimes a mid-course correction is necessary to reach a stated goal and holding one's course is not only inadvisable but dangerous; 4. <u>Inflexibility</u>---while we should be respectful of traditions (which often arise from noble origins), when they become inflexible, they restrict creativity and freedom of expression; 5. <u>Identity</u>---yes, traditions can help identify who we are, but they can also be used to distinguish quickly who the "others" are. That is because they are unfamiliar with "our" traditions or do not perform them as flawlessly or effortlessly as we do.

Lines on Leadership
In other entries, I encourage a leader to have a grand narrative that incorporates all the essential truths and values of his group and what he wants to accomplish through that group. But a leader is obligated to periodically review or have others review the practices of his group to make sure they are true to their original values more than the evolved narrative.
The Pharisees deserved Jesus' sevenfold holy audit in Matthew 23. I pray I have the openness and humility to allow others to question my group's practices and whether they reflect God's truth or man's tradition. From which one does your traditions and policies come, a given truth or an evolved narrative?

_____

_____

++

Matthew 24---Highlights: The Olivet Discourse on End Times
      The view from the Mount of Olives looking back toward Jerusalem is famous and breathtaking. Famous because one sees

the City of David, the second Temple Mount, the Dome of the Rock, and the Eastern Gate to mention a few sites that have both biblical and historical significance; and breathtaking when one realizes Jesus' teachings, miracles, trials, crucifixion, and resurrection took place there, and that this large hill is the epicenter of three monotheistic religions---Judaism, Islam, and Christianity.

In Matthew 16, Jesus chose a deliberate and dramatic setting to reveal His deity. In a similar manner, He now chooses a setting where He can reveal His destiny. Here, He can gesture in several different directions including at their feet (i.e., Zech. 14.4), and in every direction the disciples are reminded of myriad OT prophecies concerning the Messiah (Matthew wrote for a Jewish audience familiar with OT messianic passages).

The disciples asked three distinct questions in v. 3: "1) Tell us, when will these things [vs. 1-2] happen, 2) what will be the sign of Your coming, 3) and of the end of the age?" Jesus launches into an extensive discourse on His Second Advent. Unpacking all that Jesus shares has occupied the church over two millennia; to refer to the specific answers He gives, I suggest referencing several good commentaries. For our purposes, we will look at the discourse as a total unit in terms of casting vision. Much has been written about visions in many other leadership books; here are a few aspects derived from the text.

1) A vision should be compelling but not necessarily comprehensive and can have an element of the cryptic. If Matt. 24 is seen as prophecy (which it is), there are two main types of prophecy: point in time and cyclical. This vision/prophecy contains both. When cyclical prophecy is given, that means it will reoccur over and over, and usually with increasing frequency and increasing strength. The prophet can afford to be a bit enigmatic

knowing the same thing will occur often either with variations or different iterations.

2) A vision should be rooted in the past yet offer a distinctly different future than the current situation. Jesus references well-known OT apocryphal passages from Daniel, Zechariah, and the Pentateuch. He identifies Himself as the One of whom the past prophets spoke and the One who would one day in the future return to fulfill their promises. A modern-day vision caster should rely on demographics and solid research as much or more than his oratorical skills since whatever he claims as his roots or beginnings can easily be verified or refuted by anyone with a computer and Internet browser.

3) A vision should be replete with word images that are easily remembered and relatable to others. Jesus speaks of that which is familiar to his listeners (fig trees, field workers, master/slave relationship); instead of fixating on details such as the year He will return or in what manner He will return, Jesus emphasizes the suddenness and certainty of it. By using familiar images, He assures each time they see a fig tree, workers in the field, or a servant and master talking, they will be reminded of Christ's prophecy.

Lines on Leadership
Was the last vision you cast (or heard) compelling? Was it rooted in the past yet showed a distinctly different future? How did you use easily remembered word images to relate that vision to others?
_____
_____
++

Matthew 25---Highlights: Parable of the ten virgins; ministering to the least of menv.40 "Truly I say to you, to the extent that you did it to one of these brothers of Mine, even to the least of them, you did it to Me." My college days were spent at McNeese State University in SW Louisiana. One day two of my buddies and I decided to attend a three-day conference in New Orleans on the other side of the state to hear a leading apologetics speaker named Josh McDowell. Apologetics is based on a Greek combination of words loosely meaning "to speak in favor of or a word for." Josh was a dynamic defender of the Word of God we admired greatly. So, we piled in my dilapidated Opel Kadett that had a maximum speed of 45 mph and headed to the Crescent City.

We were duly inspired by his sessions, and being zealous for God we decided to go to Bourbon Street and do what is called witnessing or in the vernacular of the time "share our faith." Surely we would find someone to stop and listen to our propositional-truth-based messages of salvation. Armed with tracts and a Bible we walked up and down those streets famous for sin and sweet jazz and never got to first base with a single person. They were obviously either hardened to the gospel or impervious to it.

We wandered into Jackson Square, an iconic gathering place for every stratum of New Orleans society. We struck up a conversation with a long-haired, laid-back young man not much older than us. We thought we had struck pay dirt because he seemed interested in hearing our version of the gospel. He kept asking leading questions that fueled our desire to share more truth with him. After a while, it seemed his true purpose for his interest surfaced; he asked us if we had any money to spare. A professional panhandler, we thought; he was slick enough to try to gain our confidence and then hit us up for money. We each gave him a dollar and went on. After a few more vain attempts to share our faith, we were ready to hang it up and go back to our lodging. We found our route went back through Jackson Square where we got a life lesson.

That young long-haired man to whom we had reluctantly given three dollars had gone to the local market and bought bologna slices and was passing them out to the panhandlers and castoffs in the square. He had formed a tight semicircle of them and as he passed out the bologna, he was telling them about his love for Christ and how Christ loved them. It turns out he was a summer missionary for our denomination's Home Mission Board. We had viewed witnessing as an exercise, a duty; he had modeled the old D.T. Niles adage that evangelism is one beggar telling another beggar where to find bread[1]. We learned that compassion needed to precede conviction. We wanted to speak about Christ; he ministered to the least of these as an act of worship to his Christ and spoke in His stead to the bologna bunch on Jackson Square.

All three of us eventually went into full time Christian service: Tommy ran a Christian camp in the Northwest, Johnny eventually became a professor of youth ministry as a large seminary. I have been privileged to minister in the various ways described in these chapters. As I write, I am now a trustee for New Orleans Baptist Theological Seminary. When asked by my state convention which of our six denominational seminaries I would like to serve, it was obvious I needed to return to the city where years before I had learned a valuable lesson about Kingdom leadership.

Lines on Leadership
People are not targets, or clients, or buyers of our products and services. People are beings created in the image of our Lord (vs.

31-46) When I minister to or serve them, I learned from this incident long ago to view it as service to Christ Himself. What 'aha' moments of humility have you experienced that opened your eyes as to how you view the people you serve?

_____

_____

++

Matthew 26---Highlights: Jesus' anointing; Lord's Supper; Gethsemane; betrayal; trial; Peter's denial

This may be one of the hardest leadership examples to ponder. The simple way to express it is, "It's all about the mission." Somehow that does not do justice to what Jesus displays here by His silence.

Jesus knows His hour has come; the large crowd with swords and clubs (vs. 47-56) led by Judas came to Gethsemane, seized Jesus, and took Him to Caiaphas where a "trial" that borders on comical unfolded. They hauled "witness" after "witness" before the hastily arranged priests and Council and found no thread of continuity or veracity in their testimonies. By the lack of a rebuttal to any of the accusers, Jesus avoided giving them an ounce of legitimacy.

The high priest brought the trial to a climax with an oath (v.63) commanding Jesus to say up or down, "Are you the Messiah?" Jesus finally responded directly and specifically that He was, and quoted from Psalm 110 and Daniel 7.13 which removed all doubt as to His claim to be the Christ. This sealed His fate on a human level, as it amounted to blasphemy of the highest degree to the Jewish leaders' ears.

On a divine level (if scripted by Hollywood screenwriters) Jesus could have slain every person there by the breath of His mouth or gaze of His eyes. He chose to tell the truth and let the trials take their anticipated course. <u>It was more important in that moment for Jesus to die as the sacrificial Lamb of God than assert his power as Son of God</u>. Previously in vs. 36-46 He struggled in the garden of Gethsemane with this decision (see Lk. 22 entry) and no amount of accusations, punishment, or eventual crucifixion would deter Him from His mission of offering Himself for the salvation of mankind.

"Giving it up for the team" and "standing with my band of brothers" are in themselves good and even noble, but there is no comparison to this decision in v. 64. It is cosmic in scope. There is no way I could have stood there and taken it. I would have lashed out and said I was defending my honor and the honor of my Father, but in honest reality, I would have probably done it to save my own skin and skip the pain. This would have meant abandonment of the mission and the loss of salvation for the world if I had been in His place. I would have failed in what I was sent to do. This was a world changing, history-making decision by Jesus, to speak the truth and let the consequences come. The frightening cost was sublimated to the fulfillment of the mission.

<u>Lines on Leadership</u>
Paul admonishes us to "speak the truth in love "(Eph. 4.15). Leaders are confronted with tough decisions that might mean the loss of jobs for others, or demotions, or other setbacks for others. But the toughest decisions are when the cost will be borne by the leader himself. Jesus spoke in love for others knowing the cost of his reply to Himself, that "for the joy set before Him He endured the cross (Heb. 12.2)." What decision(s) of yours need(s) to be made in light of this passage? When has your leadership been at great personal cost?

++

Matthew 27---Highlights: Jesus before Pilate; crucifixion, burial

The crucifixion, burial, and resurrection of the Lord Jesus Christ are central to the Christian gospel and the foundation of my eternal life for which I am more grateful each passing day. True to the book's intent we will focus instead on a leadership principle that emerges from the narrative.

The main characters of Matt. 27 are Jesus and Pilate (see John 18 entry for insights from their dialogues). Woven into the chapter is a large cast of secondary characters. They each contribute significantly to the story line, and each one raises theological questions (for a related principle from a similar listing, see Mark 15 entry).

Pilate's wife--(v.19) She warned Pilate not to deal with this "righteous man" she saw in a dream. It did not dissuade him from his eventual decision, but it prompted him to ask more personal questions of Jesus before he gave into the public outcry and had Jesus crucified.

Judas--(vs. 3-10) Judas, consumed with his betrayal of Jesus, returned his 30 pieces of silver obtained by identifying Him; but the deed was done and could not be reversed. The phrase "saw that He had been condemned" gives credence to speculation that Judas' possible motive was not money but to force Jesus' hand to somehow seize this opportunity and make His Kingdom a political reality.

Simon of Cyrene--(v.32) Cyrene lies on the coast of Libya in North Africa. Perhaps Simon was in Jerusalem as a Jewish pilgrim, perhaps on official business. Regardless, he was pressed into service to carry the cross of Jesus, probably because the loss of blood and agony suffered from the scourging had already weakened His body. One of Christ's first disciples was named Simon (Peter) and now the last God follower to be near Him as He is nailed to the cross is also named Simon.

Barabbas--(vs. 15-18) He led an insurrection against the Roman government. Pilate (in his opinion) offers the crowd a choice of insurrectionists, and likely smirks at the dark humor of the choice between a man named *Bar* (son) *abba* (father) and One who claimed to be the Son of God the Father.

Centurion--(v. 54) He uttered one line in Scripture: "Truly this was the Son of God!" We cannot know if he meant the manner in which Jesus faced death, the miracles occurring around him at Christ's death (v. 51-53), or that he realized what this death meant for mankind.

Joseph of Arimathea--(v.57) The other Gospels reveal he was a secret disciple of Jesus (Jn. 19.38), a prominent member of the Jewish Council (Mk. 15.43) and opposed to the charges against Jesus (Luke 23.50). Who knows how many believers are in the halls of power in every society today? Offering his personal tomb was a way to honor Jesus and also fulfill scripture (Is. 53.9).

Mothers of disciples--(v.55-56) They had ministered to Jesus (Lk. 8.1-3) but also grieved with and for Mary His mother as fellow mothers, possibly knowing the fate that awaited their sons if they continued in the Way.

Mary Magdalene--(v.56, 61) She was there with Jesus and the disciples on the road, now at the tomb, and shortly to meet Him again in the garden as her resurrected Lord. She became the one who announced His return to the disciples (Lk. 24.10, Jn. 20.15).

Guards at the tomb--(v. 64-66) Unwitting cogs in the Roman Empire later became the first to experience the resurrection (Mt. 28.4, 11-15).

<u>Chief priests, elders, Pharisees</u>--(vs. 62-64) They became the classic example of sincere yet misguided devotion, as in their efforts to defend God they urged His Son's crucifixion (v.22).

<u>Lines on Leadership</u>
Our actions can have a double effect of clarity and confusion. We resolve some questions and generate others with each action or decision. I have no way to know how the sovereign God Almighty will take my decisions and stances as a leader and weave them into the grand narrative of life. The ones recorded in this chapter have been reviewed and weighed for 2000 years; when I make a decision I do not have that historical perspective. Do a review of your past ten decisions and public stances taken. Were they made with any thought in mind of whether they would stand up to self-scrutiny in a year? Five years? After you are retired or long gone?

_____

_____

++

Matthew 28----Highlights: the resurrection of Christ, the Great Commission

The chapter begins with the resurrection of Christ. In most novels or movies, the last scene with the principal characters has some of the most memorable lines. What would a resurrected Savior impart to His followers as their consuming mission? Christ commands in Mt. 28.19-20 to make *disciples*, not *decisions*. The verse is in the imperative mode; it is a mandate straight from the Master for **all** believers, not just an elite few like the professional clergy. Most cannot grasp a macro view of the world (eight billion+ Earth dwellers) or any one thing with large numbers (like the Federal budget). That's why movie directors and authors tell sweeping stories of epic proportions through the eyes and experiences of a few main characters; it makes the enormity of the situation comprehensible. Likewise, the idea of discipling the world is mind boggling and quickly overwhelms one's sense of being able to start such a task, let alone accomplish it, unless one starts with a micro view of discipling that is manageable. For years I have taught a framework for discipleship that allows me to operate in the micro realm with a view toward the macro one. I cannot claim credit for it but wish to share it in this form.

<u>The simple one sentence version is this: everyone needs a Paul; everyone needs a Barnabas; and everyone needs a Timothy</u>. If we taught this leadership concept within our churches and organizations, then growth would be more organic and less programmatic. In verse 16, Jesus spoke to eleven people about making disciples and the opening phrase of v. 18 is best translated "as you are going" or "along the way." He didn't say it was a 30-day miracle surefire success, but more of a lifestyle.
Because of the potential for intensity and intimacy within the discipling relationships described below, I strongly encourage their pursuit with a person of the same gender. If everyone in our churches were involved with these three relationships, we would have vibrant, healthy churches/organizations and would develop leaders from within our faith families or whatever group we lead.

    1. <u>Paul</u>—I need someone further along in their walk with Christ than I am. It can be someone local, faraway, or even from another era. My Paul is someone willing to pour into my life their collected wisdom from the Word and life and to assist me in my journey toward spiritual maturity (Col. 1.28). A person might be my Paul for a season of my life, at a certain level, or for a lifetime. My Paul might be a composite person made up of a parent, a mature believer, and an author such as C.S. Lewis, Francis

Schaeffer, Bonhoeffer, or Dallas Willard. I must exercise the spiritual disciplines of guidance, submission, and accountability to allow them to lead me down these paths; therefore, it must be someone whose integrity I trust perhaps more than their theology, because I am largely entrusting my spiritual growth to them (2Tim.1.13-14).

    2. <u>Barnabas</u>—I need someone roughly on my level of spiritual maturity who is willing to walk with me on this pilgrimage. We have each other's back; we challenge each other to persevere, to grow, to stay pure, and to incarnate what we are learning together. This is a person I know well and relate to; we know each other's struggles, weaknesses, past, and dreams. This person is committed to my success even if I might "pass him up." (Acts 9.27, 11.21-26). Given the present state of telecommunications this person could be next door or halfway around the world.

    3. <u>Timothy</u>—I need someone who looks to me for their spiritual guidance, to whom I become their Paul (see 2 Tim. 2 entry). Both Jesus and Paul spoke to the masses and had large groups of disciples but chose to invest in a few to whom they would give their prime time and effort. New believers and older ones with stunted growth may not know they need a Paul and Barnabas. Encourage these people, bring them to a fuller understanding of the ways of our Lord (like Priscilla & Aquilla with Apollos in Acts 18.24-28). This could be as simple as helping a believer to learn how to use a study Bible, how to witness, how to pray, how to serve.

    If everyone were involved in these three relationships, then that individual would also fulfill all three roles simultaneously: I would be Paul to my Timothy; Barnabas to my Barnabas; and Timothy to my Paul. Discipleship occurs best not in an isolated classroom but emerges out of a relationship.

Discipleship is not rocket science; it is living life centered on Christ in a community of faith actively engaged in the lives of others. This is why the "Great Commission" (what many call Matt. 28.19-20) is tied to the "Great Commandment" (Matt. 22.37-40).

Lines on Leadership

Discipleship is largely teaching others to teach others to teach others. The Great Commission is a local strategy with global ramifications. So as a leader who is/will be your Paul, your Barnabas, your Timothy?

_____

_____

++

MARK'S GOSPEL

Intro: Mark's gospel is breathless and straightforward. It plunges into the life of Christ and runs, not walks, towards the Passion Week and never pauses. There is a refreshing directness to how it presents the teachings and actions of Jesus. He writes as if he is the newest beat reporter hired last week by a large media firm, and his transition word of choice is "immediately."

Mark is the same cousin of Barnabas (Col. 4.10) who accompanied Barnabas and Paul on their first missionary journey, deserted them for whatever reason, and who was the subject of the divisive argument and eventual parting of ways between Barnabas and Paul in Acts 15. Barnabas took him under his wing on travels to Barnabas' home island, Cyprus (Acts 15.39).

++

Mark 1---Highlights: John the Baptist' entrance; Jesus' Baptism; Jesus begins His public ministry; healings.

"And in the early morning, while it was still dark, He arose and went out and departed to a lonely place and was praying there." (v.35) The immediacy and brevity of Mark's gospel compared to the other three gospels does indeed take one's breath away at times. In the opening verses we meet John the Baptist, see Jesus baptized, and witness the beginning of His public ministry in Capernaum. His teaching was hailed as amazing (v.22). Jesus heals the man with the unclean spirit (vs. 23-27) and Simon Peter's mother-in-law (vs. 29-31), and news spreads rapidly throughout the region of Galilee (north of Samaria and to the west and north of the Sea of Galilee). No wonder that by sunset "the whole city had gathered at the door." (v. 33) He continued to heal throughout the evening.

Such a pace could be mind-numbing and body-exhausting. It could also be ego-inflating and goal-obscuring.

Jesus knew He needed time alone with His Father. The fact that the verse says 'He arose' indicates that though He was God, 'incarnate' still means "in the flesh," and that body had to sleep. Knowing the importance of His mission (saving the world through His death, burial, and resurrection), it seems every waking and asleep moment should have been spent preaching the Good News. That is the mindset of young preachers and young leaders, to constantly be engaged in the Task, the Mission, the Goal. Jesus knew He needed to daily renew everything: body, soul, and spirit. Seeing success is inspiring, hearing great music is inspiring, being loved can be inspiring, but sometimes we need isolation (v.35, a lonely place) more than inspiration, solitude that refines direction.

Some call it a Quiet Time, others use Time Alone with God, still others use Devotionals. The name matters not: the value of a daily time to reflect and walk through what lies behind, what lies ahead, and what lies within is inestimable. A Bible and journal are always in my backpack, those plus the indwelling Spirit of God are (for me) the essential ingredients for being in His Presence as my Lord was in Mark 1.35. I try to read in His Word, sometimes systematically, sometimes favorite sections to comfort and reassure me of His promises. Sometimes I read in a treasured copy of the Word, sometimes with the convenience of my smartphone or tablet. I write a journal entry as I wrestle with the passage, for the Bible is God's revelation to man. I have done this for decades, so now it comes naturally, and I often review the past day and make plans for the upcoming one, using the insights and truth of not only that day's reading but all He has taught me and brought me through. His thoughts are so superior to mine (Isaiah 55.9) and His plans so much better (Prov. 16.2-3) that I do well to listen more than speak (Eccl. 5.2), to read rather than ramble on about my self-centered needs and condition.

Earlier in Ecclesiastes Solomon writes how there is a time to be silent and a time to speak (Eccl. 3.7b). Jesus was praying in a lonely place; that doesn't mean He was always talking. I cannot imagine the dialogues of Deity with and within itself. I can replicate neither the depth nor the detail of such an exchange. But Christ gives us here an example to follow: have a regular time morning or evening, have a place that is quiet and alone, and have communion with the Father.

It is a vital example to follow in the early stages of one's ministry or leadership and even more so in the middle and latter stages of such. The more I experience exposure or success because of my ministry or vocation, the more necessary such times of reflection become. My tendency is to quickly absorb the newest compliment or complaint and let it go deep inside of me, to identify with the latest disaster in the news or the more recent triumph in our family. The voice I need to hear and heed more than any other is that of my Father. On rare occasions, He speaks directly in revelation, vision, or promptings of the Spirit, depending on your religious background and understanding of how He communicates to the individual believer. On most occasions He speaks to me through His written Word, the Bible. Experiences and emotions are real and powerful, but unreliable as to the eternal implications of decisions to make. Circumstances are like statistics; they can easily be manipulated to mean this or that depending on my personal filters or biases. I need to hear from Him and be regular enough and patient enough to listen when He is ready to speak, not "on demand" but in His time.

Lines on Leadership

Have you ever moved to or set up shop in a new locale? Experiences pile up, take on heightened drama and importance;

everything is new or unfamiliar. Establish a regular quiet time (ex., turn off the radio on your daily commute and listen to audio tapes of the Word of God or a podcaster you trust; or get up fifteen minutes earlier every morning, read in the Word, and record what it says to your spirit that day). Find another colleague in your profession who seems grounded and secure in who they are and what they do; chances are they have a regular time of reflection. Ask them how to get started in a regular time alone (best spent in the presence of God). It works for regular times of exercise or mental stimulation (I do a crossword puzzle every morning at breakfast); it works even better for the spirit.

_____
_____
++

Mark 2--Highlights: A paralytic is healed; Call of Matthew; old/new wineskins; questioning the Sabbath

One of the best biblical examples of innovative and collaborative leadership is clearly illustrated in this chapter. Capernaum was a thriving village on the Sea of Galilee's north shore complete with a large synagogue you can visit today. Less than a stone's throw away was Simon Peter's house used by Jesus as a ministry headquarters, which can also be visited today. It was not as large as other nearby houses and Jesus followers plus the interested bystanders would easily fill it up. On one return to Capernaum, the house filled up and a paralytic's quartet of friends were determined he should have an audience with Jesus. Several avenues were available to gain His attention: they could have written petitions; caused a commotion to draw the house occupants outside ('Fire, clear the area!'); demanded the occupants leave to gain entrance; or forcibly removed the occupants. Instead, they used a tactic unique in scripture. Mark

2.4 says in the original language they "unroofed the roof." The roof was apparently in sections like tiles or other easily removed materials, creating a hole large enough to lower down a pallet upon which lay the paralytic, yet sturdy enough to hold or support the weight of his four friends.

The friends exhibited initiative and creativity; they did not demand the exclusion of others from the scene, but rather utilized space previously unused and generated the desired audience with Jesus. He responded positively to their efforts; the scripture says, "And Jesus seeing their faith spoke to the paralytic." (v.5) Faith is too often relegated to a theological transaction, to accept the truth of Jesus' claims about Himself and receive eternal life (John 3.16, 5.24, for example). There are also elements of desire, of sacrifice, of single-minded devotion to reaching a goal. Faith as stated elsewhere (see Lk. 17 entry) is not as dependent on the amount as the object of one's faith. Here the foursome's faith is clearly in Jesus' ability to heal and is fueled in part by love for their friend. Operative faith is faith in action (see Js. 2.14ff).

    Their approach was not driven by notoriety for themselves, but a desire to help another to achieve his goal. Later on in the chapter Jesus gives the famous statement about old and new wineskins (vs. 21-22) in response to his practice of dining with religiously unclean people and not following generally accepted rules of fasting. The concept of new wineskins can also be applied to the opening section of the chapter and the lowering/healing of the paralytic: Creative approaches often result in an abandonment of or a breaking out of old confines and structures. The wineskins referred to in vs. 21-22 were made from animal organs, and after the normal course of exposure to the elements outside of it and the old wine encased in it, they became brittle and inflexible. <u>When methods become more</u>

important than the Message, the gospel must find new confines and new structures in which it can expand. The fermentation process of new wine necessitates a container that can expand and allow the wine to come into maturity because of the resultant expanding gases. New ideas often need new spaces and new arenas in which to materialize and mature.

Lines on Leadership
Innovation is often initially misunderstood and unappreciated. When undertaken in tandem with others such as the four friends described above, or with a band of disciples supporting Jesus, the misunderstandings and Pharisaical pushback experienced in every incident in Mark 2 become bearable and doable. What is something you are contemplating that would require "removing a roof" or "new wineskins?"

_____

_____

++

Mark 3---Highlights: healings; selection of apostles; blasphemy toward the Holy Spirit; true family

One of the most quoted Jim Collins concepts about initial formation of an organization is to "get the right people on the bus[1]." Jesus selects twelve apostles in vs. 13-19 (twelve an obvious connection between twelve tribes of Israel and His embryonic Kingdom), and a diverse crew it is—political extremists, tax collectors, fishermen, and a future traitor. If God is sovereign and Christ is God incarnate (Jn. 1.14), then Jesus knew from the beginning how this assemblage would turn out. Judging from their repeatedly perplexed responses to Jesus' miracles and teachings, it is safe to say Jesus knew what He needed in apostles, but the apostles themselves were clueless to the true and full nature of the Kingdom of God and their participation in it. Jesus has His own inner timetable of revelation and involvement for His apostles; as an example, a man healed in this chapter is admonished not to tell anyone His identity. Christ knew the populace would call for the Roman Empire's overthrow, and his disparate disciples would want Him to fulfill their separate agendas. He needed time to introduce the values, parameters, and directions of His Kingdom before He allowed His kingship to be publicly announced. <u>Just because all the "right people are on the bus" doesn't mean they are all ready to adopt the leader's complete vision for the organization.</u>

A prime indicator of this is the separate but connected story at the end of the chapter. Jesus' own Nazareth family tried to pull Him aside from the pace and passion of the crowd saying (v.21), "He is out of his mind" (ESV, NET), "He is beside Himself" (KJV), or "he has lost His senses." (NASB) Their concern is natural and understandable: people pressed in on Him to where no one could take time to eat (v.20). They not only wanted Him to rest, one translation said they wanted to "take custody of Him" (v.21, NASB). At one point, Jesus is surrounded by a crowd and word comes to Him that his mother and siblings were outside calling for Him. He asks the crowd who are His mother and brothers and answers His own question with a key principle (v.35), "whoever does the will of God, this is My brother, and sister, and mother." It was revolutionary; up to this time (and occasionally even in current society) ancestry mattered more than ability, and brotherhood was determined by bloodlines more than buy in. Whether He glanced at the twelve apostles or the entire crowd cannot be determined; what is clear is He defines His true family as not based on genes and biological ties but obedience to the Father's will.

Lines on Leadership

The church (and to a degree other organizations) should be a place where people can find a family. Regardless of my background, dysfunctional earthly siblings, absentee biological fathers, orphan status, lack of pedigree, or 1001 other factors that distinguish our sense of "belonging" I can find love and purpose in the family of faith. A church where a person remains a consumer or a spectator and is not given a covenant bond to brothers and sisters in Christ is not a true church in my mind. How much superior to coming into work and performing x tasks for a paycheck is realizing I will be able to fellowship with and grow amid a family? What are you doing to lead your church or your organization into joining your values, your work environment, your production all into a great family environment for your members or employees? What grants them status as part of "the family?"

_____

_____

++

Mark 4---Highlights: Parables of the Sower, Seeds, Mustard Seeds, and Christ stills the Sea

Years ago, in the early stages of my NE Texas campus ministry I was introduced to the wonderful concept of summer missions: students at our Christian campus chose a site around the world for an immersive ten week where they would share their faith through servant ministry projects. Some were rural, others urban, and most dealt with a culture unfamiliar to students from the deep pineywoods of East Texas.

One student leader chose Mexico for his summer missions experience and came back ebullient. He had seen the gospel result in many giving their hearts to Christ. Don was inspired to reapply the next summer. He wanted to broaden his horizons, so he chose an inner-city assignment in New York City. Upon his return at the start of the fall semester he arrived with more questions than answers. He was quickly in my office asking what went wrong. No decisions for Christ, little response of any kind to his weeks spent in a tough neighborhood and tough circumstances. He was even questioning the effectiveness of the gospel. I simply said to him, "Same seed, different soil."

Jesus shares the Parable of the Sower and a lengthy explanation of it in Mark 4.1-20. In all four scenarios (by the wayside, rocky soil, thorny soil, good soil) the same seed is sown (which He explains is the Word of God, v. 14). It is no surprise that the different soils yield different results.

From a purely business standpoint, one would likely prioritize the soils and plant more seed in the good soil because it yields "thirty, sixty, and hundredfold" (v. 20). Why waste seed on unproductive soils? If these "soils" are the lives of other human beings, I cannot know how productive or unproductive their lives will turn out. <u>My Kingdom role is based on faithfulness and obedience instead of efficiency and output</u>. I am responsible for the sowing of the seed, not the condition of the soil. This is where ministry diverges from commerce; it is not always about production but following the Person of Jesus. If He leads me to a place where the soil is rocky, thorny, or not conducive to glorious results, then so be it. Some are called to sow their seed in a place teeming with children and growing neighborhoods. I am in a state declining in population, and marvel at the perseverance of some pastors to stay in their positions around me for decades. They understand to sow until sent elsewhere. One of our pastors went to a community that has less than 200 of a past 2000. Most are "on checks" or "on drugs." For the better part of two years, they held services there and the most that came were three. But slowly as they continued to sow, the people of the area learned of their steadfast love, their perseverance, their faithfulness. Today after over a decade of sowing on that rocky soil a work is thriving. Sow the seed.

<u>Lines on Leadership</u>
In what type of soil are you sowing? Can you describe the seed you are sowing?

_____

_____

++

Mark 5---Highlights: Gerasene Demoniac; Jairus' daughter and woman with issue of blood healed

       The eastern shores of the Sea of Galilee were considered Gentile territory at the time of Jesus. The previous chapter included the trip to this shore in the evening during a storm in which Jesus calmed the sea by speaking directly to it. This caused the disciples to exclaim (5.41), "Who then is this, that even the wind and the sea obey Him?" They did not know it was merely a prelude to the events of chapter 6.

       They encounter a wretched, tortured soul living in the region's tombs and caves, obviously known by the nearby populace but forced to live apart from them. His manacles and chains are useless to hold him as he breaks them with superhuman strength. It is soon apparent that he is inhabited by countless demons capable of such combined strength that "no one was strong enough to subdue him (v. 4)." The demons recognize Jesus for who He really is and after being commanded to leave the "Gerasene Demoniac" they ask permission of "Jesus, Son of the Most High God" (addressing Him more properly than the multitudes of people do) to enter a neighboring swine herd.

Jesus grants them permission, knowing this will greatly shorten their welcome in the region.

Once the demons enter the swine, the herd (ca. 2000) rushes over the cliff into the sea (v. 13). What a terrible yet fascinating sight to see as bleating and squealing pigs jump headlong for several minutes to their death, an inevitable outcome since the demonic delight in destruction. The leadership principle surfaces when the townspeople realize their source of economic prosperity just vanished into the foamy waters below thick with thrashing legs and bodies.

Most people are content to listen to truth or see its consequences in the lives of others as long as they are not personally affected, particularly if it is adversely. When the consequences of my actions start to affect the economic vitality of a person or a group (see Acts 19.23-28), pushback is unavoidable. It is why Jesus taught so much on money and possessions (where a man's treasure is, there also lies the individual's heart, Mt. 6.21). Jesus did not hesitate to permit the slaughter of 2000 swine to restore the life of one man to wholeness. This is an extraordinary scene. He churns the entire city into economic upheaval to bring one man to his sanity.

Lines on Leadership
Would you describe your decision making as based on expediency or conviction? What was your last decision based on clear conviction that was costly to one person or group?
_____
_____
++

Mark 6---Highlights: Teaching, the Twelve sent, the Baptist beheaded, 5000 fed, Jesus walked on the sea

This story is recounted in all four Gospels (Mt. 14, Lk. 9, Jn. 6) Jesus taught a large gathering until the hour is late. Jesus suggested they share a large sit-down meal; the disciples protested it would take 200 days' wages to feed this many people. This was money they did **NOT** have. Jesus simply asked what they **DID** have: they mustered five loaves of bread and two fish. As He blessed it, the loaves and fishes miraculously fed the large crowd of 5000. Although the author of this book is a firm believer in Christ and that the miracles reported are accurate and true, the emphasis here is not on the miraculous but on the response of the disciples and the response of the Messiah. Jesus was not interested in what they did NOT have but in what they DID have. He could use whatever they had to His glory.

We find an OT parallel to this incident. In 2 Kings 3 (one of my favorite "go-to" passages to preach on short notice) the story unfolds of three kings (Jehoram, Jehoshaphat, and the Edomite king) in an uneasy alliance. They have ventured onto a rather ill-advised route to conquer the king of Moab that has resulted in a shortage of water for the people, the animals, and the kings. The area south of the Dead Sea is below sea level, hot every day, and desolate, and now it may be the possible final resting place for a coalition army if something does not happen soon. Jehoram is the group whiner, quick to point out what they DO NOT have and blame it on the Lord (2 Kgs. 3.10, 13). Jehoshaphat does not dwell on what they do NOT have but instead on what they DO have, which is the prophet, Elisha. (2 Kgs. 3.11-14)

Elisha, after inquiring of God on their behalf, instructs them to do something totally mundane and beneath the dignity of kings: go dig ditches (2 Kgs. 3.16). Take the shovels they DO have and create trenches. This will not only provide water for them as needed (how, they thought?), but it will also have the bonus effect of destroying the enemies, the Moabites. As it turned out, a storm occurred far enough away that it was not heard, and rainfall rushed through the *wadi* there they traveled. This type of rain is here today and gone tomorrow---unless trenches are dug to retain water. The Lord's providence had the Moabites come upon the camp of Jehoram, Jehoshaphat, and the king of Edom early in the morning, and because of the angle of the sun's rays (and the fact that Edom has red sandstone formations over which the rain traveled) they perceived the trenches as pools of blood. They dropped their guard and raced to seize the battle site booty, thinking the kings had warred against each other. It resulted in not only rescuing the three armies in the desert; it contributed to the downfall of their Moabite enemy.

Lines on Leadership
The disciples' lack of faith resulted in Jesus' insistence they pick up the remains from the meal which amounted to a basket per disciple (v. 43). Sometimes the question is not 'what do I think we need?' but 'what do I have and how can I use it to fulfill the challenge before my group?'
_____
_____
++

Mark 7---Highlights: followers of tradition, the heart of man, the Syrophoenician woman

Mark, at times, seems to be the poster child for ADD, attention deficit disorder. His accounts of the teachings, miracles, and actions of Jesus are more pogo stick than pedestrian, bouncing from one story to the next. But when you connect the points where the pogo stick landed, threads and commonalities appear, such as function trumps format in Mark 7.

A rank-and-file soldier slogs through the battle, sleeps in its midst, and sees what is right in front of him at the moment. Whatever he sees his comrades doing, he learns to do as well. Traditions become ingrained from one wave of soldiers to the next. The higher up the ranks of command, the wider the range of vision required to the point the leader's perspective is often hard to grasp by enlisted men. In vs. 1-13, Jesus is chastised by the Pharisees because He and His disciples did not ceremonially wash (which was less scriptural command and more oral tradition later codified in the Mishnah, rabbinical teachings on the scriptures). They had come from Jerusalem basically to check out Jesus' activities on the west coast of the Sea of Galilee. The market where Jesus obtained the food was likely run by either Gentiles or nonobservant Jews[1]. More important in this passage is the Pharisees' disdain for Gentiles than any actual hygienic practices. Jesus calls them out as hypocrites for using what looks like religious observance to cover up their prejudice.

In vs. 24-30 the story leaps from the Sea of Galilee to the shores of the Mediterranean apparently where Jesus planned some R&R (v.24). It centers, however, on a most unusual dialogue between Jesus and a Gentile woman. On the surface it sounds rude and condescending, but in reality is a humorous and witty exchange where Jesus spoofs this disdain for Gentiles and assumed superiority of Jews over them (Gentiles being anyone not a Jew) and results in the daughter's healing. He moves up the coast in vs. 31-37 and heals a deaf-mute in a most unconventional and (at face value) rather disgusting manner. He does it by sticking His fingers in the man's ears then spitting on His fingers and touching the man's tongue. He does not associate with the "right" people and He does not conduct Himself in the "right" way.

Lines on Leadership
I worship what looks to me like a messy Messiah; messy not because He is sloppy but because I must take pause sometimes to look past the unconventionality and see the underlying purpose of His words and actions, the broader expanse of His total vision for the Kingdom of God. What ridicule and misunderstanding from others will you tolerate in order to accomplish what you as a leader know must be done, must be emphasized?

_____

_____

++

Mark 8---Highlights: 4000 fed; healing of blind man; Peter's confession of Christ;

I have often wondered if Jesus suffered from FFS—Flat Forehead Syndrome. This "syndrome" occurs when someone repeatedly hits his forehead with the palm of his hand upon hearing inane, off the wall responses, usually by subordinates or colleagues.

Vs. 1-10, Jesus again miraculously feeds a large crowd and again the disciples gather up a symbolic number of baskets (12 the first time; now, seven). As they traverse the Sea of Galilee in a boat Jesus warns the disciples about the leaven of the Pharisees (v.15) and the disciples start up a lively discussion about the fact they have no bread. After either a roll of the eyes or another palm to the forehead (vs. 17-21) Jesus proceeds to unpack what He implied by using the term leaven.

He Himself is the Provider, and the bread of life (see John 6). He is trying to divert their attention from the miracles to the Messiah Himself. It is a gentle rebuke about not understanding His Deity. It is not about filling hungry stomachs but recognizing His divine nature and ability to provide for them.

Use of symbolic or figurative speech by a speaker when the audience is zeroed in on concrete/literal terms makes for parallel lines of reasoning that never intersect. The speaker's intent is lost if the hearer's perception and understanding are not in sync with the speakers. Modern day *corporate-speak* is often more concerned with covering its backside or promoting its brand instead of paying attention to whether the customer/client is following along. Jesus took the time (for the umpteenth time) to walk through what He meant so the disciples gained understanding and insight. It is exasperating and draining to explain a third and fourth time what is so plain and easy to grasp for me, but seeing the glazed eyes turn to "aha" lightbulbs is worth it.

<u>Lines on Leadership</u>
What is an aspect of your work that you find particularly difficult to explain to colleagues or clients? What type of feedback system do you have in your day-to-day dealings with your company and the public to insure that the message is <u>not only being broadcast but understood</u>?

_____

_____

++

Mark 9---Highlights: Transfiguration, boy with unclean spirit, meaning of greatness, selected teachings

A discussion among the disciples about who was the greatest pops up frequently in the gospels, sometimes more than once per gospel (see Lk. 9.46, 22.26). It took until after the resurrection and Pentecost before they understood Jesus' kingdom was not like any the world had ever seen. Jockeying for position in a new government would have been almost unavoidable; after seeing the increasing number and scope of miracles their Leader had manifested, the unspeakable had become theoretically possible to some of them: the overthrow of the mightiest power in the known world, the Roman Empire. Empty chatter about something not even remotely possible can be dismissed as time fillers; but their discussions about pecking orders had started to take on "when we're in power" status. If Christ could control waves and storms by merely speaking to them (Mark 4.37ff), what could He do with a wave of His hand at legions of soldiers? Jesus had to address this in a manner that would quell their ambitions but also give insight into the true nature of His coming Kingdom.

He decided not to enter a military, political, or philosophical discussion. He simply stated, "If anyone would be first, he must be last of all and servant of all" (v.35; see Mt. 20 entry). Then to give a powerful visual illustration He took a child and totally disarmed all the talk about rising to prominence at His side by saying the way to His Father was not climbing a ladder of success but kneeling to serve others.

In vs. 33-37, Jesus addressed the competition within the disciples' own group. In vs. 38-41, Jesus addresses the same spirit of competition and tribalism as the disciples wanted to exclude others from being identified with them. Jesus encourages His disciples to identify allies and adversaries more accurately, and to not mistake comrades in arms for competitors.

Lines on Leadership
Who are your real allies or adversaries? real comrades or real competitors? How do you distinguish them?
_____

_____

++

Mark 10---Highlights: Teaching on divorce, rich young ruler, James/John vie for favor, heals Bartimaeus

(vs. 46-52) The healing of the blind man Bartimaeus closes the section of Mark dealing with Jesus' public teaching ministry. Chapter 11 begins with the Passion narrative as He triumphantly enters Jerusalem. He and His disciples are traveling from Galilee up the road through Jericho headed resolutely to His date with the cross and death. As He walks with His retinue through the streets of old and new Jericho, He creates quite a stir among the bystanders; the chatter and repeated whispered mentions of Jesus' name has alerted Bartimaeus that Jesus is approaching.

He uses a known messianic title for Jesus calling, 'Jesus, Son of David, have mercy on me!' (see Matt. 1.1) It is not certain why the crowd rebuked him---it could have been the use of the messianic term, it could have been, "Can't you see He is bent on getting somewhere, and is not to be sidetracked?" He kept it up, repeating the term Son of David. Jesus did notice the blind man and called him out.

The crux of the exchange is found in two short sentences: one a question, the other a response. Jesus asked, "What do you want me to do for you?" As a blind man along the side of the road Bartimaeus was used to begging and asking for alms. It would have been the natural response to say, "I'd like an extra special donation worthy of Your regional renown." Instead, I believe he had mulled over a bolder request. If we are in the presence of someone famous, powerful, or wealthy, our reasoning capacity often takes a back seat to awe, and we are reduced to basic words of adoration or commenting how fortunate we are to meet this person face to face. Bartimaeus' response is respectful, concise, and forthright. It was respectful as he called him Rabboni or Rabbi (Teacher, Master); it was concise (less than ten words); and it was forthright (I would like to see again). It was an honest request for help. Jesus granted it.

Jesus did not just ask 'What do you␣what me to do,' He asked that plus the phrase 'For you?' Part of me wants to ask why Jesus didn't just make a blanket healing of all blindness, all disease, all failings. Why doesn't He do that then, now, and for all time? He wanted the request to be personal and the response personal as well. Jesus acknowledged the man's faith in His ability to heal. When the time presents itself, I will not allow myself to be squelched. I will cry out and make my request known.

Lines on Leadership

If you are in a large church or organization where you rarely if ever have had a personal exchange with the senior pastor or the company head, and he shows up one day in your home/office, and offers to do whatever is needed in your life, what would be your reply? If you are in senior leadership, how do you handle straightforward, open, direct questions and petitions by your fellow workers?

_____

_____

++

Mark 11---Highlights: triumphal entry; moneychangers in the Temple; Questions about authority

A good leader knows a "one-size-fits-all" stump speech will not connect with everyone. Sometimes the best response is not to speak at all (vs. 1-11), sometimes it is a burst of righteous indignation (vs. 15-18), and sometimes it is the Socratic approach of answering a question with a question (vs. 27-33).

A large part of the response is to know both the audience and the situation which has been addressed elsewhere in this book. In the first passage, Jesus fulfills scripture by entering Jerusalem as it was predicted the Messiah would enter (Zech. 9.9). He says nothing to the adoring crowd, speaking only to his disciples about where to find the colt, a behind the scenes affirmation of what the crowd is shouting, that He is truly the Son of David and His Kingdom was about to be manifest to all. He knows their celebration is short lived and originates in their hope He is the anticipated Messiah who will overthrow the detested Romans.

Jesus tries to restore the Temple to a state of holiness by clearing out the moneychangers and declares publicly it is His Father's house, and that it should be a house of prayer, not a robbers' den (again a fulfillment of scripture, Isaiah 56.7; Jeremiah 7.11). The same chief priests and elders who were incensed by His action in the Temple (v. 18) sought to entrap Jesus with a trick question. Jesus, knowing his audience and their intent, exposes their trickery by turning their question on authority (designed to force His response into a yes/no answer concerning His identity) into an indirect affirmation of His wisdom.

<u>Lines on Leadership</u>
Jesus would not be deterred from His Messianic mission of being a sacrifice for the sin of mankind. His responses to the various crowds and situations were indeed different but all born of a singular drive to complete His mission of being the sacrificial Lamb of God and Lord of all nations. What is your overarching mission that must be accomplished, and are you willing to vary your response and results to achieve that mission, even to the point of being misunderstood, and receiving more scorn and

consternation than glory? Jesus was not overcome by nor taken in by the show of affirmation, knowing it would soon turn against Him. His mission was not glorification of self but of His Father. How do you make sure the mission and the person (you) are not mistaken for one another[1]?

_____

_____

++

Mark 12---Highlights: parable of the vine-growers; dialogues of Jesus with Pharisees, Sadducees, Scribes

    In a court of law, the lawyer attempts to direct the line of questioning into a narrow lane, restricting the person being questioned as to directions or variations on the response. It is akin to hiking into an increasingly narrow mountain pass to the point one cannot move or twist and can only move sideways either forward or backward, which equates to a yes/no response or the desired name or term sought by the questioner.

Three times in this chapter the vultures (Jewish leaders) fly in ever tighter circles as they believe they are closing in on their prey. Three times Jesus deflects or refutes their line of reasoning to the point they ask no further questions of Him (v. 34). Their inquiries involved fealty to God in the areas of taxes (vs. 13-17), marriage partners (vs. 18-27), and obedience to the biblical commandments (vs. 28-34).

    Jesus' replies are not novel attention diverters; they are true creative alternatives. In the area of taxes, He turns an either/or expectation to a both/and answer ("render unto Caesar what is Caesar's and unto God what is God's"). In the area of marriage, he expands the frame of reference beyond past marriage partners to show they will all be in a new set of relationships in heaven, rendering the sequence of marriage partners moot. In the area of obedience, He gives a traditional summation of the Law and the Prophets distilled down to what is generally referred to as the Great Commandment (Love God supremely and your neighbor as yourself, covering all vertical and horizontal relationships). Jesus combines a quick and innovative mind with a mastery of the very source material (the OT) used to formulate the "trapping" questions.

<u>Lines on Leadership</u>
How adept are you in the areas of content mastery, ability to counter criticism with creativity, and detecting sincere inquiry (vs. 28-34) from entrapment? How do any of these areas prevent you from engaging critics, be they church members, outsiders, or shareholders?

_____

_____

++

Mark 13---Highlights: foretelling of Temple destruction, fig tree, and predicted return of the Messiah.

Chapter 13 is Mark's version of the Olivet Discourse (see Mt. 24 entry). Today we will concentrate on the closing words of Christ in Mark 13.28-29 and 34-37 about the fig tree and the returning master. The word image is of a master of an estate who leaves on a journey and puts the servants in charge of the day-to-day affairs of the house. He specifically commands the doorkeeper to "stay on the alert" (v.34). So, the default setting is a constant expectation of and watch for the master's coming but not so intense that everyone drops their chores to peer out the windows 24/7.

Earlier in the chapter He charges the disciples to learn from the fig tree. "When its branch has already become tender, and puts forth its leaves, you know summer is near" (v.28). The budding of leaves and soon to be figs is a sure sign that the fruit is forthcoming, but it would be foolish to stop tending the plants as soon as the first bud appears. The work must continue, and no one can predict the precise day of harvest; the season perhaps, but not the date.

In modern day terms an individual or a country cannot stay at DEFCON 5 all the time with missiles and personnel on high alert: it would be a huge expenditure of money and adrenaline that would wear out a person or wear down a country. Yet to ignore the signs of the times and the sequence of events puts one at peril. An effective leader continues to strike this ongoing, ever-changing balance of one eye on the home front and one eye on the horizon, peering through a microscope and telescope simultaneously in a bifocal manner.

Lines on Leadership
The OT is replete with examples of concentrating on both the ordinary and the oncoming. In Judges 7.4-7, God instructs Gideon to use only the soldiers who kneel to drink instead of on both knees with their head down toward the water. This word image means these soldiers paid attention simultaneously to their needs yet were alert and ready to move at a moment's notice. In Nehemiah 4.9-23, he instructs those rebuilding the wall in Jerusalem to carry a load in one hand and a weapon in the other, for half of the people to stand guard while the other half continued the work.

How do you instruct your people and design your organization's infrastructure so that the work continues yet attention is also given to changing times and outside forces capable of disruption, destruction, or dissonance? How will you exhibit bifocal leadership?

_____

_____
++

Mark 14---Highlights: anointed at Bethany; Lord's Supper; Gethsemane; Jesus' trials; Peter's denials.

Most of the major events in this chapter are covered in other entries (see Mt. 26, the trials; Lk. 22, the Lord's Supper). This entry combines two of the events with similar backgrounds and different results, Jesus in Gethsemane and Peter in the temple courtyards.

Gethsemane is today a small prayer garden dotted with ancient olive trees, none of which date back to the time of Jesus. It lies on the Mt. of Olives lower down than the typical tourist overview of old Jerusalem. From this garden, the Temple Mount can be seen across the Kidron Valley. I have knelt and stood there in silence and looked over the valley toward the Temple. I wondered when Jesus prayed if perhaps He had also looked across the valley at the very place He would soon be tried and crucified. How He prayed 'not my will but Thy will be done' (v. 36) is incomprehensible to me, knowing what awaited Him.

Peter was "below [in] the temple courtyard" (v.66) after the arrest and during the various trials of Jesus. It was in this place he denied his Lord three times, cursing the last time to emphasize his dissociation with Jesus. I have often wondered if Peter looked out over the Kidron Valley and saw Gethsemane if his mind went back a few hours and thought of Jesus who did not shirk nor pretend to be someone else. Jesus did not run away; He simply allowed the Temple guards to arrest Him. It is no wonder that Peter "broke down and wept" (v.72, ESV).

<u>Lines on Leadership</u>
This is a complex situation. What if Jesus had exerted His divine nature and slipped away from the guards or overpowered them? What if Peter had died as a martyr to the cause as a fellow co-conspirator? God does not deal in the subjunctive (would of,

could of, should of); His very name is I AM, the very essence of combined volition and action. God used a deliberate sacrifice of His Son (Jesus) for the sin of mankind, and God used an act of cowardice and fear by Peter to eventually provide the early church with a transformed leader and Biblical author. The resurrection and ascension of Christ forever changed Peter and his sermons, infusing them with courage to stretch the boundaries of the early church (see all Acts entries) and change the inward sect to a global movement.

I strive to honor and obey my Father in heaven but admittedly don't always "get it right." Sometimes I make poor, unwise decisions. I pray for the <u>courage</u> of Christ when I make a decision I know will be costly; I pray for the <u>grace</u> of God when I make a decision I later regret. And I pray for the <u>providence</u> of my Father to weave all of those together in a way that will honor Him. What leadership decision to stand firm or step back looms in your future? your past?

_____

_____

++

<u>Mark 15</u>---Highlights: Jesus before Pilate; the crucifixion and burial of Jesus

Sports broadcasters often say "That will not show up in tomorrow's box score." The box score in sports is a group of statistics showing how many yards the quarterback passed in football, how many hits a batter had, how many free throws a basketball star made, or how many goals hockey or soccer players scored. It shows when points or runs were scored in which quarter or inning. It is easy to see who had a 'big night' statistically speaking. The reason the broadcaster says it is because the actions of a particular player are significant or possibly game changing yet not quantifiable in terms of the normal range of statistics. Mark 15 is replete with "secondary" persons worth noting. The "box score" is of course the trial and crucifixion of Jesus. Several side stories surround this pivotal event in the history of mankind. (For another perspective on these "secondary" persons see Matthew 27 entry)

Roman centurion--This military leader had commanded soldiers in battle and seen blood and brutality his whole adult life. This crucifixion was different enough for him to not only say the victim was innocent but "The Son of God." The difference was "In this way he breathed his last." (v. 39) It is hard to know from the text if he noticed the cry to the Father (v. 34 is a quote from Psalm 22), or the last loud cry before the last breath (v. 37), or the fact He bowed His head and yielded His spirit willingly (Mt. 27.50; Lk. 23.46; Jn. 19.30). Why this was recorded cannot be determined from the text (was he overheard by those nearby, did he convert and become a Christian, did a disciple of Christ later explain to him privately what he had witnessed); to utter a line remembered 2000 years later is extraordinary.

Joseph of Arimathea—Joseph was a member of the Jewish ruling council (v.43) yet is described as 'a disciple of Jesus' (John 19.42) and "looking for the kingdom of God" (Mk. 15.42, ESV). We do not know the full motive for his action (respect for Christ's teaching? The raw deal Jesus got (Lk. 23.51) in the trumped-up trial?), but Joseph displayed courage to approach Pilate for the body of Jesus so that he could honor Him with a proper burial. He went the second mile by offering an upper class (his own?) tomb and took the time and care to bury Jesus according to Jewish law and customs.

The Mary's and Salome--How remarkable that Mark, after the history-altering crucifixion, devotes two full sentences (vs. 40-41) to describe the women (some named like the Mary's and Salome, some unnamed) who followed Jesus all the way to Jerusalem. When everyone else had scattered dazed, shocked, and fearful after the crucifixion, who was watching to discover in which tomb Jesus was laid? Mary Magdalene, Mary mother of James, and Salome. They marked the location, intending to anoint the body with embalming oils after the Sabbath (Mk. 16.1)

Simon of Cyrene—Matthew, Luke, and Mark mention Simon was from Cyrene, the area of North Africa known today as Libya. Alexander and Rufus were named as his sons, likely the same ones mentioned as believers in the early church (Rom. 16.13[1]). Roman law allowed soldiers to conscript any passerby to perform menial short-term duties for them. It is hard to imagine what an ordeal it was for Simon of Cyrene to involuntarily participate in the very act of crucifying the Son of God his children would later follow and worship.

Lines on Leadership
None of the four mentioned altered or influenced the act of sacrifice Jesus gave on the cross, but all four were intimately involved. In varying degrees, they all showed courage or risked something to be a part of this cosmic event. None of these Mark 15 men and women sought recognition; they simply served, testified about, or honored Jesus as the Messiah. Not all leaders are CEO's and senior executive positions. If you influence one other person, you are a leader, even if it is fleeting or temporary. What box scores do you need to quit following; how can you best serve, testify about, or honor those in your circle of friends or colleagues today?

_____
_____
++

Mark 16---Highlights: resurrection; commissioning of disciples

The last chapter of Mark presents a pastoral dilemma. Modern commentaries and study Bibles point out that the last verses (vs. 9-20) do not appear in a significant number of older 1st-century manuscripts. The Bible is one of the most attested pieces of ancient literature with thousands of manuscripts of the NT alone existent, some dating back to less than decades from the actual events' occurrence. Vs. 9-20, often appear in brackets, italicized, separated, or even omitted from the body of the main text. Should I preach from this passage? Should I portray it as supplemental, apocryphal, or interesting but not inspired? Do I refer to this text only as a backup to other NT passages and use it in a secondary, supportive fashion? Do I use caution and caveats or simply avoid it?

Those in positions other than ministry might conclude this dilemma has nothing to do with their jobs. Consider these scenarios:

a) An important document from work has been lost, damaged, or deleted. Your team scrambles to find other sources that mentioned various sections of the document or from which the document was derived. The team discovers alternate versions of certain sections. Should they include all variations with footnotes and educated guesses? Should they use only what (in their opinion) is closest to what all remember as the original wording? Should they amalgamate and blend all the versions into one composite version? Will people treat the edicts and directives of this part of the document differently and with less reliance than the other parts everyone acknowledges as original?

b) The founder of the company was larger than life and many of the legends surrounding the founder over the decades made it into the core values and narrative that form the company's brand. Letters and journals are found of the founder's family members that paint a much different picture of the founder's actions and foundational statements upon which his/her life was based. Does the company acknowledge the inconsistencies, ignore them, or put distance between the founder and the company?

<u>Lines on Leadership</u>

The Craft of Research by Booth, Colombo, and Williams was considered our starting point in my Ph.D. studies concerning validity, reliability, and consequent usability: "Although you should never trust any source blindly, most of your readers will be more willing to trust print sources from reliable presses or journals than almost any source on the Internet[1]." In the margin I scribbled, "Will this change for subsequent generations?" As a leader, how do you determine the reliability of the sources you use for your decisions? How do you determine that you will stand firm on this or that piece of information and act accordingly?

_____
_____
++

LUKE'S GOSPEL

Intro: Mark's gospel displays passion; Luke's gospel reflects precision. Luke is a physician. His investigative, inquisitive style of writing shines through in his gospel and his later record of the early church found in the book of Acts. Luke's gospel is the last of the Synoptic Gospels (Matthew, Mark, Luke), which scholars agree likely used a common source document from which to write their gospels, hence their similarity in stories, parables, and teachings included in each gospel.

++

Luke 1---Highlights: births of Jesus and John the Baptist foretold and unfold; Magnificat; Benedictus

Exactness is not necessarily devoid of drama. Luke's gospel is not a dusty treatise but a beautiful and rich perspective on the life and impact of Jesus Christ. An incredible breadth of information and foundation for the story is contained in Luke 1-4 as he intertwines the lives of Jesus and John from conception to their onset of their public ministries. The reasons for Luke's gospel and his account of the early church (Acts) are found in Luke 1.3 ("to investigate everything carefully") and v.4 ("so that you may know the exact truth about what you have been taught"). Luke mentions events, names, positions held, and locations more exactly than any other NT writer. He obviously did not collect hearsay but went to primary sources such as Mary and others to compile his gospel since he was neither one of nor with any of the original apostles.

Ein Karem is the hilly childhood home of John the Baptist, son of Elizabeth and Zacharias, and lies on the western side of Jerusalem. Bethlehem, birthplace of Jesus, is on the south side, so both were born close to the Holy City. The chapter is both intimate (we meet and hear Jesus and John's parents dialogue about these unique births) and immense in scope (Hebrew fulfillment of prophecy is now coming true in their lifetimes and in their very homes). The song of Mary, known for centuries as the *Magnificat* (vs. 46-55) and the song of Zacharias, known as the *Benedictus* (vs. 68-79), are high points of praise and portent. The mother of the Messiah and the father of His messenger praise God for their offspring and their place in Jewish history. (vs.76-79 were the verses preached in 1982 at our commissioning service as overseas missionaries with the International Mission Board)

Lines on Leadership
"You have been chosen for this mission." Some people spend their whole lives waiting to hear those words; some spend every waking minute avoiding the same words. These two distinctions do not necessarily identify an emergent leader. Mary was ready to undertake this mission (vs. 38, 48), Zacharias was not so sure (v.18). Both gave us praise and prophecy that has endured through millennia. It is related to the leadership principle in Mt. 21.28-32, that ready or reluctant the bottom line for a leader is to follow through when the opportunity arises. When the mission is presented, protests, whining, trying to get out of it is allowed (see Moses' dialogue with God at the burning bush, Ex. 3-4) by God's mercy if the bottom line is submission to His will and acceptance of the task.

What God-sized task/mission looms on your horizon? If one is thrust upon you (maybe not as dramatic as the appearance of an angel, but perhaps by circumstance or a superior) would you ask for more time, an exemption, counsel, or unilaterally take it?

_____
_____
++

Luke 2---Highlights: Jesus' Bethlehem birth; flight to Egypt; return to Nazareth; Temple visit as youth

Every Christmas vs. 1-20 are read in countless church services and homes as the beloved "Christmas story" involving shepherds, angels, and a new family likely huddled in one of the hundreds of grottoes that dot the Bethlehem hillsides. Our attention will focus on v. 52: "And Jesus kept increasing in wisdom and stature, and in favor with God and men." This rare all-in-one verse embodies multiple leadership principles. The four ways Jesus matured are: 1) mentally, 2) physically, 3) spiritually, and 4) socially.

There have been effective leaders throughout history with marked deficiencies in each of those categories, especially if morality is left out of the equation. But striving for excellence in all four categories is a reliable formula for leadership preparation. The key phrase is "kept increasing." Some people are naturally gifted in one or more of the four categories. This is not an oversimplified plea for leaders to shore up weaknesses, nor is it a repudiation of strengths-based leadership. It is not an issue of 'either/or' but 'both/and,' an integrated package of the four categories. I will use my own fifty years of ministry as an example, not as a model.

1) Mentally---I have multiple degrees and respect higher education; this is not only about stretching beyond current information and expertise, but about remaining sharp and learning new ways to reason, analyze, and reflect. Reading in one's discipline is a given; reading in a transdisciplinary fashion (after retirement, I took courses in Spanish and quantum physics, learned new instruments like dobro and banjo to go along with guitar) enriches not only my knowledge but my thinking processes.

2) Physically---As one grows older, muscles atrophy, the metabolism slows, the bones break easier. On top of that, I have a job that is both stressful and sedentary, a surefire recipe for multiple health issues. I keep a Bowflex, core ball, treadmill, and TV up in the man cave and keep a regimented schedule of

exercise. Now approaching my seventies, I have incorporated Tai Chi to stave off balance issues. For pleasure I prefer hiking, canoeing, and golf, but I live where (in winter) it is -4 wind chill outside, so I combine 1) and 2) by watching instruction videos or podcasts as I exercise.

    3) <u>Spiritually</u>---as noted elsewhere in this book, a personal relationship to the Father is best maintained with regular private devotions, readings in His Word, prayer, and recording insights (my preferred method is journaling). Most of my ministry time is solitary; more so as I now work with churches in ten counties. I am on the road a lot by myself, and not under the steady tutelage of others. Private time alone with God is essential for spiritual growth.

    4) <u>Socially</u>---I am an outgoing introvert; I can flip the switch and be gregarious in a volitional way. Public speaking is something I honestly enjoy in the moment, but when the switch flips I'd rather hole up with books, guitars, and food rations to emerge a few weeks later. I've had to learn to be a better listener, to pay attention to life happenings in other lives, to attend gatherings I would label as "non-productive." There are many reasons there are over fifty uses of the phrase "one another" in the NT.

<u>Lines on Leadership</u>
What is your current plan to increase in wisdom, stature, favor with God and man? What needs to change to achieve excellence in each of the four areas? How will that change as you age?
_____
_____
++

Luke 3---Highlights: Preaching of John the Baptist; baptism of Jesus; genealogy of Jesus

    A remarkably detailed pinpoint of the time when John the Baptist began his public ministry starts the chapter (vs. 1-2).

It puts his ministry's onset from 27-29AD. The "district around the Jordan" (v.3) is where the Jordan headwaters flow into the Dead Sea, a logical area as many scholars believe he received much of his training in nearby Qumran, a famous Essene community which followed strict codes of conduct and where the Dead Sea Scrolls were found in 1947[1].

John the Baptist preached with urgency like there was no tomorrow (at least not a tomorrow that included him). He would be hard pressed to receive an invitation from any modern pastoral search committee. His words were harsh, direct, unmistakable, and unrelenting. He used Isaiah 40 as the basis for his ministry, aligning himself as the Messiah's messenger (vs. 4-6).

His responses to the crowd's questions (vs. 10-14) were intense but incomplete; he preached and demanded repentance before he would baptize someone (vs. 7-8) but did not indicate how to find this Messiah they should begin following. Later he raises their interest in the Messiah without naming Him and dashes their hopes that John himself was the Messiah (vs. 15-17). The word "gospel" in v. 18 is the 'Good News' that the Messiah is on His way. It was the classic pitch of heightening expectations without satisfying them.

His answers to three specific questions by the multitudes, the tax collectors, and the soldiers were measurable, attainable, precise behaviors for each to indicate one's repentance was sincere. The answers seem tailor-made at first glance but viewed together simply say take only what is rightfully yours and be ready to share with those who do not have as much. Staying true to his mission of paving the way for the Messiah and of sin being called sin in the lives of those in power (v. 7-8, Jewish religious leaders; v. 19, the political leader Herod) sealed John's fate (v. 20).

<u>Lines on Leadership</u>
John's choice of clothing (Matt. 3.4) suggests he was a radical and an extremist. John's sharp tongue and powerful pronouncements

about sin and about the coming Savior were deliberate attempts to rouse the public to repentance and to put them on notice change was in the wind.

If you knew your appointed mission would end like John's (prison and eventual beheading), would you maintain your boldness to pave the way for someone else (not to mention who would also take your crowds and attention), or would you moderate your words just enough to keep your position and your head?

_____

_____

++

Luke 4---Highlights: Temptations of Jesus; First sermon in Nazareth; various healings.

We often hear first impressions are lasting impressions. Jesus makes an indelible one with His first sermon in Nazareth. Fresh from His encounter with Satan in the wilderness temptations (vs. 1-13), Jesus journeyed northward to Galilee and experienced a rapid rise in popularity as an itinerant rabbi (vs. 14-15). He traveled to Nazareth, his boyhood surroundings, and the local synagogue known well to Him. He read publicly from Isaiah 61, a passage associated with the coming Messiah. Many of its phrases closely parallel the opening lines of the Sermon on the Mount (see Matthew 5 entry). In Matthew 5, Jesus' opening statements demonstrate how His new Kingdom will operate and who will be blessed by it. The Beatitudes are not quaint proverbs; they are jarring declarations that those thought to be castaways and not the 'favored' of race or power are most welcome in His Kingdom. Here in Luke 4, He begins what He continues to preach and teach throughout His ministry.

Most readers concentrate on His identification with the Messianic references in Is. 61 ("Today this Scripture has been fulfilled in your hearing" v.21). It can be argued that He did not openly say 'I am that Messiah,' but it was unmistakable that He meant the age or Kingdom of the Messiah was emerging in their midst. News of the Romans' imminent overthrow would have been welcome news to His fellow Jews. So, the congregation voiced their approval (v. 22). Six verses later, they are ready to toss their native Nazarene son over the cliff; why?

Jesus openly asserts in vs. 23-27 in the Messiah's Kingdom, His salvation shall be for ALL nations. Not once, but twice for emphasis, He points out that there was a great need in Israel, but a Gentile was favored by first Elijah and then his successor Elisha. The Zarephath widow and the Syrian general received God's favor over the "chosen" race in this pair of one-sentence bombshells.

This is one of the most important concepts in this book: <u>Jesus wanted to enlarge their frame of reference</u>. The Jews thought they were chosen because of their inherent "specialness." They were chosen of God to be His conduit through which His grace flowed to <u>all</u> nations (see Ps. 67). The shock in the Nazareth synagogue became a tsunami of rage intent on silencing this upstart heretic.

Jesus is consistent throughout the Gospels: in many of His parables, the protagonist is a half-breed Samaritan. His "Great Commission" (see Mt. 28 entry) is to make disciples of ALL nations. To the disciples on the road to Emmaus, He said, "forgiveness of sins should be proclaimed in His name to ALL the nations" (Luke 24.47). The main theme in Acts is the spread of the gospel from Jerusalem (where the first disciples tried to confine it to Jewish parameters) to the known world; God directly commissions Paul (Acts 9) as His missionary to the Gentiles. The pattern and intent are unmistakable. The local crowd in Nazareth totally rejected it; the pattern was set and repeated throughout all four Gospels. Those with the Scriptures and a unique history of God's dealings with them (see the entire OT) never saw past their own bias. Perhaps others would benefit from God's favor, but surely <u>we</u> are the preferred, <u>we</u> get the first fruits, and they get the leftovers.

This resonates strongly with the headlines of today. Social media, erosion of civil discourse, and the loss of absolute truth (addressed in other chapters) conspire to polarize segments of society into 'Us' and 'Them.' Whatever group you identify with thinks "we are Us," and everyone else is "Them;" human nature dictates "my" group is favored, or rightful heirs of whatever offerings are on the table. This is not a new phenomenon in America. Race, class, gender, geographical roots---they all play a part in establishing in our minds our tribe's inherent superiority and right to be first in line for God's bounty. Twenty-five decades into our country's history, we are still repeating this same scenario, clamoring over one another, denying other races, classes, or ethnic groupings whatever 'we' desire. American churches and companies perpetuate this self-granted status of favor, when we should repent of our stances of supremacy and rejoice that God included others besides "Us." We need to expand our frame of reference.

<u>Lines of Leadership</u>
Do you believe God should bless your church because of your own denomination? Your region of the country? Your preacher? Your inherent perceived favor with Him?
Do you believe your company should prosper because of its heritage? Because of its financial assets? Because it has you as its leader?
Where do you need to enlarge your frame of reference?

++

Luke 5---Highlights: calling of disciples; leper and paralytic; call of Levi (Matthew); new wineskins

In Luke 4, Jesus called on His hometown folks in Nazareth to enlarge their frame of reference. In Luke 5, He continues that message as He calls several disciples to follow Him. He extends their vision beyond the horizon of their lives to that point. Jesus stretched everybody and everything in this chapter.

1) He stretched Peter, James, and John (vs. 1-11). Peter was a fisherman with his own boat (v.3) and several employees/partners. Jesus could have easily displayed positional leadership and cut to the chase ("Hi, follow me because I'm the Messiah, and I'll advance your career like you can't imagine") like some huckster. Instead, He borrowed Peter's boat to teach a local crowd, then, because He's already in the boat, looks at Peter and urges him to go fishing. After an all-nighter, Peter and his men are weary, but because of the teachings and the crowd (peer pressure) who heard the suggestion, Peter relents, then hauls in a huge catch when he'd caught nothing the night before. Christ demonstrated a small facet of His Messiahship before He told Peter from now on, you will fish for men, finding a succinct and intriguing way to use Peter's skills in a new, wider arena of life.

2) He stretched the religious leaders' understanding of the forgiveness of sin and His identity (vs. 12-26, see Mk. 2 entry). He healed the paralytic, lowered through the tiles of a roof so they could get their friend an audience with Jesus, and orally granted the healed man forgiveness of sin, indirectly claiming to be equal with God (v. 21-24).

3) He stretched Matthew (vs. 27-35). After Matthew decided to follow Christ (vs. 27-28), he threw a party to honor Jesus (v. 29) and invited his tax-gathering colleagues to attend. Tax gatherers were social outcasts seen as collaborators with the Romans who gained wealth at the expense of the common people. Matthew learned that there were other kinds of religious leaders than Pharisees who condemned him, Jesus, and others for associating with sinners (v. 30). Jesus spoke truth into Matthew's life yet was willing to sit, sup, and be seen with Matthew's friends.

4) He stretched wineskins (vs. 36-39). What Jesus taught and how He conducted His life stretched everyone around him, meaning they would need a new worldview, a new lifestyle, a new way to relate to God and man. Their old worldview, lifestyle, and ways could no longer abide or contain the new ones. It was a new life, not an old reformed life. Their old lives were akin to the old brittle wineskins; a new one stretches with the expanding fermented contents (see Mk. 2 entry).

<u>Lines on Leadership</u>
Jesus brought men so far from where they were they could never go back to their original positions or mindsets. This is the essence of transformational leadership. How will you go beyond greater rates of productivity and inspiration to transform lives in your organization?
_____
_____
++

Luke 6—Highlights: Jesus as Lord of the Sabbath; Choosing of the Twelve; the "Sermon on the Plain"

Often (as you will see in subsequent entries from the Gospels), Jesus insists on confronting the religious leaders of the day about His claim to be the Lord of the Sabbath. In vs. 1-11, Jesus and the disciples eat grain out of a field on a Sabbath and rub the grains between their hands. It constituted work, which is forbidden on the Sabbath. He also heals a man on the Sabbath right in the middle of the synagogue in the middle of His teaching. His message was spot on, His methods unorthodox. What's more important, the methods or the message?

1) Instead of letting change come from the outside, we need to make the changes on the inside in order to meet the outside challenges. Churches are notoriously reactive instead of proactive. Baptists protest others' actions (Catholics have too many statues, Episcopalians too many rituals, Pentecostals too many outbursts, Methodists too many pastoral rotations, etc.) and react to perceived excesses or errant behavior instead of spending time and effort to prepare our next generation, to equip them to face the swirling changes vying for their attention. Our message must remain constant, that Jesus is Lord and all are in need of His wonderful offer of salvation, but we cannot equate our methods with the message. Our methods are but vehicles for transmitting the Message. Cars used to have cassette decks; no more. In the last 20 years, most came with CD slots; newer cars (at the time of writing) now eliminate them in favor of USB ports and Bluetooth technology. In twenty years, those cars will be laughed at as antiques. Get over it. I've got over 300 vinyl LP's and over 400 CD's. Allan, get over it. What's more important, the medium (vinyl, metal, plastic, streaming) or the music? When it comes to gospel truth, is it more important to be encased in leather, on a simple sheet of paper, on a phone app, or transforming lives? What's more important, the organ, the guitar, the soundboard, or the people engaging in worship? Do I

have to answer that? We spend more time and effort defending tradition than truth. We must decide which changes we will initiate from within, not have them thrust upon us from without. Being obedient to Christ's commands does not mean be a slave to procedure. Truth is a Person, not a Principle; I choose to follow a Person rather than a plan book. Shift your faith family from learning to be good attenders to being Christ followers[1] (Mt. 28.18-20). Teach them the proper and full meaning of a covenant relationship to Him & one another and give the next generation the latitude to express that covenant.

2) Too much of what we call "planning" is scheming to do what McNeal calls "push the present into the future[2];" in other words, we dress up our churches in future terms and clothing, but in reality it is the same church; our changes trend toward decorative, not deep to the core. The old term would be window dressing. Understand that I watch *Becket* and *A Man for All Seasons* while on the treadmill and listen to Renaissance motets in my quiet time; I have a deep appreciation for history and heritage. But I need to learn from them, not live in them. I exist in the present, true, but I'm not the same man I was ten years or ten minutes ago, and most certainly won't be the same in ten minutes or ten years from now. Neither will our churches; start now to do more preparation than planning. Churches will inevitably change from erosion by outside forces or engagement from within. <u>The question is</u>: <u>are you, as a leader, more interested in preservation or transformation</u>? When preservation becomes more important than transformation (company or church), get the will and last testament in order, it won't be long before it is read to your group's benefactors. As an associational missionary, I am often asked to pick up the pieces, retrieve the keys, and receive the deed to a church property, where a church once lived and loved until it became more

enamored of holding on to its assets and reputation than letting go and letting God change them from the inside out.

<u>Lines on Leadership</u>
Which will it be: preservation or transformation?
_____

_____
++

Luke 7 ---Highlights: Jesus heals; widow's son is raised; John the Baptist doubts Jesus as Messiah; a tribute to John by Jesus; the parable of two debtors

In verses 18-35, John the Baptist sends two of his disciples to ask Jesus some revealing questions. The Baptist had announced at the onset of Jesus' public ministry, "Behold the Lamb of God who takes away the sin of the world." (see John 1 entry) Jesus came on the scene and rose in prominence and the attention of the masses while John waned as he had predicted (John 3.30). But life in the shadows or the second tier can invite doubt and second-guessing. John may have correctly predicted Jesus' role and ascension in the public eye but now expresses puzzlement partly because Jesus doesn't fit John's expectations of the "Expected One." The Messiah had been predicted centuries ago, and with the passing of those centuries, expectations had piled up in the collective mind of the Jewish people. Jesus replied to the two inquirers by alluding to passages with Messianic overtones in Isaiah, a response designed to both comfort and instruct John that, yes, I am the One you said I was. Still, it is for Me to decide how, when, and where I will be the Messiah.

Jesus then speaks to the multitudes about John, saying he was the predicted messenger to come before the Messiah

(Mal. 3.1; Is. 40.3). However, he wasn't dressed the way you thought he should be, nor did he live where you expected to find him (v.25). He muses the public acts like fickle children playing one tune then another on toy flutes, but no one would dance accordingly. He then deftly includes Himself in the discussion as He contrasts John's method of the ministry of extremes (v. 33) with what the public interprets as Jesus' ministry of indulgence (v. 34). The chapter's last sentence is, "Yet wisdom is vindicated by all her children." (v. 35, in the parallel passage in Matthew the word "deeds" substitutes for children)

Temptations to draw utilitarian conclusions should be avoided; this is not a simple restatement of "the end justifies the means." The Kingdom He preaches and teaches about is His kingdom and He is the King; therefore, the King does not need to consult the masses as to His conduct or commerce on their behalf; He will act as only He knows to act, and only He can act because none of them are the King. The only one who knows how to be the Messiah . . . is the Messiah. If everyone is entitled to their personal set of expectations of how the Messiah or His messenger should act, He will satisfy no one.

I often consult (sometimes referee) with churches where the deacons or other groups of church leaders are at odds with the pastor. This scene in Luke 7 is at the core of the conflict more often than not. Suppose no written set of expectations (i.e., a job description) exists that can be used to evaluate the pastor's performance of his duties. In that case, it is unfair to the pastor for the deacons, elders, or whatever deliberative body is in charge to expect the pastor/leader to fulfill everyone's capricious (and often shifting) sets of expectations. There is nothing objective to use for the evaluation of the pastor's actions. If his duties are not spelled out, then it sometimes becomes a jumble of interpretations.

Jesus' life and teachings mesh perfectly with OT descriptions of the Messiah and fulfill precisely the OT Messianic prophecies. Two insights arise from this passage:

1) This passage should give Christians pause. If the Jews (who were closer students of the OT scriptures than most Christians of the NT) missed the mark on how and when the Messiah would come and who He would be, what makes Christians so sure they have it all figured out for the 2nd coming of the Messiah? We look at Luke 7 and smirk; well, sure, it's obvious the Messiah was Jesus, and then we get into discussions about our charts and dispensations and ages and pre-, mid-, post-tribulation raptures, and it becomes apparent with the 2nd coming of Christ we are right back with the children playing our pipes.

2) Stay true to character and command. If I am confident about the person I am, what my mission is, and who decided that mission, I can plot a straight line as to where I am headed instead of weaving to and fro, trying like a pinball to make sure I hit every person's expectations. Throughout the Gospels, Jesus points everything toward His death, burial, and resurrection as the way to usher in His kingdom. He could not be deterred.

Lines on Leadership
My personal mission has been and always will be to prepare the next generation of servant leaders for the Kingdom of God. What is your primary mission in your chosen vocation? What sidelines you from accomplishing it? Do you have a clearly spelled out set of expectations from those you are accountable to? If not, why not?

_____
_____
++

Luke 8---Highlights: parables of the sower and lamp; calming the sea; demoniac cured; various healings

Hermeneutics is the science of interpretation; it mostly refers to interpreting Scripture. In other parts of this book, basic principles of hermeneutics are described (ex., 1 John 2 entry). Luke 8.1-3 is a prime example of *exegesis* and *eisegesis*, fancy words for important principles applicable to business as well as theology. Eisegesis means, in plain English, to read into a text something that is not there and usually infuses it with personal bias, personal thoughts. Exegesis means the opposite: extracting from the text what is there without personal bias. That sounds simple but proves elusive. Each of us feels more objective than we are in reality; it is difficult to set aside one's accumulated total worldview with all of its experiences, teachings, prejudices, etc., and only see what is in the text and no more. Sometimes other passages shed light on the studied passage, but the same principle applies to all passages used.

Luke 8.1-3 introduces the reader to Jesus' companions as He travels from village to village "preaching the kingdom of God" (v.1). Here are some obvious observations: 1) the twelve apostles were with Him; 2) three named women (Mary Magdalene, Joanna, and Susanna) were with them; 3) "many others" who contributed financially to the preaching enterprise were also along, and 4) the named women had been healed of sickness and evil spirits. Here are some elementary inferences: 1) although Jesus often gravitated towards the poor and outcast, he also attracted some followers of greater financial means; 2) one of his followers (Mary) was from Magdala, a fishing village on the west coast of the Sea of Galilee that can be visited today, and was delivered from seven spirits; 3) Joanna's husband, Chuza, was a steward for Herod, meaning she was supporting Jesus out of funds from a Jewish governmental source; and 4) these were not casual short term followers (they appeared at the crucifixion and resurrection when many of the disciples hid or fled, Mt. 27.55-56; 28.1; Mk. 15.40; Lk. 23.49 John 19.25, 20.1)

At no point in this passage, the gospels, or the rest of the NT is one word mentioned about any romantic relationship between the women and any of the disciples or Jesus. Rumors, conjectures, and fantasies- no matter how tantalizing or plausible to a reader- cannot be anything more than fanciful speculation and a classic case of eisegesis if they are not in the text. No bestsellers about secret trysts between Jesus and Mary Magdalene, such as *The DaVinci Code,* can claim to be based on biblical texts. It is simply just not there. Hollywood has always insisted on its primary value of human love being the epicenter of the universe. The biblical texts repeatedly show that God's love is central and man's love for Him and each other is a product of His love (1 John 3.16, 4.7, 10, 19)

<u>Lines on Leadership</u>
Biblical texts, company policies, legal documents, and great literature rely on proper interpretation for their enforcement and/or influence. Is there some practice in your church or company that claims to be based on its founding documents but is more <u>eisegetical</u> than <u>exegetical</u> in nature?
_____
_____
++

Luke 9---Highlights: sending of the twelve; 5000 fed; discipleship described; transfiguration; test of greatness; further demands of discipleship

The grace of God abounds throughout scripture; its pinnacle is the gift of salvation through Christ's sacrifice on the cross for mankind's sin. We are to live a life of resultant gratitude for that marvelous grace. Some interpret the grace of God as synonymous with laxness that He lets everything slide without consequence. In Luke 9, Jesus shares two related statements showing salvation is free yet costly.

v. 23, "If anyone wishes to come after me, let him deny himself, take up his cross daily, and follow Me."

v. 62, "No one, after putting his hand to the plow and looking back, is fit for the kingdom of God."

The preacher's dilemma is to show the grace of God <u>and</u> the commitment required to follow Christ. The word halfhearted never appeared in any appeal by Christ to follow him. Oddly enough, He never used the word commitment in any of the gospels. The word commitment is overwhelmingly used in the NT in the negative sense of committing <u>acts</u> of sin or rebellion. Hebrews 3.14 and 2 Peter 3.17 speak of a wavering commitment that is more lifestyle than a single act. Jesus never asked anyone to sign a "decision card" as many do today in various church services during an invitation, a time of decision. Getting information about someone's interest in Christ or their profession of faith is useful for ensuing conversations and developing relationships, but filling out a card in no way cements a person's salvation. Discipleship for Christ was more of a process than a single isolated act.

The new birth is a concept shared in detail in John 3, so a point in time when someone decides to follow Christ is important. The vast majority of His commands are to follow and obey Him, and the cost is considerable as illustrated in these two Luke 9 verses. The cross and the plow were common sights for the Middle East, which was ruled by Romans at this time and largely an agrarian society. Those crucified on crosses were symbols of intimidation designed to discourage rebellion and often displayed alongside roads as grisly reminders of Rome's power. The plow symbolizes new life, and how much goes into ensuring it. The two concepts find commonality when Jesus says elsewhere that a buried seed's death brings new life (see Jn. 12 entry).

    Jesus sacrificed Himself in an ultimate sense and requires my commitment till the end to its inevitable conclusion. This must be a grand act of selflessness and an everyday offering of life to Him and for Him (take up his cross <u>daily</u>). If I look back in distraction while plowing, I will have crooked furrows. My eyes must be on Him (Heb. 12.2) going forward, ever toward Him.

<u>Lines on Leadership</u>
At what point do you show members of your organization what is needed to succeed and to accomplish its mission fully? Before they join, after a probationary period, at their first promotion or level of volunteering? Why?

_____

_____

++

Luke 10---Highlights: the 72 go forth to preach and return; the Good Samaritan; Martha and Mary meet Jesus

    In verse 38-42, Jesus enters Bethany, a small village outside of Jerusalem, and into the home of Martha and Mary, who are sisters. Mary stays with Jesus to hear Him either teach or engage in conversation, likely with Lazarus, whom we learn in John 11 is the brother of Martha and Mary, and they are all friends with Jesus. Mary tends to the household chores; it is not clear if she is tidying up or preparing a meal out of hospitality for their guest, or just doing what was on the to-do list for the day. Either way, she calls out Mary for practicing what we call (and what Jesus approves of) "the virtue of negligence."

Negligence can be a virtue, its mastery a worthy endeavor. Most of us use this term in a negative sense, such as, "Oops, I've let the mileage roll on without an oil change." "When did I power-wash the back deck last?" or discover a special tool out in the rain, totally rusted and useless. It may be hard to believe, but <u>we are commanded frequently in Scripture to practice negligence</u>. Pharisees are chastised for choosing to obey smaller laws while major principles of justice, mercy, and love for God go by the wayside (Mt. 23.23; Lk. 11.42), a principle repeated in various forms in Prov. 8.33, 15.32, Heb. 13.16, and most notably in Acts, where the new church leaders of a newly expanding Jerusalem church declare it is in the church's best interest for them to exercise mindful negligence (see Acts 6 entry).

Granted, sometimes those verses invoke "Do not neglect this or that" and speak in the negative. Reread the passages, and a positive interpretation emerges to guide our decision-making. The 12 apostles in Acts 6.1-7 elected to invest their time in preaching and prayer instead of potluck suppers. They consciously chose to prioritize their time according to their Kingdom values. They did not minimize providing for widows or say widows were unimportant. They delegated the work to the first deacons and looked at the church's continued increase in v.7 as a result. Elsewhere in Paul's most descriptive passage on disciple-making, a soldier foregoes everyday chores and duties to obey a commanding officer. Everyday life is not depicted as bad or disposable, but subordinate most of the time to the direct orders of a superior officer. (see 2 Tim. 2 entry)

In these biblical instances, something worthy/good languishes (or, in other words, is neglected) to achieve something else deemed more worthy of one's time. Yes, there are times when the urgent becomes all-encompassing (illness onset, loss of job, loss of a loved one), and well-planned agendas go out the window (see Acts 16 entry). But even that confirms the principle of intentional negligence. Our lives are not a patchwork of happenstance occurrences dictated by circumstances beyond our control, nor are we automatons with puppet strings attached to a universal Master. Not surprisingly, neither your author nor the sum of all the poets, philosophers, or theologians has ever found the magic formula that explains the free will of man and the sovereignty of God to the satisfaction of all. As an appointed leader within my sphere of influence, I lead, serve, and work with each decision born of principle, not convenience or personal preference.

One aspect of each decision is that attention is given to one thing at a time. A church I visit on a given Sunday means 37 others in our association I won't visit; each hour spent with a pastor or other church leader is an hour I could spend with many others. If our churches or businesses are to grow, and if we are to experience personal growth as believers in Christ, we must constantly make decisions based on neglect of some things to benefit others. I cannot be everything for everyone, everywhere, every time. There is only one Being like that in the known universe, and I worship Him. Mindful negligence can be a compassionate and Christ-like use of your time.

Lines on Leadership
Christ compressed a ministry into three years that would change the world for two millennia. He could only preach so many

sermons, heal a limited number of people, and walk from village to village. What will you neglect today to the glory of God?

_____

_____

++

Luke 11---Highlights: instructions on prayer; Pharisees confront Jesus, and He responds

Certain familiar book titles are referred to more than read (think *War and Peace* or Einstein's theories of relativity). Most people have heard of intercessory prayer and tried it off and on but have difficulty putting it into practice. The large number of biblical passages concerning intercessory prayer (1 Tim. 2.1; Mt. 18.19-20; Ro. 8.26; Js. 5.13-16; Jn. 16.23-24; & Eph. 6.18 to mention a few) leave little doubt we should intercede for others. Why do we hesitate to engage in this important Kingdom work?

1) The "**wait**" of intercession (Luke 11.1-13)—We are an impatient people; we used to say, "I haven't got all day;" I've heard someone stand in front of a microwave saying, "I haven't got all minute!" Our smartphones spit out instant results to news, sports, investments, and births---we feel between God and Google we ought to have an answer to just about any question or query we might pose---and have it now. The Kingdom of God is rarely about instant; it is always about eternal. That doesn't make it inefficient, just not likely to get on our cyber-circadian rhythms. The Father takes the heart cries of His saints very seriously, but He will answer them when, how, and where He desires; His glory trumps our satisfaction.

There is no magic formula to explain the mysterious interplay of our pleas before the throne and the sovereign will of our God; the exact role our prayers play is hard to articulate. I know when I share a specific concern with God, the more specific is His answer. At one point in our lives, my wife and I prayed for God to surround our son and his wife in Ho Chi Minh City with believers when they moved there to teach English. Soon after their move to Vietnam, we heard a presentation in a nearby WV city by a former area pastor I had never met who was doing ministry in Ho Chi Minh; we discovered they lived in the exact same neighborhood (district) as our son and the pastor was familiar with the very building in which our son and daughter in law lived and offered to help. Try explaining that away in a city of 11+ million on the opposite side of the globe. God hears; God answers.

    2) The "**weight**" of intercession (Luke11.1-13)—This may cause more to shy away from intercession than #1. To intercede for someone (a church, an approaching crisis, a country torn by war, sexual exploitation, famine, or other difficult situation) causes one to empathize, to suffer with, to sometimes buckle under the "weight" of lifting them up to the Father. The Psalms and the prophets' writings are replete with laments about the crushing, suffocating burden of crying out to the Father for someone's salvation, deliverance, or reconciliation. We also know in the back of our minds that if we intercede, we may be called upon to invest our lives in that person, which might require sacrifice.

Are you praying "safe," generic prayers without knowing if they are answered? ("God, please bless the world"). For what are you interceding, and <u>what price are you willing to pay to see it come about</u>? Be careful. You can only pray such a prayer if you are ready to back it up. God listens and answers in His own time, and His way (Jer. 29.11-13), and He will take you at your word. The church needs prayer warriors, not part-time militia, but special ops warriors ready to enter and stay in the battle, even when it is dark and desperate. May we plead for the souls of men and the hearts of nations as we linger ever longer in the presence of our Lord.

Lines of Leadership
Chapters on leadership usually focus on assets, decision-making, character traits, strategy, or the leader's abilities. Sometimes we need to acknowledge we cannot handle the situation or that something is just bigger than us and our ability to solve it. What problem or scenario has you stumped? Are you willing to humble yourself as a leader and ask God to intervene?

_____

_____

++

Luke 12---Highlights: selected parables and teachings of Jesus
    v. 15b   "One's life is not in the abundance of his possessions." v.48b "From everyone who has been given much, much will be required; and from the one who has been entrusted with much, even more will be expected." v. 56 "Hypocrites! You know how to interpret the appearance of the earth and the sky, but why don't you know how to interpret this present time?" (CSB)

    The Luke 12 parables and teaching revolve around three R's--- Redeemer, readiness, and responsibility. In a nutshell, they describe recognizing Jesus as the Redeemer who will return, to be ready for that return, and the responsibility to prepare everyone else for that return and provide for them daily. In multiple parables, Jesus identifies Himself as a master of the house who has departed and will return "at an hour you do not expect" (v. 40). In one parable (vs. 35-40), the master leaves for a faraway banquet and describes how the servants should remain alert for his return. In a curious reversal of roles, the master rewards those alert servants by serving them, becoming a servant to the servants. The servant found to be in a constant state of <u>readiness</u> is rewarded. In another parable, the master puts the household manager or steward in charge of daily allotments of food for all the other servants and lets him go about his duties. A manager who successfully completes his duties is rewarded with higher or more responsibility (v.44) "he will put him in charge of all his possessions." The manager who squanders his master's possessions and shirks his duty will be terminated as manager. Discharge of his <u>responsibilities</u> is rewarded.

In verse 56, Jesus ties all the parables and teachings of Luke 12 together with one single word in Greek. The word translated as 'time' is Kairos, which is not about a normal chronological passage of time but a specific time; the closest English equivalent is "window of opportunity." The positive side of Kairos is when a person realizes now is the opportune time and seizes it. The negative side is realizing it too late when the Kairos has come and gone.

Lines on Leadership
As in the Mk. 13 entry, leaders must strike a balance of readiness and responsibility. In the case of the Redeemer's return, expectancy must be maintained all the while taking care of the necessary activities of daily life. What is an area of your leadership where there is a balance of readiness (anticipating a future event) and responsibility (taking care of the business at hand)? Where is an area of imbalance in this regard?

_____
_____
+++

Luke 13---Highlights: call to repentance, healing on the Sabbath, teaching in the villages

Vs. 20-21 "And again He [*Jesus*] said, 'To what shall I compare the kingdom of God? It is like leaven which a woman took and hid in three pecks of meal, until it was all leavened.'" One of the seminal pieces of leadership advice I ever received was shared at a small Swiss café near Luzern, Switzerland, during a confab of American missionaries serving in Europe. I was sitting with a pastor who had planted churches worldwide and received a lot of attention across our denomination. He was at the confab to speak to us; I was a green missionary just getting started in our work in what was then West Germany.

His name was Ralph Neighbors. We sipped coffee and talked about the best way to address our present culture with the gospel. He bemoaned the prevailing mindset in most churches. He told me, "When will we get past the D-Day mentality of a broad, vast, military invasion of enemy territory (which he labeled penetration) and learn to infuse the culture with the gospel in a more biblical manner (which he labeled permeation)?" He was not anti-military, but he deplored the excessive use of military jargon and vocabulary in both hymns and sermons, saying Christians were sent into the world not to conquer it but to transform the world through servant leadership and power of the gospel by serving the world.

While I agree with his wording of penetration and permeation, it would be a wrong assumption to think yeast in dough is a more passive, quiet approach compared to frontal assaults. The process of yeast changing the dough is anything but passive and quiet. Countless mini-explosions of gas bubbles constantly occur during the rising of the bread to expand it far beyond its original shape and texture.

The gospel is, by its very nature, disruptive. When Christ bids a man to follow Him, this may initially occur out of curiosity. Still, gospel truths will soon seep into the actions, thoughts, and very identity of the follower through the power of permeation.

The Holy Spirit of God acts like yeast within the person's life, infiltrating every level and pore of his spiritual being. Sooner or later, the transformed life wants to help others experience this transformation, and they become leaven in the surrounding culture. In countries closed to the gospel, it seems at first glance the gospel itself is harmless; Christians do not go around waving rifles and demanding people pay homage to their God. They seem to be obedient and loyal subjects, not advocating open rebellion. But their changed lives begin to leaven society one life at a time. It is no wonder that the ruling party sees Christianity as subversive and anarchic in nature if their leadership ethics are in direct contrast with that of the gospel.

<u>Lines on Leadership</u>
How long is your leadership runway? Do you feel pressure to "penetrate" and overcome a certain culture in the organization, or do you have patience (and time) enough to "permeate" that same culture in your organization and see it transformed from within? Which do you think would produce more solid, long-lasting results?

_____
_____
++

<u>Luke 14</u>---Highlights: the parable of dinner guests, discipleship explained.*Math* and *values* are templates used to read Luke 14 and change the perspective and outcome of the chapter's various stories.

Math is involved in two separate plans: the construction of a tower (vs. 28-30) and the cost to wage war (vs. 31-33). An artist's rendering of a building project always looks gorgeous, with lighting, colors, and shadows strategically painted to show off the finished tower in the best possible way. But if the builder does not account for costs like environmental impact statements, laying fiber cable, sewer connections, shifting fault lines nearby, accessibility of water, electricity, bandwidth, and availability of materials (he wants to build with marble, but all that is nearby is granite), then he will likely run out of money before the project is finished. It will become the laughingstock of the town and his profession. Likewise, suppose a political leader delivers an ultimatum to go off to war without considering the simple math of can he pay for it or does he have a reliable supply line to his troops (see 2 Kings 3 for an atrocious example). In that case, he may rue the day he eschewed diplomacy in favor of deployment. Jesus did not consider discipleship an extracurricular activity or peripheral to His Kingdom. He bluntly told followers they must count the costs before they commit to Him. That which is initially attractive is not always attainable; the economy, resources, circumstances, inventory, leadership pipeline, and 101 other factors should be considered before embarking in a new direction. Going with a "gut feeling" works great in novels and movies, but decisive decision-making is usually better when undertaken deliberately rather than impulsively.

Values are involved in two related parables usually entitled Parable of the Guests (vs. 7-15) and the Parable of the Dinner (vs. 16-24). Jesus advises taking a seat of honor when it is not assured is foolish and sets a person up for possible embarrassment and dishonor (v. 7-11). In the Kingdom of God, the honored guests are the ones without a means to achieve honor: the poor, crippled, lame, and blind (v. 13). The reader empathizes with the powerless and hopes the host will promote them up closer to the seats of honor (see 1 Pet. 5 entry). If the reader was the host himself, then to be consistent with Kingdom values, he needed to not worry about the rich and powerful (v.14) and concentrate on the lower rungs of society, something Jesus preached from His very first sermon (see Lk. 4 entry).

In the Parable of the Dinner, the host's plans go awry when the invited guests start making excuses, some plausible and some outright insulting. The host (admittedly in anger, v.21) decides the party is more important than the people who "should" attend it. The host tears up the invite list, gives a whole new set of folks to invite, and when he still has seats left over, decides to make it open season for all who wish to attend his banquet; it goes from a private affair to a public one.

<u>Lines on Leadership</u>
Cold hard facts often paint a much different view of a decision to be made than the one we see through our personal desires and "gut instincts." (a brilliant argument for this is *Factfulness* by Hans Rosling[1]). Values-centered decision-making instead of bottom-line pleasing of shareholders usually yields decisions that may not satisfy Wall Street but honor the Way (see Covey's 7 Habits of Highly Effective People[2]). When in the past did facts override your personal feelings about a project, and you admitted your value system conflicted with the one you professed to follow?

_____

_____

+++

<u>Luke 15</u>---Highlights: Parables of the lost sheep, the lost coin, and the Prodigal Son

Luke 15 is a consummate collection of related parables that, like a well-composed symphony, combine in three related movements to become a powerful triumph of love and grace. Thousands upon multiplied thousands of words have been written over the centuries about this chapter, especially the beloved story known as the Prodigal Son. The theme is simple enough: a sheep goes astray (vs. 3-7), a coin is lost (vs. 8-10), a son leaves home and squanders his inheritance (vs. 11-32); the sheep is sought and found, the coin is sought and found, the wayward son is welcomed home, not rejected. In a wider context of the gospel of Luke, Jesus has been demonstrating to the Pharisees (vs.1-2; see previous chapters) and other religious leaders that every person deserves to know and experience the love of God.

Over the years, I have identified with different characters in these stories: the wayward sheep, the seeking shepherd; the mislaid coin that may have rolled off the table and the woman who tirelessly searches for it; the son who foolishly wastes his father's fortunes; the son who didn't stray but had no clue about the extent of the Father's love; and the father who constantly scans the horizon for some sign his son has returned. The beauty of these stories is how different life development stages change the roles with which I identify.

The lesson is unmistakable. The importance of the individual cannot be overestimated. At the end of each brief story (after the sheep, coin, and son have been restored), there is much rejoicing in heaven, in a village, and a family. Systems-oriented leaders who always think about infrastructure, overall vision, logistics, and procedures will probably scratch their heads and decide this is all out of proportion. The inclination is to see the needs of the many outweighing the needs of the few (or the one) when it comes to an efficient organization. The New Testament, however, is replete with stories, encounters, and dialogues showing the individual's worth to others and to God (see Philemon). Repentance was noted in each story as the catalyst for redemption (vs. 7, 10, 17-20, 32). The key is the response of the shepherd, the woman, and the father; it was not punitive but redemptive. The movie *The Martian* (2015), starring Matt Damon, illustrated this principle when he was left for dead on Mars during an aborted mission. Once it was learned he was still alive, it took a global effort to conceive and carry out a rescue of the solitary astronaut. In simple terms, we pay whatever price and expend whatever effort is needed to find and restore what was lost.

<u>Lines on Leadership</u>
Transgressions have their consequences. How do the individual members of your church or organization know they are valued, and that while some of their actions may require restrictions or reductions of privilege, it is undergirded with redemption?

_____

_____

++

<u>Luke 16</u>---Highlights: Parables of the Unrighteous Steward, the Rich Man, and Lazarus

"^{10}One who is faithful in a very little is also faithful in much, and one who is dishonest in a very little is also dishonest in much. ^{11}If then you have not been faithful in the unrighteous wealth, who will entrust to you the true riches? ^{12}And if you have not been faithful in that which is another's, who will give you that which is your own? ^{13}No servant can serve two masters, for either he will hate the one and love the other, or he will be devoted to the one and despise the other. You cannot serve God and money." ESV

Any parent who reads this passage sighs with relief and thinks, 'God, thanks for backing me up.' All the thousands of admonitions for children to clean their rooms, feed the dog, do their homework, and complete their chores seem to have been worth it for a fleeting moment. Admiral William H McRaven used this same principle as the basis of his bestseller *Make Your Bed: Little Things That Can Change Your Life...And Maybe the World*[1]. The Lord equates "unrighteous wealth" or that which is valuable in this world as the "very little" things and casts doubt on the ability of a person to handle eternal riches if they cannot handle earthly things with integrity and wisdom. One who handles the world's treasures with cavalier hands will hardly comprehend the true value of treasures from heaven.

But more than mastery of skills, the passage points towards and ends with commitment to a master. It is about devotion to God and seeing through His eyes what is valuable and what is not. This is easy to preach, hard to practice. Today's society is about multiplicity of paths for advancement, multiple affiliations at all levels of relationships, and multiple objects of love. It will find repeats in other chapters, but to become a leader, I have to become a follower, faithful to let go of any vestigial faith in or loyalty to others. The casual listener to leaders who gives cursory attention to what is said or required will rarely become a leader that commands unflagging, singular loyalty. 2 Tim. 2.4 says, "No soldier in active service entangles himself in the affairs of everyday life so that he may please the one who enlisted him as a soldier." Paul's word image about discipleship does not condemn daily routines or daily relationships, but that which is good must be dropped to attain what is great.

Salvation is free in that it is a gift, not deserved nor earned, but in another sense, it is indeed costly, for choices must be made between competing masters and values (see Rom. 6 entry). Drills and war games help soldiers learn to obey orders without reservation and to love their brothers in arms. Practices and scrimmages for athletes mold them so that when the coach calls a play during the game, it is executed both to obey and to not let their teammates down. The little things of life are not just useless time wasters; they are building blocks of obedience and character that will serve me, my Master, and my group well when the time comes to prove myself.

Lines on Leadership

Reflect on a choice of which leader to follow and emulate in your past. How have you become a leader worthy of others' loyalty and obedience? What "little things" have paid off handsomely from your training and made you a better leader?

_____

_____

++

Luke 17---Highlights: various teachings by Jesus, ten lepers cleansed, 2nd coming foretold

Some folks hear the verse about having "faith of a mustard seed and you can move mountains or mulberry trees" (v.6) and rejoice. In all honesty, many of us hear this and tend to become discouraged, thinking, "wow, mustard seeds are tiny, and I've not moved any mountains nor uprooted any trees, so my faith must be sub-microscopic." A perspective that might help you deal with a "lack" of faith is: perhaps the issue is not the _amount_ of faith but the _object_ of it.

Consider this classic yet erroneous illustration: a speaker pulls up a chair and says something to the effect, "I can talk all day about how much faith I have in this chair, but until I plop down in it, I am not exercising true faith." Then he sits down in the chair to "prove" his faith. This example is incomplete. I submit it is irrelevant how "much" faith the person has in an object. It matters much more about the object's worthiness, or in the case of said chair, the sturdiness of it. I can have all the faith in the world that the chair will hold me, but if its metal is riddled with rust, or is wooden and termite ridden, or just poorly constructed, I can sit down with the fullest confidence imaginable and still wind up sprawled on the floor when the chair collapses.

In terms of salvation, the world is filled with millions who have placed their faith in everything from religious systems to themselves and have done so with totally pure motives or intentions. The mantra for decades on college campuses has been, 'it doesn't matter what you believe, as long as you're sincere.' I can have all the faith in the world that a set of rituals, an idol, a set of principles, or a particular relationship will deliver me; however, according to my understanding of the Word and the exclusivistic nature of Christianity (which I wholeheartedly affirm in this instance), In regards to salvation, if the object of my faith is not Jesus Christ, heaven is not within my reach (Jn. 14.6). 'If I only had enough faith, if I had the gift of faith' . . . televangelists have always preyed upon this worry in the back of a person's mind and appealed for people to make an actual show of faith by supporting their respective ministry. It is not the amount; it is about the object of faith. Here is another image: you find yourself hesitantly edging out on some frozen river to try to cross. Maybe you're on all fours, afraid to extend an appendage, slowly inching your way across. All of a sudden, an ATV comes barreling through the woods drives straight across the frozen river with two passengers and disappears into the forest. Even though you feel a bit foolish on your hands and knees, the end result is both of you cross the river. The amount of faith was not the issue. It was a simple fact of physics about how thick and solid the ice was. Was the ice trustworthy? It could also be about experience, knowing from prior dealings whether or not that object of your faith will hold up.

You exercise faith all day, every day: when you drive on any highway, you place your faith in the hundreds of car drivers passing by you to stay in their lanes and not plow you under. When you take a drink from the tap water and deposit your paycheck in your bank, you are showing faith; again, you might have full confidence in those drivers, your water company, or your bank, but they have to prove themselves to be worthy. "**Worthy** is the Lamb that was slain to receive power and riches and wisdom and might and honor and glory and blessing." (Rev. 5.12) In my life, He has proven to be a trustworthy object of my faith, regardless of if that faith is smaller or larger than a mustard seed.

Lines on Leadership
As a leader, I must ask myself periodically: do I offer my associates a worthy object of their faith? Only after the question of the reliability of the object of faith is settled can the conversation begin about moving mountains.

_____
_____
++

Luke 18---Highlights: Parables on prayer, a Pharisee and a publican, the rich young ruler, the blind man sees

In the last chapter's Lines on Leadership, the question was raised about becoming a worthy object of faith for the followers. The first of many Luke 18 parables on prayer (vs 1-14), priorities (vs 18-23), and possessions (vs 24-30) sheds further light on being that worthy object of faith. It is often labelled the parable of the importune or persistent widow, and Luke instructs the reader in v. 1 the parable is written, "to show that at all times they ought to pray and not to lose heart." For those who identify with the widow pleading her case, it is indeed an effective illustration of persistence, or what was called "praying through" by older believers.

For leadership purposes, however, the focus switches to the two dispensers of justice in vs 1-8: the unrighteous judge (v.2)

and God (v.7). The contrast could not be more apparent. The unrelenting pleas of the widow wear down the judge, the emphasis being the widow's efforts. God is described as one who will surely exceed the unrighteous judge in dispensing justice and is quicker to hear the cries of His children; the emphasis is not upon the petitions of believers but on the character and compassion of God.

God is not a softie, a pushover, or an easy mark. He is *El Shaddai*, the sovereign and almighty God. Throughout the Old and New Testament, He is described as just and willing to do the unthinkable for His people (the sacrifice of His Son for the sin of man). Jesus referred to this earlier in Luke 11.13 ("If you then, being evil, know how to give good gifts to your children, how much more shall your heavenly Father give the Holy Spirit to those who ask Him?"). No one has been <u>for</u> His people more than God. When I think about what He has done for me through Christ Jesus and how He indwells the believer through the Holy Spirit, I can rest assured He will provide for me passionately.

<u>Lines on Leadership</u>
As a follower, I look for a leader who will see me not only as a cog in the wheel of his company's machinery but sees me as an individual of worth, who has my back, and will balance the needs of the one and the needs of the many with justice. As a leader, I need to be proactive in dispensing justice, not waiting for followers to petition or clamor for their needs to be met. They need to know I have their back.
How do our teams/church members/employees know we respectfully disagree as leaders have their best interests at heart?

++

Luke 19---Highlights: Zacchaeus, ten minas parable, Jesus' triumphal entry into Jerusalem, Temple cleansing

Zacchaeus is one of the better-known secondary figures of the NT. The subject of countless Sunday School lessons and children's songs, Zacchaeus is depicted as "a wee little man" who climbs in a sycamore tree to glimpse Jesus. He is seemingly chosen at random by Jesus from among the roadside throng for a home visit and rewarded for his initiative to perch above the crowd.

From a leadership perspective, I offer this possibility. Jericho, at the time of Jesus, was not just a wide spot in the road; it is one of the oldest walled cities in the world[1], having appeared notably in the Biblical narrative in Joshua 2-6. In NT times, Herod the Great had expanded its prominence with "aqueducts, a fortress, a monumental winter palace, and a hippodrome[2]." This was not just a village but a place of wealth and notoriety. The term "chief tax collector" (v. 2) applied to Zacchaeus is only used this one time in the entire NT. I propose that Jesus did little to nothing that was random. In a public ministry that spanned but three years and altered the course of history and millions of lives, Jesus spoke and acted with deliberation and forethought. Instead of Zacchaeus being a winner of a happenstance glance, I believe Jesus deliberately chose him to bring about the maximum impact and most significant influence in Jericho. Here was a man known well to the populace because of his unique title and place in society, despised as tax collectors usually were. Jesus strategically chose Zacchaeus to drive home his consistent message that the gospel was for all strata of society (see Lk. 4 entry) with particular emphasis on the broken, the despised, the rejected, and the forgotten.

Jesus called Zacchaeus a true son of Abraham (v.9) not because of his place in society or his ethnic identity but because of his transformed heart, demonstrated by his transformed priorities as he announced the giving of half of his possessions and four times restitution to those he had defrauded. He did not buy his salvation; his generosity evidenced his transformation. Jesus had not only come to his house but into his heart. As leaders, we must simultaneously be open to all around us with our message and not only seek out the high and mighty to the exclusion of the lowly; yet we must also be mindful of strategic encounters, strategic conversations, and strategic decisions that can be leveraged for the maximum impact.

Lines on Leadership
What encounter, conversation or decision do you need to seek that will have a marked impact on your congregation or company? Reflect on attaining a balance of serendipity and strategy in your leadership.

_____

_____
++

Luke 20---Highlights: Questioning of Jesus by religious authorities

A definition of diplomacy is "skill in managing negotiations, handling people, etc., so that there is little or no ill will; tact.[1]" This is NOT what Jesus practiced in chapter 20. His clear intention was to expose the religious leaders' faults of each posit used in their repeated attempts to entrap Him.

He artfully and deftly handles each attempt by the religious leaders (origin of His authority, vs. 1-8; obligations to earthly power, vs. 19-26; continuity of relationships from this life to the next, vs. 27-41) to entangle Himself in His own words. For good measure, He throws in a parable (vs. 9-18) that euphemistically identifies the religious leaders as the primary culprits in His coming demise and simultaneously affirms His claim to be the Son of God. The parable delights the masses and infuriates the religious leaders (v.19, "And the scribes and the chief priests tried to lay hands on Him that very hour, and they feared the people; for they understood that He spoke this parable against them").

Jesus uses a different technique in every round of inquiry. When questioned about His authority, He responded with another question. While they pondered His response, He took advantage of their pause to paint them in a corner verbally with the parable of the vintners. They countered with a surefire yes/no question about ultimate loyalty to God or Caesar; He responded with an all-encompassing answer that shifted the focus from ultimate loyalty to proper priorities. Their last attempt was intriguing, but Jesus showed their faulty understanding of marriage and its relationship to eternity.

The scribes acknowledged His answers by saying, "Teacher, You have spoken well." I have often wondered what would have happened if Jesus had left the dialogue at that point. He didn't. He took the occasion to turn the tables and become the inquisitor, asking them to explain a familiar OT passage (Ps. 110). He often cited that, if correctly interpreted, it provided further evidence for His godly Sonship (vs. 41-44). No response was forthcoming. Perhaps He wanted to show He had plenty in reserve; they had not exhausted His knowledge nor stretched Him to the limit of His wisdom. They had merely scratched its surface. The chapter ends as Jesus addresses His disciples and recaps a familiar negative portrait of the religious leaders in plain, unmistakable language (vs. 45-47).

Lines on Leadership

Muhammed Ali was a great boxer in the 20th century. He became famous for the "rope-a-dope" technique; he would allow the opponent to flail away and hit him with blow after blow while up against the ropes lining the ring. The elasticity of the ropes helped Ali absorb the punches and minimize their effectiveness. After wearing out his opponent, Ali would wait for the proper moment to turn the aggressor, coming off the ropes strategically to deliver the convincing blows to win. Reflect on a time in your leadership when you could have postponed open conflict and perhaps been more effective by utilizing one of the multiple approaches described in this chapter.

_____

_____

++

Luke 21---Highlights: the widow's mite; Luke's Olivet Discourse account (see Mt. 24, Mk. 13 entries)

Most parables and incidents recorded in the Gospels convey a central truth. In verses 1-4, a familiar story unfolds of the widow who gives her two mites (coins) and is commended by Jesus for doing so. Consider the place, the people, and the perspective of each in this scene.

The place is the Temple, the central building in old Jerusalem. Thirteen receptacles were placed throughout the grounds for the purpose of receiving the offerings of worshippers. The trumpet shape had a practical use, small at the top and wider at the bottom to thwart the occasional hypocrite who thought about thrusting his hand in the receptacle pretending to donate while attempting to take coins others had donated. The receptacles were made of metal, so if someone wanted to "trumpet" his offering (Matt. 6.2), the person sent the coins cascading into it to it, the noise assuring the attention of passersby[1].

The people were the rich, making sure others knew they were giving by the noisy coins; the poor widow who gave coins worth 1/64 of a day's wages, hardly making a sound in the receptacle and attracting little or no attention; the Lord, the silent observer of both; and those to whom He made His observation (likely the apostles, possibly random listeners as he taught daily in the Temple (vs. 37-38)).

The <u>perspective</u> was that Jesus uses the smallest coin known (the lepta) and compares the widow's offering to those of the rich as "more than all" (v.4), <u>implying not true impact but true worth in the Kingdom of God</u>. Throughout the NT and especially in the Sermon on the Mount (Mt. 5-7), Kingdom values are often upside-down mirror images of what the world touts as worthy. <u>He notes her total sacrifice as opposed to the surplus of the rich</u>. The blessing for the widow was the act of giving itself; elsewhere, Paul reminded his Ephesians elders that Jesus said, "it was more blessed to give than to receive" (Acts 20.35). A sacrificial offering given as a spiritual act of worship releases a person's spirit; it frees them up to listen and draw close to the Father. It is not done to attain or maintain one's salvation but as a simple sign of love for God. Giving without the need for recognition has a way of purifying one's motives and heart.

<u>Lines on Leadership</u>
The Kingdom of God is not about promotions, advancements, titles, or raises. It is about serving, giving, and honoring the King out of gratitude. Televangelists promise if you give (to them), you receive great rewards and material riches. The widow teaches and Jesus observes that we should give sacrificially out of love and gratitude. We give not as some fast track to collect celestial crowns but as a true act of worship. What have you given to your organization that was meant to be seen of men? What have you given as a leader meant to honor Jesus as Lord, for His eyes only?

++

Luke 22---Highlights: The Lord's Supper instituted; Gethsemane; Judas' betrayal of Jesus; arrest and trial

Turning points in our lives are usually not measured in minutes or hours but in moments. They are the arresting, deeply engraved memories that elicit a visceral response from us upon every remembrance. Those moments drive us and form us. They are more often than not unscheduled and unexpected.

As a worship leader, several of those moments have come during a celebration of the Lord's Supper (vs. 14-23). I serve Southern Baptist churches and love their dedication to the Word of God and their love of evangelism and missions. However, one area that is often diluted as to impact is their observance of the Lord's Supper. In most of those churches, a small plastic cup of grape juice is served along with a tasteless, tiny square of unleavened bread, the preacher reads a few verses of scripture, the congregation partakes all at once, and often the observance is buried at the end of a service or done more obligatory than as a true act of worship. It is amplified further by COVID forcing many churches to use individually packaged grape juice and wafers, so no one touches it except the church member. Three of those pivotal moments in my ministry were during a Lord's Supper observance and all three as I was an interim pastor. This will be a longer entry than usual due to its deeply personal nature.

1. Early in my campus ministry, I was an interim for an interim (he suffered a heart attack, and I preached for six weeks in his stead). The small Disciples of Christ church celebrated the Lord's Supper weekly. The elders fanned out from the altar to

distribute the elements to the rows while the pastor stayed behind the altar. The first time we did this, I felt self-conscious and awkward with nothing to do, so instinctively, I looked down to begin praying. There was a large brass cross on the altar directly in front of me with a circular, convex brass base. I saw a reflection of my face at the foot of the cross. When I think of degrees obtained, tasks accomplished, or recognition received, my mind's eye goes back to that cross with me standing on the outside but kneeling humbly on the inside.

    2. During our missionary time in Germany, our church in Trier celebrated communion with a common cup passed through the rows of congregants. I was the interim there for several months between pastors (I was there to work at the Universität Trier and help plant churches) and was used to the way we observed "Abendmahl." One day we purchased a new metal common cup. It passed through the rows and came to me last as pastor. It was unscratched, new, and shiny pewter inside and out. As I held the cup and gazed inside it, I saw my reflection through the wine on that new surface and froze. Symbolically I saw my face covered with the blood of Christ. It was likely seconds, but it seemed like hours to me until the worship leader called me back to the task at hand in front of the people. We often sing in hymns about having sins washed away by the saving blood of Christ (1 John 1.7), but it became more real than ever in that moment.

    3. In the same Texas town where I was the local college minister, I was asked to be an interim pastor for the Evangelical Presbyterian Church. I had preached there often as it was in my neighborhood, and I knew many members. The first time to celebrate the Lord's Supper, I was instructed to let the elders distribute from the sides of the altar where prayer benches were placed. I was told to stand behind the altar and distribute to those who could not kneel at the benches. At first, it looked like

I would serve all the stiff-legged and gray-haired members. Then a young man came to the altar with his sister. Our families knew each other. Jacob had recently drowned, staying under the water for over ten minutes. I had been at the emergency room when the EMTs brought him in. He suffered significant brain damage and was in the beginning stages of rehab. As he picked up the portion of bread, he got it halfway before his sister had to help him get it to his mouth. She gently wiped the crumbs from his mouth. He repeated the motion with the cup, getting it halfway up when his sister again helped him guide it to his mouth. By this time, I am openly weeping, and everyone can see it. His sister's name was Grace. When a child of the King could not experience the presence of the King on his own, Grace enabled him to do so. It was a holy moment[1].

Lines on Leadership
The Lord's Supper has been celebrated worldwide for over 2000 years since its inception. Those three moments described changed the way I worship and believe. What moments in your life and career were truly life-changing for your leadership and why?

_____

_____

+++

Luke 23---Highlights: Jesus before Pilate, then Herod, then Pilate; crucifixion and burial of Jesus

There is often a proper response and a political response to any posed scenario; any overlap between them is usually coincidental. Pilate examined Jesus after His arrest and saw no reason to impose the death penalty. The proper response would have been to release Him. Instead, to kick the proverbial can down the road, upon learning Jesus is allegedly a Galilean (v.6-7), Pilate sent Him to Herod. Pilate exhibited indifference and expedience; he could have easily looked up the Roman records of birth and taxation to find out that Jesus was born in Bethlehem (Lk. 2.1) and raised in Nazareth.

Herod wanted a circus sideshow, not a real trial (v. 8); when Jesus would not perform miracles on cue to save His own life, Herod returned Him to Pilate. Pilate brought all of the Jewish chief priests and elders into the mix (v. 13) to tell them Jesus was not a candidate for the death penalty, a fact upon which he and Herod agreed (v.15). He thought he could pacify the crowd with a few lashes and other forms of punishment; Pilate judged wrongly that their obvious jealousy and hatred of this man would dissipate after seeing Him suffer painfully.

So intense was the hatred for Jesus among the chief priests and elders that they dropped any pretense of wanting justice and sought revenge (vs.18, 21, 23) for all the times He had bested them in dialogue, criticized them openly to the multitudes, and made them the villains in parable after parable. Pilate spoke to them three times (v. 22), each time extending the Roman brand of mercy to Jesus and to them. Each time the clamor and fervor grew to the point, v. 24 shows, Pilate was thinking politically about poll numbers instead of justice: "And Pilate pronounced sentence that their demand should be granted."

Lines on Leadership
It could be argued that Pilate was concerned about overall peace among the perennially rebellious Jewish people he governed, that the needs of the many outweighed the unfortunate needs of this one innocent man. Have you ever made a similar decision that was politically motivated instead of doing what you knew

was proper? If so, would you make the same decision today? Is it ever proper to use a scapegoat, someone or something upon which a collective group's anger (or the sin, or the frustration) can be successfully transferred to deflect their attention from you?

_____

_____

++

Luke 24---Highlights: The resurrection, Road to Emmaus, appearance to the disciples, the ascension

      For believers, the death, burial, and resurrection of Christ (vs. 1-12) constitute the most significant cosmological event of all eternity. It made salvation accessible to all who accept His incredible gift of grace. The Lukan account contains a unique epilogue to the resurrection story involving Emmaus, a small village to the west of Jerusalem (vs. 13-35), and two of its residents heading home confused and bewildered. They had witnessed the death of the One they had hoped would be the Messiah and redeem Israel (v. 21) yet had heard reports from some of the "women among us" (v.22) to whom angels had announced He had risen (v.6). Since the inner circle of the disciples had refused to believe it (vs. 9-11), these two travelers did not know what to believe.

      The post-resurrection Jesus began to walk alongside them. Whether He was perturbed or amused by this scenario, He decided not to reveal His identity and walked alongside them for what must have been several hours as His questions probed the source of their sadness (v.17). They had obviously been a part of the larger following of Christ (v.24) and wanted so much to believe the impossible reports of the women (Mary Magdalene, Joanna, and Mary mother of James, v. 10) and subsequently some other disciples, yet could not allow themselves to do so because no male disciple had actually seen Him (v.24). Jesus patiently explained the identity/purpose of the Messiah from the entire OT; everything that had transpired and looked confusing was what had been precisely predicted in Scripture.

When they reached the village of Emmaus, the day was waning, and the two invited Him (partly out of common hospitality, partly out of curiosity to hear more) to stay with them. He was the guest of the house, but when He assumed the role of host to break bread in front of them (v. 30), something in His manner, actions, or words caused them to realize He was indeed the One of whom they had spoken for hours on the road. When he suddenly left their sight, even though the evening was upon them, they rushed back immediately (v.33) to tell the gathered disciples. As they related their revelation, Jesus appeared among them, ate with them, and, as He had done with the two from Emmaus, He explained the messianic passages of scripture to them. He had no doubt gone over and over them repeatedly in their three+ years together on the road; now, with the burial, death, and resurrection fresh in their minds, these Scriptures came together with new light and new meaning. He commissioned the disciples to be His witnesses "to all the nations, beginning in Jerusalem" (v.47) before He departed them. This scene opens Luke's account in Acts of how these disciples began to fulfil that commission.

Lines on Leadership
Two aspects of Jesus as a leader in this passage are:
1) instead of rushing to the "Big Reveal," He exhibited patience to hear the hearts of the two on the road to Emmaus. With further patience, He took time to teach them the Word. How many times as a leader have I rushed to the task at hand and not

taken time to hear out what troubled my colleagues or fellow workers or taken time to listen and discover what the exact need was that I could provide?

2) when Jesus appeared to the eleven, the other disciples, and the Emmaus duo, He took the time to once again explain the Scriptures concerning His Messiahship. How many times as a leader have I balked at sharing with people for the umpteenth time something they should have "caught" much earlier?

Perhaps they needed the unexpected trauma of the recent events to crack open their minds' understanding of that which had been in front of them all the time. Are we willing to patiently take the time, that one more time, to explain what we have lived, taught, and exemplified in front of people for years in order that some might finally "get it" and believe?

_____
_____

++

JOHN'S GOSPEL

Intro: John wrote his gospel many years after Matthew, Mark, and Luke wrote their gospel accounts. It, therefore, does cover the same ground content-wise as those three and majors more on the teachings of Jesus. For that reason, it makes an excellent starting point for a new reader of the NT. John was one of the original twelve apostles and is often called the "beloved apostle." He also is the author of three minor epistles (1 John, 2 John, 3 John) and the Revelation.

++

John 1---Highlights: prologue on the deity of Christ, a testimony of John the Baptist, first converts of Jesus

I apologize for not addressing the magnificent prologue of this gospel (vs. 1-18) with its matchless description of Jesus as God come to earth clothed in flesh, full of grace and truth. Instead, we will concentrate on John the Baptist's small but pivotal statement as he paves the way for Jesus' public ministry. In verse 30, the Baptist declares, "This is He on behalf of whom I said after me comes a Man who has proved to be my superior because He existed before me."

<u>We are all interim</u>. Death, retirement, demotion, resignation, dismissal, financial ruin, or debilitating illness will eventually force us to give way for a replacement, absorption, or elimination of one's position in a particular group.

My current ministry during the production of this book is to coordinate work among churches in a ten-county region in the heart of Appalachia. This area does not have the transitory population of other US areas (except for the slow attrition of folks leaving WV after losing coal-related jobs). Many of our churches are manifestations of extended families that reach back generations in their hollers or counties. The majority have pastored over ten years in one church, several over twenty, two over thirty, and one forty+ years. I once conducted a search committee orientation for a church in a neighboring county where the pastor retired after 55 years in one congregation. Here the illusion of permanence can be especially strong. I rejoice in the stability of our shepherds as they tend their flocks, but over the years, as I help them navigate heart attacks, church splits, retirement, or a move to other fields of service, I am often reminded <u>we are all interim</u>. As I write, I am 69 and had announced July 1, 2023, as the date to step down from this post and transition to a slower pace and other venues of ministry. My health is good, my mind is sharp, and I'm one to dream and always ask, "what if. . .?" Working in a maintenance mode/treading water mentality is not for me. But I want to embody and emulate the example given to us in this opening chapter of John.

John the Baptist (not the author of this gospel account) is a striking figure, a true countercultural force that made initial waves with his preaching, his clothes, his unorthodox style, and his uncompromising message. He was there to pave the way (Is. 40.3) for the Messiah. In the latter half of the chapter, John has a vibrant ministry and has attracted followers. When Jesus arrives on the scene to begin His public ministry, John does not react with jealousy (they were related, Lk. 1.36) but announces Jesus as "the Lamb of God who takes away the sin of the world" (v.29). He repeats it the next day (v.36), knowing full well he will lose disciples, fame, and influence. Two chapters later, he utters the immortal words, "He must increase, but I must decrease" (Jn. 3.30). We will never know if he fully embraced his pronouncement of Jesus as the Paschal Lamb of God or if he had premonitions his sharp tongue would soon result in the loss of his head in prison (Mt. 14.1-12).

I want to follow John's example of knowing when someone has come whose message is more needed than mine or builds upon what I have said, a person to whom I should allocate my resources, my experience, my following, and my leverage. I realize I do not own a position; I am at best a steward of that Kingdom position, and now it is someone else's time.

When leaders realize their interim status (regardless of their present situation or success) they will acquire additional urgency about their work and a deeper sense of peace; it's not all about me, but about the cause or the Christ. Many pastors and senior management look at other staff members as rivals instead of potential successors in whom they should invest, train, equip, and groom for future success. In business (and especially in ministry), if we adopt this attitude of interim status, we become more open to actively developing others to take our place.

Lines on Leadership
Mike Krzyzewski is the most successful college basketball coach ever at this writing. He is affectionately known as coach K (most do not dare to pronounce shu-chef-skee) and has brought national prominence to Duke University through the Blue Devils' consistency of excellence, numerous championships, and countless players who went on to become an NBA player or coach. The day I wrote this chapter, he coached his final regular season game ever. He announced several months prior that he would step down at age 75, and no hoopla or guesswork was generated since his longtime assistant would move one seat over at center court to assume the head coaching position. He had determined the time was now to pass the torch. We are all interim. What will your inevitable exit strategy look like: years-long phase-out, a sudden departure, an allowance of erosion, and years to decrease your effectiveness? Will you be man or

woman enough to recognize someone will come along better suited at that time to take the reins and go forward without you in the saddle?

_____

_____

+++

John 2----Highlights: wedding at Cana, cleansing of the temple

John's gospel is the theological equivalent of Maurice Ravel's *Bolero*, a 17-minute-long musical composition where the same incessant melody passes from section to section with a constant increase in volume. From the very first chapter, John's motif of Jesus as true Light, Life, Truth, and Love begins with the prologue. It continues to rise until the climax of the crucifixion and resurrection narratives. Here in John 2, we see a recurring corollary: that speaking the truth can be confusing to the masses and costly for the speaker.

This may sound irreverent, but Jesus starts early in John's gospel by trying to pick a fight. He continues (see Jn. 5 entry) to make claim after claim about Who He is and what he came to do, and people react with either bewilderment or disbelief that eventually gives way to rage. In v. 13, Jesus decides to go to the temple in Jerusalem for Passover. The temple of His day was a massive structure. It was not only at the core of the city but the fulcrum of the entire Jewish culture and near to the heart of every practicing Jew. Even today, no visit to Jerusalem is complete without extended time spent at the temple's Western Wall, the Southern Steps, and viewed from below in a tunnel tour. Jesus wades into the midst of the merchandise hawkers and creates quite a scene; he swings a scourge of cords and turns over tables of goods, doves, and other animals squawking and flying everywhere. The astounded merchants say (my paraphrase),

"Who in blazes do you think you are to come in here and start a ruckus, destroy our way to make a living, and act like you own the place?" He replies in v. 19, "Destroy this Temple, and in three days I will raise it up." We cannot ascertain from the text if the merchants convulsed with derisive laughter or thought the lights were on, but nobody was home. We do know they said, "It took 46 years to build this structure, and you think you're powerful enough to not only remove it but rebuild it in just three days?" John writes the gospel in approximately 90 AD, so he has the benefit of knowing how this all turns out, as he notes Jesus meant another type of temple altogether (v. 21).

    This passage dispels some of the myths about how a servant leader behaves. There are seminal passages mentioned elsewhere in this book (see Mt. 20, Jn. 13, Phil. 2 entries) where servanthood is closely attached to Jesus' leadership. Being a servant does not mean being a pushover or a doormat. Jesus remains steadfastly focused on His identity and His mission by clearing out the Temple. His proclamation is not understood until later, but His actions are burned into the memories of all present. Make no mistake; He knows full well where this will lead. To state one's purpose as a leader, to back it up with action, and to know the full consequences of what the public may do to you because of your words and actions inspires and terrifies me. Jesus knew His repeated Messianic claims and repudiations of the religious leaders of the day would land Him in their crosshairs and cost Him His life on the cross.

    Many of my journal entries over the years are filled with this question: when the time comes, will I stand and make what Paul tells Timothy (1 Tim. 6.13) is the "good confession?" At the end of this gospel account, Jesus stands before Pilate and could have said, "No, I didn't really mean all that bluster and bravura. I was just making a name for myself" ---He doesn't. Instead, He stays the course and speaks truth knowing the cost, from the start of His ministry to the end. I pray I will remain true to my Master and my mission from beginning to end.

Lines on Leadership
When the situation arises, do you speak the truth, take the appropriate action, and take the consequences?
_____
_____
++

John 3 ---Highlights: new birth dialogue with Nicodemus, John the Baptist's last testimony

The third chapter of John contains arguably the most famous single verse in the entire Bible, Billy Graham's signature sermon anchor, John 3.16. The verse is at the center of one of two dialogues in the chapter: 1) between Jesus and Nicodemus, a Pharisee, and 2) between John the Baptist and his disciples.
The dialogue between Nicodemus and Jesus consists mainly of a protracted word image. Jesus declares the only entry point into His Kingdom is to be 'born again' (vs. 3, 5, 7), a phrase that today has unfortunately acquired many innocuous and harmless meanings reducing 'born again' to a mild cathartic attitude adjustment or a term for an "aha" moment. Jesus brilliantly takes a universal human experience to which everyone has strong emotional attachments and uses it to illustrate the upside-down priorities of the Kingdom of God (see Mt. 5 entry). The second half of the Nicodemus discourse emphasizes the two distinctions of mankind in the new Kingdom. It will not hinge on race, gender, power, wealth, nationality, or any other metric humanity uses to distinguish its groupings from one another. It will simply be those who place their faith in the 'only begotten' Son of God, a phrase

Jesus uses twice (v.16, 18) and those who do not. During His entire ministry (see Lk. 4 entry), Jesus tears down artificial categorizations of mankind and shows there are but two: those who believe and those who do not.

The dialogue between John the Baptist and his disciples picks up this theme and uses yet another word familiar image, that of bride and bridegroom, to describe his relationship to Jesus in regard to their ministries, and proceeds to reinforce Jesus' separation of mankind into two simple groups summarized in v. 36, he who believes in the Son has eternal life; and he who doesn't (repeated and rephrased in 1 Jn. 5.12).

Max dePree's little masterpiece, *Leadership is an Art*, begins by saying <u>the first duty of a leader is to define reality</u>[1] (see Mt. 10 entry). This finds repetition in other sections of this book. Both Jesus and John the Baptist define the new reality of the Kingdom of God (a phrase they both used in their first public declarations; John first in Mt. 3.2, Jesus in Mk. 1.15), and they do so with a powerful and enduring word image, tying the spiritual principle to a shared human experience.

Organizational leaders spend millions in research and advertising to formulate an image, a mythos, a grand narrative that portrays the values and mission of their organization. A good leader finds a way to make a point here and there with an appropriate illustration. A great leader finds a word image that burrows its way from the organization's corporate consciousness down to every cell's DNA, where it reproduces itself in every conversation, project, and publicity piece to get across its reason for existence.

Lines on Leadership

What word image are you currently using in your everyday interaction with group members to portray your company/church/group's values and purpose?

_____

_____

++

John 4---Highlights: Jesus and the Samaritan woman at a well and His disciples; Jesus heals

John devotes most of chapter 4 to an extended dialogue between Jesus and a woman that results in many of her townspeople believing in Him. For Christians, this is one of the clearest examples of personal evangelism in the NT. For leaders, the Jesus of chapter 4 is a convention-defying trailblazer, further establishing a new order of how things will be done in His kingdom.

From Jerusalem to Galilee, the most direct route was through Samaria (today's West Bank), but because Jews detested the "half-breed" Samaritans, travelers usually detoured by crossing the Jordan River and adding miles and time to a more roundabout route to avoid Samaria. Verse 4 says he "had" to travel the direct route; we don't know if floods prevented Him from crossing the Jordan River on the "Jewish" route or if He had determined to break with convention; in context, I suspect the latter. It could also be that as Messiah, He knew if he went this way at this time, He would meet the woman at the well. He comes to this crossroads town known in OT passages as Shechem. Many OT patriarchs are connected to this area (v.5). Joshua led the Israelites into the Promised Land and set up an antiphonal reading of the Law, blessings (from Mt. Gerizim) and curses (from Mt. Ebal) on both sides of Shechem, called Sychar in

John's account (v.5). With His first words in v. 7 Jesus has defied multiple conventions:

> 1) He speaks to a woman (v.7); 2) He speaks to a Samaritan (v. 9); 3) He speaks to her in public; 4) He speaks to an unaccompanied woman; 5) He speaks to an unclean woman known by the town as morally loose (v.6, it is noon, a time when the proper women of the village would not draw water); and 6) He sent his disciples into the local town to buy food likely not kosher (properly prepared according to Jewish law and custom) (v.8)

Jesus brilliantly engages the woman using the immediate surroundings of a well (see Jn. 7 entry) not only to begin the conversation but to turn it from physical need to spiritual need and eventually to declare His identity as Messiah (vs. 7, 10, 13, 26). She perceives He is an unusually gifted man and asks in v. 19 why different places exist for Samaritans (Mt. Gerizim) and Jews (Jerusalem) to worship God. Most commentaries agree this was a diversionary tactic, an attempt to sidetrack Jesus because He had addressed some very personal issues (her marital status, vs. 16-18). Samaritans had a shrine on Gerizim and followed the Pentateuch as the Law (first five books of the Jewish OT)[1]. Perhaps her inquiry was not diversionary but sincere, just sincerely incomplete. Jesus does not reprove so much as reveal what is coming, the new order where the Person not the place is the important aspect of worship (vs. 21-24), that instead of people traveling to meet God, God had come to dwell in their midst. Jesus wades through the mixture of truth and tradition in this entire exchange to arrive at the stunning declaration in vs. 25-26 that He is the Messiah awaited by all men (and women).

He does not pedantically spell out everything for her but rather answers with intrigue, mystery, and just enough information to make her figure out on her own the actual import of what He has claimed. Instead of demanding she bow down in the presence of divine royalty, He allows her to deduce slowly what is transpiring in front of her. He is being a good fisher of men/women (see Mt. 4.19). He presents the lure and waits for the woman to respond. I have tackle boxes full of lures and live in some of the country's most picturesque mountains and rivers, but I've always had trouble presenting a fly or lure or even a worm. I always try to reel them in at the first encounter with the bait. It is a sheer act of the will for me to wait and allow the fish to decide when to engage with what is presented. Jesus was the master of not only content but the moment and method of delivery.

    Jesus speaks to her situation, her need, and offers a new avenue of worship (Himself) as a solution. Granted, if He is anyone other than the Messiah, He is deceived or deceitful. On the strictly human plane of existence, leaders who can describe a dilemma or scenario with keen powers of observation are commonplace; those who can offer a vision of a better way forward are rare. Rarer still are those leaders who will invest themselves totally in the fulfillment of that solution, and ever rarer is a leader who will be so humble as to place himself at the mercy of the one he wishes to help[2] (Jesus has no bucket or container and must rely on the cooperation of another to draw any water from the well). As I write, one such individual in the news is Jim "Mattress Mack" McIngvale, the founder of a large furniture store in Houston, TX. Whenever natural disasters come that way, such as hurricanes, floods, subfreezing temperatures with attendant loss of power, heat, and water, Mattress Mack can be seen all over the news offering people a place to sleep, rest, get warm, get fed, in essence turning his stores into rescue shelters. When asked what he would do with all of the furniture the masses slept and sat on, he said we would have some gigantic, discounted sales. A reporter asked him, "aren't you losing money every time you do this?" He replied, "this is not about making a profit. It's about making a difference[3]."

Lines on Leadership
Where have you addressed unhealthy mixtures of tradition and truth, prejudice, the denial of truth or resources to a people group because they are not "like you?" How have you invested yourself as an integral part of the solution?

_____

_____

++

John 5---Highlights: healing at Bethesda; multiple claims for Jesus to be Messiah

The present-day pools of Bethesda are a spectacular site next to the Church of St. Anne near the Sheep Gate in old Jerusalem. It is a true highlight to walk among its ruins and realize you are standing where this chapter took place.
When the gospel of John is read as one unit, it has this inexorable, building momentum as it cements the identity of Jesus as the Son of God, Messiah, God come to dwell among His people. Jesus was not coy, waiting in the corner to be asked and pled with to take this position. From the first chapter, He displays His supernatural wisdom (1.48), creative powers (2.11), purpose (3.16), intimate knowledge of each person's life (4.18) and identity (4.26). The incident in chapter 5 shows His choice in chapter 4 to travel through Samaria was deliberate. He is intent on declaring He is the Christ and Lord of all. In Chapter 5, Jesus knew full well what day it was (the Sabbath) and that doing any form of work, miraculous or otherwise, would incur the wrathful attention of the religious establishment (it does, v.16,18). Christ initiates the

conversation with the man who has waited daily for 38 years at this pool to be healed (v.5) and takes the initiative to heal him without being asked.

The bulk of the chapter takes on a courtroom atmosphere. Jesus proceeds to offer multiple witnesses to His identity as Messiah, John the Baptist (vs. 33-35), Jesus' works (miracles, v. 36), God the Father (vs. 37-38), and the Scripture (vs. 39-47). You don't eat the menu; you eat the entrée. The Scripture is seen as testifying of Jesus (v.39). He is to be worshipped, not the Bible.

Jesus picks a fight with the religious leaders, and it won't be the last time; He makes a habit of healing or working on the Sabbath to show He is the Lord of everything, including the Sabbath. Indeed, probably the most explosive sentence in the chapter is v. 17. He has gone past the point of no return. He challenges their concept of doing no work on the Sabbath (if God didn't work on the Sabbath, how could you breathe, have light, be warm, have crops grow, etc.) and equates Himself with a God who would work on the Sabbath ('My Father is working, and I'm doing the same;' they got the inference immediately as v. 18 indicates), all in one sentence.

Adaptive leadership is a 21st-century approach to leadership espoused primarily by Ron Heifetz of Harvard[1]; I highly recommend reading anything he writes. Adaptive leaders (for the sake of oversimplified brevity) divide solutions into two camps, technical and adaptive. *Technical* solutions are the ones that have been proven, written, codified, and executed from a manual or past experience. Find the solution, insert, implement, and be done. *Adaptive* solutions are needed when the solution does not easily present itself from past instances. It emphasizes a group approach to problem-solving, and the leader, more often than not, forces the issue to stay front and center by creating a *deliberate disequilibrium*. The status quo is upended, a new disruptive scenario is introduced to the situation, and the group is compelled to confront the disequilibrium by finding a way previously unknown or unused for that situation. The primary leadership skill is to keep the disequilibrium front and center but without totally blowing the top off the situation from pressure and to not give in to the temptation to "solve the problem for them." It is messy and can be inefficient if time is of the essence, but in the long run, allows the group involved to be at the center of the process to arrive at a solution, and encourages buy-in from all involved.

Lines of Leadership

Jesus presented the religious leaders with a concept of the Messiah that did not fit the religious leaders' framework. He presented a deliberate disequilibrium by healing on the Sabbath. The technical solutions of the religious leaders could not address the dilemma Jesus had posed. What perennial issue in your organization could benefit from this adaptive leadership approach?

_____

_____

+++

John 6---Highlights: feeds 5000; Jesus Walks on Water; Bread of Life; Where else can we go?

The perspective for this chapter will be future leaders, the disciples of Jesus. The sections of this chapter comfort me as Jesus meets needs and again declares His claim to Messiahship in a poetic, figurative way. From the vantage point of the disciples, this is a terrifying sequence of events.

First, Jesus, as a consummate teacher as well as Savior, asks a question. He knows the answer, but He asks mainly to furrow the disciples' brows and make them squirm. V. 10 states there were 5000 men, so if any women and children were present, this is by any measure a large crowd by the shore of the Sea of Galilee. He asks, "Where will we get enough bread to feed this many?" Oh, to have an actual on-site video of how Andrew said all we have are a kid's fish and barley loaves. Jesus exposes their lack of faith by giving out so much food to the masses that the apostles pick up a "driving-home-the-point" twelve baskets, one for each apostle.

In addition to this puzzling incident, they got into a boat and rowed during the night toward the northern shore, and Capernaum---and Jesus walked on water to join them in the boat (see Mt. 14 entry). As soon as He entered the boat, they were <u>immediately</u> (v.21) onshore at Peter's hometown. Fear magnified the frustration of the early evening feeding, and they ceased to search for explanations. The recipients of the miracle meal sought Him out and asked how Jesus arrived so quickly in Capernaum (v.25). Instead of an explanation or reference to His miracles, Jesus launched into a mysterious, lengthy discourse in the synagogue on why He was the Bread of Life (v.35) that befuddled the grumbling Jews, then He turned the Bread of Life metaphor on its head by saying He was <u>living</u> bread (v.51) of which they would have to partake in order to have eternal life and seemed to add in the bonus gore of drinking His blood. Many of the disciples could not take this any longer and left (v.66); miracles or no miracles, free meals or not, this was too bizarre.

From a leadership standpoint, the crucial verses are 66-68. As some disciples leave, Jesus a) does not run after them, saying, "Come on back, I was just messing with you, here's what I really meant," and b) asks the twelve, "'Are you taking off as well?" Peter in the last twenty-four hours has seen and heard nothing that makes sense, yet he says in v. 68-69, "Lord, to whom shall we go? You have words of eternal life. And we have believed and have come to know that You are the Holy One of God." Peter didn't understand any more at that moment than he did the day before regarding a rationale for what he had experienced. But he knew he stood in the presence of Someone extraordinary enough

Peter was willing to suspend his search for logic, step out in faith, and continue to follow Him.

Some may object and say this sounds suspiciously like many cult followers say; their leader is so mesmerizing, charismatic, charming, or fearsome, if they follow him/her, they will find peace, or glory, or whatever each one seeks. There is no crazed look in Christ's eye, no ego demanding subservience, no command to grovel at my feet; Peter thought, here is a Rabbi capable of meeting physical needs, who is not bound by the laws of nature (gravity or space/time constrictions), who somehow (I can't figure it out) is willing to sacrifice Himself for us in a way that right now seems out and out weird---but Peter senses all these mounting miracles, discourses, and I AM statements will slowly come into focus. He cannot articulate it entirely, but Peter's admiration for Christ is slowly turning to adoration. He is the only one who speaks here, but he obviously speaks for the group (to whom shall <u>we</u> go---<u>we</u> have believed).

Lines on Leadership

I cannot command the commitment of future followers if I cannot commit myself (see Lk. 16 entry). This is an "I'm in" moment for Peter; what if he had not spoken up? Would some of the twelve have slowly drifted off into the darkness with the other doubting disciples? How many meetings have you attended where the outcome or a vote count was in doubt until someone said, "I'm in," or "we're on board with this?"

Would others describe you as a person of commitment? To whom or to what are you committed beyond yourself and your own personal success/stability/sustainability? What was the tipping point for that commitment?

_____

_____

++

John 7---Highlights: Jesus tangles with Jewish leaders; declarations of His Deity; springs of living water

At the time of this book's publication, the US 14th Amendment guaranteed anyone born within the boundaries of the United States is at birth a US citizen regardless of his/her parents' origin. How important is it where a person is "from?" I was born on Luke Air Force base near Phoenix, AZ. We were there for less than two years as a family, and I did not visit the state again until my 45th wedding anniversary trip. My "growing up" years were in southwestern Louisiana, where I learned to love Cajun food and music along with their *joie de vivre*, but I would never say I was remotely Cajun. After college, I married a Texan and had two stints of living in that state for a total of 32 years as bookends to our six years of mission work alongside the Evangelische Freikirchliche Gemeinde in Germany. My most recent years have been in the heart of Appalachia. My accent does not betray any particular region except that I am NOT from where I currently reside. Where am I "from?" Where I currently reside? Where I spent the most time? Where my ministry bore the most fruit? Where they dress and sound like I do?

For both the scorners and adorers of Jesus, Galilee was the site of His sermons and miracles being discussed in Jerusalem, so they identified Him as from that region. The prejudice of the Jewish rulers toward Galilee as inferior is apparent as they scornfully say (v.52) no prophet has come from that region (even though several likely did: Jonah, 2 Kg. 14.25; possibly Elijah, 1 Kg. 17.1; possibly Nahum, Nahum 1.1). If they could convince the public Jesus came from inferior stock or an inferior place, it would be easier to dismiss His teachings.

Jesus had a heavenly origin (vs. 28-29) and an earthly ministry, one more part of the dialectical tension that comes from a message of a Kingdom that has arrived in Him but is not yet visible to the masses. He reinforces that "now but not yet" tension in vs. 37-38 as He promises if a person follows Him, He will give "rivers of living water." John comments in v. 39 this was because the Holy Spirit had not yet come as He would at Pentecost (see Acts 2).

Gerolstein is a small town of less than 10,000 nestled in Germany's volcanic born Eifel mountain range. World-famous Gerolsteiner mineral water has been produced there since the late 1800s. German Baptists organized a multi-town evangelistic effort in the 1980s. The Gerolsteiner Mineralwasser factory parking lot was where the city fathers gave permission for a tent revival (see Mt. 9 entry). I had the privilege of preaching during that revival. The hills surrounding Gerolstein produced water that promoted health and became the number one "Sprüdel" in terms of sales in Europe; there was no doubt vs. 37-38 would be the subject of the first sermon during that revival. I spoke of the living water promised by Isaiah (44.3; 55.1; 58.11) and personified in Jesus as a present reality for everyone there and a future reality if the Lord allowed us to establish a church there. Through many adventures, the church was founded and exists to this day some 35 years later.

The "mother" congregation for the Gerolstein church was our church in Trier, an hour away by train in the Mosel River valley. Gerolstein was a small town nestled in the hills far above Trier; the Swiss pastor of the Trier church and the American missionary were both from "somewhere else." Together we co-pastored the mother and daughter congregations for several years. Between his Schweizer Deutsch and my butchered German pronunciation, it was a miracle that the congregation grew. But where we were from and how we presented the gospel did not overshadow the living water of the gospel, satisfying the thirst of a people hungry for the Word. With Jesus, the Jewish leaders allowed the alleged culture of His ministry (Galilee) to overshadow His message's content. I thank God the members of the Gerolstein church looked past our odd accents and vocabulary to hear the Good News we brought.

Lines on Leadership
What do your colleagues or members know about "where you're from?" Does the recounting of your alleged starting points or country of origin clarify or confuse the message/narrative you wish to communicate?

_____

_____

++

John 8---Highlights: adulterer caught in the act, Jesus as the light of the world, the truth shall make you free

"You shall know the truth, and the truth shall set/make you free." This quote from v.32 has found its way onto the entrances of university lecture halls, public libraries, and churches. Truth seems to be a diminishing concept as people lose faith in absolute truth, and current society embraces "my truth," that whatever I declare to be truth is truth for me. For others, it is a disembodied, non-attainable Platonic idea for which we only have contradictory examples. Some believe it to be a king-of-the-mountain approach: whatever narrative about an event or phenomenon survives all the other comers will become truth. Still others follow Hegelian syntheses, with each truth having an "anti-truth." From those two opposing statements a synthesized truth emerges that will also have an "anti-truth", and on it goes. Added to this confusion is the mounting tsunami of misinformation and disinformation that pervades our media.

One wonders, how will I recognize the truth that will set/make me free?

We could dive into *epistemology*, the study of knowledge and its acquisition, or dive deeper into *alethiology*, the study of the nature of truth. V. 32 does not begin with a capital letter as a new or independent thought. It is a continuation of v. 31, where Jesus said, "If you abide in My word, you are truly My disciples, and you will know the truth, and the truth will set you free." (ESV) Other translations use verbs like 'if you continue' or 'remain' in My word (see Jn. 15 entry). To establish the truth in a statement, I must trace it back to its source. In John 1, the Word is introduced as the living Word (Jesus) and written Word (Scripture). In John 17, Jesus says in prayer to His Father, "Your word is truth" (v.17). If you believe God is real and that Jesus is His Son, these four simple words have monumental importance. God becomes the source of truth; whatever He says is truth, or as several people have said through the years, "all truth is God's truth" because they consider God the source of all truth. Jn. 1.17 traces the source of truth back to the law of Moses but does not stop there; in a "Back to the Future" moment in Scripture, it says that "grace and truth were realized through Jesus Christ." This section (Prologue) states that in the beginning (pre-Creation, pre-earth, pre-human) was the Word. Later in that section, He is called the true light, and He was "full of grace and truth." (v.14)

This seems like an example of circular reasoning, of assumptions posing as fact and being used to prove their own existence. When traced back to their source, mathematical axioms are not birthed by an equation but a faith proposition. The truth will make you free, but ultimately it will rely not on a set of facts but rather a faith in Something or Someone, a first Cause or First Person. Metaphysics deals with first principles and first causes. The spiritual realm is often called metaphysical not because it is antithetical to the physical universe but because it goes beyond it or after it.

Lines on Leadership
What is the source of the foundational truth for your life, vocation, day to day conduct? Can you identify it? Are you willing to stake your church/company, reputation, and family's welfare on it/on Him?

_____

_____

++

John 9---Highlights: healing of a blind man on the Sabbath; Pharisees' questions: Jesus declares His deity

Jesus repeatedly made a point to heal on the Sabbath (Mt. 12.8, 10; Mk. 3.1; Lk 6.6; Lk. 13.10; Lk. 14.1ff; Jn. 5.9). John 9 shares yet another detailed account of such a healing, again on a Sabbath (v. 14), this time with multiple questionings of the formerly blind man by the religious authorities. This issue of healing on the Sabbath has been discussed in other chapters (see Lk. 6, Jn. 5 entries).

The emphasis in John 9 for today is the variation of how Jesus healed. In this instance, He "spat on the ground, and made clay of the spittle, and applied the clay to his eyes" (v.6). In other instances of healing, He verbally commanded a person to be healed without touching them Himself (Mt. 9.2; 12.13; 17.18; Mk. 2.11; 3.1; Lk. 6.10; 9.40; 17.14; Jn. 5.9); He laid hands on some (Mk. 6.5; Lk. 13.13; 14.40; 22.51); healed without being present (Mt. 8.13; 15.28); or took a dead person's hand to restore life (Mt. 9.25). Some were healed by touching the hem of His garment (Mk. 6.56; Lk.4.40; 8.44), and one was healed by a two-step process of directly spitting in a man's eyes and then touching the eyes with Jesus' hand (Mk. 8.22-25).

The method used to heal in John 9 is unique because of its complexity and the number of elements involved. Jesus used spit of His own, the ground, took time to mix them (a form of kneading, which was forbidden on the Sabbath as a category of work[1]), applied the rudimentary poultice to the man's eyes, and then instructed him to go wash in a specific pool (Siloam). The man did as instructed and received his sight. Instead of rejoicing with the man, the religious leaders pressed him repeatedly to denounce Jesus as a sinner, charlatan, or anything but the Son of God (9.13-34).

The bottom line is people were healed, and the leadership principle is that there were many ways to accomplish it. Jesus often spoke of what would result from the healing or why He healed, but He never explained His methods except His deliberate timing to heal, often on the Sabbath (not to rebel but to declare that He was Lord of that Sabbath). This is not a validation of the "the end justifies the means" method of leadership; Jesus was scrupulous to observe OT biblical admonitions, just quick to point out where men had embellished or ignored them for laws of man's origins.

Lines on Leadership
In the churches where I minister, I often say the message remains the same (the gospel), but our methods must change to address the current culture, region, circumstances, etc., if they do not compromise biblical truth (see Mt. 15 entry). What unorthodox or unaccepted methods have you used to achieve your goal(s)? Would you use any of those same methods today?

++

John 10---Highlights: Parable of the Good Shepherd; Jesus claims equality with the Father

There are seven 'I AM' statements in the gospel of John that purposefully link Jesus to God the Father; John 10 contains two. Jesus said He was 'the door' (v. 9) and 'the good shepherd' (vs. 11, 14). After a visit to Bethlehem in 2019, I understood them much better as the two metaphors combined into one.

Hundreds of small grottos dot the hillsides of Bethlehem (see Mt. 2, Lk. 2 entries). They were ideal locations for a shepherd to shelter his livestock. Many have a small entrance through which a person must carefully enter; inside is a large rock room perfect for protecting the animals at night. It was perfect because the single entrance allowed the shepherd to be both the door and the shepherd as he would stand, sit, or sleep in the entrance and silently announce to foe and predator alike: to get to my sheep/cattle/goats, you must get past me.

Jesus contrasts Himself with two types of non-shepherds, a thief (v.10) and a hireling (vs. 12-13). The thief actively wants to harm the sheep, and the hireling could care less about them; one wants to grab sheep to turn a quick profit, and the other one thinks sheep are simply a means to grab a paycheck. The shepherd, however, "lays down his life for the sheep" (v.11), and later Jesus openly talks about doing the same for all of mankind, a willful choice (vs. 17-18) to sacrifice His life for them. When we were in Germany, I met a pastor from one of the state-supported denominations who lived in our neighborhood. We struck up a friendship and one day talked about the topic of hirelings and shepherds. He listed colleagues from his denomination who were believers and those who were not. Incredulous, I said how can you be certain? He replied they told me themselves! State-supported means part of one's income tax goes to the church, even as a non-attender. We were part of the Freikirche (free church) denominations, churches that do not receive monies from the federal income tax. That pastor friend related that many of his colleagues got the training but exhibited no calling and claimed no salvation relationship to Christ; it was just a job for them. I cannot think of a better definition of a hireling.

Later in the chapter, Jesus continues the sheep/shepherd analogy to dually assert His deity and identify who is in His fold. The voice of Jesus identifies Him as the great Shepherd the sheep will follow (vs. 4, 27; Heb. 13.20). Those who do not recognize His voice are not of His flock, which automatically excluded the Jewish temple leaders (vs. 24-26). He finishes the section off with the blockbuster statement that "I and the Father are one." (v.30), which flies in the face of those who claim Jesus never equated Himself with God (the leaders acknowledged it when they said, "You, being a man, make Yourself out to be God." I want to recognize and follow the voice of Someone who would sacrifice Himself on my behalf.

<u>Lines on Leadership</u>
Would your organization's fellow workers/members describe you as a shepherd or a hireling?
_____
_____
++

John 11---Highlights: the raising of Lazarus; the conspiracy to kill Jesus develop

This chapter is pivotal in the life and ministry of Jesus. The die was cast as the Jewish religious leaders viewed Jesus' ever more remarkable miracles not as joyous occasions but as signs of their waning influence among the populace (v. 48). Many conflicts in organizations revolve around the "C" word, control, as noted in other chapters. The leaders, to ensure their place in society is not lost, determined that day to kill Jesus (v. 53) and ordered the people to inform them of His whereabouts if seen (v. 57).

In the midst of this development, Jesus was approximately 12 hours by foot away from Jerusalem at the site of John the Baptist's baptisms on the Jordan River east of Jericho (Jn. 10.40-42). His good friends in Bethany (v.18) have sent word that Lazarus is sick unto death. Two factors come into conflict at this moment. 1) Jesus genuinely loves this family (Jn. 11.3, 5, 33, 35, 36, 38). They have exhibited friendship for and faith in Jesus (Jn. 11. 21, 24, 27, 32; 12.1-3), so naturally, He would like to help them in a way only He could. 2) He knows the clouds of conspiracy are gathering in Jerusalem near Bethany. What should He do?

The disciples all reminded Him out of fear of what awaits Him in Jerusalem (vs. 8, 16), yet Thomas encourages them to disregard the danger and says let us follow Him to our deaths, a somewhat prophetic statement in light of the next chapter (see Jn. 12 entry). Jesus did the unexpected. He sublimated His personal feelings for Lazarus and tarried, allowing Lazarus to die (v.6). Jesus purposefully waited until four days had transpired before His return to Bethany to speak life back into Lazarus.

As an example for leaders, Jesus openly allowed His true affection for this family and His friend Lazarus to show, yet was not deterred from the mission to give God honor and glory. To have come immediately to Lazarus' bedside and healed him would have been an occasion for rejoicing, but to raise him from the dead would immortalize this story read by millions of readers millennia later. The right decision made at the wrong time diminishes or even negates the good that can come from that decision. The timing is almost as important as the decision itself. Jesus showed a long-term understanding of the total situation and went far beyond the parameters of friendship alone.

Lines on Leadership
What is a decision you made in the past that was the right decision but was made or implemented at the wrong time? What decisions loom over the horizon that needs to be seen in their larger context and possible consequences?
_____
_____
++

John 12---Highlights: Entrance into Jerusalem, Jesus' death foretold

v. 24, "Truly, truly, I say to you, unless a grain of wheat falls into the earth and dies, it remains by itself alone; but if it dies, it bears much fruit." After multiple elusions of the Jewish leaders' attempts to confront or capture Him, Jesus announces in v. 23 that "the hour has come for the Son of Man to be glorified." Instead of stepping into the spotlight with music swirling to a climax and thunderous multitudes roaring their approval, Jesus announces that being glorified means dying and that out of His death, life will spring forth. He then invites others to follow Him, and that to follow Him means to tread the same path He will take ("where I am, there shall My servant also be," v. 26). The Lk. 9 entry describes this as a process and lifestyle; in Jn. 12, it is a moment of truth when the person commits to Christ to the point where the person will follow Him wherever that leads. Christ is very plainspoken: it leads to death that will bring life to others.

On a spiritual level, this is the essence of Christianity; eternal life is a gift given only when one is willing in faith to die to self and be raised in the power of Christ to follow Him.

On a secular level, I am a guitar player of modest ability and an avid guitar collector, particularly those made by Appalachian luthiers to reflect my current surroundings. Many desired tonewoods used to build guitars are endangered species or are increasingly difficult to obtain. In an interview conducted with Bob Taylor of Taylor guitars, a company known for the innovative use of tonewoods, I was struck by a statement he made concerning sustainability. Mr. Taylor spoke about the need to plant trees systematically for the future. Most high-end guitar parts suppliers roam forests to find isolated trees they hope can produce boards suitable for guitar making. Instead of happenstance wanderings through forests, he said his company has started to plant trees in such a way that they would ensure the types of wood they want will be available. It would be a sustainable manner to honor the environment yet provide enough wood for the next generation to build quality guitars. He knew he would never see those trees grow to maturity; their normal lifespan would easily surpass his. He was willing to invest in a future he would never see[1].

Lines on Leadership
In John 10, Jesus spoke of laying down His life for His sheep. In John 11, He declared He was the Resurrection and the Life. Later in John 14, He will declare Himself to be the Way and the Truth as well as the Life. As a leader, I pray when the time comes, or the situation arises to follow Christ's example and give my life to

give life to others, I will be willing. It may take the form of investing in others, sacrificing time, energy, and resources, or giving life itself. This is the ultimate test of servant leadership. What area of your leadership needs reexamination in light of Jesus' analogy, that of a seed dying in the ground to see life spring up anew so that future generations may live and continue the work of the Kingdom/your organization?

_____

_____

++

John 13---Highlights: Washing of the disciple's feet by Jesus; institution of the Lord's Supper

    The concept of servant leadership is unmistakably displayed in John 13 through a deliberate, repeated gesture that resounds through the centuries. During the last meal with His disciples, before the arrest, trial, crucifixion, and resurrection, Jesus rises from supper (v. 4), strips down to essential clothing, bends His knee, and washes the feet of every disciple. It is difficult to imagine which emotion was stronger: the humbling of the disciples, their Master doing what they should have offered to do (vs. 6-10), or the sorrow Christ felt as he washed the feet of his future betrayer, Judas Iscariot. (see Max Greinke's sculpture, The Divine Servant[1])

    After rising, Jesus says of this act of servant leadership, "If I then, the Lord and Teacher, washed your feet, you also ought to wash one another's feet. For I gave you an example that you also should do as I did to you" (vs. 14-15). Later, He says more broadly, "A new commandment I give to you, that you love one another, even as I have loved you, that you also love one another. By this all men will know that you are My disciples, if you have love for one another" (vs. 34-35). Love is shown by our service.

Oscar Thompson rephrased it by simply saying, "Love is meeting needs[2]." Wilkes counts servanthood as the first requisite of leadership[3]. Nouwen sums up this principle in his little yet impactful book on Christian leadership, declaring:

> It is not a leadership of power and control, but a leadership of powerlessness and humility in which the suffering servant of God, Jesus Christ, is made manifest. I, obviously, am not speaking about a psychologically weak leadership in which Christian leaders are simply passive victims of the manipulations of their milieu. No, I am speaking of a leadership in which power is constantly abandoned in favor of love. Powerlessness and humility in the spiritual life do not refer to people who have no spine and who let everyone else make decisions for them. They refer to people who are so deeply in love with Jesus that they are ready to follow him wherever he guides them, always trusting that with him, they will find life and find it abundantly[4].

Lines on Leadership

The Leadership Challenge, the best overall book on leadership for a church or corporate setting, uses Five Practices of Exemplary Leadership with ten overall commitments[5]. Model the Way is the first practice, and its two commitments are 1) clarify values by finding your own voice and 2) set the example by aligning actions with shared values. Kouzes and Posner open chapter 4 with an example of how to Set The Example.

Steve Skarke was brought in to be a plant manager at a facility with the self-proclaimed goal of becoming a "World Class Plant". He started reminding everyone to clean up after themselves with little positive results. He went to the hardware store, purchased a large plastic bucket, and went through the plant picking up trash in front of the employees, dumping it in the proper container, and saying nothing on a regular basis. Before long, other managers were buying their own buckets and doing the same. Soon completely new ways to position workers and trash receptacles were in place. His example became the norm without mandated policy reviews or meetings dedicated to a solution[6].

This is a tricky balance. On the one hand, we are told to do our almsgiving, prayer, and fasting in secret (Mt. 6), yet in the same Sermon on the Mount, Jesus says to "let your light shine before men in such a way that they may see your good works, and glorify your Father who is in heaven" (Mt. 5.16). Jesus performed a highly visible gesture of service. Nouwen points out that the key is our intent is not to improve our self-images but humbly emulate Christ. What is one way your servant leadership example (viewed by others) could spawn a new norm in your group?

_____
_____

++

John 14---Highlights: Comfort for the disciples; oneness of Jesus and the Father; the role of the Holy Spirit

John 14 is an oft-quoted Biblical passage at funerals as Jesus promises (v. 2) to prepare a place for believers in "My Father's house." Later He utters one of the most often quoted "I AM" statements when Jesus declares He "is the Way and the Truth, and the Life" and further states that salvation is exclusively granted by Him: "no one comes to the Father but through Me (v.6)." These two concepts are central to most preachers' evangelistic sermons.

Less accentuated is the bulk of the chapter when Jesus describes the emerging role of the Holy Spirit (see Jn. 16.7-15). He uses a particular term to describe the Holy Spirit (v. 16, 26) that appears in various translations as Companion, Counselor, Advocate, Intercessor, Friend, and most often as Helper or

Comforter. The Greek word used is *Paracletos,* literally "one who walks alongside". Para is a prefix, meaning "alongside" and appears in words such as paramedic, paratrooper, etc.

We do not have extensive descriptions or physical portraits of God the Father, the Son, or the Holy Spirit. They are one in essence but three in offices or functions, a statement debated for centuries. Any organization of two or more people (spiritual or corporate) does well to read this chapter over and over to see the intertwining, interaction, and interplay of the Father, Son, and Holy Spirit with each other and with believers. The affirmation, alignment, and advocacy of one for another is a perfect model for all human relationships. The believer who learns to follow the commands of God is granted the eternal fellowship of His presence (v. 21, "He who has My commandments and keeps them, he it is who loves Me; and he who loves Me shall be loved by My Father, and I will love him, and will disclose Myself to him; v. 23, "If anyone loves Me, he will keep My word; and My Father will love him, and We will come to him, and make Our abode with him.") This hearkens back to v. 2 where Jesus promises to prepare a "dwelling place" ("room" in modern translations, "mansion," KJV). Followship engenders fellowship. The King of the Universe extends an offer to live with Him forever. I just need to recognize when He is speaking to me, leading me, and follow whether He speaks or walks beside me as the Father, the Son, or the Holy Spirit.

Lines on Leadership
It is a rare leader who commands the respect and obedience of his group yet is deeply beloved by them to the point they long to have him/her around and live life together. Do your fellow workers desire your help and presence, or do they avoid it? How do they know you have their best interests at heart and do

everything you can to give them the best work environment, the best team, and the best future?

_____
_____

++

John 15---Highlights: Jesus as the Vine, the disciples' relationship to each other and with the world

    This chapter is, without a doubt, one of my favorites in the whole Word of God. It always takes me back to a certain hillside in then-West Germany.

    I grew up in Lake Charles, LA, from first grade through a bachelor's degree in music education. Nutria, moccasins (snakes, not shoes), alligators, and gar stand out in my memories as well as flat, flat, flat land covered by towering trees interrupted by bayous and lakes. A small shower meant days of standing water in the yard and, later, mosquitoes. I was never far from water but worlds away from vineyards.

    We were commissioned in 1982 by our denomination's then Foreign Mission Board (now the International Mission Board) to be its first missionaries (along with the Jenkins family) to do German language work in partnership with the Evangelische Freikirchliche Gemeinde (German Baptists). Prior missionaries had done primarily English language work with churches planted after WWII. After a year in language school at Lüneburg, we moved to Trier, the oldest city in West Germany (founded by Romans in 16BC) to work with the local congregation and begin a collegiate ministry. Our townhome was in a new neighborhood near the Universität Trier.

    I soon learned that our neighborhood, Trimmelter Hof, was once a Roman settlement outside the city. The Romans had planted vineyards there. As I started to explore our neighborhood on daily walks, two streets over, I discovered an active vineyard on the steep hillside, and from there, I could see multiple hills and countless vineyards. This was a magnificent new sight for a transplanted swamp lover.

Our landlord lived further down the Mosel River and was a vintner. One day he came to visit us, and in his car trunk he showed me new rootstocks he was about to plant back in his vineyard. He explained the parts of the individual grapevine. His commentary on the plant and my re-reading of this passage in my German Bible made John 15 come alive. The rootstocks in his car were the trunks of the vine and were planted in the ground. By themselves, they were gnarly, uninteresting, bereft of beauty or a hint of greenery. At a certain point in the growth, a shoot forms of a completely different color and texture, as if someone had attached it with glue. As it continued to grow and extend, a dowel rod was thrust into the ground, around which the vine twisted and curled upward towards the sun. Leaves formed, and eventually, small clusters of what would become grapes.

Most English translations for verse 5 approximate 'I am the vine, you are the branches.' In German the verse says, ich bin der Weinstock, Ihr seid die Reben. (I am the trunk of the wine, you are the vines). Now I understood; Jesus was that gnarly, unattractive connection to the land and its nutrients. I was the shoot coming off of it. In v. 5, the KJV has the word *abide*; in modern translations, the word *remain*. "He who abides in Me, and I in him, he bears much fruit." As long as the vine remains in living, vital connection with the trunk, the nutrients flow through, and the grapes grow. The vine is but the conduit of the nutrients and water that become the fruit. The end of the verse cements this: "for apart from Me you can do nothing."

On a faith level, I realize that whatever talents I possess are relatively inconsequential compared to having the life of

Christ flow through me into the lives of others. The rest of the chapter convinces me my purpose in life is to reproduce the life of Christ in others: in unbelievers, it is called evangelism; in believers, it is called discipleship (see 1 Tim. 2 entry). On a secular level, I realize that whatever position of leadership or status I achieve in life is not so much due to brilliance as to all those before me from family, school, work, and friends who poured their knowledge, wisdom, and love into shaping who I am; again, I am but a conduit of their wisdom to pass it on to the next generation.

Lines on Leadership
Believers and nonbelievers alike owe an ongoing debt of gratitude to those who have invested in us, be it our Lord or our lineage. I am thankful for every living, vital connection and want to remain in that relationship for the rest of my life: I want to make my predecessors proud and produce fruit to His glory, and I want to make my successors grateful I preceded them. What influenced the type of fruit your life is producing, and how are you producing fruit that will result in future generations?
_____
_____
++

John 16---Highlights: Jesus teaching on the Holy Spirit; His death and resurrection foretold

One thread that unites John 14, 15, 16, 17, and 18 is the concept of truth. Throughout John's gospel, truth is closely connected to God the Father, God the Son, and God the Holy Spirit. In the prologue (1.14) we read, "The Word became flesh and dwelt among us . . . the only begotten from the Father, full of grace and truth," with the living Word identified as Jesus. The written Word of God sets the truth free for the one who abides in it (Jn. 8.31-32) and is equated with truth (Jn. 17.17). Jesus as the living Word equates Himself with truth ("I am the Way, the Truth, and the Life," Jn. 14.6). The Holy Spirit as the *Paracletos* (see Jn. 14 entry) is called the Spirit of truth (Jn. 14.17; 15.26). This Spirit of truth in John 16 will lead the disciples into all truth (v.13). At Jesus' trial before Pilate, He is asked point blank, "What is truth?" (see Jn. 18 entry). John sees all truth as God's truth; another way to state that is that all truth has its origin in God[1].

Each time in John's gospel truth is either identified with one person of the Godhead or spoken by a member of the Godhead. <u>Truth explained is almost never as effective as Truth incarnated</u>. Even as Jesus taught the disciples this one last time, they had a hard time following their Master's line of thought (v.17). The truth of the new birth was not evident to them until Jesus had died, was buried, and rose again. Now, this idea of a Helper who will come after Christ is gone befuddles the group.

In vs. 7-15, Jesus explains the threefold role of the Holy Spirit when He comes as their *Paracletos*. The Spirit will convict the world of sin, righteousness, and judgment. Simply put, He will show the world it has been wrong about sin (that it's not about a balance scale of good and bad but belief or unbelief in Jesus as the Son of God), about righteousness (it cannot be attained but is a gift of God through Jesus Christ), and judgment (he who believes in the Son has eternal life; but he who does not obey the Son shall not see life, but the wrath of God abides on him, Jn. 3.36). Later in John's epistles, he repeats, "He who does not have the Son of God does not have the life." (1 Jn. 5.12) Like pretty much everything in the last three chapters, most of this flies right over the heads of the disciples and makes little sense until the death, burial, resurrection of Christ, and the coming of the Holy

Spirit at Pentecost (see Acts 2 entry). Everything the Spirit does and says will point back to Jesus ("He shall glorify Me," v. 14).

Lines on Leadership

A remarkable, completely seamless arrangement of the Trinity comes together in John 16. There is an indescribable distinction of function yet total unity in the Father, Son, and Holy Spirit. There is no hierarchy, no ladder rungs, and no flow chart necessary for the Godhead to be the Godhead. The nearest depiction yet inadequate illustration is possibly the ancient diagram attributed to Athanasius of Alexandria[2] (see diagram). Without

Christian representation of the Trinity. 1

any blasphemous comparisons to deity, how would you describe the working relationship with the senior leadership of your group? How would each of your colleagues describe the working relationship? How does the truth emerge from that working relationship?

_____

_____

++

John 17---Highlights: The Lord's Prayer

The term "the Lord's Prayer" popularly refers to Mt. 6.6-9 as Jesus teaches His disciples a usable framework for prayer that has endured over the centuries. Some consider John 17 a more accurate "Lord's Prayer" because it is a prayer only Christ could pray. It is intensely personal, describing His mission and His relationship with Father God in a manner only His Son could dare address.

In one way, the prayer is about Jesus: there is no one else in the chapter, no furtherance of the narrative of events or nurturing of the disciples, and no description of His whereabouts. It is a Son speaking to a Father in the most unique relationship of persons in the entire universe. The time has come for that which has been discussed and planned in the hallways of heaven before eternity (Eph. 1.3-14). It signals the eve of a great battle, the calm where resolve and decisions meld to create a resultant reality.

His disciples are at the heart of His petitions. He refers to them as men (v.6) and afterwards only as "they". The language is disarmingly unadorned. The weight of the moment tends to simplify one's vocabulary. He twice prays for the disciples to enter into a unity (vs. 21, 23) that approaches the unity He has with the Father. Christ speaks the central truth for the body of Christ, which is its unity, one of the strongest witnesses available of the existence of a triune God. Christ also prays for their protection and provision (v.15) and that they not be taken out of the world but shielded from the evil one.

Lines on Leadership

Persecution tends to purify; combat or engagement with an adversary tends to solidify covenant bonds between those fighting on the same side (ask any former combat solider). Jesus exemplifies a good leader as He demonstrates His ultimate willingness to sacrifice Himself for His mission and to uphold the honor of His Father and His faith family. He is ready to pay the price necessary for victory. The next time you tell your fellow members of your organization, 'I'm not asking you to do anything I wouldn't do myself," will this chapter come to mind and have a bearing on your following statements and actions?

_____

_____

++

John 18---Highlights: Betrayal of Jesus, His arrest, trial, Peter's denial, Jesus before Pilate

One of the deepest, most profound questions in all of Scripture (perhaps in all of life) was uttered by Pontius Pilate as he interrogated Jesus. In v.38, Pilate directly asked Him, "What is truth?" It seems more difficult than ever in today's society (where absolute truth is deemed mythic) for people to answer that question. The branch of philosophy concerned with truth as a subset of its discussions is *epistemology*, the study of knowledge[1]. Without getting technical, the search for truth hinges on: How will I recognize it if I am looking at it? In that sense, Pilate was not too far off base, mainly because he was staring it in the face.

Pilate's question was poorly stated. People search for truth in systems, books, or philosophies. He should have asked, "WHO is truth?" Jesus is neither an embodiment nor a repository of truth; He IS truth. He did not come to teach truth, He IS Truth (Jn. 14.6). Truth is a Person, not a Precept or Principle: not the Jesus of fairy tales, not the distorted Jesus who is the darling of social media posts, but Jesus Christ, Savior and Lord, Son of God (Mt. 16.16; Phil. 2.5-11; Col. 1.15-21). He is the Alpha and the Omega, the starting point and end destination of any search for truth, the foundation of everything in our lives, including marriage, family, vocation, health, wealth, and eternal life (John 15.5; Col. 1.27).

In a later epistle, John states, "And we know that the Son of God has come, and has given us understanding so that we may know Him who is true; and we are **in** Him who is true, **in** His Son Jesus Christ. This is the true God and eternal life (1 Jn. 3.23)." According to this verse, when I look at Jesus, I gaze upon the

Truth. Therefore, the more I contemplate the Person and Character of the living Christ, the more accurately and intimately I will know the truth. If Jesus Christ is truth, then truth is not a static concept but a dynamic, alive entity. Truth not only exists, but it also moves, it expresses itself, and it has a heart for mankind. Truth is not some objective, neutral, unfeeling force of nature; it is an eternal, living Person, and that Person gave His life for mankind out of love for the Father.

For Pilate to have stood that close to the Truth and think he could extinguish it on a cross because it bled and seemed ill-suited to resist, the might of Rome missed it altogether. All the truth of God's character and will is bound up in the Person of Christ. In the previous verse to Pilate's question, what is truth, Christ says simply, "Everyone who is of the truth hears My voice." We are to walk in the truth (2 Jn. 4; 3 Jn. 4) because we walk (live) in Christ.

<u>Lines on Leadership</u>
What (or who) is the *Urquelle* (source) of your leadership? To what foundational statement or truth can every facet of your leadership be traced?
_____
_____
++

John 19---Highlights: Pilate condemns Jesus, the crucifixion

At multiple points of the arrests, trials, and beatings leading to the crucifixion, Jesus had opportunities to back out of the proceedings. On numerous occasions, He had easily eluded attempts to capture or contain Him (Lk. 4.30; Jn. 8.59; 10.39). When the Roman soldiers and officers from the chief priests came to arrest Jesus in the garden (18.3), Jesus, "knowing all the things that were coming upon Him" (18.4), could have once again easily evaded their grasp. He stood His ground. When they asked if He was Jesus the Nazarene, John uses an unmistakable "I Am" statement to indicate Jesus' answer implied deity as it has the previous times He had said 'I Am' (the door, the good shepherd, the light of the world, etc.). A wave of the hand or one command as God in the flesh could have slain them or pushed them aside; indeed, the second time He said it, the entire entourage fell to the ground (18.6). The revealing statement is when He says to Peter, "the cup which the Father has given Me; shall I not drink it?" (18.11)

In chapter 19, Pilate made more than one attempt to punish and release Jesus instead of crucifying Him, and upon learning of His claims to be the Son of God, Pilate increased his efforts to free Him. Even after being impaled on the cross, Jesus could have delivered Himself. Instead, He paid the debt He did not owe and paid the price I could never pay for my sin and the sin of the world. John purposefully phrases the death of Christ on the cross as Jesus saying, "It is finished," meaning the price had been paid, the sacrificial Lamb of Passover had been slain, and He "bowed His head, and gave up His spirit" (v. 30), implying it was a willful laying-down of His life instead of succumbing to the horrors of the execution.

In my younger years, I admit that I looked at this sequence of events and wondered why Jesus did not display His power like some superhero saga's protagonist; or I actually doubted His power, that in His weakened, emaciated state, the trials, lashings, and humiliation of it all had overwhelmed Him. In my early adult years, I saw this as a theologically amazing fulfillment of so many OT scriptures. In my later years, I have come to realize how mind-numbingly courageous and terrifyingly awesome this decision was: He followed through with His plan to save mankind regardless of the cost to Himself. Aside from all the medical descriptions of the pain and suffering He endured, I cannot imagine the spiritual realm of demonic taunting and cries of victory Jesus heard and saw. His sheep were scattered, the movement was finished, and at that moment, no one understood what He knew had to be done, and no one else could do it.

<u>Lines on Leadership</u>
There will be one supreme moment in every leader's life when he/she will have to stand their ground and follow through on a decision that will be painful, result in loss, and perhaps end a career, but must be done for the good of all be it their church or their company. No one will understand it, nor will they acknowledge its inevitability. The decision will be questioned even by one's closest associates. How will you prepare yourself for that moment so that when it comes, you do not falter but follow through?

_____

_____

++

John 20---Highlights: The Empty Tomb; the disciples' reactions to the resurrection; Thomas' declaration

The resurrection is **the** pivot point for Christianity; without it, the faith collapses and degenerates into a mere set of moral teachings (see 1 Cor. 15 entry). I stake my entire ministry and eternal life on the resurrection being a historical fact and total reality.

For leadership purposes, this will be the "Now I Get It" chapter. In rapid succession, Mary Magdalene, then Peter, then an "unknown disciple" (v.8, John, the author of the gospel) react to the empty tomb. Seeing the empty tomb does not automatically result in a belief in the Resurrection. The disciples went to their own homes (v. 10): maybe they were in shock, couldn't grasp what it meant (v. 9), or thought, "someone stole the body, and now they will come for us." Mary obviously didn't "get it"; she was outside the tomb weeping (v. 11-18). Even after seeing two angels inside the tomb (in a position that recalls the Ark of the Covenant, Ex. 25.18), her response to their question (and subsequently to the man she thinks is the gardener) is apparent she is not thinking about resurrection but grave robbers.

It is not until the "gardener" speaks to Mary in such a tone, manner, or inflection that she recognizes it is indeed Jesus. Exploding with joy, she wants to cling to Him, who was lost and now is in her presence. She goes to tell the disciples the good news. Apparently, they can't grasp it or don't believe her (Lk. 24.11) because the next scene has them cowering behind closed doors (v. 19). Jesus short circuits their reasoning and belief when He appears among them (closed doors again). Thomas was not there, and when the now-believing disciples tell him Jesus is alive, he scoffs and says he has to see it for himself. A week transpires, and Jesus once again appears in their midst behind closed doors (v. 26), this time with Thomas present. Jesus presents His hands and feet for inspection, then Thomas proclaims the immortal 'My Lord and my God!' confession. The chapter ends with an invitation to the reader to make his/her own decision about Jesus being the Messiah and the Son of God and to believe in His name.

Lines on Leadership
Pastors, presidents, professors, and parents alike wish each time they issued a sermon, a policy statement, a teaching, a command, or a pronouncement that everyone within hearing

range "got it". Different learning styles, different biases against or for the new circumstance, and different levels of resistance to change (not to mention the free will of man) all play a part in how quickly something (that seems to the pastor, prof, parent, or president perfectly obvious) sinks in and becomes truth for an individual. Effective leaders use multiple ways to ensure their followers "get it" and exhibit patient persistence until they do.

Jesus used parables with multiple levels of meaning when He spoke to the public and then explained the parables in detail to the disciples in private. He used repetition and object lessons (wheat, pearls, fig trees). Concerning the Resurrection, He sent emissaries (the angels) and appeared to many of the disciples. What are your usual indicators that your 'audience' gets it? What are some indicators you may not be heeding? What are some you need to incorporate?

_____

_____

++

John 21---Highlights: Jesus meets the disciples by the sea; Jesus threefold questioning of Peter

The last chapter of John's gospel contains one of the strongest leadership lessons in the entire NT. It is a master class in rebuke and reclamation, a perfect blend of chide and challenge. The location is called Tabgha on the NW shore of the Sea of Galilee/Tiberias (v.1). To have stood on that shoreline and relived this chapter is a special memory for me. It was forever cemented in my heart as I lingered in the small chapel built over the rock where local lore says Jesus served breakfast to His disciples (vs. 12-14). My spirit can still hear the worshipful praise chorus sung in that chapel by a Russian Orthodox group of pilgrims as I lingered among them.

Jesus uses sensory impressions as well as memories to frame what He will soon do with Peter. In the semi-light of predawn, He calls to some of His disciples not far from shore after their fruitless night of catching no fish and gently goads them into admitting their luck was nil (v.5). He instructs them to cast on the right side of the boat, and they haul in 153 fish, which reminds Peter of an earlier encounter with a young Rabbi who did something similar (see Lk. 5 entry). Christ employs smell, one of the strongest evokers of memories, by using what some translations describe as a charcoal fire (v.9). The same word is used in Jn. 18.18 as Peter experiences his 3x denial of Christ. The combined memories reminded Peter how limited his understanding was of Jesus' power, His mission, and his relationship with Jesus.

      The threefold denial comes full circle as Jesus asks Peter three times, 'Do you love me?' Peter answers three times, "Yes, Lord", and John notes that the third time He grieves him (v.17) because of the painful, unmistakable reminder of his denial. Yet Jesus does not tell Peter he is disqualified, or He is assigning Peter to lesser tasks: He tasks Peter three times with an imperative, feed my sheep, be a shepherd to them. Instead of being rejected as Peter likely had expected, he is not only restored to Jesus but he is also reclaimed and given the responsibility to lead out and to tend the flock. Peter has no clue what that really means (see the book of Acts) in terms of global impact. It is enough at this seashore breakfast to know he is loved and trusted not on account of but in spite of his past words and actions.

<u>Lines on Leadership</u>
Grace is costly to offer and difficult to accept. Finding the right balance and sequence to help a fellow worker review his

shortcomings, recant them, and re-engage in the work at hand is often elusive. To take the time to provide the right setting and ambience to help him/her through this process can be costly. But if it revives a relationship that is strained or dormant, it pays off dividends for everyone involved. This goes way beyond ordinary evaluations; Jesus had a unique place in His heart and Kingdom for Peter, and this relationship was crucial to that Kingdom's early growth after Pentecost. What breaches in your relationships need the care and time Jesus put into the restoration of Peter?

_____

_____

++

BOOK OF ACTS

Intro: Acts is Luke's record of the birth and expansion of the early church. It is the second of two NT books authored by Luke. Acts is the best manual available for any church planter or starter; it also contains marvelous lessons for leaders at any level. It picks up the narrative immediately after the resurrection of Christ with His ascension and the subsequent arrival of the Holy Spirit. It introduces us to St. Paul, the architect of many early churches in the known Middle East and Europe and also the author of the majority of NT books.

++

Acts 1---Highlights: Ascension of Christ; prayer in the Upper Room; selection of Matthias

Wait. Really? Seriously? After everything that has transpired in the last few days, wait? Jesus has been crucified, risen from the dead, was in full miracle and rabbi mode in their midst, and just when it looked like He was ready to finally "restore the kingdom of Israel" (v. 6, if He can conquer death, the Romans should be no match for Him). He had just ascended into heaven right before their collective eyes. Wait?

Yes, wait (vs. 12-14). After what they had been through, it was best to come together in a corporate season of prayer to process what new set of rules were in play and how the Lord's last instructions would come to pass. This was not a passive time of simple contemplative meditation. This was fraught with fear of the unknown: their leader was suddenly no longer among them; they didn't have a game plan beyond a vision statement that encompassed local to global proportions with no details on how to do it (v.8). Scripture could never be interpreted the same way again, every miracle and teaching of the Master had to be relived in light of the His death and resurrection, and their mandate (to herald the good news of His Kingdom's arrival) had to be carried out. How?

Acts 1 is the post-resurrection/pre-Pentecost interlude. There had been times of instruction (Lk. 24.27), of fellowship (Jn. 20.19, 21.9-12), of restoration (Jn. 21.15-17), and displays of power (Acts 1.9). In a symphony or opera, such an interlude is usually soft and slow, yet both the audience and the musicians sense the coming crescendos and quickening tempi. The lack of decibels does not mean a lack of tension or energy about to explode forth. The Upper Room, where these days of prayerful waiting took place, was a place of fear and wonder mixed together, of unspeakable joy and unspoken questions.

Peter stands as spokesperson (v. 15) and says, let's get down to business, fill Judas' position, get back to full strength, and get ready. This appears consistent with his 'speak first, think later' approach exhibited many times in the gospels. How will they fulfill what we call "the Great Commission", Jesus' call for global evangelization? This is not someone who has the group's next few years mapped out in strategic detail. What he does know is their ranks have been depleted with Judas' betrayal and sudden demise. He understands the parallel with twelve apostles/twelve tribes and the need to fill this now vacant position. He has no clue how they will carry out the Lord's wishes, but he is determined to be ready for the when's, where's, and how's. He's not planning; he is preparing. The mandate is clear, but the method is not. The Lord told them to wait (vs. 4-5).

Lines on Leadership

In Reggie McNeal's book *This Present Future,* he advocates spending less time planning and more in preparation in our current atmosphere of rapid change and unforeseen turns[1]. Reflect on an event or series of events that created a new frame of reference for everything that has ever happened in your organization or church since the event (COVID would be a good example). Was your group ready for adaptation, flexibility, and unforeseen outcomes? Had your group planned or prepared? How can you prepare for a future you cannot predict?

_____

_____

++

Acts 2---Highlights: tongues of fire; sermon at Pentecost; initial practices of the early church

The event of Pentecost in Acts 2 is seen by many as the birth of the NT church. The chapter begins in a united session of prayer as disciples were gathered in one place (v. 1), awaiting leadership from God as instructed in Acts 1.5-8. Tongues of fire descend on all, and this is interpreted as the coming of the Holy Spirit since they can now all speak in different languages. Peter preaches the first post-resurrection sermon from the Southern Steps of the Temple Mount, thousands believe the message (v. 41), and the chapter ends with this new community, establishing a now centuries-old pattern of devotion to their leaders' teachings, fellowship, worship, and prayer (v. 42-47) that has become (and should be) the focus of corporate church life.

One aspect of this remarkable event is the missional breaking of barriers. Missions is a subset of ministry and evangelism that deals with crossing into unknown territory. For the gospel (or any message) to spread beyond one's native group, there are several borders/barriers to cross:

1. Linguistic (v. 8). To speak gospel truth to the heart of another, he/she should hear it in their heart language (see Acts 21 entry). This time, it is done miraculously; learning to speak another's heart language is normally a difficult challenge. To go

beyond basic words to nuance, to different values, and ways of expressing the same thought takes years of learning by a missionary or a corporate worker in his new country.

2. <u>Geographic/topographic</u> (Acts 1.8). Some of those countries listed in chapter 2 were far, far away from Jerusalem, with different climates, altitudes, crops, etc. At one point, the author, when deciding which country he would choose for mission work, participated in a mission trip to Brazil. He had suffered a heat stroke several years before it and found he could not tolerate the heat and humidity. This helped determine his final destination would be then West Germany. Any leader going to a different climate must take stock of his advantages and limitations in that climate.

3. <u>National</u> (v.9-11). Pentecost was a miraculous way for people of many different nations who were in Jerusalem for the festival of Pentecost to hear this Good News and take it back to their respective countries. The incarnational approach is still the standard to go and live in another country, but the superior approach is indigenous, for nationals from a respective country to reach their own.

4. <u>Cultural</u>. Any time cultures try to co-exist, clashes and discrimination are inevitable. (Acts 6.1-6)

5. <u>Religious orthodoxy</u> (Acts 15.5; see Acts 10 entry). While standards of religious practice are necessary, they sometimes prevent adherents from recognizing God is moving in a new way.

6. <u>Technological.</u> The apostles and Paul used every mode of travel and communication known at that time to proclaim their message. All organizations face the need for expansion of their digital footprint in the 21st century. What used to be a peripheral luxury for an organization's programs and resources has now become essential to reach the younger generation. The

printing press revolutionized religion and politics in the 16th century of Martin Luther[1]. The smartphone has altered not only individual lifestyles but total societies; with artificial intelligence (A.I.) coming over the horizon, how will organizations incorporate it into their message[2]?

<u>Lines on Leadership</u>
In retrospect, we see the Pentecost event in Acts 2 and marvel at the results of the language and conversions, but, in all honesty, it took the nascent church several years before it started to cross the missional barriers listed above. What is your organization doing to cross barriers that currently hinder and hobble the proliferation of its message?

_____

_____

++

Acts 3---Highlights: Healing of Beggar; Peter's post-Pentecost sermon

Peter has just experienced a phenomenal event in Acts 2 as 3000 people responded to his sermon preached simultaneously in multiple languages. In Acts 3, he was approached by a beggar seeking alms at the temple gate. The apostles learned throughout the pages of Acts what this new indwelling of the Holy Spirit would mean to their daily lives. The possibility of speaking in Jesus' name and seeing a person healed by it stretches Peter's faith; it is the first healing recorded in the book of Acts post-Pentecost. Peter was learning his role as ambassador, as an intermediary, and that he was not the one bringing about the healing or the conversions.

One fundamental of leadership is to know who I am and who I am not. This has many moving parts:

Age: Maturity can open up areas of my abilities previously untapped or undeveloped. Age can also erode abilities.

Physical, intellectual, emotional, and spiritual: We must be honest with ourselves about our capabilities in each of these four categories and how they influence each other. One example would be I may have the intellectual prowess to understand a problem but not the emotional capacity to address it properly.

Connectivity: The obvious dimension of this is whether or not I can connect with a group or an individual naturally or have to work at it. It can also mean my ability to convey an idea cognitively or affectively.

Character, Competence, Calling: (see 1 Tim. 4 entry) Do I know both the depth and the outer limits of these three in my life?

The list can fill many pages, and the reader is encouraged to explore other additional areas where a leader needs to know who he/she is and who the person is not. The two main ways a leader discovers who he is and who he is not is by internal and external examinations: internally as a self-evaluation and when others measure or give feedback as to my leadership capabilities. While reflection is an invaluable tool for improvement, and scores of reliable tests exist to gauge my effectiveness as a leader, the best indicator of who I am and who I am not as a leader is in-the-field experiences.

After the healing draws a crowd (it seems the beggar was a well-known fixture at this particular gate), Peter launches into his 2nd sermon in Acts. He could have easily convinced the crowd the power was in his hands, his touch, his voice, or some magical incantation he would repeat for a price so as to gain wealth. Instead, he rightly gave all credit and honor to Jesus (v. 16) and proceeded to preach the good news of salvation and forgiveness of sins to be found in following Jesus as a risen Savior. A servant leader knows who he is and who he is not, and to Whom he owes everything he has and accomplishes.

Lines on Leadership
It is a delicate balance between having confidence in one's abilities and giving God praise and thanks for those abilities (v.6). What is a recent example where you had the opportunity to give God or someone else credit for your accomplishment? How did you handle it?

_____

_____

++

Acts 4---Highlights: 1ˢᵗ arrest of Peter and John; their release; things in common; intro of Barnabas

My favorite NT character is Barnabas. The most important person in the NT is unquestionably Jesus, of course, but I gain great inspiration from Barnabas and his approach to leadership. Paul, Peter, and John are giants of the faith, far beyond anything I would dare hope to attain. But Barnabas seems accessible, the guy in the room I could most easily listen to as well as relate to. Acts 4 is our introduction to him; we learn a great deal from his one-sentence resume in vs. 36-37.

His proper name is Joseph, a Hebrew name that is translated as "one who increases" or "adds to". He is from the priestly tribe of Levi, meaning he is comfortable with and well-versed in matters of religion and the temple. He comes from Cyprus, an eastern Mediterranean island crossroads of commerce, meaning he was comfortable with different cultures and people from "somewhere else". He was a man of considerable wealth, described as a landowner, and apparently generous as he sold a tract of land to benefit the fledgling congregation. His nickname is <u>Barnabas</u>, the "son of encouragement". Nicknames usually come from repeated comments about one's appearance (Shorty), accomplishments (the Finisher), or reputation. In this case, he builds up people by infusing hope or bringing out the good in them. That reputation is burnished throughout the NT as he interacts with Paul, Mark, and others.

It is too simplistic to assign the title "second banana" to Barnabas. It is Barnabas who vouches for Paul after Paul's conversion (see Acts 9 entry). It is Barnabas who is mentioned first in the pairing after they launch out as the first-ever Christian missionaries (Acts 13). He was revered in the Jerusalem church; they trusted him to investigate the growing Gentile church in Antioch (Acts 11.22). When there, he had a positive influence on the church yet decided to bring Paul on board, knowing what the outcome would be for him personally (see Acts 11 entry). Rather than cause a scene with Paul over their eventual schism (Acts 15), he took the high road and began over again with Mark as his apprentice, repeating the process with him he had done with Paul (Acts 13.4; 15.39). Barnabas was capable and an asset to everyone who met him, secure in his place in the Kingdom in whatever role the Lord gave him to fulfill.

When we were forced by medical issues to return from the mission field early in our ministry, I felt it was a huge step backward; little did I know I would land at a Christian university where I would have the privilege to disciple hundreds of students and help them discern a calling and direction in life with Barnabas as my role model.

Some leaders are the "starters" for an organization, those who can grow it in the early stages and are secure within themselves to know when it is time to hand off the leadership so the organization can go to the next level. Some leaders are happy to "wash, rinse, and repeat", so instead of making a name for themselves, they pour their lives into countless others, content to repeat and infuse the basics of leadership in their followers and fellow pilgrims, "adding to" their training. Entrepreneurs, church planters, and charismatic personalities can initiate and inspire but not necessarily sustain or grow a group past a certain level. Barnabas should be the patron saint of every senior vice president, associate pastor, or professor who lovingly nurtures the potential of succeeding generations within their company or church.

Lines on Leadership
Who has been a Barnabas in your development as a leader? With whom have you been a Barnabas?
_____
_____
++

Acts 5---Highlights: Ananias and Sapphira; imprisonment of apostles; release; Gamaliel's admonishments

I have lived in several areas near the battlefields of major wars. I have visited Bannockburn, the site of Scotland's hard-won yet short-lived freedom from England in 1314, made famous in the movie Braveheart; Culloden in northern Scotland, the site of the decisive defeat in 1746 of the Jacobite uprising; scores of castles that withheld or succumbed to sieges; Masada atop a majestic mesa near the Dead Sea where Jewish zealots robbed the mighty Roman army of a victory by committing mass suicide; Antietam, Gettysburg, Fredericksburg, Vicksburg, and Appomattox where the campaign for the soul of America was waged. Walking those grounds, retracing the steps of bravery and foolishness that resulted in the loss of life and formation of nations—it brings a person to silence reflection. Perhaps the most sobering is to stand on Mt. Carmel or Tel Megiddo in Israel and gaze upon the Plains of Megiddo, knowing that multiple battles have been fought on this crossroads of the Middle East across the millennia and knowing one day, an epic battle of good and evil will take place there—Armageddon. (Rev. 16.16)

Peter and the apostles—no mention of how many of them—were scrambling as the miracle of Pentecost and the explosion of the church in Jerusalem were in full swing. They had taken a stand for truth and integrity that cost the lives of Ananias and Sapphira (vs. 1-10), which resulted in further growth in the young church (vs. 11-16) with miracles, worship, healing, and salvations. The Jewish religious officials decided enough was enough and had them imprisoned (not the first time, see Acts 4), yet they were delivered by an angel (vs. 17-25). The officials rearrested them and forbade them from teaching about and in the name of Jesus (vs. 26-28). Peter responded with one of the most memorable lines in Acts: "We must obey God rather than men (v.29)."

The battlefield and the reason for the battle should be chosen carefully. Gaining the high ground, selecting which field on which to stage the troops, the timing of an advance (such as Pickett's charge and Little Big Top in the battle of Gettysburg), and making sure the army knows what the stakes are...these are all crucial to the success of a battle. Consider two perspectives on choosing the right plan, place, and timing of a battle:

1. Apostles. They had a heavenly messenger's mandate (vs. 19-20) to preach, and it trumped the admonition by earthly rulers to cease and desist preaching (v.28). This group (vs. 18, 29, 40) had witnessed countless miracles, the resurrection of Christ, been filled with the Holy Spirit (Acts 2), and seen thousands

respond to their preaching. They not only believed their message, but they are also willing to act on it regardless of the consequences (they "rejoiced that they had been considered worthy to suffer shame for His name" v.41).

    2. <u>Gamaliel</u>. Instead of giving in to the crowd's anger and indignation, Gamaliel gave sage advice: choose your battles wisely. If God is in this, you don't want to be found waging war with the Almighty; if He is not in this, its influence will quickly dissipate, like the examples he cited (vs.33-39).

<u>Lines on Leadership</u>
When you engage in a new culture or new set of circumstances, first investigate what is entrenched within that culture or set of circumstances so deeply that a crusade against it is futile or so costly it becomes a Pyrrhic victory. Second, is God in the midst of this leading the way or warning you to hold off, back off, or shove off? What battles are you currently considering whether or not to start or finish?

_____
_____
++

Acts 6---Highlights: Choosing of the first deacons; arrest of Stephen

    The church exploded in Acts 2 from a single group in the Upper Room to a megachurch with 3000 professing faith in Christ after one sermon—for every pastor, a dream to preach, a nightmare to administer the day after. The embryonic movement grew rapidly in the coming days (Acts 2.44-47, 4.32-37). By the time the narrative reaches Acts 6, the church leaders have some important decisions in light of that growth. At least two main leadership principles emerge in the selection of the first associate ministers (some would call them deacons).

A. <u>Leaders should concentrate on what only they can do or do best and delegate the rest</u>. The apostles declare their priorities as threefold: 1) the Word of God (v. 2), 2) prayer, 3) and ministering the Word to others (v. 4). To scramble and teach the Old Testament in light of the recent events of the resurrection and Pentecost was then and continues today to be a consuming task (they didn't have the NT we do today, it wasn't written yet). How many times do people at work buckle when asked to "wear one more hat" or take on one more role, and they collapse, quit, or are terminated because they could not handle so many tasks or do them all at the required level of excellence? That doesn't mean the newly chosen associates' duties are demeaning or "beneath" the leaders' dignity to perform. Leaders should be willing to mix in and identify with all levels of workers in a given organization as servant leaders (see Matthew 20, 1 Peter 5 entries). There are 168 hours in each week, and grace is not a chronological concept; young leaders always think they can cram one more thing into the day, but in reality, there are only so many hours in a week and no more. A wise leader knows his priorities and areas of giftedness and operates within them. It does not mean the delegated tasks are "for someone else to do the demeaning or dirty work;" it simply means to be the most productive as a group, the leaders have to do what only they can do best and get help with everything else.

B. <u>Ignore cultural aspects of any decision at your own peril.</u> In Acts 6.1, the Greek-speaking Jewish widows were perceived as neglected in favor of Hebrew-speaking widows in the daily food distribution. Apparently, many transformed by the miracle of Pentecost lingered in Jerusalem instead of going back home. Each culture has its unique take on concepts of time, personal space, superiority, muted prejudice (I will tolerate that group over there as long as they behave or speak like us), leadership (autocratic or collaborative), style of music—order of widows being served...the list is endless1. The dominant group of widows spoke Hebrew. Would the voices of a new group be heeded or told they are perpetual guests, not part of the "inner" circle which sets the norms?

In 1982, our young family sold everything we had to become debt free and move abroad to minister. Our mission board graciously provided not only living expenses but required us to wait on ministry until we had attended language school for a year. It was brutal studying just one subject all day, every day. After that year, we moved to our primary location. Our ideas of being proficient in the language were shattered quickly when we had to learn the local dialect, when people started talking to us as if we were actually fluent, and especially when the conversation drifted into abstract areas—like spiritual things. We always felt on the defensive—did we hear this or that correctly? Did we miss intent? —and hesitant to jump in with any confidence. When we came back to the states due to medical issues after several years, my wife taught English as a Second Language (ESL) in TX public schools for over two decades. The lessons we had learned about humility and patience of being treated differently because we didn't speak or think like the indigenous population served her well.

The leaders in Acts 6 showed wisdom by 1) having the congregation choose the new associates (v.3); 2) giving practical but neither exhaustive nor overly restrictive guidelines for their choices; and 3) ensuring both groups involved in the dispute found representation among the associates chosen (v.5). The growing Gentile sector of the church in Acts had to be addressed, not suppressed (see subsequent chapters in Acts). Take a close look at the names of those chosen; they are predominantly Greek names, meaning not necessarily that they were all from outside of Israel, but their names would open doors for them among the Greek-speaking Jewish widows. (A subsequent example is Saul, introduced at the end of Acts 7, who becomes Paul later in the book. Saul is his Hebrew name; Paul is his Roman or Gentile name. If he was to minister to the Gentiles as commissioned by God in Acts 9, he would need a name that denoted 'I am one of you,' or 'I am sympathetic to your language and culture.')

<u>Lines on Leadership</u>
Delegation to and empathy with the different subgroups within my organization go together. In what ways do you identify with each group within your organization? What tasks have you clung to instead of empowering others to do in order to free up your giftedness and priorities?

_____

_____

++

Acts 7---Highlights: Defense by Stephen; Stephen's martyrdom

Stephen offers a lengthy narrative of the Jewish people in Acts 7 he knows will result in his death. Many who would have stood in his place would have mollified the crowd, played to their sympathies, softened the story to reflect their viewpoint, or some other technique designed to curry favor or strike a bargain with the Jewish high council. Instead, Stephen retells the details familiar to everyone present about the most seminal event in their history, the Exodus, and makes sure they understand that Moses, Joshua, and David foreshadowed the coming of Jesus as the Messiah. He uses deliberate words to describe Moses ("the one whom God sent to be both a ruler and a deliverer, v. 35") to allude to Jesus' claims to be a ruler (His constant referral to His Kingdom) and a deliverer (Jn, 4.25). He then turns to the most iconic symbol of God's presence and the Law (the Ark of the Covenant) and shows his audience and jury have turned their back on both the Law and the Lord Himself as its embodiment.

It could be said that Stephen hoped for the long shot, overly optimistic result, that the council might become convicted of their wayward misplaced faith and recognize the truth of who Jesus was. In light of the pressure and actions of the Jewish religious leaders toward Jesus and His disciples during and after His ministry, this is beyond naïve. Stephen knew full well his fate if he took this approach for his defense. The courage and conviction of the moment are high points of the New Testament; <u>his martyrdom is a watershed event for the young church as it ushers in the dispersion of the believers and the accompanying acceleration of their message's reach beyond Jerusalem</u>.

Stephen's fortitude and firm stance echo the way His Lord Jesus answered Pilate ("the good or timely confession," 1 Tim. 6.13, Jn. 18), speaking the truth with full awareness of what consequences awaited. Proverbs 25.11 states, "Like apples of gold in settings of silver is a word spoken at the proper time." Most often, we think of this proverb as something wise, witty, humorous, comforting, or appropriate, with everyone nodding their heads in approval at its wisdom, wit, etc. In this case the "word spoken at the proper time" results in a single person's death and the expansion of a movement. Stephen is compelled in v. 55 to speak aloud what he sees with his eyes of faith, words that seal his fate; he sees Jesus standing at the right hand of God and declares it to those assembled around him.

Lines on Leadership

This example of life and death being in one's response (Proverbs 18.21, "Death and life are in the power of the tongue, and those who love it will eat its fruit") is sobering. It can take the dimension of mortality being in the balance as here, or it can involve a promotion, a prison sentence, or a disqualification from a contest. When the time comes, and your response will be the tipping point, what will likely be your reply, your recantation, or a sign of your resolve?

_____

_____

++

Acts 8---Highlights Saul persecutes the church; Philip preaches in Samaria; Philip & the Ethiopian Eunuch

How do I know the Acts 8 leaders in the Jerusalem church had accepted the Lord's message (the gospel was for ALL nations)? When they started preaching to the Samaritans, considered a half-breed, inferior type of "black sheep" to Jews. Here are some thoughts on those "other people" in our lives (vs. 1-24), followed by a principle of divine appointments (vs. 25-40). Them. *That* group. "They" don't pull their weight. Someone should do something about "them." *Objectification, Vilification, and Annihilation* is a documented pattern of dealing with those "other" than "us." 1) <u>*Objectification*</u> makes people faceless, less than human, individuals who melt into an entity without distinguishing characteristics except for an overwhelming one "we" find annoying, then offensive. Once a group is objectified, it is easier to speak in generalities about it and boldly about its shortcomings. It can be a race, a class, language speakers, a team, or a competitor business; the shapes & sizes are endless. When the "other" is not a person or group of persons but an object, it is easier to assign disdain and usually involves a lessening of the "other's" value. 2) <u>Vilification</u> occurs when the object seems to pose a threat by its very existence or proximity. We begin to find faults, flaws, and shortcomings to research until we find a bad example and then extrapolate that to represent the entire group that has now become an object. 3) <u>Annihilation</u> is all too often the outcome of objectification and vilification. The object is vilified to the point someone says, 'Who's going to rid "us" of this menace?' and someone takes up the challenge, even envisions themselves as a crusader anointed to personally exterminate the "other(s)."

This pattern has become all too recognizable in contemporary life. Each election cycle exceeds the previous one in assailing opponents to where the issues are lost amid the mud-slinging. Segments of our society are casually labeled "enemies." Dictators have a favorite diversionary tactic to keep evil deeds hidden; they declare *x* or *y* (usually the U.S.) an enemy trying to subvert their government, create a bogeyman, and galvanize their citizens to fight this invader trying to do away with "our" beloved country. Hitler wrote of the Jews' inferiority and other objectified groups in *Mein Kampf* (a poorly written but revealing polemic) long before he was chancellor. When he found a receptive audience to his ideas, he utilized pseudoscience and paraded every parody imaginable of Jews in front of his followers until they were convinced Jews were a true plague that had to be eradicated. In the USA in 2018, a man interrupted a baby naming ceremony in a Pittsburg synagogue, screaming all Jews deserve to die, and then eleven did at his hand before police ended his life. Objectification led to Vilification which led this man to Annihilation. During the early decades of the 2000s several mass shooters issued manifestos using this very sequence directed toward African Americans, Jews, Asians, or whatever the targeted "them" was[1].

Who are your "Samaritans: Millennials? Migrants? Arabs? Christ-Killers (an old derogatory term for Jews)? Druggies? Democrats? Republicans? A company offering similar products or services? Jesus said to love my neighbor (Mt. 22.37-40)—even the ones not in my homeowners' association, my country, my race. We are sinners mercifully saved by the grace of God and must use every ministry avenue possible to share that grace with "them". (we were once "them," Eph. 2.11-22). More love, fewer labels.

We first meet Philip in Acts 6. He is one of the seven chosen to oversee the equitable distribution of foodstuffs to the different language speakers among the widows. There is no way to know if this was a stretch for him or if he accepted the assignment gladly. Apparently, he met the criteria laid down by the apostles (a good man, full of the Spirit and wisdom, and able to lead, Acts 6.3). Perhaps this interaction with other language speakers opened up Philip's eyes and spirit to accept others not like himself so that when the persecution came in Jerusalem (v.1), and the leaders were scattered, Philip (apparently working as a team with apostles and other leaders, v.20) started preaching to Samaritans.

This brings us to the second leadership example in Acts 8. The gospel was well received in Samaria as Philip and his associates were on their way back to Jerusalem (v. 25), preaching all the way. Philip was instructed by an "angel of the Lord" (v. 26) to go not only on a detour but what looked like a wild goose chase out in the desert. He meets a eunuch headed home to Ethiopia. Apparently, the eunuch had a high position in the Ethiopian court and had been to Jerusalem on court business; he also had a personal interest in spiritual matters, for he read a scroll from

Isaiah while in his chariot. He read from one of the most obvious Messianic passages in Isaiah (Is. 53) and invited Philip to help him understand it. One of the simplest yet profound sentences in Acts, v. 35 states, "and Philip opened his mouth, and beginning from this Scripture he preached Jesus to him." The eunuch becomes a baptized believer and goes his way rejoicing.

In Christian circles, this is often labeled a "divine interruption". It can be a minor annoyance or scale up to a major upheaval of one's day. But when the Lord jars me out of my routine and brings into my life an individual with a need for my Christ, I need to heed Phillip's example of obedience and willingness to be used, even when inconvenient. On paper, this makes no sense to deviate from a well-established pattern of success, to leave success behind for fruitless wandering in the desert that winds up being a solitary encounter. Even though it didn't appear at first to be as productive as the path Philip had been on, <u>his faithfulness to the Master meant more than his schedule</u>. In secular terms, this could be seen as a long-shot opportunity to open up a new segment of a company's market for its products or services. Whether you call this a prompting from the Holy Spirit of God or a gut instinct, sometimes you must be willing to risk looking foolish to be where and what the Lord desires.

Later in the NT, Paul repeats this principle (see Col. 4 entry) and 2 Tim. 4.2, where he exhorts his young understudy to preach the word in or out of season. Peter picks up a similar call when he admonishes the reader to be ready at all times to give a response when others ask about our faith (1 Pet. 3.15).
Be willing to see people through God's eyes and be willing to share what you have with those He places in your path. Acts 8 shows us that empathy and evangelism should be willing partners.

Lines on Leadership
How have you ever participated in the objectification, vilification, and annihilation of another group/company? How have you combined empathy and engagement towards a group for which you previously had no feelings and with whom you had no previous meaningful contact? Have you ever had what you would call a "divine interruption"?

_____

_____

++

Acts 9---Highlights: Paul's conversion, Ananias & Barnabas assist Paul's new ministry, Peter in Joppa area

The dramatic conversion of Paul on his way to Damascus dominates Acts 9. Few people would dare to compare their careers to Paul's missionary impact. But Acts 9 offers additional portraits of two men who provide more attainable models for most leaders. Let us examine the boldness and bravery of Ananias and Barnabas.

1. Ananias entered Paul's life (vs. 10-19) with hesitancy and fear. How many times throughout the OT and NT alike, when God speaks to an individual, is the first reaction of the hearer fear and trembling? Part of this is surely from the scene itself being so out of the ordinary (angels, burning bushes, visions), but another fear inducer is the task itself, usually God-sized (see Moses' story in Exodus 3 and Gideon's story in Judges 6). Ananias is well aware of Paul's reputation and the expected results if he does the Lord's bidding. God revealed to Ananias what Paul's purpose in His kingdom would be before He revealed it to Paul (confirmed by Paul in Acts 22.12-16 when he recounted this scene in his trial testimony). He made the courageous decision to obey God and speak truth into the life of a man he had previously feared and

avoided. Ananias did not know the circumstances of Paul's Damascus road encounter; Paul did not know the 'why' behind this encounter. Ananias knew the <u>purpose</u> of God for Paul, and Paul knew the <u>power</u> of God through direct experience. How many individuals came to me and spoke words of affirmation to me in my early years as God's calling became more evident to me? Thank God for every Ananias' in my life who helped me refine God's purpose for my life.

2. <u>Barnabas</u> entered Paul's life (vs. 26-31) as Paul's early preaching evoked strong suspicions. Paul's previous life as an enemy of Christians overshadowed his newfound declaration of Jesus as the Christ, and as Paul came to Jerusalem, he found it difficult to meet the disciples, who scurried away when he arrived. In terms of change, Barnabas was what is called an "early adopter". Perhaps he was inclined to always give folks a second chance ('Barnabas' is his nickname meaning son of encouragement, see Acts 4); perhaps he saw the potential in Paul for the Kingdom others did not yet see. Whether he was a man of simple compassion or great vision, Barnabas showed courage in advocating for Paul to the apostles (one of the great "buts" in the NT, v. 27, BUT Barnabas). What if Barnabas erred in judgment and had "allowed the fox into the chicken coop"? If that had happened, Barnabas would be mentioned in the same breath as Judas pointing out to the officials where to find Jesus. There was a certain element of risk involved in Barnabas' decision. Paul had the gift of proclamation and the ability to stir passions with it. Barnabas had the platform (inner circles of leadership) where Paul could find acceptance for his message. Barnabas was probably also involved in the decision to send Paul back to his hometown Tarsus (v. 30) for further preparation and also for his protection.

In my roles as a college campus minister and now as an associational missionary, I have advocated for hundreds of young ministers who needed someone to stand beside them, be a catalyst or cheerleader, open that door to an inner sanctum, recommend them to a pastor search committee, put in a good word here and there, or be a resume referral. Some faded, some blossomed, and some excelled way past their advocate.

I am so grateful for each Ananias and Barnabas in my life and for the privilege of being an Ananias or Barnabas to another Kingdom brother or sister. The repercussions and rewards of these two men's boldness will be seen in subsequent chapters.

Lines on Leadership
When have you been an Ananias, the person whose task is to inform someone God has a higher purpose for their life than they presently pursue? When have you been a Barnabas, risking your reputation to advocate for a potential Kingdom partner?
_____
_____
++

Acts 10---Highlights: Vision of Cornelius, Peter preaches at Caesarea, Gentiles receive the Gospel

Peter has already stayed several days in Joppa—a seaside community on the Mediterranean about thirty miles south of Caesarea Maritima—with a man named Simon the tanner. He has witnessed healings and conversions in this city in the previous chapter and perhaps has taken a few hours up on the roof to relax, pray, and smell the salty breeze mixed with the odors of a tannery while food was prepared below. I've always wondered if those aromas influenced his dreams because he has a series of three separate visions of clean and unclean (according to Jewish law) animals descending on a sheet and is ordered by a voice he deems as the Lord telling him to eat all of them. Upon waking, perplexed and unclear as to the meaning, men from Caesarea arrive and ask him to accompany them to the home of a Roman centurion. All of this is out of the norm for Peter, but he goes with them, and after hearing how the Lord has spoken to Gentiles as well as Jews, he utters these words: "I most certainly understand now that God is not one to show partiality, but in every nation, the man who fears Him and does what is right, is welcome to Him." (vs. 34-35). He expanded his frame of reference in regard to who receives the favor of God (see Lk. 4 entry).

The churches I work with in ten WV & VA counties voluntarily band together in an association. They had never organized an association-wide mission trip. I had extensive relations and experience with similar churches in Alaska through years of taking college students there to lead in statewide youth leadership conferences. We worked with the Alaska Baptist Convention's state Evangelism Director named Jimmy Stewart (it is always fun to say, pardon me, but I have a call from Jimmy Stewart). The citizens there were rugged individualists like WV'ans, and it was a cold and mountainous region like WV (but much larger in scale). That, plus the fact it was far enough away to still be a disparate culture, and we didn't need a passport to visit it, made me think our Appalachian folks would relate well to our northernmost state. The exploratory meetings generated great interest. One couple from a church named Lorton Lick BC (that is the real name) came and explained they had never slept in another bed for the entire 40 years of their marriage. That may sound extremely rare in current times, but not that uncommon in our region of Appalachia. West Virginia is officially "the Mountain State" and unofficially "Almost Heaven", and with its tight folds of hills and hollers, streams and deep forests, one can make a case for "why should I go anywhere else?" We will call the couple the DQs.

We took 35 people and had a great mission experience. The group split into three teams: one on the Kenai Peninsula to help area churches and communities; one in Anchorage to conduct Backyard Bible Clubs in public parks; and one in Willow, two hours north of Anchorage, to assist in Disaster Relief for a recent fire that destroyed over 200 homes. So, of course, I sent the DQs to Willow, the nastiest work of the three, where they slept on air mattresses in a tiny church. Six weeks after we returned from Alaska, Mr. DQ showed up in my office saying, "When do I get to back?" I said, "That's one reason we do mission trips, to expand your frame of reference on what the Kingdom of God looks like and how it operates." He not only went back the next summer, but he also recruited and led a group of five men from his church who went with him. Now when we announce the deployment of our Disaster Relief teams to help with hurricanes or floods, who's the first person to sign up? Mr. DQ had expanded his frame of reference about the size and scope of the Kingdom of God.

Three leadership principles intertwine in these stories:

1. <u>Expanding frames of reference</u> (collectively for our church or company and individually for my worldview) <u>allow us to see beyond our artificial borders of bias, small thinking, or lack of experience to discover new horizons of thought and experience</u>. Expansion implies addition or increase, but the scary side of that expansion is a corresponding loss factor: we lose some sense of security, of knowing something was so true and solid but now is deflated, flattened, diminished, or deleted. The loss is real (see Lk. 4 entry; for a fuller explanation, see Jim Collins *Built to Last*[1]).

2. <u>Expanding frames of reference involve trust</u>. Peter's vision made no sense to him. He knew it was significant but had no idea where it was leading him. He had to trust the voice behind the vision and the veracity of the visitors' accounts of yet another connecting vision in order to make the decision to go to Caesarea. It helped change the course of Christianity, as we see a few chapters later in Acts 15. Mr. DQ had to trust me, a (to him) new leader—who had been on 80+ mission trips on four continents—that this would be positive and life-changing.

3. <u>Expanding frames of reference often show up with total indifference to our schedule, time, or place at which we find ourselves</u>. No offense to present residents of Joppa (Jaffa, south of Tel Aviv) or Mercer County in WV, where I currently serve, but they are not exactly the epicenter of this or any other universe. Moses didn't plan on a burning bush turning his world upside down, Gideon had no plans to lead any military campaigns (see Acts 9 entry), and Jesus' disciples thought they were meandering on the shores of the Sea of Galilee on temporary leave from their jobs to hear the latest wandering rabbi. You cannot predict the time or place when God will turn your world around by expanding your frame of reference.

<u>Lines on Leadership</u>

At what points(s) in my understanding of the Kingdom of God (or how my company operates) do I need to expand my frame of reference?

_____
_____

++

<u>Acts 11</u>---Highlights: Peter recounts his Joppa experience; gospel comes to Antioch; Barnabas seeks Saul

This chapter contains two catalytic decisions that fueled the explosive growth of the early church, two decisions that confront many leaders today.

1. Peter recounts at length to the home church in Jerusalem (vs. 1-18) his remarkable insight from chapter 10, where his vision at Joppa and encounter with the house of Cornelius convinces him <u>the gospel is not just for Jews only</u>. The church responded with, "God has granted to the Gentiles also the repentance that leads to life" (v. 18). Without any means of fast communication, those who had been scattered about the region after the persecution in Jerusalem were still preaching to the Jewish communities only, unaware of Peter's experience (v.19).

Verse 20 introduces us to nameless men identified by home regions, Cyprus and Cyrene, who cross over the line of demarcation between Jews and Gentiles and begin preaching to the Greeks in Antioch. Antioch was at that time the third largest city in the Roman Empire (behind Alexandria and Rome) and quite cosmopolitan[1]. Cyprus (see Acts 4 entry) was an island in the eastern Mediterranean where cultures, languages, and ships of many countries mingled constantly. Cyrene was an important town near the coast of North Africa in current-day Libya[2]. It was a few miles inland and served as a connection point for trade between the sea and the interior. Men from these locations would be comfortable speaking to people from disparate cultures. Because of their witness, the gospel took root and took off in Antioch (v.21). They were willing to break out of the usual parameters and not wait until the "head office" (Jerusalem) gave its official blessing or made it "company policy". Planting churches and establishing beachheads for new advances requires an entrepreneurial spirit. Until one has lived in a culture unlike one's upbringing, it can be a jarring experience to find out that your norms, values, and reactions are not universal in scope but often confined to your culture. Every church/company needs some folks from Cyprus and Cyrene.

2. The success is such that news of it filters down to Jerusalem, and the mother church sends Barnabas to investigate. Peter's experience was extraordinary in Acts 10; if the same phenomenon is occurring in Antioch, then a definite turn in how the church will grow is afoot. Sending Barnabas is a crucial step in confirmation, and what happens next will set the stage for what culminates in Acts 15 and changes the church forever. That is well and good in terms of church history and the advance of the gospel, but if Barnabas had not done what he did after arriving in Antioch, the growth there could have remained local and taken many more years to connect with what was happening in Joppa and Jerusalem.

Barnabas' decision is monumental. Verse 24 relates that Barnabas had a stellar resume: He was a good man and full of the Holy Spirit (character), and "considerable numbers were brought to the Lord." Because of his reputation in the Jerusalem church and because of what was happening in Antioch, he could have easily become the main figure within this movement, the lead pastor of the church at Antioch. Verses 25-26 change the course of history for the church: instead of becoming the main figure in Antioch, Barnabas goes to Tarsus, Saul's hometown, and brings him to Antioch. This is absolutely remarkable. Barnabas was fully aware of Saul's enormous potential from Acts 9 and knew what would inevitably happen. They forged a wildly successful partnership that resulted in a church-planting movement (see Acts 13-14); it didn't take long before Saul eclipsed Barnabas in stature and influence.

Barnabas willingly stepped into an arrangement he knew would result in taking a back seat to Saul. He knew his limitations; he was self-aware enough to recognize someone else could take this further than he could. It is reminiscent of George Washington after his second term in office as the first President of the United States; at that time, Washington could have continued on as long as he wished, but he knew his decision to step down and created an orderly transition of power would set a precedent for others to follow. Barnabas earns my admiration for putting God's Kingdom ahead of personal accolades or gain.

Lines of Leadership
1. Who are the "men of Cyprus and Cyrene" in your church/company? Are you one of them?
2. How committed are you to the goals of your church/company? Would you ever willingly seek out others to help "the cause", knowing they could possibly supplant you?

_____

_____

++

Acts 12---Highlights: James executed; Peter freed from prison; Herod struck dead

There is so much to unpack in this chapter. Space allows but two principles to be addressed.

1. James, an apostle and brother of John, was executed by Herod the Great's grandson (also Herod) to please the Jews (vs.1-3). He then seized Peter, a chief spokesperson for the growing movement, and had designs to execute him also to further please the Jews and quell this "rebellious sect". The narrative shows that Peter was under extraordinary security yet was freed by an angel of the Lord (vs. 6-17).

By some lines of reasoning, it would seem obvious God loved Peter more than James, or that Peter was more valuable than James, or in crass terms, less expendable. This is easily dismissed when one considers James, Peter, and John were the three disciples in whom Jesus invested the most time and that Jesus had predicted such a fate for James and many others who followed Him (Mt. 10.39). This was not a surprise but an expected consequence when a message of redemption can be heard as one of sedition by the current government. The surprise was the degree of direct divine intervention.

Our best combination of intellect and spiritual discernment amounts to tic-tac-toe when compared to the chess of God's purpose and will for mankind. This is very personal for our family. Our first son was born in 1981 with a cephalohematoma, a blood hemorrhage between the skull and skin. The doctor told us in the office that 99% are absorbed and disappear without incident[1]. We are the 1 %ers. We were in the midst of selection by our denomination's mission board and asked several doctors if it could be removed (people were calling him conehead). We finally persuaded a neurosurgeon to perform what was thought to be cosmetic surgery on a five-month-old. As mentioned, this was in 1981. The day of his surgery was the day the board was to vote on us as missionaries. Thirty from our church surrounded us in the waiting room as we prayed. The doctor gave the classic pronouncement: I have good news and bad news. They got it "all", but "all" included an unseen cyst that had penetrated the skull and was growing toward the brain. They had to remove a significant portion of his skull. He said to call your mission board; you would not be going anywhere; it may heal up with bone in 1-2 years if it ever would; he would need to wear a helmet when he started to crawl. Within six weeks (we have the X-rays to prove it), the skull was completely healed up. The doctor had never seen anything like this; we told him our God was capable of anything, including this. Needless to say, we rejoiced. If we had opted to wait and operate at 4-5 years of age on our first missionary furlough as advised, the surgeon said Joel would have had permanent brain damage or died.

Our second son was born with a rare but benign form of muscular dystrophy. It was mistakenly diagnosed at the beginning, and we took a long journey of trial and error with therapy and hospitals before we learned he basically had few "fast twitch" strength muscles and mainly "slow twitch" fine-tuning type muscles. He has had trouble running, lifting, and anything requiring strength; athletics took a back seat, and the arts came to the fore as he is an excellent singer, guitar player, pianist, and thespian.

One son is dramatically healed, but the other is not. It does not mean God is capricious or that He favored one son over the other. It means we live and breathe to serve Him in whatever circumstances we find ourselves in (Phil. 4.11), and "whatever my lot, Thou hast taught me to say, it is well with my soul[2]." I don't write that glibly; my wife has two incurable and potentially fatal diseases (systemic lupus and cutaneous T-cell lymphoma). We have seen our share of ups and downs in life, but as Job announces at the beginning of the oldest book in the Bible, The Lord giveth, the Lord taketh away, blessed be the name of the Lord (Job 1.21). This is not fatalism but rather a deeper level of trust in the love and purpose of the Father. Do I question Him? Often and loudly beat on His chest now and then? I think God would rather us be honest with Him than pious on the outside and churning on the inside. I trust Him to fulfill Rom. 8.28 not as a platitude but as a deep promise to me, His son in the faith.

2. Herod thinks he is large and in charge (vs. 20-23). A rebellion of a different sort than the one led by James and Peter has arisen, and he has the upper hand. Herod shows up in his royal robes (which were silver and gleaming in the sun to radiate light and give him a "heavenly" glow) and begins pontificating to

the masses. They acclaim him as a god, and he revels in their showered praise; God strikes him dead on the spot. What just happened?

In the Old Testament, there is a long line of kings in the divided kingdom of Israel who did evil and "committed the sins of Jeroboam" (1 Kings 12ff). The repeated phrase invites the question, what were the sins of Jeroboam? He instituted places of worship to substitute for his people having to travel to the temple in Jerusalem, which was in the southern kingdom of Judah. He instituted new religious festivals to take their mind off of going south to celebrate. He then recruited whoever wanted to sign up as priests and created a new order of religious leaders. In light of some of the political shenanigans of today, this might seem quaint and trivial to some, expedient to others.

Both Jeroboam in the OT and Herod in Acts 12 committed the same sin: <u>Anyone can speak **about** God; some are ordained as His representatives to speak **for** God, but no one except God can speak **as** God</u>. Jeroboam begins his public career as a valiant warrior (1 Kings 11.28); pastors and corporate leaders begin with humble positions and noble aspirations. Along the way, they see their decisions affect lives, and their importance becomes dopamine and serotonin to their spirits. This or that became a reality because of <u>my</u> role, <u>my</u> words, <u>my</u> decision, and <u>my</u> influence. Power accrued while soaking in praise of others is intoxicating. The line of demarcation between speaking on His behalf and speaking instead of Him is faint yet consequential, as Herod and Jeroboam both discovered.

<u>Lines on Leadership</u>
In reference to Peter and James: how willing are you to place your life at the disposal of your King, your company, and your

cause? How willing are you to speak truth regardless of the consequence?

In reference to Herod and Jeroboam: Accomplishments should be celebrated and rewarded; how much of the credit/glory you receive do you keep, and how much do you defer to your Lord? How much do you share with those on your team, in your company, or in your church?

_____

_____

++

Acts 13---Highlights: 1st missionaries appointed; preaching in Cyprus, Pisidian Antioch; opposition rises

This chapter marks a watershed moment for the burgeoning movement and has personal connections to our family's history. The first missionaries are selected, Barnabas and Saul (v.2), which would seem to be logical choices given their leadership within the church at Antioch (see Acts 11 entry). For Christians, it is important that the first missionaries were appointed out of and by the local church.

Barnabas and Saul sailed to Cyprus, Barnabas' country of origin (Acts 4.36). We have no way of knowing if Barnabas felt more at ease in his homeland, if it afforded them contacts, or if Barnabas desired that his countrymen hear the gospel first on this missionary journey. John Mark, the eventual writer of the second Gospel and cousin to Barnabas (possibly nephew, Col. 4.10), had tagged along when Barnabas and Saul left Jerusalem to return to Antioch and accompanied them part of the way on this first missionary journey, an important fact later on in the dissolution of the Barnabas and Paul partnership.

This brings us to the subtle yet important development in verse 9. Luke casually mentions, "But Saul, who was also known as <u>Paul</u>..." From this time forward, in Acts and all of his epistles, he referred to himself as <u>Paul</u>. Saul is his Hebrew name, and if his new life's mission was as a missionary to the Gentiles (as declared by God (Acts 9) and confirmed by his work in Antioch, Acts 11), he would need a name more amenable to the culture. Paul or Paulus was his Roman name. He could speak multiple languages and dialects (Acts 21.37-40), but if introduced to a Gentile audience with a Jewish name (Saul), many would have likely dismissed him and his message.

A lighthearted story illustrates this principle. When we moved to our present position in the heart of Appalachia, we left a Texas college environment. Professors there were known as Dr. A, Dr. J, Dr. D, using the initial of their first or last names. It was a term of endearment that also showed respect. I had just finished my Ph.D. before we moved, and this state's "vanity" license plates were inexpensive, so I decided to give Mr. T (a popular TV character of years gone by) an upgrade and get Doctor T. So I did. At the first pastors' meeting, I showed the license plate to some of them. They shook their heads and said, "Hmm, looks like you don't know." "Know what, this doesn't sound good." They replied, "Dr. T is the guy who owns the porn shop out by the landfill." Hmmm. I quickly found out they were right, and that name was widely known in our area as a person who not only owned the porn shop but bars and related businesses.

Three years elapsed before I could renew the plate. I was repeatedly asked if I'd gone "mobile" or what I had in the back seat to offer. When I could, I changed it to DR ALLAN, which by this time was what most of the pastors called me anyway. I had failed to take the local culture and context into consideration and paid for it with some good-natured ribbing that lasted several years.

Lines on Leadership

In the board room, the classroom, the church, the family, and the neighborhood, we are known by certain names. Those names or titles can open or shut doors for our careers. Hollywood celebrities adopt new names to better connect with their new audiences. What name or title do you use? Does it connect with your colleagues? Subordinates? Associates? New clients? New target group? Is your name/title a bridge or barrier to your desired audience?

_____

_____

++

Acts 14---Highlights: encounters in Iconium, Lystra, Derbe; return to Antioch

21st-century Social media has the ability to create a persona or brand with millions of followers within days or even hours. A reputation used to take a lifetime to craft; now, it can be generated with a single video or text submission strategically placed. If it "clicks" with people, it is shared and re-shared with countless others at blazing speeds, thanks to fiber optics and wireless connections. This same phenomenon has created volatile and sudden swings from popular to pariah and back again depending on the latest entry by the person seeking fame or a determined fan or foe who attacks the individual.

This is not a new phenomenon but a repeat of Acts 14. Paul and Barnabas embark on a missionary journey to several area municipalities to share the gospel. They evoke strong reactions from believers and opponents alike. In one city named Lystra (vs. 8-18), healing occurs, and Paul and Barnabas are proclaimed gods. Barnabas was named Zeus, perhaps because of his age or stature, and Paul was labeled Hermes because he did most of the talking. The local Zeus priest gets into the act and upgrades the occasion with food and festivities. Sudden adulation can feed the ego and be incredibly intoxicating (see Herod in Acts 12 entry). Here Saul and Barnabas wisely decided this would serve no purpose but to obscure their real reason for being there and rebuffed the crowd's adoration, rejected their newfound deified status, and had trouble convincing the gathered multitude of their mortality.

At this moment, with the crowd showing some bewilderment and likely asking itself, "Well, if they're not gods, then who are they, really?", the determined detractors (who had taken the time and effort to follow Paul and Barnabas all the way from Antioch) swayed the crowd to not sacrifice to these new gods but instead stone them. To their credit, they chose not to accept the worship of the crowd and also not to give up on their quest after such a painful setback. Verses 20-22 show they viewed these extraordinary happenings through a longer-term lens, telling the newly appointed leaders of the area churches, "Through many tribulations we must enter the kingdom of God" (v. 22). Salvation may be obtained as a free gift of God, but it has some attendant post conversion costs.

Paul and Barnabas teach us several valuable lessons in this chapter. 1) Every public pronouncement that challenges the status quo will draw criticism, justified or not. If I believe in this cause, I have to take the blows as well as the accolades and steer a steady course toward the realization of that cause. 2) They took time to develop leadership for every church they had planted (vs. 22-23) before departing the region. Creating growth without sufficient infrastructure to sustain that growth is a surefire recipe for collapse. 3) When they did return to Antioch, their home base for the mission efforts, they had the integrity to report everything that happened to them, not just the high points; but they also had the wisdom to portray the journey overall as God opening "a door of faith to the Gentiles." (v. 27)

Lines on Leadership
There was a balance in the actions and attitudes of Paul and Barnabas. They were not locked onto the lows of setbacks or the highs of victories but the goal, which was taking the gospel to the Gentiles. Those who remain out "in the field" but don't come into home base occasionally to report, refresh, and regroup tend toward eccentricity and rough edges; those who remain behind the fortress towers without venturing forth occasionally to let their message mingle with the reality of the world tend toward complacency and softness. What are some of your recent setbacks and victories? Do they amount to an advancement of your cause/message?

_____

_____

++

Acts 15---Highlights: Jerusalem Council; Paul and Barnabas reshuffle missionary partners

The Council of Jerusalem represents the moment when the discoveries of Peter and Paul in previous chapters of Acts (that the gospel was not just for Jews) were codified and made official; developing orthopraxy led to developing orthodoxy instead of vice versa. How remarkable to think that several future authors of the New Testament were likely present or nearby: James, half-brother of Jesus; Paul; John Mark; Peter; and others (vs. 2, 4, 6, 22, & 37; see Gal. 2 entry). The reports of the unforeseen (yet highly prophesied) implications of Pentecost (that God was painting outside the lines) had been heard by the church in Jerusalem. Those from within that church who wished to keep the Good News confined to Jewish practice and jurisdiction arrived at Antioch (v.1) to show these new "Christians" (Acts 11.26) the error of their ways, ran into the formidable duo of Paul and Barnabas, (v. 2, "dissension and debate"), and everyone decided the time had come to find out what God was actually up to.

    The Council of Jerusalem was not a unanimous celebration but more like a raucous, rancorous extension of the Antioch discussions (v. 7, "and after there had been much debate"). The gospel had upset communities all along the eastern Mediterranean seacoast. The apostles and elders in the church, in their wisdom, knew this was a critical decision: Was this a potential rift that could become permanent and fatal, or an extraordinary opportunity to fulfill the scriptures (Ps. 22.27; 67.2; 72.17; 96.3; James quotes from Amos and Jeremiah)? Was this a family squabble or a true game-changer? When the stakes are high, and the participants have deep but divergent convictions, the outcome is often gridlock or, worse, a splintering of the body/company. The issue of slavery in 19th century America, the issue of a company tipping toward more business abroad than in its home country, or the issue of a religion tied to one ethnic group or for all nations is fraught with looming failure. The apostles and elders under the leadership of James arrived at a solution that both acknowledged God's endorsement of the Gospel spreading to the Gentiles and the concerns of those with a background in Jewish law.

    News of this decision was heartily welcomed by the church in Antioch (vs. 30-31). In the early 1980s, we were still in language school in then-West Germany, and the pastor of the German Baptist church in Lüneburg had become the executive director of the European Baptist Mission, a body that represented the mission work among Baptists from all European countries. His name was Horst Niessen. Periodically, the Foreign Mission Board (FMB) of the Southern Baptist Convention, the group that sent us to Europe at the invitation of German Baptists, held a worldwide meeting of like mission boards in Richmond, VA. Because of its size and scope, the FMB was always regarded as the senior partner at these meetings and usually dictated the agenda and the decisions made. A recent change in leadership at the FMB had been made, and this was the first such meeting for that new leadership. I will never forget Horst coming back to Germany and blurting to me, "They listened to us! They listened to us!!" He excitedly related how different this meeting had been; the new leadership had said there was no agenda at the meeting except to hear how God was working in each region of the world and to hear it from those experiencing it. The respect bestowed to each of those mission boards by this action was evident on Horst's smiling face.

The leadership at Jerusalem and at Richmond, VA had one thing in common: They had no idea where their decisions would eventually lead, but they knew it was the right and good thing to do. The scriptures supported them, the timing was appropriate, and it was a good gesture to show that servanthood and initiative were both present.

Because I have a personal affinity for Barnabas, I will take an author's license to add a second principle to this chapter. The Jerusalem Council was a huge success for Paul, an affirmation that he was on a good path of preaching a gospel for all people. Antioch was in a flourishing situation, and his work had been acknowledged at this council. It was time to take a second missionary journey and build upon what had already been done. Barnabas, whose prior endorsement of then Saul to that very same Jerusalem church leadership had made it possible for Saul to even have a ministry associated with the home church, now wanted to extend to John Mark a second chance and have him join this second trip. Paul would have none of it: John Mark had left them during the first one. We have no idea why, he just did (homesickness, couldn't keep up, didn't agree with tactics used, all speculation). Paul and Barnabas ended their successful partnership and took on new partners: Paul with Silas and Barnabas with John Mark.

While I am sure there were regrets (we know Mark became useful to Paul later on in his ministry, 2 Tim. 4.11) and a sense of personal loss, both pairs were successful in their respective endeavors. Paul and Silas continued to extend the boundaries of the gospel's reach, and Barnabas and Mark went to familiar territory in Cyprus (v.39). Some partnerships are for a season. I like to think of that season as "seasoning". There may have been things Paul needed to learn from Barnabas, and Barnabas from Paul that would find better fruition in a new partnership. Barnabas influences the writers of most of the NT (Paul's epistles and Mark's gospel, plus perhaps James or other apostles in the Jerusalem church). Silas is a co-author of several of the Pauline epistles.

Lines on Leadership

1. What decisions loom on the horizon for you that will have far-reaching consequences? Have you taken company policy, governing documents, and cultural circumstances into consideration? What decision would affirm the most people or groups involved in its ramifications?

2. Consider partners from past seasons in your career. Where did they contribute, for good or bad, to your understanding of how to be a better leader?

Acts 16---Highlights: Paul meets Timothy, Macedonian Vision, 1st European convert, Philippian jail

In the midst of Paul's second missionary journey (vs. 1-13), he experienced a phenomenon I've seen over and over in my years of ministry. Preachers have a term for it: "the Macedonian Call." If you plot on a map the places Paul had preached up till then, he intended to systematically crisscross Asia Minor with the gospel. God had other plans. In Acts 16, it was clear to Paul that he and Timothy were forbidden to enter certain districts (Phrygia, Galatia, Bithynia, Mysia, vs .6-7). A person can turn in any of 360 degrees and start walking; it won't be long before you find a need you can address with the gospel. However, in *Experiencing God,* one reads that "The need does not necessarily constitute the call[1]." Paul showed sensitivity to the Spirit by going to Troas, thinking he would minister there, but instead was told by God to traverse the Aegean Sea over 100 miles to land on the Macedonian peninsula; there, he would soon converse with and win Lydia to Christ as the first European convert (v. 14). The "Macedonian Call" is about two things: being obedient while looking for the Spirit's leadership and being flexible when it seems one command is succeeded by another one in a different direction (see Abraham and the almost sacrifice of Isaac Gen. 22, and the many direction changes during the Exodus).

I had planned for months in 2017 for an associational Cuba mission trip and submitted our ten visa requests over two months before departure as instructed. Ten days before our flight (we never received a reason why), we learned our assigned Cuban venue's building permits were denied. The next 24 hours of calls and prayers produced another venue twenty miles from our original destination. There we assisted in the same ministries we had planned for (VBS, adult discipleship, and construction for which the church already had a building permit) in a smaller town (approx. 15,000). In God's timing and wisdom, he placed us in a location not as much on the government's "radar" where we had more opportunity to share our love more freely for God with our new Cuban friends.

This marked at least the fifth time this has happened to me in mission settings. 1) In 1996, I took a college group to assist in the Atlanta Olympics. We were assigned to a dead-end location with little to do; after much prayer (and I'll admit, some behind-the-scenes lobbying), we were placed on the busiest location of the Olympics, where 80,000 passed us each day on Congress St. 2) In 1997, my college mission team was scheduled to airdrop into remote mountain villages of Albania to show the Jesus film; civil war broke out two months before our departure, and we had to switch countries winding up in former East Germany where my German language fluency was a huge help. 3) In 2003, our college group was to go to an East Asian country when the SARS virus exploded across the scene. We had to postpone the trip six months from the summer to the Christmas semester break. We scrapped our original premise and learned a dramatic reading of Dickens' Christmas Carol to present in university English classes, which we did ten times and spoke to hundreds of students outside of class, many resulting in gospel conversations. 4) In 2016, we had scheduled a mission trip to Miami that was cancelled due to several factors. I had no way of knowing in God's timing we would be called upon during that same time frame to minister with multiple Disaster Relief teams during the deadly WV floods.

Each time we had taken the initial step of faith to cross a (for us) barrier to share the Gospel with one group, only to be redirected in various ways toward another place and need. Churches and organizations now operate in an environment that changes more rapidly than at any other time in history due to technology, pandemics (COVID-19 in 2020), increased mobility, and social media, to mention just a few. Long-range planning is not as important as being prepared, flexible, and heeding whatever voice you deem reliable as to the direction your group should go. For Christians, this means every undertaking should be bathed in prayer before, during, and after the task at hand. We serve at His request, in His timing, wherever, however, and whenever. Plan, but always be prepared for that unexpected mid-course correction. God is not capricious, but He can be relatively spontaneous. <u>The written Word of God is not so much a manual as it is a toolbox</u>; it gives insights on how to better worship and follow the living Word of God. I don't worship pages in a book; I worship a Christ who is on the move. Listen for the Macedonian Call.

<u>Lines on Leadership</u>
Paul encountered a place he didn't expect (come to Macedonia and help us), a person he didn't expect (Lydia as the first European convert), and a prison situation he didn't expect (thrown in a Philippian jail). Is this extraordinary or normative for your leadership career? What is your attitude toward constant contingency thinking? Where does flexibility rate in your hierarchy of leadership attributes?

_____
_____
+++

Acts 17---Highlights: preaching in Thessalonica, Berea, Athens; discourse on Mars Hill

Paul and Silas, accompanied by Luke, took their leave of Philippi and continued preaching in a series of towns down the eastern coast of what is today Greece. After the agitation and riots in Thessalonica and moving on to Berea, the trio split up for safety's sake, with Paul escorted by sympathizers by sea to Athens. On the surface, it seems the same overall pattern emerges each time the gospel is presented: Some are persuaded (vs. 4, 12, 34), some scoff (vs. 5, 13, 32), and some treat it as the latest, greatest novel teaching *de jour* (vs. 19-21).

There is an old adage, 'business before pleasure.' I have taken over 80 groups on what would be called mission trips, which usually center around ministry or service to a local community and, out of our service, earn the right to share the Good News of Christ. The trips are taken in the US and abroad, but usually in a culture with varying degrees of disparity with the home cultures of the trip participants. For many years I practiced that adage, get our goal accomplished, and then tack on some "reward" or "down" time doing something fun or entertaining. After a few years, I started to see the wisdom of reversing the sequence to 'pleasure before business', not for recreational purposes but because of what we see in Acts 17.

When we were in a foreign country, the first few days would be spent in a city known for tourism and where a group of Americans would not draw as much attention as it would in smaller villages or the interior. That way, our group could accomplish several preliminary but important goals: 1) They could overcome jet or road lag and not look like zombies when we interacted with our primary group; 2) they could absorb the shock of being surrounded by an atmosphere of a foreign language; 3) they could acquire some elementary cultural cues and language interaction; 4) and visits to significant national sites provided some important future conversation starters and common points of interest. This was productive in two ways: It lowered the anxiety level of our mission trippers and gave us time to relate the truths of the gospel to the culture in which we found ourselves. To go with locals on a scavenger hunt in Tibet, scale the Christ the Redeemer statue overlooking the Rio de Janeiro harbor, or ride the Chicago subway are adventures that bond and teach much better than any lecture or video lesson.

These principles remain effective when transferred to US soil; taking folks from the deep South or Southwest to the Northwest, the inner cities of Chicago or Boston, or to a community of a different ethnic composition than their hometowns jar their collective systems. They need time to adjust; instead of just plowing ahead with what amounts to a canned sales pitch, they learn to adapt and connect gospel and culture. It also forces mission trippers to confront whether the gospel they were sharing was American, white, Southern, or Baptist instead of biblical; if it is truly for ALL nations, it must be shared in a way to which indigenous people groups can relate.

Paul used his power of observation and days spent wandering Athens to relate to his crowd (v. 22), to become familiar with their artists (v. 28), and relate the gospel to philosophical topics and language since many of his hearers were from various schools of philosophy (v. 18). He did not soft-pedal the crux of his message, the resurrection (vs. 18, 31-32). But he understood his audience; he spoke to Jews in synagogues (vs. 1, 10) and Greek scholars on Mars Hill.

Lines on Leadership

Does the presentation of your message take into account what makes each audience for that message unique? What preparatory steps could you take to help the message and audience mesh together better?

_____

_____

++

Acts 18---Highlights: Paul in Corinth

An oft-mentioned leadership principle is to do what only you can do (or what you do best) and to delegate the rest when possible and feasible (see Acts 6 entry); this chapter is a fitting example.

Paul met Aquila and Priscilla during his ministry in Corinth, discovered they had the same vocational skills (tent making or possibly working with leather) and spent time getting to know them (vs. 1-4). They were from Rome; therefore, he knew they were neither averse to travelling nor living abroad. Whether or not they were Christians before or after their time with Paul is not known, but by v. 18, they accompanied Paul to Ephesus on the west coast of Asia Minor, and by vs. 24-28, they were discipling Apollos "in the way of God more accurately" (v.26). When Silas and Timothy arrived on the scene in Corinth after their follow up work strengthening the new churches in Thessalonica and Berea (Acts 17.14-15), Paul devoted his next eighteen months to full-time evangelism and discipleship in the region.

This was his method, to be the vanguard, the spear point, and to have trusted disciples who could, in turn, strengthen the new believers (see 2 Tim. 2 entry). Paul's repeated admonitions in his letters to stay the course, correct false doctrine, and handle the Word of God accurately were written to associates such as Silas and Timothy and now Priscilla and Aquila, as well as the local church. He put great faith in his disciples to continue the work he blazed across the various cities he visited.

Another aspect of this process can be seen in the life of Apollos. He was being effective with what he knew to proclaim that Jesus was the Messiah, but he needed others to instruct him more fully concerning His Lordship and other aspects of His teachings. He was willing to be taught, even though he had had success and was recognized as an effective apologist (v. 28) for the gospel. To his credit, he was willing to be taught by Paul's associates, such as Priscilla and Aquila, instead of demanding Paul himself.

Lines on Leadership
Multiplication of my efforts as a leader begins with trust in those who will continue what I have started. In whom have you invested your trust and wisdom to the point they can instruct others as well or better than you about your group's mission?
Many times I have attended a conference or a church service to hear Person X only to be told that Person X could not make it but had sent his associate in his place. Using Apollos' example, I had to rethink: Am I here just to be in the presence of a known personality, or am I here to gain knowledge? Am I chasing fame or the facts?

_____

_____

++

Acts 19---Highlights: Paul's adventures in Ephesus

Demetrius was a maker of idols purchased by the residents of Ephesus. Paul's gospel had made sufficient inroads in the hearts and conversations of the populace to affect Demetrius' business. He riled up the business community by saying, "²⁵Men, you know that our prosperity depends upon this business. ²⁶ You see and hear that not only in Ephesus, but in almost all of Asia, this Paul has persuaded and turned away a considerable number of people, saying that gods made with hands are no gods *at all*. ²⁷ Not only is there danger that this trade of ours fall into disrepute, but also that the temple of the great goddess Artemis be regarded as worthless and that she whom all of Asia and the world worship will even be dethroned from her magnificence."

Instead of engaging in an intellectual discussion or an objective search for truth, Demetrius ignited a marathon (2+ hours) pep rally, which has become the norm in the era of social media: shout at each other instead of talking to or with each other. There is no record of nor a reason to believe that Paul taunted or personally goaded Demetrius, and when the pep rally began, Paul's people wisely held him back from responding (v. 30), possibly to keep the fray from escalating, more likely to protect Paul from personal danger.

Paul had used Ephesus as a headquarters for reaching Asia Minor with the gospel, speaking in a public hall for over two years (v. 10). The contrast between the two styles is marked: Demetrius incites, Paul informs by daily reasoning (v.9). The phrase "all the residents of Asia heard the word of the Lord" could mean either Paul's reputation grew to the point people made an effort to travel to Ephesus to hear his teachings, or that Paul established Ephesus as a base of operation and took several excursions in various directions throughout western Asia Minor on speaking tours.

The bottom line is that Paul's teachings were not mere intellectual exercises in points of philosophy or theology. They had a measurable impact on individuals' behavior to the point they affected the local economy and religious identity. Transformed lives garner all types of attention.

Lines on Leadership
What measurable impacts have your teachings and directives had within your organization, within your immediate community, or within your city? (Take time to walk through your tenure there and be honest). If none, why not?
Is the resistance your teachings face due to an offensive/abrasive demeanor, their content, or their contrast to the prevailing community values?

_____

_____
++

Acts 20---Highlights: Paul in Macedonia, Greece, Miletus; Paul's farewell to Ephesian elders

Paul is on his way to Jerusalem and knows in his heart what awaits him there (arrest, trial after trial, imprisonment) after multiple warnings and prophecies. From the coastal town of Miletus, some miles south of Ephesus, he calls for the Ephesian elders to meet him there. What follows is the lengthiest, most personal, and most emotional charge to leadership from a NT figure other than Jesus. He foregoes a hero's welcome in Ephesus and meets with the leaders to reaffirm his love for them and faith in their leadership of a beloved congregation. A selective but not exhaustive list of leadership qualities he exhibited in this passage are:

1. <u>The prioritization of his time</u>: If he makes a stop at Ephesus, where he taught for over two years (Acts. 19.9-10), he knows it will slow down his journey toward Jerusalem.

2. <u>Discretion on when to wade into confrontation and when to avoid it:</u> His last episode in Ephesus had resulted in a riot and almost gotten out of hand (Acts 19.23-41). His multiple scrapes with the law and the public in Acts clearly demonstrated his courage, but he would not be deterred from his primary goal of reaching Jerusalem.

3. <u>The acknowledgement of leadership succession</u> (v.29): As stated in other places in this book, we are all interim (see John 1 entry). In campus ministry, I had two years of a student's gen ed. classes to pour into him/her before the person disappeared into his/her major. Sometimes they stayed in leadership of our campus ministries, but inevitably they all graduated, dropped out, or transferred. I had a finite time with them and knew I had to train them before their inevitable transfer or graduation. From the very moment our two sons came into this world, we prepared them for the day they left our home and became productive, self-sufficient adults. In my work with churches in WV, I told them from day one I would give 100% every day for ten years and then would walk away in transition (I don't use the word retirement). Another corollary of this passage is the painful realization many have when they shift from a single pastorate to a multi-staff setting or when a manager goes to a senior management position. It affords a greater opportunity to effect change, but it signals a loss of interaction with the rank and file of the church or organization. Some leaders become convinced that they and only they have the message and influence to lead their group. This may be true in the short run, but in the long term, I must acknowledge the gifts of others and their ability to lead in my place; if I've done my job right of developing leaders, they will succeed in ways either better or in new directions than I would have taken the organization.

4. <u>The balance of the professional and personal</u>: Paul acknowledged the goals and warnings he needed to give about the work but took time to affirm his genuine love for them, witnessed by the emotional display in vs. 36-38. We came to WV in 2013 in obedience to God's calling; I had no family here and no previous connections of any type in our ten counties. The floods of 2016 in our state just above our area killed 23 as torrential rains gorged normally small streams and transformed them into deadly rushing walls of water. As I coordinated multiple training and deployment of Disaster Relief teams, my ministry here went from professional to personal. Colleagues became brothers; strangers became faith family.

5. <u>It really is "more blessed to give than to receive"</u>: Paul ends his remarks to the Ephesian elders with Jesus' famous maxim in v. 35. Countless televangelists have used that maxim to line their own pockets and promise you'll receive more than you give, everyone profits from it. Paul doesn't say your sacrifice is guaranteed a material reward; your joy is a byproduct of sharing your life with others. The satisfaction of investing in a cause or another individual far exceeds any material remuneration I would receive for offering my time and effort.

<u>Lines on Leadership</u>
If you left your present post of leadership, would you have a similar gathering as Paul? Have you prepared your current leadership staff for your eventual promotion, departure, retirement, or reorganization? What contingencies are in place when one of those things inevitably happens?

_____
_____
++

Acts 21---Highlights: Paul sails from Miletus toward Jerusalem; warned repeatedly danger awaited him there; Paul is seized in the Temple

Paul is determined to go to Jerusalem. He sailed directly from Miletus past Cyprus, straight to Tyre. Different disciples warned Paul not to go to Jerusalem, first during an extended stay at Tyre on the coast and then in Caesarea, where they stayed with Philip (see Acts 6 and 8 entries). Upon arrival in Jerusalem and consultations with the church leaders there, Paul made his way to the Temple, heeding the precautions urged upon him in previous chapters. Paul had made many enemies during three missionary journeys and teaching in major cities in Asia and Europe, while in the Temple, he was recognized by some of them. Trumped-up accusations were flung and a riot ensued so grievous the Roman military was called in to quell it. A tribune (commander of 1000 troops) took charge and was about to take Paul back to the barracks for questioning or worse when Paul spoke to him in Greek, then asked to address the crowd, which he did "in the Hebrew dialect". (v.40)

The narrative bleeds over into chapter 22, but for now, an important leadership principle has already been displayed. Paul has calmed a potentially deadly situation by a simple technique called head and heart language. (see Acts 2 entry)

When we moved to then West Germany in 1982 to do German language mission work, we knew three German words: kindergarten, danke, and sauerkraut. That was it. After an intensive year of language school, we could communicate much better, and we retained a weekly tutor for our entire time there to continually improve our German. German students learned English in school from fifth grade on, so carrying on a basic conversation with most neighbors and acquaintances was possible in English. So why go to the trouble of learning German?

Because it was the **heart** language of the folks to whom we wanted to minister. English was their **head** language, meaning they could perhaps understand on a cognitive basis what we were saying in English, but to reach deeply into their spirits, we needed to speak to them in their heart language. Conversely, the opposite was true for us. To speak in their heart language was, for us, our head language. No matter how many lessons we took, books we read, conversations we led, television shows we watched in German, and fluent we became, it would always be our second language, our head language. Our neighbors, church members, and acquaintances appreciated our efforts, and an effort it was most days. They much preferred to have us trip and stumble over words than them do the same in English. It also placed them in the driver's seat as to the conversation speed and direction.

When Paul found himself in the midst of a riot, there was no time to pull out the Greek/Hebrew/Latin dictionary. The preparation, years of dialogue in a foreign tongue, and observations had to all be committed deeply into Paul's ability to converse. His language proficiency had to be to the point, not only informational but also persuasive, to relate not only facts but also convince a group of his true intentions. Israel was located in the Middle East along major trade crossroads and had been conquered by many different civilizations; not to learn the heart languages of different cultures would have put one at a distinct disadvantage. Americans think because English is the current worldwide language of commerce, they have no need of learning a second or third language. If Christians want to make disciples of other nations, they need to learn the heart language spoken by every non-native group.

Another corollary to language proficiency in speaking to a group of which you are not native is temperament. When we spoke in a secondary or tertiary language, it was our experience that anytime emotions rose to the surface, vocabulary and syntax disappeared from our brains and tongues—they just vanished. So discipline was necessary not only to conjugate and decline properly but to rein in emotions so we could communicate well. Space does not permit mentioning variations and countless dialects within each language.

Leaders take time to learn the <u>heart</u> language of their intended audience or group they will lead. The language gap could be because of age or socioeconomic class as well as nationality or ethnicity. Learning enough of the group's <u>heart</u> language to be understood is wise; trying to pawn myself off as a native speaker (when I clearly am not) crosses the line to become a caricature or opens me up as a leader to ridicule. Even though I spent many years relating to college students, as I write, I already collect Social Security payments; for me to try and sound "cool" or "dope" or "hip" or any other outdated term to show my solidarity with the group would be met with scorn or worse. Learning the <u>heart</u> language of a group can open empathetic doors or at least create temporary openings for further dialogue.

<u>Lines on Leadership</u>
Which colleagues, neighborhood, extended family, or target group speaks a heart language you need to learn in order to be heard affectively as well as cognitively?
_____
_____
++

<u>Acts 22</u>---Highlights: Paul's first defense

There is no substitute for first-person narratives, testimonies, or accounts of a particular event. History is thankfully not written solely by those who were involved since they are usually too busy creating it. Most would write with terse, raw words of action or description, and the interpretation and reflection would be missing.

The conversion of Saul, the former Jewish persecutor of Christians, was detailed in Acts 9 in a dramatic third-person narrative. In Acts 22 (after many years of mission work and reflection on that seminal event in his life on the "road to Damascus"), Paul relates the same conversion experience in a first-person narrative. Much greater detail is given of his conversation with the Lord and subsequently with Ananias, the first person of faith to interact with the former sworn enemy of believers. While people often embellish and burnish a story in its repeated retellings, the additions found here in Acts 22 over the Acts 9 account are more the product of sorting out what happened on that life-altering day over the period of many years.

The missionary journeys, the violent reactions of the crowds, the imprisonments, beatings, desertions, and stones hurled as his body all find their way into the manner and inflection of his voice. When the Lord appeared to him in Acts 9, and he was blind for several days, Paul's mind was a jumble of thoughts and emotions while wrestling with letting go of everything he had held to be true up to that moment. Through study, preaching, travels, and interaction with multiple cultures and countless people, Paul had had time to ponder not only the 'what' of that foundational day in Damascus but the 'why.'

He speaks with incredulity and fear in Acts 9. He speaks here in vs. 3-21 with measured tones and quiet conviction. And he knows precisely what trigger word will ignite the throngs present: Gentile. Just as Jesus in Luke 4 had incited the hometown crowd by inferring God loved Gentiles as well as His "chosen" people, so Paul, in his missionary journeys, had seen

God grant salvation and favor to the Gentiles. It is the overall theme of the entire book of Acts that God will not be confined to human-made parameters; He extends His grace to all men.

Lines on Leadership

Several years elapsed between the actual conversion event and the account given here in Acts 22. What pivotal moment in your life has taken you a long time to unravel, explain, or understand? If it was traumatic, it might take therapy, prayer, counsel, and the healing of time for it all to come into perspective. If it was a springboard for your success or the fulfillment of a life's purpose, how did you reflect on its importance? Journaling? Talking it out with a friend? Meditation? What crucial time in your life would deserve this amount of examination?

_____

_____

++

Acts 23---Highlights: Paul before the Sanhedrin; a conspiracy to kill him; moved by Romans to Caesarea

Claudius Lysias was the Roman commanding officer of the garrison assigned to Jerusalem, the one who initially apprehended Paul during a disturbance in the Temple in Ch. 21 and in Ch. 22 decided to get the truth out of him by scourging. Upon discovering Paul was a Roman citizen, out of fear (v. 29), he released him to the Jewish chief priests. He did not give him total release because he was savvy enough to know that doing so would have caused great unrest to keep growing among the Jews. So his decision to have Paul speak to the Sanhedrin was a political calculation and in keeping with his desire to get to the truth (Acts 22.30).

When the Jewish leaders erupted in an intractable argument among themselves that Paul cleverly instigated (23. 6-10), the commander wisely excised Paul from the growing unrest and took him to the Roman barracks for a cooling down period with the intent to start the whole process up again. Upon learning of a plot by forty Jews to kill Paul the next time the commander brought him to the Sanhedrin, he devised a plan to take him to another venue where Paul might receive a fairer hearing. He ordered an extraordinarily large contingent (two hundred soldiers, seventy horsemen, and two hundred spearmen, v. 23) to ensure the safety of Paul as he brought him to Caesarea Maritima. The largest portion of the group went as far as Antipatris, halfway to Caesarea, and returned, leaving Paul with the horsemen to continue on to the coast at Caesarea (vs.31-32).

Verses 26-30 include a letter the commander wrote to Felix (procurator/governor of the Roman province made up of Judea and Cilicia, the area of Paul's hometown of Tarsus). Whether Luke heard it read out loud, Paul later recounted it, or he saw a copy of it is pure speculation. On the surface, it sounds perfunctory and businesslike, outlining the commander's reasoning and conclusions concerning this action of transporting Paul from Jerusalem to Caesarea. He paints a positive picture of his actions toward Paul, describing how he rescued Paul, conveniently omitting the details of almost scourging him before finding out Paul was a Roman citizen entitled to certain legal rights.

<u>Lines on Leadership</u>
Writing letters of importance and "word-craft" are lost arts at the time this book was written: most contemporary communication is spur-of-the-moment snippets shot into cyberspace as texts,

emails, "tweets," and social media, written with little regard to consequence or how the other person will react to it. A formal letter that decides the fate of a man/company/organization should be carefully thought out and carefully worded to achieve its intended goal. Precisely because most communication is electronic these days, a formal or handwritten letter, by its rarity alone, gains much attention.

The commander should not be commended for his omission of certain details of his proceedings with Paul so as to cast himself in a more favorable light. He did, however, show how to state the situation in a manner that seemed forthright and sensible and considered his audience for the letter (Felix, a legal superior). What was the last letter of consequence you composed? Did you consider all the ramifications for all the parties involved? The overall tone of the letter? Was the vocabulary used insightful or 'inciteful'? Did you read it aloud or have a third party read the letter to see if it was well stated and if the intended impact would indeed be delivered? Evaluate the possible outcomes of your letter and what could have been improved.

_____
_____

++

Acts 24---Highlights: two appearances by Paul in the court of Felix at Caesarea Maritima

In this chapter, Paul is brought twice to the court of Felix, once to hear and refute the trumped-up charges brought against him by Ananias and the temple lawyers from Jerusalem (v.1) and once to explain his faith in Christ to Felix and his wife (v.24). It is openly acknowledged that the evidence presented against him is flimsy at best and nonexistent in reality, but to placate the political situation Felix retains him in Caesarea for over two years

(v. 27) not in hopes of wearing down Paul's resistance to the charges but in hopes of extracting money from him (v.26).

The average person (including this author) would feel like this was time wasted and likely experience a frustration level that reached a boiling point. Paul had an exciting, adventurous life as he shared the gospel and saw lives transformed from city to city and region to region. Now he languishes in what amounts to house arrest (he is allowed to have visitors, v. 23) and his only audience for his preaching is a procurator seeking bribes more than truth.

But Paul had received assurances in Acts 23.11 from the Lord Himself that he would one day have an audience for the gospel in Rome, the seat of power for the known world. He knew this was not his final destination, nor was it "the main act". This is the paradoxical nature of each time a leader shares his convictions. It should be given full attention, full mental and spiritual focus, and the highest level of energy. Each time our message is on display (whether in a legal sense as here or in the court of public opinion), it deserves all that, yet it is simultaneously a learning period, a building block, a next step in the progression of a *Lebensbotschaft* (life message). Each time is important, but if I believe in a sovereign Father who is able to take every thread in my life and weave it into a God-honoring tapestry (Rom. 8.28), it must be seen as continual preparation for the future. Paul is more interested in the propagation of the gospel than his personal freedom or agenda; Christ is more important than his circumstances.

Lines on Leadership

The natural progression in a successful career is perceived as appearances in ever larger arenas or larger situations than before. To go from preaching on multiple continents to confinement on the seacoast and considered quasi-entertainment for government officials would look like a failure on most resumes.

What periods in your life have seemed like someone else was putting their foot on the brakes of your career? How did those lulls add to or dilute your *Lebensbotschaft*?

_____

_____

++

Acts 25---Highlights: Paul's defense before Festus, then Agrippa

When a person visits the Holy Land multiple times, it cannot be predicted which moments will overwhelm one emotionally. Places where Jesus was baptized, taught, and crucified, are dear to all Christians. In 2019 as a Holy Land tour group leader, I had one of those moments as we visited the Mediterranean coast at the site of Paul's dramatic encounter with Festus in Acts 25. I stood on the original floor of the place where Paul (sensing a repeat of the plot to ambush him if taken back to Jerusalem, vs. 2-3) appeals to have his case heard before Caesar (vs. 10-11).

I stood there for a long time, wondering if I would have the courage to say: Put me in the presence of the most powerful ruler of the known world to witness to him and his courtiers, all the while gazing out over the Mediterranean toward Rome. This was neither a tactical error nor an impetuous decision but rather an act of obedience to the Lord's revelation in Acts 23.11: Paul would be a witness for Him in Rome.

Courage and fortitude figure large in decision-making, traits no doubt displayed by Paul in this courtroom scene. But logic also plays a role: Paul knows if he goes to Jerusalem and the extraordinary measures of security afforded him in Acts 23 are not repeated, he will likely be ambushed and killed. If he goes to Rome and is not well received, he is again likely to meet a mortal fate. His stage and impact will both be greater if he goes to Rome, so he chooses Rome. Thinking a decision through logically may make its resolution easier to reach but not any easier to execute. Many notable political and business figures speak openly about "going with my gut feeling", which could involve emotions, instincts, and inner drive; others, particularly in the world of sports and manufacturing, are data-driven, crunching the numbers to come up with a rational and evidentiary-based conclusion. Judging from the responses he gives from Acts 23, Paul incorporates both in his decision to appeal to Caesar.

Lines on Leadership
Reflect on a decision that turned out to be pivotal or memorable. Was it based on emotion and instinct or logic? What is your default mode for decision-making, to trust the numbers or go with intuition? Or a blend of the two?

_____

_____

++

Acts 26---Highlights: Paul's defense before Festus and Agrippa

This is the third Acts narrative of Paul's conversion experience and the second time he has personally recounted it. This account is by a man at peace with his persona and his place in the world. He provides a portrait of his life before, during, and after the conversion with great precision. He appeals to Agrippa's ego and his royal position by often referring to his kingly title; he is not preaching to gain his freedom but theirs from sin.

Agrippa and Festus are clearly surprised at this "defense" Paul mounts; in all likelihood, if Paul had pled more strongly about his innocence than the attempt to show Jesus as the fulfillment of all the prophecies Jews had longed for, he would have gone free (vs. 31-32). Festus protests in v. 24 that Paul's great learning has driven him mad, and Agrippa, in v. 28, deflects the proceedings by saying he is almost persuaded to accept Paul's claims about Jesus as true.

Paul speaks honestly about his zeal to capture and silence Christians before his conversion. In this instance, it is entirely possible as he told of hunting them down, he was channeling memories of Stephen's defense (see Acts 7 entry), and the story comes full circle: after seeing a young man speak so forcefully and clearly about Christ, knowing the outcome of his testimony, Paul now stands in the same scenario. He gives the "good confession", something he refers to later in his ministry to young Timothy as he exhorts Timothy to do the same thing whenever the time would come (1 Tim. 6.12-13).

Lines on Leadership
Just a few chapters previous to this speech, we read the letter sent by the Roman tribune Claudius Lysias (Acts 23.26-30). In it, he made sure he was seen in the best light possible, conveniently omitting the fact that he almost had Paul scourged before discovering he was a Roman citizen. Paul does not try to burnish his image or boost his personal stock; he does not withhold the damning truth about his own actions. Indeed, he shares his despicable crusade against Christians in detail to show how off-kilter his zeal and resolve had become.
Throughout history, when a strategic moment had arrived, men and women from the Diet at Worms to the bridge at Selma, AL have decided to take the courageous stand knowing the consequences that awaited them. Martin Luther and Martin Luther King had their respective shortcomings but proved true to

their convictions when the situation arose. Paul looked to Stephen, and Timothy was encouraged to look to Paul as an example. Who will you emulate as your model when your turn comes to take a stand for the truth? Is your leadership such that others would be inspired to take a stand for the truth as they follow you?

_____

_____

++

Acts 27---Highlights: Paul's travels and adventures on the way to Rome as a prisoner

<u>This extraordinary chapter is one of the most detailed and action-packed in the NT and serves as a case study in crisis leadership</u>. The richness and variety of the vocabulary describing the ships, the rigging, the maneuvers, and the locations indicate that Luke was not just recounting others' collected accounts but was personally knowledgeable about all aspects of sailing. Indeed, most of the "we" sections of Acts from chapter 16 on involve maritime travel. Luke's intimate narrative not only displays familiarity with but first-hand experience on the high seas and heightens the unfolding drama.

During the ill-fated voyage, Paul slowly gains the confidence of both the Roman centurion named Julius and the passengers (see his words in vs. 10, 21-26, 31, 33-34). He exhibits shrewdness and compassion in the course of the weeks-long crossing of dangerous waters during a dangerous season. He demands neither their acknowledgment of his leadership nor acceptance of his Lord Jesus. He does not claim any authority by virtue of his position or reputation but rather earns their trust over the course of the trip.

Paul gives us a prime example of how to give testimony to our relationship with Christ amid adversity and crisis. He does not try to elevate his own importance; he does not speak from false modesty; he simply and clearly speaks with conviction about what God has shown him and that God is not just interested in saving His "own", but His grace extends to the entire crew. They can follow his advice and live or perish. At all times, he considers the needs of all the various elements of crew and prisoners. All his training, his past trips, his fluency in several languages, and his prior multiple times of deliverance from adversity in prisons, stonings, and riots come together as he leads this group to safety amidst impossible circumstances and odds.

<u>Lines on Leadership</u>
Paul wisely took time to foster a relationship with the centurion. At the beginning of the relationship (vs. 9-11), the centurion was more inclined to listen to the ship's pilot than Paul. By verse 31, he is heeding Paul's admonition to keep the crew in the boat against their wishes. By v. 43, the centurion saves the entire group of passengers' lives by keeping the soldiers from slaughtering them (if prisoners escaped, it would surely end the soldier's careers and likely their own lives) and primarily to preserve Paul ("but the centurion, wanting to bring Paul safely through . . ."). Paul multiplied the scope and the strength of his leadership by investing in and gaining the trust of the centurion. In which superior/adversary/possible ally do you need to invest time and trust in order to multiply your leadership? Would you be one of those huddling in the corner of the ship, hoping the soldiers and the crew didn't see you, or would you stand up and show the group a way that, while no guarantee, might be a way out?

_____

_____

++

Acts 28---Highlights: Paul heals and is healed at Malta, arrives in Italy, and enters confinement in Rome

The book of Acts ends as it began, with the declaration that the Gospel of the Kingdom of God is for all men, Jews and Gentiles (v. 28), which Paul bolsters with an oft-quoted OT passage from Isaiah 6 about the stubbornness and refusal of God's chosen people to accept this message.

Paul exemplifies consistent servant leadership throughout this chapter as he gathered sticks for the fire (v.3, he had just led the group to safety through a wretched shipwreck and deserved the respect of others doing the work), healed the father of a leading civic figure (v.8), and then received and helped all on the island who came for healing. He could have easily said he was "off duty", that he did not want to be deterred from his final destination, or that he didn't have time for the "little people" since he was about to hit the "big stage" of Rome, but he graciously spent time with groups of believers who met him at every port on the way from Malta to the capital.

Upon his arrival in Rome, he settled in with a Roman guard in his private quarters and called for the "leading men of the Jews" to share with them why he had come to the Eternal City. Notice he couches his speech in terms familiar to them (v. 17-20, speaks of the 'hope of Israel' (v.20) without naming it as Jesus) and appeals to their sense of a common tradition and heritage ("I have done nothing against <u>our</u> people, or the customs of <u>our</u> fathers," v. 17). When they return in large numbers, presumably coming and going over the course of two years (v.30), Paul uses every opportunity to share Jesus from the Old Testament.

The four Pauline prison epistles are Ephesians (treatise on what the church is and does), Philippians (servant leadership and deep abiding joy), Colossians (brilliant contrast of competing worldviews), and Philemon (a master class on evangelism and relationships). Instead of doubting God's decision for him to come to Rome, moping about his diminished visibility, or wringing his hands every time one of the Jews in Rome rejected his preaching about the kingdom of God and Jesus (v.31), Paul takes the circumstances dealt him and remains consistent in his message and life.

<u>Lines on Leadership</u>
It was a pivotal life point for our family when we had to leave the European mission field in the late 80s to return to the states for medical reasons. I thought my ministry was diminished and restricted. I had no idea I would wind up as a campus minister at a Baptist undergraduate college where I would have the privilege of discipling hundreds and multiplying myself on the mission field through students who have far surpassed me in terms of effectiveness and longevity. This parallels but in no way equals what happened to Paul. What major life change looked like a reduction or even a cessation of your duties but turned out later to be a shift that created new ways to share your message or created new audiences?

_____

_____

++

LETTER TO THE ROMANS

Intro: The book of Romans has been called the "most profound work in existence[1]." This epistle is considered the pinnacle of Paul's NT letters. All opera singers have specific operas they wait to undertake until they have reached a certain level of competence, maturity, and ability to bear up well under its import. Most preachers view Romans in the same light: not because of its complexity but rather its gravitas. It singlehandedly spawned the Reformation as Luther wrestled with the first chapter to understand how man lives by faith and not by works. Romans 1-11 is a single comprehensive treatment of the universal need for Christ; its apex is the 8th chapter which borders on sublimeness. Romans 12-16 is the practical section of the epistle where Paul shows how a person's faith in Christ unfolds in everyday life, the *Auswirkung* of one's salvation. All of Paul's epistles are arranged in the NT by length, not by date of authorship, with Romans being the longest and Philemon the shortest.

++

Romans 1---Highlights: just live by faith, the gospel is the power unto salvation, the consequences of unbelief

Vs. 16-17—"For I am not ashamed of the gospel, for it is the power of God for salvation to everyone who believes, to the Jew first and also to the Greek. For in it the righteousness of God is revealed from faith to faith; as it is written, 'But the righteous man shall live by faith.'"

Every good research proposal, dissertation, essay, or organizational white paper has a thesis statement or hypothesis, that one assertion or axiom on which the author's total argument depends and from which the rest of the paper's thoughts and conclusions flow. The book of Romans is generally acknowledged as Paul's masterpiece and one of the high points of the NT. While several of his epistles are written to local congregations and address local issues, Romans resembles more of a general treatise than a personal pastoral admonishment. The book of Romans is essential to NT theology, and Rom. 1.16-17 is its thesis statement.

The gospel (the Good News that God has come to us in Jesus Christ and through His death, burial, and resurrection we can obtain forgiveness of sin and eternal life) in vs. 16-17 is:

1) <u>The power of God unto salvation</u>---It is not to be adorned, camouflaged, diluted, spiced up, or soft-pedaled: It is pure and simple the vehicle through which God announces His salvation has been granted.

2) <u>Where the righteousness of God is revealed</u>---When our fallen nature is transformed by hearing and responding to the gospel, we start to realize by faith the true nature of God as love and grace, that through some inexplicable depth of love for us as Creator He became our Redeemer in Christ Jesus. Matt. 5.8 states, "The pure in heart [those transformed by the gospel] shall see God." The gospel saves and then helps us see Him more clearly as He really is.

3) <u>The catalyst for a life of faith</u>. The gospel saves, then helps us see more clearly the one who saved us, then sanctifies us as we live daily a life of faith directed toward the God who offers that Good News (see 1 Cor. 1 entry).

<u>Lines on Leadership</u>
What seminal statement defines your organization? Do the branches and divisions of your organization flow from that statement? Does every member/employee know this statement? Can they articulate what it means to them and to the

organization? Do they act and decide with this statement in mind?

_____

_____

++

Romans 2---Highlights: everyone is without excuse

Vs. 28-29 "For he is not a Jew who is one outwardly; neither is circumcision that which is outward in the flesh. But he is a Jew who is one inwardly, and circumcision is that which is of the heart, by the Spirit, not by the letter; and his praise is not from men, but from God."

<u>The law requires what it cannot produce itself</u>. Obedience to and fulfillment of the requirements of the law are not found in ritual but in repentance, in submitting to the Spirit of God and allowing Him to transform a person's life.

In a corporate setting, I can adhere to the company dress code, wear the company logo on my suit lapel (or, for younger generations, have it tattooed in a conspicuous place), memorize the company policy manual, and still not be a "company man or woman". Countless employees can spout the company mission statement to insure their place of employment but loathe everything it stands for. Outward conformity is not a reliable indicator of inward compliance, as evidenced in the proverbial situation when the mother demands a young toddler sit down in his high chair, and the resultant glare says, "I may be sitting down on the outside, but I'm standing up on the inside."

This translates to a church setting as well. As I talk with pastors in our association, I often hear about church members who know the language (Christianese), know the songs, and know the routine but are clueless as to the who and the why they go through the motions and other than the social acceptance or some faint hope they are doing something helpful.

<u>Lines on Leadership</u>
Paul spoke of circumcision of the heart to denote an inward transformation. In this instance, the inward transformation results in outward actions, the reverse of doing certain rites or rituals in order to hopefully effect an inward transformation.

This is light years beyond external vs. internal motivation. Do people in your group work together merely "to keep their place in line" or because they truly believe in your company/church/Cause? As a leader, how do you distinguish between the two groups?

_____

_____

++

Romans 3---Highlights: universal effects of sin, justification by faith

v. 20 "... by the works of the Law no flesh will be justified in His sight; for through the Law comes the knowledge of sin. [21] But now apart from the Law the righteousness of God has been manifested being witnessed by the Law and the Prophets, [22] even the righteousness of God through faith in Jesus Christ for all those who believe; for there is no distinction; [23] for all have sinned and come short of the glory of God . . ."

One of the staple plot twists for literature and cinema is the person who cheats the system, saves his crew at the last minute by finding a heretofore-hidden loophole in the system, or devises a way to make the system work for him. While this makes for exciting narratives and increased ticket sales, it does not apply to real-life or scriptural truth. Notice the all-encompassing words in the passage quoted above: "<u>no</u> flesh", "<u>all</u> those who believe", and "<u>all</u> have sinned". There is no exception; there is no escape clause within the closed sphere of man's efforts to find a way out on his own. Paul builds a case for the inevitability of it from both the Psalms and Isaiah (vs. 4, 10-18) and also provides the solution to that inevitability: it is not a way to cheat the system, find a loophole, or make the system work his way. The solution is not found in the Law or man's efforts but in a life of faith in the promises of God (see Rom. 4 entry). The answer is not within a system or within man; it is a gift from God accepted by faith.

Life principles apply to work, family, or personal fulfillment. They are true across the board, and the person who tries to outsmart or outmaneuver those winds up on the short end of things. It boils down to who makes the rules of engagement. If every person dictated the consequences of his own actions, the world would be in total chaos. Someone has to set the parameters to maintain order and sanity within the organization; it is why laws are written, to maintain order in society, and to provide for personal safety, interests, and aspirations. In an organization, it can be by committee, by policy, by tradition, by fiat, or by whatever the CEO says, goes.

Having the absolute last word in any given situation sounds like a dream for most leaders, but in Daniel 6, it backfired on King Darius. According to "the law of the Medes and Persians", whatever a ruler decreed or signed was inviolable even by himself. To save a friend (Daniel), Darius could not undo his injunction and signature. It took an intervention by the Almighty. God's Word will never expire (Is. 40.8). God never goes against His Word. He alone can create a way to allow "all have sinned and fall short of the glory of God" to find that glory. It is not an escape, a loophole, or a way to game the system. It was not His patchwork on-the-fly improvisation to make up for an inferior system of man's creation with no way to achieve salvation on his own. God's method "from the foundation of the world" (Eph. 1.4) was to have Christ provide the way to achieve what man on his own could never do.

Lines on Leadership
What have you done to create an atmosphere in your organization of making consequences known and how they will be enforced? What process or mechanism exists within your organization for forgiveness and for redemption, and how does a person receive it?

_____

_____

++

Romans 4---Highlights: justification by faith in the OT; Abraham's faith reckoned as righteousness

v.3 "Abraham believed God, and it was reckoned to him as righteousness." vs. 21-24 "... being fully assured that what He had promised, He was able also to perform. Therefore also it was reckoned to him as righteousness. Now not for his sake only was it written, that it was reckoned to him, but for our sake also, to whom it will be reckoned, as those who believe in Him who raised Jesus our Lord from the dead."

It would be hard to overestimate the importance and impact of Abraham. Judaism, Islam, and Christianity all find their roots in this ancient patriarch. The distinctive of Christianity, however, is the topic of Romans 4.

The life of Abraham is chronicled in Genesis 12-25. He was wealthy and influential. He dealt with kings of the earth (Gen. 12.15-20) and spoke directly to the King of the universe (Gen. 12.7; 15.1ff). His fortune was considerable, his fame widespread, and his family tree provided the seeds for three religions. Judaism, Islam, and Christianity all count Abraham as an important link in their respective lineages. Yet what Paul writes about Abraham in Rom. 4 as enduring is not his fortune, fame, or even his family, but his faith. Paul quotes the OT in chapter 1 that the righteous shall live by faith. He continues to show throughout the book of Romans that faith in the promises of God is the distinctive of Abraham's life and the model for every believer, that he/she should place their faith in the promises of the Lord.

Lines on Leadership

Abraham could not have known during his lifetime that millennia would pass, and yet his life would be revered on a global scale. His decision-making was often questionable (passing off his wife as his sister, not once but twice, Gen. 12 and 20; trying to "help God" by getting Hagar to bear a son for him, Gen. 16). He was an obscure merchant wandering in search of a land and a promise's fulfillment he would never find (Heb. 11.13, 39-40).

The faith of Abraham, typified best by his almost sacrifice of Isaac (Gen. 22), is his greatest contribution to subsequent generations. He was willing to entrust himself to the guidance of God, even to the point of sacrificing what was most precious to him. As mentioned elsewhere (see Mk. 2, Lk. 17, 1 Cor. 13 entries), it was not the amount of faith nor was it the quality of Abraham's faith that mattered; it was the object of his faith (God) and his reliance on His provision that was reckoned to Abraham as righteousness (vs. 3, 21-24).

As a leader, what has been your lifelong quest? Most prized possession or accomplishment? Are you willing to place it, a career, rewards, or even your life on the line to show your faith in the providence of God? Are you willing to do that once or multiple times to forge a lifestyle of reliance and faith in Him?

_____

_____

++

Romans 5---Highlights: the results of God's justification; His Spirit poured out in our hearts

v.8 "But God demonstrates His own love toward us, in that while we were yet sinners, Christ died for us."

"The person who takes personal responsibility to live into the future in a transformative way, in relationship to others in the system, is the leader[1]." A collective, collaborative method of leadership is suitable for many 21st-century scenarios and the preferred choice of leadership for younger generations. There will, however, always be a need for the one person who initiates action, introduces bold thinking, or offers a way no one else either could take or had previously shown to the group. The remarkable aspect of v. 8 (from a <u>human</u> perspective) is that Christ took the path he took before anyone indicated they would follow Him. Today's leader takes polls, conducts interest groups, and consults big data before making any decision or launching in a new direction with his organization. From a heavenly perspective, Christ died for us as part of an eternal plan (see Rom. 3 entry; Eph. 1.4). It was not a calculated risk; it was part of His unfathomable obedience to the will of God the Father.

As a leader, I would in no way compare myself to Christ or my mission to His Kingdom. But many times, as a leader, I have to launch out and initiate a direction for the organization no one else sees or can envision. It is a solitary launch, as noted repeatedly in v. 15 ("one Man"), v. 17 ("the One, Jesus Christ"), and v. 19 ("the One"), that only He could make.

Bolsinger in *Canoeing the Mountains* prefaces the quote used above with, "because we are hard-wired to resist change, every living system requires someone to live into and lead the transformation necessary to take us into the future we are resisting[2]." Newtonian physics dictates that more energy is needed to take a body from being stationary to being in motion than the energy needed to keep the body in motion. I know the energy, prayer, time, money, and creativity it takes to help a church find renewal and experience new life; to lead mankind to a transformational salvation on an eternal, cosmic basis is beyond my comprehension. A key phrase in Bolsinger's second statement is "requires someone to live into". Christ did not make salvation an offer from afar, a transactional "deal". He came to dwell among us (Jn. 1.14) and empathize with our plight (Heb. 4.15) before He offered to save us "while we were yet sinners".

Lines on Leadership
What is something you feel so singularly passionate about that you are willing to make it your life's work, even if no one else is on board with it? For those in the twilight of their effective leadership years, what was something you felt so singularly passionate about you were willing to make it your life's work, even if no one else was on board with it?

_____

_____

++

Romans 6---Highlights: meaning of baptism, inevitable master, one verse gospel

v. 23 "For the wages of sin is death, but the free gift of God is eternal life in Christ Jesus our Lord." v. 16b, ". . . when you present yourselves to someone as slaves for obedience, you are slaves of the one whom you obey, either of sin resulting in death, or of obedience resulting in righteousness."

"Well, it may be the devil or it may the Lord, but you're gonna have to serve somebody[1]."

Every teenager dreams and schemes toward the day they are out from under parental, educational, and vocational authority. They operate under the illusion that they will one day be "free" in their minds, meaning from constraint. It would be understandable to read v. 23 as being freed from sin, unshackled, liberated . . . and all of that is true. But nothing in the verse promises an unbridled, unfettered future answering to no one but oneself.

The gift of eternal life is indeed free, but when read in the context of the entire chapter, it is apparent the Lordship of Christ comes into play. Going backward through the chapter, <u>the topic raised by v. 23 is not only what I've been freed **from** but also what I've been freed **to**</u> (see Gal. 5, Col. 1 entries). I have been freed to finally become what I was created to be, a citizen of the Kingdom of God. I have been freed from the control of sin over my life and willingly taken on a new Master of my soul. Vs. 16 and 18 declare I was a slave of sin and now have become a slave of righteousness (see 2 Cor. 2.14 and Col. 1.13).

I would never second guess anyone writing under the direct inspiration of God, but in our current society, the term 'slave' sounds negative, punitive, and downright terrifying. The emphasis needs to be taken off the individual and placed on the new Master. In a quick comparison of their track records throughout the biblical narrative, how is a choice between sin and the Savior as a master anything but a no-brainer? One lord is bent on dominating and crushing me, one bent on serving me and sacrificing Himself for my release from the previous one; I'll gladly serve that kind of master—and trust that He can do a much better job than either me or sin managing my life. The sooner I quit chafing at the thought, "I gotta serve somebody", and realize what a privilege it is to serve and work with Christ in His Kingdom, the sooner I'll learn to rejoice at this wonderful offer and live it out.

Lines on Leadership
What have you done as a leader to let your organization know you provide an environment for growth as well as security? How do your followers know you have their back? How have you combined clear choices and requirements for your organization with sacrificial love and devotion for them?

_____

_____

+++

Romans 7---Highlights: conflict of the two natures in man
Everyone has the same primary conversation partner. No matter where you live, what age you have reached, what profession you pursued, or what friendships you nurtured, everyone has the same person they talk to more than any other person. That conversation partner is self.

This is compounded for a Christian by the NT teaching that a person who is born again has two selves, an old or former self (Rom. 6.6, Eph. 4.22, Col. 3.9) and a new self (Eph. 4.24, Col. 3.1, 10). The ongoing dialogue within a person of these two selves is central to this chapter but maddeningly difficult to articulate. On the one hand, Paul begins the chapter with a description of a married woman being obligated to her husband until he dies, and then she is free to marry another, which dovetails with the word image of baptism in chapter six, of dying to the old self and being raised to new life with a new self. Both of those analogies talk about the finalities of death and new life.

Yet Paul willingly acknowledges in vs. 14-25 that the old self doesn't go quietly off into oblivion but instead demands and holds onto "squatter's rights". To add yet another analogy to this scrambled panoply of word images, it is like the deed of ownership to the house called 'my life' has been transferred to another owner, yet the former occupant refuses to leave the premises. He flits from room to room, demanding to be allowed to stay and continually disrupts the new owner's plans.

Preachers quote parts of vs. 24 and 25, "Wretched man that I am! Who will set me free from the body of this death? Thanks be to God through Christ Jesus our Lord!" to get a rousing amen and approval from the congregation. Yet the pesky conclusion of v. 25 cannot be ignored, "So then, on the one hand I myself with my mind am serving the law of God, but on the other, with my flesh the law of sin."

This is not so much a dichotomy of being as it is a continuation of chapter six (always read in context) and a springboard into the glorious peak of Romans, chapter eight. Paul is pointing out the futility of life if we live it in a closed system of thinking that I'm in control of things, and the struggle is purely internal, between the old self and the new self (the OT equivalent is the book of Ecclesiastes: if the perspective is the repeated phrase "under the sun," meaning I look at life strictly from an earthly perspective, it is futile; if I allow a heavenly perspective, to fear God and obey His commandments as in Eccl. 12, then I have hope). Sin is in control; the Law was given to point out its sinfulness and expose the destruction it wishes to wreak, yet it cannot free the person from sin's grip. There is an external way out, one alone (Jn. 14.6), and His name is Christ Jesus. The dilemma Paul describes in chapter seven is intractable unless the person acknowledges the entrance of Christ into his life and lives out that new life in the manner described in chapter eight.

Lines on Leadership

As a leader, have you ever taken time to write down the ongoing dialogue between the old self and new self? To see on paper the warring thoughts that race through your head daily? To see how much those thoughts sap your time and energy away from leading your organization forward? To Whom or to what do you reach out to help propel you forward in life? Describe in detail this struggle occurring between destructive and constructive forces at work within your organization.

_____

_____

++

Romans 8---Highlights: our deliverance and victory in Christ

v. 1-2 "There is therefore now no condemnation for those who are in Christ Jesus, for the law of the Spirit in Christ Jesus has set you free from the law of sin and of death."

The 1986 Oscar-winning movie, "The Mission", portrays in a visually stunning fashion the corrupt relationship between politics and religion in the European colonialization of South America. Robert De Niro's character Mendoza is a man of action who has committed grievous offenses. He seeks release from his guilt and follows a priest deep in the jungle, where he has heard he can deal with his past, present, and future. In a rugged and brutal display of penance, he carries a huge cumbersome weight attached to him by ropes up cliffs, through the jungle and across streams. The weight contains all his worldly possessions, including his armor and weapons and makes the journey laborious and even dangerous for the entire group. The climax of the scene is when a member of the indigenous tribe (which is helping the priest, his order, and Mendoza to scale the heights), in a dramatic and sweeping gesture, finally slashes the rope connecting Mendoza to the weight that besets him and the group. It tumbles down the path into the rapids, never to be seen again. The released misery, the background music, the intensity of the moment, the tears of terror turning slowly into tears of joy, and the fellowship of forgiven brothers embracing him is an unforgettable moment[1].

If we are set free from condemnation through Christ Jesus, can anything return us to condemnation? Paul ends Rom. 8 with a resounding 'no'; nothing external or internal, nothing present, past, or future, nothing in this world or ones to come can separate us from the love of God in Christ Jesus (vs. 37-39).

Lines on Leadership
It is said the hardest person to forgive is oneself. In a life of leadership, I will inevitably think and act in ways that are regrettable. They can debilitate and neutralize my effectiveness if I cannot get past them. This is not a call to dismiss them, forget them, or pretend they never happened. Romans 8 shows Christ's incredible ability through His sacrifice and resurrection to release me from the requirements of the law and the wrath of God, so much so that nothing can separate me from His love (including my failures, my sin, my 'regrettables'). A leader who can go forward with this confidence (that everything ever done or will be done is covered by Him, and not even the leader can separate himself from Christ's love) can lead with freedom. This does not mean my thoughts and actions are without consequences; I may still pay the price for past indiscretions or poor decisions and even suffer loss because of them, but I can still have them forgiven by God; that is indeed priceless.

What weighs you down and neutralizes your ability to lead in terms of past sins, past decisions, and past situations? Can you accept His offer so magnificently described in Romans 8 of no condemnation by and no separation from the love of Christ?

_____

_____

++

Romans 9---Highlights: Grace and Israel

v.3 "For I could wish that I myself were accursed, separated from Christ for the sake of my brethren, my kinsmen according to the flesh."

The previous chapters build this incredible narrative of a life-changing and mind-bending new life in Christ. The power and the preciousness of that new life are repeated over and over. Chapters 1-7 are a cohesive, comprehensive argument that no one sector of mankind has a credible exemption from sin and its results. Chapter 8 is the epitome of what life in Christ is. All is well, cue the hallelujah chorus.

That choir comes to a jarring halt and collective stoppage of breath as Paul, instead of continuing the exultation of chapter 8, pauses to lament the inability of his kinsmen (Jews) to understand and embrace its truth. His sorrow is so overwhelming he utters the unthinkable in v. 3 that he would give up everything he has described in chapters 1-8 in order for his people to have their eyes opened and receive the gospel. The same sentiment is echoed in the OT in Exodus 32.32. Moses, thoroughly frustrated with his people for their stupidity (building the golden calf) and furious at Aaron for his utterly stupid reply (I threw it [gold] into the fire and out came the calf), could have understandably called for their wholesale destruction and a do-over (which God offered to do at another time and Moses refused). Instead, he rises to the response of a mature and long-term leader by saying, "But now, if Thou wilt, forgive their sin; and if not, please blot me out from Thy book which Thou hast written!" (Ex. 32.32)

God has a similar response to both men. In Ex. 32.34, God says to Moses, "But go now, lead the people where I told you." There is no explanation for their actions, no granting of Moses' request: stay on mission, stay on task. In Rom. 9, God shows Paul he is pleading for the wrong people group; to God, Israel is not an ethnic grouping or a specific geographic location but those who obey the commands of the Lord (vs. 6, 25-26, 32-33). Stay true to the mission I gave you, stay on task.

<u>Lines on Leadership</u>
As a leader, I am not very confident that if I reached a goal, achieved a long-cherished standing, or amassed a great fortune, I would be willing to give it for the sake of my appointed group. This causes me to ask myself two questions: 1) what price would I be willing to pay for an individual, a group, a company, or a church to come to its senses, repent, and start heading in the right direction (see Lk. 11 entry)? In light of Moses' and Paul's example, what question should I be asking if #1 is not the right question or about the right group?

_____

_____

+++

Romans 10---Highlights: further ramifications of salvation

v. 9 "if you confess with your mouth Jesus as Lord, and believe in your heart that God raised Him from the dead, you shall be saved." vs. 14b-15 "how shall they believe in him whom they have not heard? And how shall they hear without a preacher? And how shall they preach unless they are sent? Just as it is written, 'how beautiful are the feet of those who bring glad tidings of good things!'"

The pastor of one of our flagship churches was known throughout the larger area as a community pastor; he was everyone's pastor, young and old, attended countless civic events, was sought by all denominations to speak, and had a positive word for everyone (especially if they were fans of the Crimson Tide Alabama football team). His was the first voice I heard when our association called me to become their director. We became friends and were often in each other's office, home, and occasionally on the golf course together. We counseled, corrected, and encouraged each other.

In 2019, David developed pains and went from doctor to doctor until it was discovered the core cause of his discomfort was esophageal cancer. By the time it was discovered, it had metastasized into several organs. He and his wife decided not to begin treatment, knowing it was a matter of months before he would succumb to it. In Sept., he grew increasingly frail, and it was obvious the end was near. On his last night in his own house, several area pastors gathered at his home to pray over him. I have rarely heard such strong and personal prayers at one time. What broke the dam of emotion and honesty before God was when David stood, leaning on a walker as he admonished us to preach the gospel with our last breath. It was a holy moment for us all.

The days ticked away, and he refused treatment and food while in the hospital. The last time I saw him in that hospital room, he was surrounded by family and friends. His voice was hoarse, but he was aware of our presence. On his nearby bed table was a stack of gospel tracts; he gave one to every new hospital employee who came to his aid. Even near death, he shared the Good News with anyone he could. As he was dying, he lived out his challenge to us a few days earlier. That day as his attention was diverted to his son in conversation, I quietly kissed his exposed foot and mouthed the words of v. 15 to him, 'How beautiful are the feet of those who bring Good News.' His last acts were emblematic of his evangelistic nature. It was simply who he was, someone always ready to share Christ and His gospel with every man, woman, and child.

Lines on Leadership
What matters most to you as a leader? If that subject will be on your lips near death, is it the main topic of your thoughts, conversations, and actions in the midst of your life?
_____
_____
++

Romans 11---Highlights: Israel and its salvation
v.36 "For from Him and through Him and to Him are all things. To Him be the glory forever. Amen."
A book I give away at every opportunity is *The Call: Finding and Fulfilling the Central Purpose of Your Life* by Os Guinness (no relation to the beverage). A theology of "the call" is, at times, elusive and mysterious. Consider the following perspective: "Our primary calling as followers of Christ is by Him, to Him, and for Him. First and foremost, we are called to Someone (God), not to something (such as motherhood, politics, or teaching) or to somewhere (such as the inner city or Outer Mongolia[1].") The Latin word 'to call' is *vocare* from which we derive the English word vocation, which should mean our calling. Somewhere along the way (Industrial Revolution?), our vocation began to be defined by what we did to earn a living. Here are typical opening lines among males: "Hi, my name is ____." "And

what do you do for a living?" We are identified by our company, our skill set, and our location (i.e., a dairy farmer from Monroe County), but our primary identity is a relationship to God (1 Jn. 4.19).

God calls us primarily to Himself, not a task or a location. When we are rightly related to Him, what we do, when we do it, and where we do it will fall in line. "For you have been called for this purpose, since Christ also suffered for you, leaving you an example for you to follow in His steps" (1 Pet. 2.21). His call to His side does not guarantee success; it guarantees eternal life. The 1 Peter verse is in the context of suffering while fulfilling the will of God. <u>The will of God is not a sequence of events (something) but a relationship with Him. Likewise, the Kingdom of God is not a location (somewhere) but a relationship with Him. You are first and foremost called to Him</u>.

Our speech often betrays a hierarchy of calling, as if the layperson in the pew occupies the lowest rung on a ladder that usually goes upward like this: nursery worker, Bible teacher, deacon, pastor, home missionary, international missionary. In the business world or in the military, there is a definite hierarchy of authority or responsibility from assistants and associates (enlisted men) to executive vice presidents (officers) to CEOs (generals, admirals). This should not be confused with calling. We all have the same primary calling to His side, and we need to understand our Lord is dynamic, not static. Ro. 11.36 denotes a God that is active and on the move. We need to get in step and in sync with Him.

Archbishop William Temple underscored this danger sternly. To make the choice of career or profession on selfish grounds, without a true sense of calling, is "probably the greatest single sin any young person can commit, for it is the deliberate withdrawal from allegiance to God of the greatest part of time and strength².″ (The Call, p. 46)

      Our calling is from Him, through Him, and to Him. (Rom. 11.29-36). To Him be the glory forever.

Lines on Leadership
How would you describe your relationship to God, your calling from God, and the relationship of both to your leadership?
_____
_____

++

Romans 12---Highlights: the practical consequences of salvation
The formula for Paul's epistles presents theological content and then transitions to its practical applications. Romans 12 merits 10+ installments on its own but will be confined to one unified concept. In great cities, there is one main place where all rail lines converge and re-emerge, such as New York City's Grand Central Station. A large airport operates in a similar fashion; in the body's nervous system, the brain is the master cluster of neurons, dendrites, and axons, with signals constantly traveling in both directions. Romans 12 serves such a function: It is one of the most densely packed NT chapters regarding practical areas of everyday living and the gospel's impact on them. Each topic mentioned by Paul has multiple passages in other NT passages where he or other writers expand that topic mentioned in Rom. 12. Here is my dozen with partial examples; feel free to construct another:

      v. 1-my life is to be a living sacrifice to God (Eph. 4.1, Gal. 2.20, Col. 3.3)

      v. 2-be transformed instead of conformed to the world (Eph. 4.17-18, 1 Pet. 1.14-16) vs. 3, 16-have an accurate sense of self-worth compared to Christ (Phil. 2.1-11)

vs. 4-8—benefit the body of Christ with spiritual gifts (1 Cor. 12; Eph. 4; 1 Pet. 4.10-11)

v. 9---flee from evil; embrace good (1 Tim. 4.12; 2 Tim. 2.22)

v. 10---be devoted to and love one another (Jn. 13.34-35)

v. 11---serve others proactively (Mt. 20.28, Gal. 5.13)

v. 12---exercise hope, perseverance, devoted prayer (Col. 4.2-4, Heb. 10.32-36, 2 Pet. 1.6)

v. 13---practice hospitality as a virtue (1 Tim. 3.2, Titus 1.8, Heb. 13.2, 1 Pet. 4.9)

v. 14, 17, 19-21—bless one's enemies without retaliation (Mt. 5.44, Lk. 6.27-35)

v. 15—empathize with the pain and joy of others (I Cor. 12.26)

v. 18—be at peace with all men (Eph. 4.29-32)

Lines on Leadership
Where is the nexus/reference point/info hub where information, policies, directives, and strategy flow in your organization? If this list was used as a diagnostic by a review board of your leadership, how would you score?
_____
_____
+++

Romans 13---Highlights: relationships to God and government

On Monday, Sept. 19, 2022, the state funeral for Queen Elizabeth II was watched by over two billion people on various media, making it one of the largest audiences in broadcast history. She reigned for 70 years as the longest-tenured monarch in British history, passing on to glory at the age of 96. It was a remarkable combination of pageantry, pomp, and personal witness for Jesus Christ. She approved every detail of the ceremonies down to every hymn, and every hymn sung was clearly chosen to give Christ all the glory. The Archbishop of Canterbury provided both a tribute to Elizabeth and a clear gospel call using her life as a shining example. Westminster Abbey was the setting for the funeral, and the committal service was in St. Georges Chapel within the confines of Windsor Castle. At both services, truth from Romans 13 was on full display.

v. 8, "Let no debt remain outstanding, except the continuing debt to love one another, for whoever loves others has fulfilled the law." (NIV). "Owe nothing to anyone except to love one another; for he who loves his neighbor has fulfilled the law." (NASB) The Archbishop shared during his sermon that, "Her Late Majesty famously declared on a 21st birthday broadcast that her whole life would be dedicated to serving the Nation and Commonwealth. Rarely has such a promise been so well kept!" He further added, "In all cases those who serve will be loved and remembered when those who cling to power and privileges are long forgotten[1]."

v. 1 "Let every person be in subjection to the governing authorities. For there is no authority except from God, and those which exist are established by God." At Westminster, the Archbishop said, "In 1953 the Queen began her Coronation with silent prayer, just there at the High Altar. Her allegiance to God was given before any person gave allegiance to her[2]."

Just before the queen's coffin was lowered to the vault below St. Georges Chapel, a silent ceremony took place that symbolized Rom. 13.1. The crown jeweler, with great care and devotion, removed the scepter, the orb (a globe with a cross on its top), and the crown from atop the coffin (each affixed in an inconspicuous way) and after each symbol of power was removed it was given to the priest. The priest then slowly placed each symbol upon a pillow on the altar. When all three rested on the altar, the off-screen commentator remarked the obvious, that the symbols of power were placed on the altar to signify all power and authority come from the sovereign power and authority of God.

<u>Lines on Leadership</u>
At some point, every leader must step aside, step down, or pass away. Will people honor your leadership as one of service and devotion or otherwise? When was the last time you acknowledged to the Father that all you have and ever will have comes from His hand?

_____

_____

++

Romans 14---Highlights: principles of conscience
     v. 17 "for the kingdom of God is not eating and drinking, but righteousness and peace and joy in the Holy Spirit." Romans 14 parallels 1 Cor. 8 on not becoming a stumbling block to others. It explores more dimensions than just eating meat sacrificed to idols (1 Cor. 8) and how one's witness can be neutralized or negated by doing something perfectly legitimate (from a biblical standpoint or from a personal conscience standpoint). I have to learn to manage my desires or preferences for the good of the organization and for the good of the Kingdom.
     One issue we encountered during our years of working alongside German Baptists was the issue of alcohol at meals. Biblically speaking, one cannot make a case for total abstinence; overseers and deacons in 1 Tim. 3 are both required to not be

addicted or given to much wine and not be teetotalers. I grew up in a home where my mother was a caterer; I had tasted many liqueurs and alcoholic beverages, helping prepare and serve meals. I was never drawn to them, and from a personal conscience perspective, I was neither in favor nor opposed to them.

But I knew we were in Europe to represent 45,000+ Southern Baptist churches and many thousands of church members who were adamant about total abstinence. Practicality dictated it was impossible to explain otherwise to every one of the fifteen million Southern Baptist individuals who supported us as international missionaries, so it was easier not to imbibe at all. But the local culture in which we ministered saw absolutely nothing ethical or sinful about having wine or beer at a meal. If a neighbor or even a German Baptist church member offered a beverage they had purchased just for our evening meal, with us as honored guests, to not imbibe could be impolite to offensive and was viewed at the least as asocial. What were we to do?

I was there to represent my denomination, but also to represent my Lord and honor His Word, to avoid (as I read Rom. 14 and 1 Cor. 8) making my refusals a stumbling block to conversations or relationships that could lead a person to Christ. After prayerful reflection, we adopted the following practice; in our own home we would not offer anything alcoholic, guests or no guests. If we went to another home and were offered an alcoholic beverage, we asked if we might have water instead (most homes had some brand of Mineralwasser on hand). If they consented, the situation could be averted. If we sensed there was puzzlement but openness to discussing why, we gently discussed the subject and tried our best to respect the culture and heritage (for example, our landlord was a vintner, see John 15 entry). If we sensed an affront, we accepted their offer.

I learned to appreciate my German Baptist pastoral colleagues as men of God. I admitted a bit of initial hesitancy to fellowship with them when every one of them quaffed a brew at our first large meeting. But when I heard them pray in earnestness and fervor and saw the way they shared their faith openly on the street and in the course of their daily lives, I learned the deeper dimension of Rom. 14.17, that the kingdom of God was not eating and drinking, or festivals and rituals (Colossians 2.16-23) but love and peace and joy in the Holy Spirit.

<u>Lines on Leadership</u>
You may or may not agree with my stance described above. At some point in your leadership you were or will be confronted by a "damned if you do, damned if you don't" scenario. Your personal influence in other lives sometimes clashes with your professional initiatives. How did/will you relate Romans 14 to that intractable situation?

_____
_____

++

Romans 15---Highlights: the denial to benefit others; missionary intent

vs. 18-20 "For I will not presume to speak of anything except what Christ has accomplished through me, resulting in the obedience of the Gentiles by word and deed, [19] in the power of signs and wonders, in the power of the Spirit, so that from Jerusalem and round about as far as Illyricum I have fully preached the gospel of Christ. [20] And thus I aspired to preach the gospel not where Christ was already named, that I might not build upon another man's foundation; . . ."

An improper frame for this chapter is to contrast an ambitious leader ("Give me the highest hurdle, the deepest challenge, the biggest mountain to overcome") with a not-so-ambitious leader ("I'll take what the big boys don't, I'm just the B team"). Wherever you are on such a spectrum is irrelevant to vs. 18-20 above. Paul obliterates a hierarchy of prominence concerning a place everyone knows (Jerusalem) and a place you would have a hard time finding on a map (modern-day Illyricum is Albania).

I have said this so often I want this sentence etched on my tombstone: <u>Every point on this earth is equidistant from the heart of God.</u>

Paul does not care where God sends him as long as he is able to further the gospel. He is being consistent with God's call on his life (see Acts 9 entry) to be God's missionary to the Gentiles. Anyone with an entrepreneur/explorer's heart identifies with v. 20 to go where others have yet to tread (cue the Star Trek theme song). Paul does not see a <u>hierarchy</u>; he only sees a <u>heeding</u> of the original call. He is willing to go to a metropolitan nexus of trade (Jerusalem) or plant himself in places like Illyricum, which for me, corresponds to the current outer limits of our association in hills and hollers with names like Isaban, War, Matoaka, or Iaeger. He will not limit God as to the 'where' portion of his call.

My denomination initiated a nationwide shift in its "home" mission priorities several years ago. Its mission board for North America devised a shift built on a data-supported premise: For the first time in human history, more people live in cities than in the countryside[1]. If that was true, it made sense to concentrate strategic and financial resources on urban versus rural ministry, particularly in the area of church planting. From a missional standpoint, I understood. That invited, however, a bias toward rural as less worthy of prime resources and prime personnel. The shift was initiated at a pace and scope that proved disruptive across the country at my level of ministry: the association, a voluntary banding together of local churches to cooperate in missions and ministry. Subsidies of associational work dried up; drastic decisions as to personnel and ministry needs had to be made over the last ten years.

This chapter is personal to me. Before I started working in the coalfield country of southern West Virginia, a state official actually said to a group of pastors from there, 'I don't have time for the little churches.' He subscribed to hierarchy thinking. Yet these 'little' churches back in the hollers have produced some wonderful ministers, and our association currently has four couples from them on the mission field around the globe. We rejoice in the idea of every point on this earth being equidistant from the heart of God. My 23 years of collegiate ministry on American soil were on one of the (then) smaller liberal arts campuses of Texas Baptists. Hundreds of young men and women scattered from our hill tucked on the outskirts of a small county seat in the deep pineywoods of East Texas to faithfully serve Christ across this globe. Every point on this earth is equidistant from the heart of God.

Lines on Leadership
Henri Nouwen, a Catholic writer who left Harvard for L'Arche, a home for adult disabled men, speaks to this concept when he says:
"The way of the Christian leader is not the way of upward mobility in which our world has invested so much, but the way of downward mobility ending on the cross. This might sound morbid and masochistic, but for those who have heard the voice of the first love and said yes to it, the downward-moving way of Jesus is

the way to the joy and the peace of God, a joy and peace that is not of this world²."

As a leader, this does not mean I should automatically eschew promotions, ambition, or excellence. It says I must be willing to go and do whatever, wherever, whenever, and however to fulfill God's purpose for my life. It is not about going up or down some success ladder; it is about going where Christ beckons. Describe your agreement/disagreement with this perspective on where life has placed you in terms of your ministry/career.

_____

_____

++

Romans 16---Highlights: final greetings and a roll call of those who helped Paul

"I remember Richard Nixon back in 74, and the final scene at the White House door//and the staff lined up to say goodbye, tiny tear in his shifty little eye//He said, "Nobody knows me, nobody understands; these little people were good to me. Oh, I'm gonna shake some hands." Chorus: Somebody line 'em all up, line 'em all up, line 'em up, line 'em all up (2x)" --- James Taylor, Line 'Em All Up¹

Paul names an extraordinary thirty+ people in the twenty-two verses that close out Romans. In contrast to the satirical lines of Taylor's song, Paul does not consider these folks "little people" who furthered his ministry. Paul not only mentions names, but he also describes their place in the kingdom of God and lauds them all. There is genuine admiration and appreciation in his descriptions of Phoebe (vs. 1-2) and of Prisca and Aquila (vs. 3-5). There is no social media at the time of Paul's dictation of Romans (v. 22), so these commendations serve as valuable letters of introduction to the believers in Rome.

The last major section of Kouzes and Posner's Five Exemplary Practices is entitled *Encourage the Heart*. The two subsections are Recognize Contributions and Celebrate the Values and Victories[2]. To receive cursory acknowledgment of one's work is better than nothing at all, but Paul goes the second mile in this chapter as he recounts the ways Phoebe has served many and how Prisca and Aquila "risked their own necks" for Paul, a fact known to "all the churches of the Gentiles" (v.4). He recognized their contributions.

He celebrates the values and victories when he points out that Epaenetus is the "first convert to Christ in Asia" (v. 5); when Andronicus and Junias are singled out as "fellow prisoners" and spiritual predecessors of Paul ("who also were in Christ before me," v.7), showing they shared his values and indeed exhibited them before Paul had even become a Christ follower himself. He uses distinctions such as beloved (vs. 8, 9, 12), approved in Christ (v. 10), fellow worker (vs. 9, 12, 21), kinsman (vs. 11, 21), a choice man (Rufus, v. 13), and hard worker (vs. 6, 12).

Kouzes and Posner further elaborate that we should recognize contributions by showing appreciation for individual excellence and celebrate values and victories by creating a spirit of community. Excellence is noted when he describes Andronicus and Junias as "outstanding among the apostles" (v.7). Community is noted when he describes the churches associated with Prisca and Aquila (v.4), Aristobulus (v.10), Narcissus (v.11), the brethren of Asyncritus (Uv.14), and all the saints with Philologus (v.15).

Lines on Leadership
Paul did not hand out participation ribbons or cheap, tiny trophies. He is authentically in debt to many of these people and

grateful for them all. Describe the ways in which you recognize contributions and celebrate values and victories within your organization. How do you know your people see your actions as genuine and from the heart?

_____
_____

++

1ST LETTER TO THE CORINTHIANS

Intro: The church at Corinth was simultaneously precious and problematic for Paul. This letter contains the depths of depravity yet one of the greatest descriptions of love in any language (chapter 13) as a pagan culture and Christianity collide within this local church. Pastors and corporate leaders alike will identify with the admonition/affirmation blend of leadership Paul espouses in this epistle.

++

1st Corinthians 1---Highlights: appeal to unity; the wisdom of God is Christ Himself

<u>Holiness and salvation are not the same. Let me elaborate.</u>

Salvation is a gift of God to all who call upon His name and confess Him as Lord (Rom. 10.9-13). Our salvation is secure (Eph. 1.13), and for that, I am grateful to God. 1 Corinthians 1 is bookended by a term that some have trouble connecting with salvation, the word 'sanctification'. Let's explore just one aspect of what it means to be sanctified.

There is a saying among preachers: "I was saved, I am being saved, and I will be saved." They are not saying salvation is by installment plan and is partial until I get the last installment. The statement means I was saved (totally, by regeneration), my salvation unfolds in increasing areas of my life (sanctification), and one day, I will shed this earthly body and experience my salvation in a complete way unknown to me in this existence (glorification).

Let's concentrate on the second part of the three. Sanctification and holiness come from the same Greek base word. They both imply a simultaneous separation "from" and a separation "to"—a separation *from* sin and a separation *to* the

Father. Holiness is not some mysterious, rapturous state of consciousness I achieve just by reading, praying, or playing Gregorian chants while burning incense. <u>Holiness-sanctification is aligning my life one step at a time with the heart, actions, and mind of my Christ</u>. Here is an alliterative sequence that helps me gain a handle on the concept of sanctification:

1) <u>Loss</u>---Some losses are external and traumatic (a loved one passes away; a financial debacle makes my IRA shrink, etc.). Some losses are choices to let something go, a prized possession, or a possible opportunity. 2) <u>Lord</u>---Each time we experience loss, we have a choice to make, to look away from or toward the Lord as we deal with the loss. It seems easier to look away, blame God, and fester in my bitterness, but in the end, when I look toward the Lord, I initially receive comfort and wisdom and, sometimes, an eventual answer to the perennial question (why?). 3) <u>Love</u>---When I see, touch, and feel the world through His eyes, His Word, and His Spirit, I learn to love myself and others as He loves me/them. Of course, when I love like the Lord, agape love is a sacrificial one, best typified by the gift of His Son, Jesus Christ, to us as the Lamb of God. When I love like God loves, I will experience inevitable loss, and the cycle repeats. 4) <u>Loop</u> (Loss, Lord, Love)—The more I allow this cycle to operate in my life in a series of looping, ongoing circles, the more I conform to His image (Rom. 8.29), and the process of sanctification continues as He refines me toward Christlikeness. Each loss leads me to the Lord for guidance which leads me to love and be vulnerable to more loss. Sanctification occurs when I stay in this holy 'loop'.

<u>Holiness---sanctification is not earned; it is acquired</u>. At the point of salvation, there is a sense of being set apart by God unto Himself. From that point on, there is a sense of process as the Loss/Lord/Love cycle repeats without end, and we become more like our Christ. Baptists tend to emphasize the immediate

sanctification at the new birth, and many other denominations tend to emphasize the process. It is not either/or but both/and. Leaders within congregations need to rejoice in what is theirs in Christ and ask for continued patience with them as leaders as they strive toward conformity to the image of Christ.

Lines on Leadership

Devise a simple table of characteristics of Christ or professional skills you want to possess or exhibit. Mark an annual or periodic day when you will take a personal assessment as to your progress or stagnation in acquiring or exhibiting those traits/skills, of aligning yourself with Christ or becoming more like those traits and skills you desire.

_____

_____

++

1ˢᵗ Corinthians 2---Highlights: sources of wisdom, the contrast of the world and the Holy Spirit

Vs. 1-2 "And when I came to you, brethren, I did not come with superiority of speech or of wisdom, proclaiming to you the testimony of God. For I determined to know nothing among you except Jesus Christ, and Him crucified."

In Michael Pollan's book, *In Defense of Food,* he invokes what he calls the 'great grandma rule', to not eat anything she wouldn't recognize as food. He expands it to be fourfold: avoid food products containing ingredients that are a) unfamiliar, b) unpronounceable, c) more than five in number, or d) include high fructose corn syrup[1]. Modern society and globalization have unwittingly conspired to make food shippable and consumable by adding preservatives, taste enhancers, and chemical concoctions that allow food to be packaged and transported to the four corners of the world during all four seasons of the year (with the end result a populace obsessed with fitness and nutrition winds up ingesting unhealthy products). We have learned to be filled as inexpensively as possible is more important than being nourished. Pollard's main statement ("eat food, not too much, mostly plants", p. 1) is explained later as eating <u>real</u> food, not the industrialized, mostly processed versions of everything on our present grocery shelves[2].

When I see the proliferation of books, programs, videos, and presentations of what passes as gospel today, I often wonder if two thousand years of preaching, pontificating, and adding to the gospel have rendered it as unrecognizable to the Lord and the first-century believers like modern processed food. I wonder, what have we added and substituted and ground into the gospel, always with good intentions of preserving and shipping it to the four corners of the world and making it available in all four seasons? How many organizations continue to add to their message or their products until the originals are no longer recognizable?

Paul obviously doesn't mean to just repeat v. 2 as some mantra and only speak that one sentence, "Jesus Christ and Him crucified". Throughout the two letters to the Corinthians, he addresses many different subjects; but every one of them is seen through the lens of and measured by the gospel, that God has sent His Son to be the sacrifice for our sins on the cross, rose in triumph from death, and offers us eternal life through that death, burial, and resurrection. The message must remain at the fore and be the core of my ministry or my vocation. Whatever seems to encrust it (my oratorical skills, my strength of personality, my competence, v. 1) needs to take a back seat.

Lines on Leadership
In terms of ministry, would the Lord Jesus recognize His gospel in my version of it? In terms of business, would the founder of my company recognize his core message in my version of it? If not, why not? What have I added to that original message that needs removal or revision?

_____

_____

+++

1st Corinthians 3---Highlights: factions in the church

Reflectional Leadership was written when American society was more concerned with ideology and identification than information and insight. Groups of people sling insults and names at each other, trying to identify them with a certain ideology (be it religious, political, or sociological) that supposedly end an argument that never got underway in the first place. Attempts to discuss or ascertain what the issue really is rarely get traction. The overall goal of moving forward in a mutually beneficial direction gets lost in the social media blitzes. They are focused more on claiming higher ground than finding common ground.

This is not a new phenomenon. Paul accurately described the same scenario as immature (vs. 1-3) when the members of the Corinthian church divided themselves into separate camps aligned with Paul, Apollos, Peter, or Christ (1 Cor. 1.12-13; 3.4). Using the common image of agriculture, he reminds them the matter at hand is not who sows or who irrigates but that growth occurs (v. 6). The role is not as important as the result (v.7). The team is more important than the individual members; yes, they all have their individual style and receive their own respective reward (v.8), but the emphasis is unmistakably God: God's growth (v. 7), God's workers, and God's field (v. 9).

In Kingdom work, I can never forget to whom the Kingdom belongs. Paul switches metaphors in midstream from plowing to construction (God's building, v.9b) and doesn't skip a beat by summing it all up in the statement: "No man can lay a foundation other than the one which is laid, which is Jesus Christ (v.11)." This does not mean we are faceless and just a part of the machinery; there are an infinite number of building materials, infinite number of architectural designs, and an infinite number of living arrangements. But they all have one thing in common: Christ as the foundation. The metaphors continue from fields in which we plow to buildings in which we live to the very bodies we are, with God inhabiting each as His own temple (v.16).

Human nature tends to set one's "own" group as the norm and all others as deviating from that norm see Acts 8 entry). This can produce unique healthy markers such as music, art, food, clothing, and language, but it can also lead to artificial distinctions used to leverage my importance or significance as opposed to those "other people". My task as a leader is to help my team worry less about distinguishing themselves from all others and concentrate more on finding truth and insight, regardless of who provides it.

<u>Lines on Leadership</u>
An oft-quoted prayer of St. Francis of Assisi seeks "to understand more than to be understood[1]". Are the groups within your organization experiencing healthy or unhealthy competition and distinction from one another? Are they expending more energy on labeling each other or in learning from one another?

_____

_____

++

1ˢᵗ Corinthians 4---Highlights: describing servants of Christ

The author asks for forgiveness for his repeated use of the minister's main mnemonic, alliteration. It often comes across as a contrivance more than an aid, but sometimes it emerges from the text itself, as in this chapter. A leader in 1 Cor. 4 can be a (possibly) faithful, foolish father figure filled with power.

1. Faithful—in v. 1, Paul depicts leaders as servants of Christ and stewards entrusted with the message of the gospel (mysteries of God). The primary characteristic of a steward is his faithfulness (v. 2) to both Christ and His gospel. In ministerial circles, this word often has the connotation of longevity (he's pastored that church for x decades), which is an admirable trait, but in this context, Paul is more concerned with fidelity to the Messiah and His Message. Endurance becomes the sign of faithfulness rather than momentarily demonstrated loyalty[1].

2. Foolish---v. 10, "We are fools for Christ's sake." A main principle in Wilkes' book on servant leadership is that I am able to take risks because I belong to and am forever joined to Christ[2]. I rest in the security of that bond, and because of it, I can go ahead and take risks without regard to how foolish I appear in the eyes of others. We can afford to become "scum of the world" and "dregs of all things" (v. 13) because we belong to Him. If I have assurance from my organization's boss, I can take risks, and I can bomb out time and again until something clicks/sticks, all without fear of reprisal or dismissal; it is emboldening and liberating.

3. Father---v. 15, at some point in my leadership, I have to think of myself primarily as the head of my family instead of the perpetual learner and subordinate. Yes, I am always my father's son; there is always something to learn, and I should

always be a Timothy to a Paul in my life; but there comes a time when I have to see myself primarily as the patriarch (providing the most visible and observed example; hence v. 16, "be imitators of me") How many times did church members receive a sermon or teaching from Timothy and smile, thinking, "it's a younger Paul in our midst"?

  4. <u>Filled</u>---Paul uses this concept both in satire and as an example. In v. 8, he mocks the Corinthians for their self-proclamation about how rich they are; in vs. 19-20, he says rather forcefully I am coming in your midst, and we will see how powerful you are and your true source, if it is from your own haughtiness and self-appraisal or from the Lord, "for the kingdom of God does not consist in words but in power." This does not encourage a Machiavellian approach to becoming a spiritual king of the mountain, grasping and maintaining a command post, but is an acknowledgment of the source of my authority. Daniel Day-Lewis, in his Oscar-winning portrayal of Lincoln in the 2012 biopic *Lincoln,* thunders in a climactic scene that he is "the President of the United States, clothed in immense power[3]." Lincoln was not a haughty, arrogant man; he understood that his recent reelection and the Constitution were his sources of authority, not some inward personal strength, wealth, or right. <u>It was imputed, not inherent</u>.

<u>Lines of Leadership</u>
As a leader, how many of these characteristics (faithful, foolish, fatherly, or filled) would colleagues use to describe you?
_____
_____
++

1st Corinthians 5---Highlights: immorality addressed

Redemptive statements or restrictive statements are equally inept and ineffectual without enforcement. The terms to receive redemption come from the one providing the redemption. Those being redeemed do not dictate the length, quality, or nature of the redemption. If there is no power to back up the redemption or the restriction, the one in charge is an "emperor without any clothes".

1 Cor. 1-4 speaks of holiness and being conformed to the image of Christ. If someone will not get with the program in a given workplace or organization, there has to be a means by which the person is shown the standards to be met, the way to meet them, and given ample opportunity to align himself with those standards. Here in 1 Cor. 5, Paul explores the rather uncomfortable reality that not everyone in the Corinthian church is on board with conforming to Christ and His holiness, and they must be dealt with in a proper manner (vs. 5, 7, 9 -11).

The words Paul uses seem harsh to our ears (v. 5, deliver such a one to Satan). It is a difficult balance as a leader to be in search and rescue mode (leave the 99 sheep and seek out the stray, Lk. 15), which shows compassion yet understands there are consequences. Yes, in Lk. 15 Jesus' emphasis is on the lostness of the sheep and the rejoicing when it is found. But elsewhere in Scripture, David as shepherd shows the other side of helping that stray sheep end its straying days. Psalms 51. 8 reads, "Make me to hear joy and gladness, let the bones which You have broken rejoice."

V.6, "Do you not know that a little leaven leavens the whole lump of dough?" In terms of discipleship and evangelism, this image has positive connotations. In light of this chapter, it has a negative impact that cannot be ignored: Errant attitudes, behaviors, and actions left unchecked will spread throughout an organization, the proverbial bad apple that ultimately rots the entire barrel. A mark of an effective leader is being able to create a balance of redemption and restriction with clear rewards/repercussions.

Lines on Leadership
Describe your tendency to be either overly compassionate or quick to judge, punish, and reflect on ways to achieve this balance of redemption and restriction in dealing with the members of your organization.
_____
_____
++

1st Corinthians 6---Highlights: lawsuits for Christians; relationship of body and spirit

(Rarely have I gained so much satisfaction from painful confession as I did from this 2015 column written to personally illustrate 1 Cor. 6.12; the leadership principle is obvious enough from the content alone. In years to come, it will likely become more quaint than satirical.)

V. 12 "All things are lawful for me, but I will not be mastered by anything." Different translations render that phrase as "dominated" (ESV) or 'brought under its control' (KJV). Principles of biblical interpretation say to view this passage in the context of sexual relations, but Paul also talks about appetites in general (v. 13), unholy unions with unbelievers (2 Cor. 6.14) and expands it in his second letter to the Corinthians to a general statement on spiritual warfare to take "every thought captive to the obedience of Christ" (2 Cor. 10.5). Okay, that's simple enough. Nothing but Christ should be in charge of my life, got it. But there is this small rectangular object in my pocket that spews out endless useful information, keeps my day ordered, and wakes me up. It helps me buy and sell whatever I want whenever, teaches me how to mount kayak wall hangers or play new guitar chords (it even tunes my guitar), and books flights or rental cars. It conveys my thoughts to anyone else with a similar device at all hours, stores and plays my music collection, does all of my mathematical computations, allows me to see my son halfway around the world in a foreign country in real-time, is a portable library, shares my daily Bible verses (written or audio, choose your translation), shines light in dark corners, records my life in photos/videos and shares it instantly with others, has more computing power than the Apollo spacecraft onboard computers, and, oh, I almost forgot . . . it makes phone calls. Yes, a smartphone. It has insidiously woven its functions into my everyday life at a level unimaginable only ten years ago. It has become (now the confession part):

Communicator-in-Chief---Rolodexes, phone directories, maps, Bible translations, endless videos, radio, writing paper, books, and magazines: I don't have to carry them; they all fit in my hand. Recently, I stood in my bathroom texting a person in Singapore about a person in London with whom I was simultaneously on Facebook. I usually exchange texts/emails with pastors before I eat breakfast.

Companion-in-Chief---It is often the first and the last thing I see during the course of a day. If I'm in the office, out and about, walking, or at home, it is the one constant entity with direct eye contact with me. Wilson, Tom Hanks' volleyball "friend" in the movie *Castaway*, has nothing on my cell phone.

Commander-in-Chief---Sometimes I feel like the phone has gone from servant to master (hence the verses above) and from a liberator (its mobility) to a leash. It blurs lines between private and public, work and relaxation, and often replaces reflection with reaction and concentration with distraction. Every invention or discovery of man, from fire to the printing press and advanced weaponry to automobiles, can be used for evil or good. How then should I handle this thing that can allow me to send encouragement to a loved one yet also be used to remotely detonate car bombs?

    People had great ministries, marriages, friendships, and families for centuries before smartphones; this portal to the world in my hand can enhance or hinder all that is truly important to me. I need to know what God, not Google says about this. Lord? Wait a minute, Lord, incoming text; a guy is calling, no, two are calling at the same time; someone sent a book recommendation and became Facebook buddies; can I get back to you on this, Lord? Wait, I'll schedule you in my digital calendar...as soon as I read this article, look at these photos, listen to a new tune, watch this movie trailer, read the newspaper, check the weather before leaving, check my email, check in with the office, check my investments, check my heart rate, check my . . . (☹, my battery died). Lord, you still there?

Lines on Leadership
Is the personal communications device in your pocket (i.e., a smartphone or its successor) a liberator or a leash?
_____
_____
++

1st Corinthians 7---Highlights: states of marriage, social standing; when to stay, when to flee

    Chapter 7 begins a several-chapter run on the sense of balance and nuance a leader must display and how to balance biblical truth with the infinity of individual human conditions. This culminates in the soaring beauty of 1 Cor. 13, Paul's unmatched description of love as the supreme virtue. In this one chapter, Paul tackles marriage, sexual intercourse, divorce, slavery, work relations, remarriage, singleness, and widowhood. Apparently, some strangely extreme views concerning sexuality and social standing had arisen within the Corinthian congregation, and Paul addresses them head-on (vs. 1-16). Some had taken the stance that one should refrain from sex, even between marriage partners, in order to fully devote oneself to God. Paul quickly refutes this and says sex is a gift from God, and to participate in it within the moral confines of marriage is not distracting from God but honors Him (vs. 32-40). The balancing act begins: Paul acknowledges he has more time to devote to his mission and does not need to give time to a wife or consider her as he constantly travels or pulls up stakes for the next city. But he also acknowledges that not everyone can keep up this pace or this arrangement.

As I write this, I have just completed an intense two-week period of a Peru mission trip and a trustee meeting at New Orleans Baptist Theological Seminary. Home is wherever my wife is, and has been for 47 years. I could probably accomplish more as an openly admitted workaholic in regards to workload if she were not part of my life, but precisely because I tend to keep piling it on, I need someone there to speak to me of rest, of comfort, of taking a break, someone with whom I don't have to be "on" all the time as the leader. Her go-to solution to slow my breakneck pace of life is to go camping. It takes about the second day before I can honestly unwind and breathe deeply. I chafe at it every time and simultaneously acknowledge the need for it.

Paul repeats a similar argument about work relations (slave/master, vs. 21-24) and about religious rites (vs. 18-20). The encapsulation of the examples is the statement, "Let each one live his life in the situation the Lord assigned when God called him" (v.17, CSB). As a leader, I can fully expect a person's loyalty and hard work, but I must be willing to consider his life situation in regard to family obligations, work background, and religious beliefs. A Christian leader reading this chapter must exercise patience and understanding about whatever a group member brings to the table as his life situation, especially if he/she is a new believer.

Lines on Leadership
Human Resources policies and federal hiring practices make knowledge of the categories mentioned above difficult to impossible to learn when employing new colleagues for a work environment, which is different than granting church membership to fellow churchgoers. How can you as a leader eventually learn each life situation for your group members? What is a discovered sociological or spiritual situation that you know would make decisions as a leader difficult for you in regard to your group members?

_____

_____

++

1st Corinthians 8---Highlights: individual liberty and sublimating it to serve others

    This chapter continues the narrative of chapter 7 in describing a further balancing act a leader must master. Chapter 9 shows the aggressive side of becoming all things to all men in order to bring them to Christ. Chapter 8 shows the passive side of self-imposed restriction; that <u>sometimes I must curtail one or more freedoms I have in Christ to gain the right to share the gospel with another person</u>. The balancing act comes when I try to keep condescension out of the equation.

If I have a fuller knowledge about a subject (in this case, meat sacrificed to idols, vs. 4-13), and I am in the presence of another person who does not possess that "fuller" knowledge, my "fuller" knowledge can easily lead to haughtiness and condescension. 'Why, you poor person, you are obviously unenlightened; here, let me enlighten you with my superior knowledge.' My attempts at trying to enlighten the person usually end in defensiveness, being cut off, or barriers erected. I can also mistakenly try to enlighten him with my enlightened practices: ('Maybe if he sees me eating this meat sacrificed to idols, and he knows I am a believer, I can convince him my God is bigger than his god.')

Paul adapts Jesus' command to go the second and third mile of effort on another's behalf to a second and third mile of self-restriction for the sake of others. He refrains from doing something perfectly legal and ethical that could be mistaken by a friend as an endorsement of his idol worship (or whatever useless practice or endeavor he does to gain the attention and merit of God). And <u>he must do so with grace, not a showy display of his holiness</u>. Paul concludes this section with v. 13, "Therefore, if food causes my brother to stumble, I will never eat meat again, so that I will not cause my brother to stumble."

As a leader, the words "weaker brother" should never cross my lips in the presence of whomever I consider a "weaker" brother. That reeks of superiority, especially in this era of hypersensitivity to everything from body shaming to criticism of people's eating habits, clothes they wear, choices they make, etc. My eating and drinking of anything forbidden (by another's value system), from meat (pork) to beverages (wine, beer) to actual food sacrificed on an idol's altar, should not become a stumbling block to a person learning more about my Christ. (see Rom. 14 entry).

Lines on Leadership
What is something you need to refrain from doing or saying in the presence of those you lead in order to keep them from stumbling? Conversely, what is something you know you need to do or say in their presence to help them be more receptive to your message but might personally restrict yourself?

_____

_____

++

1st Corinthians 9---Highlights: proper use of liberty in Christ

One ramification of leadership is to be constantly misunderstood. The new vocabulary you try to introduce is met with resistance. The actions you take are seen through the filter of old ideas; they are seen without the necessary patience to grasp how those actions define a new reality, not affirm an old one. The directions in which you take your organization are criticized no matter which compass point shows up. To be misunderstood is a natural corollary to being a leader.

Paul desires to "become all things to all men that I might by all means save some" (v. 22), and again, even though he is "free from all men, I have made myself a slave to all, so that I may win more" (v.19). This is not a "bottom-line-is-all-that-matters" (ends justify the means) approach to leadership, to do "whatever it takes" to get a customer or to maintain a relationship. Vs. 19-27 are driven by Paul's woe in v. 16 ("woe is me if I do not preach the gospel"). He is more interested in the result than his reputation. He is willing to be misunderstood (see Mt. 11 entry) like John the Baptist and Jesus because he is compelled to get the gospel understood by as many as possible. He is driven more by empathy and compassion than he is by quarterly poll numbers. Paul will become and say and do whatever makes sure the gospel is received, understood, and implanted in a person's heart—as long as it does not violate biblical integrity (vs. 24-29, he competes in a way so as not just to participate but to win, which must be done in accordance with the rules governing that particular race). If in doing so I am misunderstood, I am misunderstood.

Lines on Leadership
Who is someone in your group you are trying to reach and know you will need to adopt an unfamiliar role or uncomfortable stance to reach? Who is someone in your group you know will require an orthodox approach to gain or sustain his trust in order to finally get your message through to him? Are you willing to be misunderstood to do so?

_____
_____
+++

1st Corinthians 10---Highlights: mistakes made by Israel as well as by individuals

Vs. 23-24---"All things are lawful, but not all things are profitable. All things are lawful, but not all things edify. Let no one seek his own good, but that of his neighbor." 1 Cor. 6 has a related verse that spotlights the "weaker" brother. In Chapter 10, the focus is on the "stronger" brother. As in other chapters, the context is key. This is not a blanket permission to do whatever comes to mind because of my freedom in Christ. Just because I have permission to do something doesn't make it desirable. The two verses taken together make it obvious that the profitability is not about my personal "bottom line" but whether it is profitable for another.

The ensuing verses narrow the illustration to eating meat sacrificed to idols and learning how to curb my freedom when it leads a weaker brother astray or hinders his growth in understanding what freedom in Christ means. The principle can be expanded to other areas of life as the concluding chapter verse says, "Whether, then, you eat or drink or whatever you do, do all to the glory of God" (v.31). Paul repeats this principle in Galatians when he summarizes that, ". . . you were called to freedom, brethren; only do not turn your freedom into an opportunity for the flesh, but through love serve one another" (Gal. 5.13).

This tension between my personal desires and the needs of others lies at the foundation of society. As I ascend the ladder of success and leadership within a group, the temptation is to think I can forget my obligations to others and reap the rewards of my labors by doing what I want to do and letting the "little people" fend for themselves. Nouwen calls it the "temptation of power", where "power offers an easy substitute for the hard task of love[1]." That power can come from increasing authority, from resources, or from knowledge, as in this Corinthian chapter. <u>Our power is not ours primarily to serve our desires but to meet the needs of others</u>. As I grasp the next rung of the ladder or the next outcropping of rock on the way up, my other hand must continue to be extended downward to help others attain their upward climb. Love and faith both require an object. My love and faith cannot stop at self-love or faith in myself, legitimate as those things are; we are created and wired to relate to others in the image of God, and this requires me on my journey toward sanctification to look upward to glorify Him (v. 31) and to look downward to my brother and meet his needs (vs. 23-24).

In closing, I offer this extensive, well-known quote from 1984 as the antithesis of 1 Cor. 10:

"The Party seeks power entirely for its own sake. We are not interested in the good of others; we are interested solely in power, pure power. What pure power means you will understand presently. We are different from the oligarchies of the past in that we know what we are doing. All the others, even those who resembled ourselves, were cowards and hypocrites. The German Nazis and the Russian Communists came very close to us in their methods, but they never had the courage to recognize their own motives. They pretended, perhaps they even believed, that they had seized power unwillingly and for a limited time, and that just around the corner there lay a paradise where human beings would be free and equal. We are not like that. We know that no one ever seizes power with the intention of relinquishing it. Power is not a means; it is an end. One does not establish a dictatorship in order to safeguard a revolution; one makes the revolution in order to establish the dictatorship. The object of persecution is persecution. The object of torture is torture. The object of power is power[2]."

Lines on Leadership
What are some things perfectly legal and moral for you in your current leadership position that you need to sublimate, suspend, or postpone in order to meet the needs of others? What safeguards have you built into your value system to prevent your life from resembling or incarnating the Orwellian quote?
_____
_____
++

1st Corinthians 11---Highlights: Christian order, marital relationships, the Lord's Supper instructions

"Be imitators of me, just as I also am of Christ (v.1)." The eleven words beginning 1 Cor. 11 sound arrogant but express a core leadership quality. Earlier in this book the statement is made: Everyone needs a Paul, a Barnabas, and a Timothy in their lives (see Mt. 28 entry). I need someone to follow, someone as a partner, and someone to train. The need to obey and imitate Christ is made clear throughout the NT, as we are often commanded to follow Him. Every leader's first leadership lesson is 'learn to follow'. When I am in the Timothy role to my Paul, or every believer to their Lord, followship makes sense. But for me to have a Timothy, someone who depends on me to train them and bring them to spiritual maturity, that means I have to grow into a Paul figure for my Timothy. I need to grow into a leader worth following. <u>I need to openly declare my life worthy of imitation.</u>

This seems to fly in the face of repeated NT emphases on humility and demurring to the Lordship of Christ. Paul addresses this in Phil. 2.3: "With humility of mind, regard one another as more important than yourselves." Note that he does not say better or higher but more important. 'I believe in you so much I want you to come as far as I have, then exceed me, to surpass my achievements. Learn how I got to this point and then go beyond me. That means I can help accelerate your learning by showing you what has worked and what has not, to help you avoid all the pits and detours I had to take to get here. If you look at my life, it should point to Jesus. The end goal is not to have you following me; that is but an intermediate step; the end goal is to help you follow Christ better.' This principle is undeniable as the NT writers repeatedly refer to an imitation of the author or those in authority over you (1 Cor. 4.16; Phil. 3.17; 4.9; 1 Thess. 1.7; 2 Thess. 3.7, 9; Heb. 13.7; 1 Peter 5.3).

It also means my life is open to examination by my Timothy. If all I show my Timothy are the triumphs and successes of my life, I give him a partial portrait that is inaccurate. I must allow him to see my failures and shortcomings. The higher up a person is in leadership circles, the harder it usually is for him to give his followers full access to his life. Power and authority seem to cloak a person with an aura of invincibility and distance that glosses over failure (Wow, he got this far, he must have been incredible in his field to get to this level, made all the right decisions, and pushed all the right buttons).

Probably, the scariest part of full access to my life is the lack of control over what my follower chooses to imitate. It cannot remain simple access; to become a true mentorship, I must take time to advise what in my life to imitate, take time to field the inevitable questions, and not get defensive when they become personal. It takes investment as well as disclosure when discipling by imitation.

<u>Lines on Leadership</u>
What aspects of your leadership are worthy of imitation by your followers? What needs to be improved before allowing others access to your life for imitation?
_____
_____
++

1st Corinthians 12---Highlights: Spiritual Gifts, many members one body, baptism of the Holy Spirit

Three areas of argumentation arise when this chapter is discussed within Christian circles.

1) One area is whether or not the spiritual gifts listed are operative in today's world. Some say the gifts were operative

until the NT canon was completed (consensus within the larger body of Christ was reached as to which written documents were truly inspired by God and declared His new covenant to supersede the Old Covenant or OT) and were no longer needed. Others believe strongly that all the gifts are operative today, as in NT times. Still others believe some gifts were meant for apostolic use and some gifts (listed in some translations as the best or the better gifts) were meant for general use by the entire body of Christ.

    2) The second area perennially discussed is: can a person have more than one spiritual gift? Are the listings of gifts (this chapter; Romans 12; and 1 Peter 4.10-11) exhaustive, meaning there are no other gifts other than what is listed in the NT? Since many of the gifts listed in these passages are also commanded of us as believers in other NT passages (to witness, to teach, to serve), I tend to teach we have a primary gift, and there is no set number of gifts one should exercise. The command in this chapter is to exercise our gifts, but the emphasis seems to be on the corporate body exercising them in a coordinated, synergistic fashion like the different members of the body, an emphasis repeated in Rom. 12.

    3) The third area of contention is the nature and purpose of a spiritual gift. Some believe a spiritual gift is something supernatural conferred by the Holy Spirit after conversion. Others believe it is a talent or natural proclivity of a person that becomes sanctified by the Holy Spirit after conversion. Still others would rather label a pre-conversion spiritual gift a latency that needs the touch of the Holy Spirit to become active.
Natural ability, latency, talent, unique set of strengths, number of gifts, are they still valid—the terminology can be confusing. This may not shed light for anyone else other than myself, but I humbly submit my definition of a spiritual gift: <u>A spiritual gift is</u>

<u>the path of least resistance in my life through which the grace of God flows into the life of another person</u>. I tend to think in terms of natural forces having spiritual parallels, be that electricity, water, light, or gravity. Within this chapter, Paul uses an extended analogy of that which is common to every person on earth (having a body) and uses the body to describe how all the different gifts work together, as do the members of the body. So you can use whatever force of nature you relate to the most, water, electricity, light, or gravity, and when the path of least resistance is found, the grace of God flows easier through that path in my life into the lives of others. This, in part, avoids the discussion about whether the gift is a talent, capacity, etc.

In my years of college ministry, we had from twenty to twenty-five different ministries on and off campus led by student leaders. Those leaders were responsible for recruiting other fellow students to help out with their ministry. We irreverently called it "divine dabbling": work with children in area apartment complexes; sing with a performing group; learn sign language; lead a freshman Bible study; and tutor after school at a local elementary school or a score of other ministries. After a semester, try something else. Sooner or later, you would find something that **a)** you would rather do than eat, or **b)** something where others noticed a joy on your face when you participated, or **c)** others would affirm that people resonated with the way you handled that ministry. Those might be indications you were closing in on your spiritual gift in a clinical diagnosis, trial and error method. I loathe so-called "spiritual gift inventories" because they tend to show what you have been exposed to: Protestants score low on the "charismatic" gifts (miracles, healing, tongues), and charismatics score high on them, what a surprise!

More and more businesses are using more sophisticated aptitude testing and HR departments that can help fine-tune a match between openings in a company and a person's strengths. Churches need to catch up. Most churches scramble every year with their nominating groups to "plug holes" in their volunteer charts for Sunday School, mission education, and committees based more on willingness and availability than giftedness. It reminds me of my dad telling me about how he got chosen in the USAF during WWII to be a mechanic. The C.O. went down the line of recruits and said, "You, you, and you are typists; you, you, and you are mechanics; you, you, and you will work in the kitchen." Building a culture of people operating out of their giftedness would make the nominating group less onerous and much more productive regardless of the organization!

Dive in to serve in a variety of ways within your local church or your organization. It may seem chaotic and inefficient at first, but when people work out of their giftedness to the glory of God, the body/organization/company is more profitable for the Kingdom (or the shareholders).

Lines of Leadership
Reminisce about times in your past when people commented on your having excelled or reveled in something. Perhaps hidden in those comments is a key to your spiritual gift, as described in 1 Cor. 12.

_____
_____

++

1st Corinthians 13---Highlights: the love chapter
    v. 13 "But now abide faith, hope, and love, these three; but the greatest of these is love."

1 Cor. 13 stands tall in theological and literary circles as one of the greatest descriptions of love ever penned. I am unable to add anything of significance to the centuries of commentary on it. Rather I offer a humble reflection on v. 13 and extended analogy to relate its trinity of virtues to leadership.

<u>Faith</u>—the <u>amount</u> of faith one exhibits is not as important as the <u>object</u> of one's faith, a statement explored in several other chapters (see Mk. 2, Lk. 17, 1 Cor. 10, James 4 entries). I am an avid canoeist (Mad River, Explorer 15). When stepping from a dock into a small boat, there is that unmistakable moment of transference, when the weight of the body shifts from primarily on the dock to the boat, and the direction of motion is irreversible; you are committed to the act of landing in the boat (or capsizing it and getting wet). When I place my feet (and subsequently the largest portion of my body weight) in the dead center of the boat, keeping the weight and my center of gravity low and in the middle, it keeps the boat from tipping, and it remains stable. Even though I am experienced at this maneuver, it always contains a moment of trepidation!

The bigger the boat, however, the less I think about shifting from the dock to the boat. A larger vessel does not sway and rock as quickly; it is more stable. When it gets to the size of a sea-going ship, a boat that dwarfs the dock, I do not give a second thought at all to walking onboard. If that is true with boats, and I start to reflect on the immensity of the love of God, the grace of God, and the track record of God in Scripture, why would I ever hesitate or hold back faith in His love, grace, or track record?

<u>Hope</u>—Size alone is not an indicator of a boat's seaworthiness. The dimensions, materials, and quality of workmanship all factor into my faith in that vessel. An additional factor is my faith in the experience and competency of the crew

and boat's leadership, likely the captain. Once those factors are considered and satisfactory, then I can turn my attention to the journey and the desired destination. Hope is the present contemplation of and appropriation of a future reality.

<u>Love</u>—There is no set sequence of interaction between faith, hope, and love. One reason love is considered the greatest of the three by Paul is that it most often trumps faith and hope (V.13). If I've been on enough journeys in a given vessel and have grown to respect, follow, and eventually love the person in charge of that vessel, be it a boat, a company, or a church, I tend to not pay as much attention to its seaworthiness anymore, to the quality, the ability to reach its destination, etc.

Recently I visited one of our many southern WV churches' worship services. As far as sermons go, it was lacking in good hermeneutical principles and tightness of reasoning. But the pastor has been there for over a decade and is much beloved. The congregation has learned over the years to fill in the gaps in his sermons with either their collective knowledge of the Word or the love in their hearts for their pastor.

<u>Lines on Leadership</u>
In your organization, where is the <u>faith</u> of the followers placed? In what direction is their collective <u>hope</u> pointed? And would <u>love</u> be out of place in describing their relationship to you or your relationship to them?

_____
_____
++

1st Corinthians 14---Highlights: confusion from speaking in tongues

Vs. 8-9--"For if the bugle produces an indistinct sound, who will prepare himself for battle? So also you, unless you utter by the tongue speech that is clear, how will it be known what is spoken? For you will be speaking into the air." v.11 "If then I do not know the meaning of the language, I shall be to the one who speaks a barbarian, and the one who speaks will be a barbarian to me."

Have you ever attended a conference where the speaker was obviously from another planet (because you had no idea what he/she was talking about)? The program topic looked promising, but the vocabulary used was foreign to you. Have you stood by your car on the repair shop hydraulic rack when the mechanic tries to explain the mysteries of torque and engine displacement? Or sat in the doctor's office when the Latinized terms start flying, and you are not certain if he is describing your ailment, its treatment, or his investment strategies (probably all three)? In all three settings, the person's competence and expertise are unquestioned, but they have become comfortable in their specialization "insider terms", words people within the profession understand, but no one outside their select circles does.

This can happen in any profession: musicians, plumbers, coaches, politicians, ministers, and business executives. If everyone in the group has the specialized experience and knowledge base I do, I can speak in terms they all understand. But if the circle is widened to those with less experience or exposure to the specialized vocabulary, I lose their interest or support if I don't adjust my vocabulary and approach accordingly. As a professor in the classroom, a preacher in the pulpit, or a presenter at a civic group, I strive to make sure the mature student/believer is challenged <u>and</u> the most elementary seeker stays engaged.

The recipients of this epistle, the Corinthians, were a boastful, haughty bunch. Paul has taken three chapters (12-14) to explain that 1) speaking in tongues might be spectacular but not necessarily superior (chap. 12); 2) that love is the greatest and surest of all manifestations of God's grace in my life (chap. 13); and 3) the gifts were given to edify the church and glorify God, not advance my own cause (chap. 14). My second language is German, and I can converse and read in it all day long. After about the second sentence of my speaking 'auf Deutsch' to an average non-German speaking audience, I go from amusing to annoying to arrogant. There are areas of my heart, especially in my prayer life, where I feel more comfortable speaking to God in German, not English. That is when I speak to Him as His child and a follower of Christ. But when I speak to anyone as a leader, I must speak in a manner that not only displays my competence but does so with clarity. Only then can my group follow my lead with confidence.

<u>Lines on Leadership</u>
Next time you speak to your group of followers, enable someone who is NOT an expert in your field to critique the vocabulary you used as obscuring, cluttering, or clarifying your message.

_____
_____
++

1st Corinthians 15---Highlights: the resurrection and its ramifications

Vs. 13-14 "But if there is no resurrection of the dead, not even Christ has been raised; and if Christ has not been raised, then our preaching is vain, your faith also is vain."

My ministry (on the mission field, college campus, and the hills and hollers of Appalachia) has been marked by what I term elsewhere in this book as the 'creative alternative' (see Mk. 12 entry). The creative alternative approach to ministry and leadership says there is rarely just one either/or answer to a problem or issue at hand. I try my best to help the person wrestling with the problem to change perspectives, enlarge their frame of reference, juggle the elements of the problem, relabel everything, resize each element, isolate the factors, and try just anything possible to see the problem as solvable by more than one obvious or one inevitable solution.

Since problem-solving lies at the heart of leadership, leaders tend to be forward thinkers, the goal being to arrive at a workable solution, always in forward mode. And the approach of 'creative alternative' has worked well for me—helping others not to stop at the first plausible, workable solution but to seek out multiple ones and realize there are usually more ways than one to succeed at a given task or problem. But the quoted passage above (vs. 13-14) looks in the opposite direction. It forces the gaze in reverse toward the origin, page one, the beginning upon which a ministry or career is built. All belief systems, all company mission statements, and all personal codes of conduct can be traced back to some foundational truth, some guiding principle. Some would call this an *axiom*, which by definition is "a self-evident truth that requires no proof; a universally accepted principle or rule[1]." That foundational truth, that guiding principle is rooted in faith as well as logic. The resurrection of Christ is foundational for Christianity; according to 1 Cor. 15, it rises and falls on the truth of the resurrection. It is, in a sense, an irreducible complexity: If the resurrection is not true, then Christianity tumbles as if the trusses and frames of its infrastructure had just been removed.

Lines on Leadership
What is the irreducible complexity, the foundational truth, the origin statement upon which your ministry or your leadership position rests?

_____

_____

++

1st Corinthians 16---Highlights: closing remarks

Vs.13-14 "Be on the alert, stand firm in the faith, act like men, be strong. Let all that you do be done in love." This sounds like a bland motivational poster or bumper sticker formula for team building that borders on triteness, but the five imperative phrases blend well to provide a well-rounded, common-sense approach to leadership.

1. Be on alert. As a stand-alone command, this could be taken several ways: in light of Paul's other epistles, this could mean to always be on the lookout for false teachers who will come into a flock to lead them astray; it could mean to keep looking forward to the future for what is to come; it could mean to continually examine the infrastructure of the organization periodically. To summarize, constantly look inward, look forward, and look outward, always striving to be aware of what is and what is about to happen.

2. Have a firm faith. Know what your foundational values are and act upon them (see 1 Cor. 15 entry). It always amazes me how few people in any given church or organization can articulate with certainty what the foundational truths are upon which the group is built and is building.

3. Act like men. Of the five commands, this seems to be the most difficult because, in our society in the early 21st century, gender and gender expectations are in flux and questioned at

every level and every turn. Reviewing multiple translations makes it clear this command has to do with courage and bravery, which imply defending either something or someone. As I write this chapter, the spring 2022 Russian invasion of Ukraine entered its third month; over five million Ukrainians had fled the country as refugees and emigrants. The vast majority of refugees were women and children, as all males of fighting age stayed in the country. They "acted like men".

    4. <u>Be strong</u>. Be decisive. When a decision is made, it should be clearly articulated and clearly implemented. This speaks not of brute strength but of unity of effort and unity of direction. Being strong is not always about might; in this passage, it is more about unity and purity.

    5. <u>Do everything in love</u>. It is noteworthy that divergent leadership books come to the conclusion that love must be at the core of all that is done within and for an organization[1].

<u>Lines on Leadership</u>
Taken together as a quintet, the five commands may at first be like keys to a golf swing where it is problematic to try to think about each one simultaneously. Taken in sequence, the five commands would make an excellent checklist at the end or beginning of a week as the leader reviews the past week in his/her organization. How did you do this past week?

_____
_____
++

2ND LETTER TO THE CORINTHIANS

Intro: The rich word images of 2 Corinthians have long been a treasure trove for preachers and for leadership development. There are five sets of multiple epistles to one location or person in the NT: 1&2 Corinthians, 1&2 Thessalonians, 1&2 Timothy, 1&2 Peter, and 1, 2, &3 John. In each set, the first epistle is the longest and has more "moving parts" to its content. In each set, the second epistle reveals a more personal side of the writer and is often a second installment in the writer's thoughts that necessitate a more thorough treatment.

2 Corinthians is a passionate, protracted defense of Paul's apostolic credentials. At some point in a leader's opposition, scoffing, denial, and outright attacks will surface, the most painful coming from those who were formerly close and in agreement with the leader. Paul was rather severe in his treatment of the Corinthian church in the first epistle, and after several years' absence, he decided to send this letter ahead of his return to Corinth to reestablish his status and in the case of some to establish it in light of their resistance to his apostolic standing.

++

2nd Corinthians 1---Highlights: heavenly comfort; the questioning of Paul's integrity and identity

v. 4-5—"He *comforts* us in all our affliction, so that we may be able to *comfort* those who are in any kind of affliction, through the *comfort* we ourselves receive from God. For just as the sufferings of Christ overflow to us, so also through Christ our *comfort* overflows." (CSB, italics mine)

Comfort and affliction are inseparable. Leaders are viewed outwardly as highly motivated by success, reward, victory, wealth, or personal fulfillment. But inwardly, many are driven by the interplay of affliction and comfort. If everything is going well, a leader rarely feels the need for comfort. When everything craters or shudders to a halt, especially when it is costly to us financially, physically, or spiritually, we seek comfort, something to hold on to, something that will give us security in the midst of chaos, something that points a way out of bleakness into brightness.

A mature faith-based leader acknowledges that a sovereign God is involved in both our afflictions and our comfort. From the earliest book of the Bible (Job) through the last book of the New Testament (Revelation), suffering and comfort have a close relationship. Both assurance and consternation result from reading such verses as Eccl. 7.14, Prov. 16.4, Lam. 3.38, Is. 45.7 ("The One forming light and creating darkness, Causing peace and creating calamity; I am the LORD who does all these things.") and 2 Cor. 1. Note the promise of Paul's words, comfort comes from God through Christ. <u>Comfort is not always equated with nor attached to understanding</u>. The understanding comes eventually through the exercise of comforting others with the lessons and comfort I received.

That comfort can manifest as a ministry of presence, encouragement, instruction, inspiration, or joining in someone's difficult walk alongside them. The week I typed this chapter, our family transferred the matriarch of my wife's side, her 97-year-old mother, from assisted living to skilled nursing care. It was a short trip from one floor to another in terms of distance in our local nursing home, but financially it was a leap from $3500/month to $11,000+/month in expenses. General wisdom we had been told was that we would have to exhaust her checking account and personal assets down to $2000 before we could even apply for Medicaid (our government's medical care for those unable to afford it). Our nursing home staff was kind enough to give us a contact in our state who knew otherwise.

The contact's mother had done exactly that in her later years, blowing through her life savings to afford those last months of intensive care. When he saw the trauma and anxiety it caused the whole family, he vowed not to let that happen to others and started a Medicaid advisory group to share with others what he learned. His fee has been worth every penny as he found ways for us to apply <u>now</u> for the mother-in-law's Medicaid instead of using up all of her assets. This removed the financial trauma and drama from her last days and allowed us to concentrate on comforting her.

A few months after the above paragraphs were written, my mother-in-law passed on to glory. My wife and I were privileged to sing hymns of hope to her during her last three hours. While we sang "Face to Face with Christ my Savior", she breathed her last breath. It was, for us, a holy moment (see Lk. 22 & Rom. 10 entries). My father had passed on two years earlier at age 99. The grief and sorrow of that earlier experience with an aging parent going on to glory prepared us well for Rubye's homegoing. Out of our affliction God granted us comfort as we led out in the organization of the services and resultant estate settlement.

<u>Lines on Leadership</u>
Learned or accrued comfort is a wealth that leaders need to not hoard but give away. In the giving away of our comfort, we enrich ourselves. Who needs or will soon need your comfort so you can lead them to comfort others?

_____

_____

++

2nd Corinthians 2---Highlights: extended analogy of a military victory parade

v. 14a: "Thanks be to God, who always leads us in His triumph in Christ." Many thanks are owed to Ron Dunn (former pastor of MacArthur Blvd. Baptist Church, Irving, TX and conference speaker) for his memorable sermon, "Chained to the Chariot", which was my first introduction to this rich passage of scripture[1].

Vs. 14-17 contain a rich series of word images that center on an ancient Roman victory parade. If a Roman general waged a significant and successful military campaign, he was rewarded with a parade down the main street of Rome with all appropriate fanfare and pomp. Three word images relate to leadership and different perspectives on it.

1) The victorious general would lead the parade, and chained to his chariot would be the vanquished armies' commanders walking behind. Leaders can identify with both perspectives: a) we usually prepare ourselves for adversity and struggle, but seeing ourselves as victorious and not only contributing to the victory but leading its processional reward is a position hard for some to envision. Paul describes us elsewhere as "more than conquerors" through God (Rom. 8.37). The converse position is to be one of the vanquished foes. As a Christian, I realize my participation in a victory comes after I surrender to the Lordship of Christ; the falling confetti, flowers, and music are not for me, but for the one firmly in charge of the chariot (v. 14). Paul uses the same phrasing in Col. 2.15 ("He made a public display of them, having triumphed over them through Him[2, 3]").

2) Surrounding the general's chariot were people swinging incense holders, which emitted a special fragrance reserved for these occasions. The crowds instantly recognized it

as the smell of victory. To one side of the conflict, it smelled like victory; to the other side, it smelled of death and destruction (vs. 15-16). Smell is one of the strongest memory triggers. What memory triggers will people in your group use to remember your singular victory?

3) Peddlers would strategically work the crowd selling their wares. Because the masses were in a festive mood, they did not mind or were not aware they had paid for diluted wine cut with other fluids to increase the peddlers' profits or that they were not getting the genuine products but instead some inferior copies (v. 17). Paul encourages the reader to speak with integrity because we speak "as from God, we speak in Christ in the sight of God." (v. 17) The Gospel is not a product to peddle but a treasure to proclaim and should be handled as if it was indeed precious.

Lines on Leadership
Good leaders can take whatever posture is required by the situation, either the victor or the vanquished. Our accomplishments give off an aroma of success or failure, depending on the perspective. Our message must be heralded with integrity. How have you (as a minister or business leader) taken the roles of victor/vanquished/incense swinger/hawker of goods? Are you willing to take the vanquished as well as the victor's position in order for your group to succeed? (For the Christian, it is of no consequence whether the person leads the parade or is the object of derision; the main thing is that Christ triumphs) What is the "aroma" of your group in the greater community in which it exists? When you share x presentation with others (peddle your wares), what do you add or take away to make it more palatable or profitable? What degree of integrity is present?

++

2nd Corinthians 3---Highlights: aspects of the new covenant

Vs. 17-18 "Now the Lord is the Spirit; and where the Spirit of the Lord is, there is liberty. But we all, with unveiled face beholding as in a mirror the glory of the Lord, are being transformed into the same image from glory to glory, just as from the Lord, the Spirit."

When I applied for the Ph.D. program at Dallas Baptist University to be in their second-ever cohort, the director of the then-fledgling program repeated one word that caught my ear and imagination—transformative. She assured me the same person I was when I started the doctoral program would not be the same person who graduated with the degree. She said the transformation would not end at graduation but continue for the rest of my professional and personal life. She was right. There were certain rights and privileges that come immediately upon completion of a terminal degree, but learning how to behave and think like a leader, to carry the title of leader (not as an imposter masquerading as one), and come to see myself as a true leader, that came much later (see Gal. 4 entry).

Most clichés are truths trivialized from repetition, and the one repeated at almost every graduation ("this is not a culmination but a beginning") is a prime example. Paul's word image in vs. 17-18 speaks of both point and process (see 2 Pet. 1 entry). In the Matrix movie series, the protagonist Neo is in one way transported to a different reality from the one he is used to as "Mr. Anderson". The transformation to Neo starts dramatically and swiftly, but learning how to operate within his new reality is a constant revelation and learning process[1].

Salvation is both a point in time when the transformation begins and a process in which we are continually being conformed to His image. 2 Cor. 3 describes the beginning of the journey; 2 Cor. 4 and then chapter 5 speak of a lifelong transition: a) from life on earth without Christ, b) to life on earth with Christ continually conforming me to His image, c) to life with Him in eternity.

Lines on Leadership

A key to a transformation's beginning and process is found in v. 6 when we read the famous "for the letter kills, but the Spirit gives life", a concept gloriously expanded in Romans 8. The letter (a stand-in term for the Law) can only condemn, can only point out what needs to be done and gives no way to ultimately do anything but break it. The Spirit is what transforms a person. As a leader, the quicker I realize that policy manuals show followers how to transact, but leaders show followers how to transform, the quicker I'll see true transformation in my group. Paper begets paper, policies beget policies, programs beget programs, life begets life.

_____

_____

++

2nd Corinthians 4---Highlights: qualities of a good leader

Chapter 4 is bookended by chapter 3, where Paul extols the mystery and glory of Christ coming to dwell in a believer as Lord (3.16-18) and chapter 5, which describes our relationship to Christ after this life (5.1-9). Chapter 4 is what we are to become in between chapters 3 & 5. It contains one of the most comprehensive sets of characteristics for a leader found in the New Testament. It became a staple lesson on leadership in many venues and is offered here in a much-abridged version applicable to church and corporate settings alike, with vocabulary adjusted to fit your situation.

<u>Leaders are to be</u>:

1. a **Student** of the Word. V. 2 admonishes us not to "adulterate" the Word of God. The original language term refers to wine merchants who would often dilute or "cut" the wine with other products to stretch their profits and swindle the customer. Not only are we to refrain from diluting or twisting the Word ("walking in craftiness"), our lives are to be "manifestations of the truth" as we live by what we discover in it. (see Jn. 13, 2 Cor.2 entries)

2. a **Servant** Leader. v. 5, "We do not preach ourselves but Christ Jesus as Lord, and ourselves as your bond-servants for Jesus' sake." In a recent conversation, some teens related to me how they so deeply wanted a certain position with a certain title to denote they were now recognized as a leader. According to Paul in this passage, the "title" we are to seek is to be known as servants of Christ, with the emphasis not on our servanthood but on our Lord.

3. a **Steady** Influence. The chapter begins with "therefore, since we have this ministry, as we received mercy, we do not lose heart" and continues in v. 16, "we do not lose heart, thought our outer man is decaying, yet our inner man is being renewed day by day". In researching my scores of journals, it is breathtaking how many times circumstantial deep valleys and soaring summits occur within 24 hours. Maintaining a steady outlook does not deny passion or frustration, ecstasy or despair, nor is it about an averaged-out "end of the day" score; it is about keeping our eyes laser-focused on the Lord.

4. **Secure** in his/her limitations. In v. 7, we are described as "jars of clay" or "earthen vessels", depending on the

translation. A leader should have enthusiasm and optimism in abundance but have a realistic assessment of his physical, mental, financial, social, and educational parameters, which ones can be altered over time, and which ones are there to stay.

5. a **Sacrifice** (vs.8-12). Leaders must be prepared to be the shock absorbers in life. This goes way beyond "taking one for the team". Jesus gave the ultimate example as the One who sacrificed Himself to satisfy the requirements for our sin and allowed us to break its power over us. <u>The majority of a leader's sacrifice of time, effort, reputation, and lost opportunities for self-promotion will be known only to him</u>. You have to decide for whom or for what x sacrifice is worth it all. The tribulations and adversities of this life provide the fiery kiln in which those jars of clay are hardened into useful vessels for the Master.

6. **Selfless,** v. 15, "For all things are for your sakes, so that the grace which is spreading to more and more people may cause the giving of thanks to abound to the glory of God." A succinct, chiastic definition of this is: "True humility is not thinking less of yourself, it is thinking of yourself less." (attributed to but not likely to be from C.S. Lewis)

7. a **Standard** of conduct. All of these qualities will make the leader's life a standard against which others can measure themselves. In other NT books, we see this spelled out more clearly using Paul as that standard (1 Cor. 4.16; 1 Cor. 11.1; Phil. 3.17; Phil. 4.9; 1 Thess. 1.6; 2 Thess. 3.7-9) or other leaders among the church members (Heb. 13.7).

<u>Lines on Leadership</u>
In what ways has your life been an example of being a student, a servant leader, a steady influence, secure in your limitations, a sacrifice, selfless, and a standard of conduct? What needs to change to become such a leader for your group?

++

2nd Corinthians 5---Highlights: the temporal and the eternal contrasted "For we walk by faith and not by sight" is my "life verse" (2 Cor. 5.7). That is the reason there are 50+ walking sticks on display in my office; people who knew my "life verse" donated to my global collection of sticks over the years. Let's explore what "walk by faith" means on a daily basis.

     The diagram below is an overly simple visual of this principle. The rectangle represents the passage of time, be it days, months, or years, and from left to right. When I enter a new area of life in which I have no experience, the grace of God is dominant in that He guides my every step and provides close supervision. I feel His presence strongly in this new endeavor as I lean on His Spirit's leadership (Gal. 5.16-25); every new believer has sensed this at the beginning of their spiritual pilgrimage. Our heavenly Father watches over our every step in this new area of life, much like we guide a child's steps as he learns to walk, clean a room, or ride a bike.

However, the diagonal line shows (over the passage of time) that grace gradually takes a back seat to wisdom. This represents what happens in all parenting situations: We guide with words, hands, and facial expressions extremely closely. Over time the child is expected to learn how to walk, how to clean the room, and how to ride a bike. He/she is to acquire wisdom, what we are oft instructed to do in the entire book of Proverbs (I read the book of Prov. every January). In terms of "feeling" or "sensing" the Spirit, it can be mistakenly perceived as if God draws away from us. Relax, He is always with us, even to the end of the world (Mt. 28.18-20). He wants us to grow and mature in Him, acquire wisdom and order our lives accordingly. It doesn't replace grace, as the diagram might mistakenly seem to represent (I'm not an artist, and I would welcome suggestions to improve it). After He determines I've had enough time to acquire wisdom, He expects me to use that wisdom to order my life. If you fall into a hole over & over, and He miraculously lifts you out of it, you learn little. If, after the third time, you have to crawl and pull your way out of the hole, it doesn't mean God abandoned you; it means He thinks it's time to acquire wisdom enough to avoid falling in, and He allows you to gain that wisdom in a way you will become more careful! (see Phil. 4 entry)

So, walking by faith (v. 7) is continuing to launch into new areas of my life, much like when the priests' feet touched the Jordan River in Joshua 3.13. When I'm in a new area of life, He intercedes and guides me much more closely and intimately; after a while, I am to learn the ways my Father operates in this realm and walk in a similar fashion (1 Pet. 2.21). <u>Leaders think in the comparative mode (longer, faster, deeper, stronger, quicker, better), always looking for a new way to increase production or stretch resources</u>. As a Christian, this grace/wisdom concept has always lowered the fear factor for me when launching into a new territory of leadership. I know my Father will initially guide me from close at hand, showing me when and where to step, and will give me His allotted time to acquire wisdom on how to continue in that once new, now familiar area.

A pronounced manifestation of this is when a person lands in a disparate culture with a new language to acquire. The cognitive connections just aren't there to form the words. So, I have to rely on the Lord, on others, and on trusted friends. At first, they guide me closely until I become acquainted with the right words to say, the right gestures to make, or the right direction to go. Missionaries describe the first year of language study and work in the field as both challenging and exhilarating because of a heightened dependence on and sensitivity to the Spirit of God as language and culture acquisition occurs. This cycle of grace and wisdom repeats over and over as they venture into uncharted territory for them linguistically, culturally, and strategically.

Lines on Leadership
Describe a time when grace was clearly evident in your life and then when it took a back seat to godly wisdom in your decision-making.

_____

_____

++

2nd Corinthians 6---Highlights: the ministry as a balancing act

v.14, "Do not be unequally yoked with unbelievers, for what partnership has righteousness with lawlessness, or what fellowship has light with darkness?" (ESV) v. 14a "Don't become partners with those who do not believe." (CSB)

There is a delicate balance here for a leader. Becoming partners with those who do not live by nor incorporate the gospel is not only discouraged but strongly admonished. Paul clearly distinguishes the two groups as righteousness and light as opposed to lawlessness and darkness and continues the analogy in the following verses. Yet one does not lead in a theoretical vacuum with the faithful and the faithless as clearly separate. Leadership, whether sacred or secular, must engage the world at some point. We buy or sell to the world; we sometimes are forced to form alliances with those who do not share our values in order to achieve a greater good or to honor a previous pact of a previous generation (see 2 Kings 3, Jehoram and Jehoshaphat, Jehoshaphat and Ahab).

I admire the attempt of any church to maintain fidelity to its doctrines and practices to keep the Gospel pure in its proclamation. But sometimes, in a church's desire to stay pure, it becomes paranoid about becoming tainted. Its desire to stay unstained by the world if left unchecked causes it to be uncooperative and to stay in its self-constructed monastic bubble of purity. This is unsustainable if we are to engage the world with the gospel; it is unsustainable in business where one often deals with companies or individuals whose desires are less savory than the leaders'. Paul often speaks of false teachers and, later in the Pastoral Epistles, admonishes Timothy and Titus to beware of those who infiltrate the church with false doctrine. At the same time, Jesus speaks extensively in the parable of the wheat and tares (Matt. 13.24-30) about letting the two crops grow mixed, with their disparities coming clear when the plants mature.

The key word in this verse is "yoked". If I have a gospel, a product, or a service I want to offer to others, I want as much interaction with as many people groups as possible. Entering into conversation or commerce with as many as possible is desirable for every leader. However, he must be careful with the ones to whom he enjoins himself, enters into a symbiotic partnership, and offers the trusted bonds of a covenant relationship. To be unequally yoked with those who do not share my values can, in time, dilute or corrupt my values or, to the outside world, make my values hypocritical and hollow.

To see this explained succinctly from an ecclesiological standpoint ("we can only engage a pluralist and secular society if we have clarity about what it means to be the church"), see Gordon Smith's *Wisdom from Babylon*[1]. To see this explained from a missiological standpoint, see Newbigin's *Foolishness to the Greeks*[2].

Lines on Leadership

In reviewing past "yokes" in ministry or business, which ones were or were not advisable? As a leader, are you prepared to leave a contract or partnership on the table if you feel the two parties are "unequally yoked?"

_____

_____

++

2nd Corinthians 7---Highlights: the heart of Paul is bared

v. 10 "For the sorrow that is according to *the will of* God produces a repentance without regret, *leading* to salvation; but the sorrow of the world produces death." True moral guilt versus false guilt may sound like theological calisthenics to some, but it is crucial to understand as a leader. Paul refers to the multitude of issues within the Corinthian church, often in both epistles, sometimes with forceful language, and that is the main subject matter of this chapter. The key is to discern the sources of the admonition and its intent.

If the admonition comes from the world, it comes from an endless number of sources for an endless number of reasons; it weighs down the soul, suffocates it, and gives no room for response or attempts to understand it; it just comes as an unending avalanche. Social media and instant feedback from anonymous authorship multiply the severity and weight of the sorrow from unrelenting criticism till it crushes a person ("the sorrow of the world produces death"). The only defense seems to be "shut it off", but to have interaction with any portion of the world (professionally or personally), one cannot remain totally cut off from it. The world heads everything toward entropy (see Col. 3 entry) because it is convinced the self is superior to anything God could possibly have to say; so to have hundreds to thousands of selves speaking in admonition results in chaos.

The paragraph above is hypothetical. In today's world, it is impossible to remain unconnected to anyone and be successful. Indeed, the very nature of leadership connects one to others, and by virtue of their connection, they have input into the life of that leader. The key is making sure the voice I heed first and foremost is that of God. He speaks to me primarily through His Word and His Spirit and secondarily through His people (the church) and His providence, which I experience through circumstances[1]. Throughout scripture, God demonstrates His love and His desire to redeem. The entire biblical narrative declares He paid the ultimate price to restore His creation unto Himself in Christ Jesus; therefore, any word of admonishment from God will have redemption at its core. God's edicts can seem at times harsh and inscrutable, but they lead to life (Mt. 7.13-14; 1 Jn. 5.12).

Lines on Leadership

One day as I drove our SUV down a curvy back road, I came across a young mother tightly grasping the hand of a screaming, unhappy daughter. As I slowed down, I saw not only sorrow but anger on the face of the child: How could this spiteful adult hold me back from running free? The mother's face seemed to say, 'Thank you for understanding. I am not a bad mother.' Her actions saved that child from running in front of my vehicle to certain destruction. As a leader, I must undergo discipline administered by my Father, knowing it is for my good (Heb. 12.4-11). As I learn the value of this approach, I eventually treat my followers accordingly: Restrictions and reprimands are always undergirded by redemption. Consider the last time you had to correct a person in your group. Was redemption the foundation of your decision?

_____

_____

++

2<u>nd</u> <u>Corinthians 8</u>---Highlights: Macedonian offering, the collective voice of the churches, mutual respect

There are three (at least) areas of leadership in 1 Cor. 8: abundant generosity, beginnings of associational life, and cultivating respect.

1) Abundant generosity: Paul commends the Macedonians (a city-state well known to the Corinthians) not only for their generosity but for their sacrifice (they "gave beyond their ability of their own accord", v. 3), for their eagerness to help (v. 4), and for their priorities ("They first gave themselves to the Lord and to us by the will of God," v. 5). It is a best practices model to share with all of the established house churches strewn across Europe, Africa, and the Middle East. It shows a group that

gave way beyond any expectations, practically begged to participate and saw what they were doing as an act of worship.

2) Beginnings of associational life: In vs. 18-19, the development of Christianity had grown to the point that the churches banded together and made a united decision to send "the brother" (widely thought to be Luke) to accompany Paul. The following verses show the brother was sent to assist Paul and also hold him accountable for the offering being gathered from the various churches throughout Asia Minor and Europe for the church in Jerusalem. Instead of edicts issued by "the top down", this is a collective voice of the local churches being expressed to Paul, the most prominent leader of the movement. As I write, I work with around 40 churches in ten counties, and I see this passage as crucial to the formation of what we call an association, a voluntary banding together of local churches so they can do more for the Kingdom synergistically than separately.

3) Cultivating respect: Paul extends a measure of respect to persons and to groups. He commends Titus and the unnamed brother to all the churches as to their purpose and character. He shows respect to the Gentile churches and does not treat them as second-class in relationship to the "mother" church in Jerusalem. He hopes to show the Jerusalem church the genuineness of the Gentile churches' faith by gathering this offering from town to town. He does not pit one church against another but instead commends each one to lift up and edify each other. They are all full Kingdom partners.

<u>Lines on Leadership</u>
This chapter outlines much of what I do as an associational leader. I often relate best practices I see in one church to encourage others to adapt that model for their use. I help churches make decisions to voluntarily pool their resources to

mutually benefit themselves and others beyond themselves. I try my best to lift up our pastors to their flocks both for their commendation and for their prayerful support. As a leader, what are you doing within your organization to relate best practices, encourage mutual input and collective decision-making, and show respect up and down the corporate ladders?

Bonus: This is all summed up in v.9, "For you know the grace of our Lord Jesus Christ, that though He was rich, yet for your sake He became poor, that you through His poverty might become rich."

_____

_____

++

2nd Corinthians 9---Highlights: insights on giving

v. 6 "Now I say this: the one who sows sparingly will also reap sparingly, and the one who sows generously will also reap generously." This verse has been ripped out of context by televangelists eager to fatten their coffers and by those who want to prove the Bible speaks of karma. Taken alone, it sounds pretty common sense that you get out of something what you put into it. Both groups violate a basic principle of hermeneutics: always read a verse in context.

The following verses 9-15 show a now familiar pattern: My generosity will be amplified and expanded beyond what I can imagine if God is involved and <u>gets the credit</u>. The generosity is neither key nor catalyst; it is a junior partner in the process (see Mt. 11 entry). Through my generosity the grace of God flows into the lives of others, much in line with the previous definition of spiritual gifts (see 1 Cor. 12 entry). This continues as long as we teach along with our generosity for others to continue in our example that the grace of God may flow into as many lives as possible. Any benefit I derive from my generosity must remain secondary; the moment I think first about what rewards I get for my generosity, it all dries up. Let me explain with a simple exercise I've used many times to illustrate this principle.

Push the chairs and tables in a room to the side and have the group stand together in the middle. Hand out several coins to each person. Tell them on the count of three to start giving away what they have to each other and concentrate on making sure others have coins around them until you shout STOP. When it begins, go about a minute and listen to the laughter and the joy. After shouting STOP, don't ask how that felt or what did they experience. Immediately announce now on the count of three; I want you to amass as many coins as you can and hold on to them. Go! The mood in the room flips quickly to fear, suspicion, or open anger. It's best not to let them go as long as the first round; it can get out of hand! Once they have done both rounds, have them sit down and talk through the exercise.

Later in the chapter, Paul mentions how the Lord loves a cheerful giver (v.7). The joy comes from seeing the recipients not only benefit from my gift but learn to do the same for others. His grace abounds as He takes what I give and multiplies it so I can "abound in every good work" (v. 8). God is always the source and the sustainer, as summed up in verses 10-11, "Now He who supplies seed to the sower and bread for food will supply and multiply your seed for sowing and increase the harvest of your righteousness; you will be enriched in everything for all liberality, which through us is producing thanksgiving to God." It is the full circle we also see in Romans 11.36, "For from Him, and through Him, and to Him are all things. To Him be the glory forever." As long as my personal benefit remains a side effect and not the main reason to give, God will bless it. God gave freely and completely in the death, burial, and resurrection of Christ; how can I do anything but follow in those steps and give freely and completely so others can live and prosper and triumph? And pass it on to others?

Lines on Leadership

In the coin exercise, why was one round full of hilarity and the other one ugly? Is your church or organization geared toward serving others or themselves? Are the products of your ministry or business primarily to make money for your group or designed to serve and benefit others?

_____

_____

++

2nd Corinthians 10---Highlights: spiritual warfare, the relationship of Paul to outside influences in Corinth

Preachers love to dive into vs. 3-5 that deal with spiritual warfare (v.4, "For the weapons of our warfare are not of the flesh, but divinely powerful for the destruction of fortresses.") and rail against satanic forces seeking to nullify and destroy the church. They are correct on a spiritual plane; however, a more complete reading of the entire chapter reveals Paul was likely defending himself as he was taking the high ground against unseen forces of evil.

The lines of demarcation between cooperation and competition are often murky and overlapping. As an itinerant missionary/preacher on the move in the Mediterranean world, Paul knew when he left a particular location that others would come after him; he could not be in all the churches all the time where he had shared the gospel (no video conference calls back then). He knew some of these people would be honorable and some would not; some would continue to teach in a manner consistent with his gospel, and some would add to, dilute, substitute, thwart, and twist the teachings he had so carefully laid out to them. He also knew that some would come after him and not only reap the harvest sown by his labors, but they would also claim credit for it and not acknowledge his contributions.

It is difficult in leadership to discern where people are truly cooperating in and contributing to the same cause as you, using your efforts to slingshot beyond you and boost their own careers, or worse, subsume your work and claim it as their own. Walter Isaacson describes the fluid nature of these work relationships in *The Code Breaker*. He lays out a full treatment of colleagues who can become competitors and the speed with which those transformations occurred in the race to decipher the human genome and begin gene editing (such as the unbelievable pace to find the COVID-19 vaccine). He also explores through the main character (scientist Jennifer Doudna) how she interacted with those who proved to be chameleonic depending on whose papers got published first and the lengths to which people resorted, including herself, to be the first to the finish line with breaking developments[1].

In my current ministry, our associations of churches have a geographical locus but no specific boundaries like county or state lines; my ten counties in which I work have several other associations that have churches in near proximity to our churches. Three of our associational churches are dually aligned with other associations and even other state conventions. In a day when geographical proximity gives way to connection points in terms of affiliation, this means I have to maintain good relationships with other counterparts even when their church planting efforts may "intrude" or "overlap" mine. In Paul's case, the murkiness involves doctrine; in Doudna's case, it involves data and its use; and in my case, it involves the possible duality of allegiance with possible overtones of "turfism".

Lines on Leadership

'Trust but verify' has been attributed to everything from Ronald Reagan to Russian proverbs[2]. Paranoia about every little difference between colleagues has often alienated them or made them into competitors (as I see in many independent churches). Blind trust of every colleague and their intentions as being honorable is an invitation to disaster (for a fuller treatment, see Covey's *Smart Trust*[3]). In light of this chapter, what is your attitude toward colleagues and their interaction with your work/reputation/legacy?

_____

_____

++

2nd Corinthians 11---Highlights: Paul's defense of his apostolic credentials

2 Cor. 11 is a continuation and intensification of the concerns in chapter 10. Paul goes as far as to compare the false teachers to demonic beings in the memorable phrase, "For even Satan disguises himself as an angel of light" (v.14). I often joke that my spiritual gift is cynicism, but after fifty years of ministry I have seen my share of charlatans and connivers who have the vocabulary and presentation down so well they sound sincere; they hold the Bible with one hand and quietly pick your pocket with the other. Diligence is required to find out what is 'veneer' and what is 'core' with colleagues' motives.

Paul contrasts their motives with his in one of the most dramatic and personal words of testimony in the NT. Vs. 22-28 describes the cumulative sufferings he has endured for the sake of the gospel, including beatings, shipwrecks, constant danger, and deprivation. He enumerates them not to evoke pity but to bolster his claims of integrity in contrast to the false teachers, and the climax of the litany of these experiences is v. 28, where, above all, he carries the burden of concern for all the churches. None of the lashes or nights spent on the open sea compared to the heaviness of his heart for the viability of the churches. He offers this as strong evidence of his true motives toward them. Earlier in the chapter, he reminds them he came without charge since the Macedonians had provided for his needs (v.7), likely in contrast to those who taught for fees.

This teeters on bragging and being audacious, but such assertions are biblically legitimate if the focus of the boasting is not the one boasting but God. "Let not a wise man boast of his wisdom, and let not the mighty man boast of his might, let not a rich man boast of his riches; but let him who boasts boast of this, that he understands and knows me, that I am the LORD, who exercises lovingkindness, justice, and righteousness on earth." (Jer. 9.23-24)

Lines on Leadership
In both ministry and corporate work, background checks are a necessary component of rooting out those who might appear to be assets when they are, in reality, liabilities. Mastery of competencies is trumped by the purity of motive in this passage. Too many companies and even more churches dispense with background checks thinking they are intrusive, an invasion of privacy, and confrontational. I not only want to know if their record is clean but if it is pure. How do you determine the true motives of those you bring into your work or ministry group?

++

2nd Corinthians 12---Highlights: Paul's heavenly vision; his thorn in the flesh

Paul had just about had it. The false teachers he knew would follow him to Corinth (as they had all across Asia Minor) and would draw and keep crowds with fanciful visions that had the teachers at the center of the story. Many ministers can be drawn into what some call "top that testimony", where ever more spectacular and grandiose narratives are produced to keep the attention of one's followers. Paul did not want to get stuck in such an endless cycle ("Boasting is necessary though it is not profitable," v.1) but also did not want to back down and slip into the shadows. So the first verses (1-6) describe an incredible journey into the highest of heavens that would be hard to top without immediately naming the person having the vision ("I know a man who. . ."). It becomes apparent by the chapter's end that Paul is the person in the roundabout claim and further establishes his apostleship to the Corinthians.

To make sure the readers understand Paul is not out and out bragging and that there is no danger of him getting the proverbial "big head", by receiving this vision, he describes his "thorn in the flesh", which keeps his feet firmly and humbly on the ground with no danger of him floating off into celestial ecstasy. It is not stated what the thorn is (disease, annoying person, speech condition) or if God sent it, but it is permitted by the Lord as Paul prayed three times for release from its presence and was denied all three times (v.8). Whether it was God ordained or God allowed is theological gymnastics when one's sufferings curtail strength or neutralize efforts.

When a thorn pricks or pierces the flesh, it demands one's total attention and crowds out every other thought. On a trip to the Holy Land, our guide pointed out the shrub/tree thought to provide the branches for Christ's crown at the crucifixion. Everyone's eyes opened wide as we saw and felt the several inches long thorns on the branches. To barely touch them induced pain; to contemplate them pressing into the flesh caused more than one misty eye.

One state (the thorn in the flesh) can occupy one's thoughts to the point of uselessness because it becomes all-encompassing. The other state (caught up to the third heaven, "whether in the body or apart from the body I do not know," v.3) can equally occupy one's thoughts to the point of uselessness from the viewpoint of day-to-day work. Paul did not know if he was on earth seeing heaven in his mind's eye or vice versa. This is not about moderation, achieving a healthy blend of the two; in that case, they would balance each other out. It is about acknowledging the reality of both being in my life and learning how each one informs the other so that I might deal rightly with the gospel entrusted to me as a minister. The gospel message I am to proclaim is susceptible to embellishment and attachment of my ego to it to gain stature; it can also become a crushing weight under which I often struggle. As a leader, I need to not only find a healthy co-existence of these two tendencies (so I stay "on message") but also acknowledge it can also be about the sequencing or seasons of the two.

Lines on Leadership
What enduring image, vision, or story compels you to lead further? Which thorn in the flesh keeps your ego in check?

++

2ⁿᵈ Corinthians 13---Highlights: get in line with the truth

Vs. 2b-4 "²ᵇIf I come again, I will not spare anyone, ³ since you are seeking for proof of the Christ who speaks in me, and who is not weak toward you, but mighty in you. ⁴ For indeed He was crucified because of weakness, yet He lives because of the power of God. For we also are weak in Him, yet we shall live with Him because of the power of God directed toward you."

Paul came to the conclusion that if the Corinthians wanted a display of power, he would give them one, but he preferred softer diplomacy to a raw show of authority. An isolated yet crucial element of leadership is to possess a working knowledge of the surrounding culture's value structure. Some cultures value strength and valor; some honor a more genteel approach to one's position of leadership. Some cultures advocate a softer approach yet, in actuality, reward the stronger one. In our time in Germany, we were often forced to take a passive position in discussions mainly because of our language proficiency, not as a sign of maturity or choice of behavior. Not knowing the cultural cues also puts one in a defensive, passive mode; for several years, we were never sure if our words or deeds were being received as offensive or inconsequential. We decided it was better to be thought of as too benign rather than too belligerent, so we adopted an attitude of patience and deferment in dealings with our German supervisors. This often put us at a disadvantage because the people we dealt with had strong honored tactics and strong personalities in their leaders more than acts of service and humble hearts.

The servant leadership advocated throughout this book (because of its numerous Biblical examples) can often give the impression of weakness, a posture easily misinterpreted as docility. The same Christ on His knees washing His disciples' feet in John 13 is the same Christ revealed as the triumphant Lamb of God in John's Revelation. His servanthood is not servitude; it is a chosen behavior to love His people with their knowledge of His power as the background. The disciples had seen Him perform miracles over and over again, command the elements, heal broken bones, open silent mouths, and restore leprous bodies to health. They knew He was the Christ, the Son of the living God; for Him to willingly become their Servant and ultimately a Sacrifice on their behalf drove them to show power through their weakness.

<u>Lines on Leadership</u>
What is the prevailing culture of your church or company in regard to strength being shown in weakness? How does it affect your leadership's display of discipline, celebration, and service?

_____
_____
++

LETTER TO THE GALATIANS

Intro: The location of Galatians was southern Asia Minor (modern Turkey). Galatians has often been referred to as the Reader's Digest version of Romans. Indeed, some of the same themes appear in both books, but Paul is definitely addressing a local church here, its attendant local issues, and local happenings (such as dressing down Peter on one occasion, 2.11ff). He interprets events from far away such as the council at Jerusalem (see Acts 15 entry) to the local church. Galatians contains some of Paul's richest word images and the believer's relationship to the Holy Spirit which results in the fruit of the Spirit (5.22).

++

Galatians 1---Highlights: purity of the gospel, Paul's credentials as an apostle

One of my early mentors in ministry often talked about climbing the corporate ladder, only to discover it was leaning on the wrong wall. In his particular case, he was rising up the ranks of a then-large telecommunications company when God called him into full-time ministry. In vs. 13-18, Paul describes a similar situation where he had gained stature among Pharisees and notoriety for his persecution of this new rebel sect that called themselves Christians. His frame of reference was not just expanded but shattered on the road to Damascus (see Acts 9). Yet he did not dive immediately into the God-given task of bringing the gospel to the Gentiles; he purposefully went away to gain perspective and distanced himself in both location and time from the initial event (v.17).

The parallel between Moses and Jesus is striking. Moses needed years in the desert to prepare for the task of delivering the Jewish people from bondage in Egypt to life in the Promised Land. Jesus came to earth from heaven as the pre-existent Christ and needed years to adjust to life on a human plane before delivering His Kingdom from bondage to freedom through His teachings, death, burial, and resurrection. Paul wisely chose not to immediately preach this new (to him) gospel but instead to wrap his head and heart around the enormity and complexity of his assigned task. He mentions three years in Arabia and Damascus (v.17) and again an interval of fourteen years (Gal. 2.1). His years of preparation resulted in the masterpieces of theology (study of God), missiology (study of missions), ecclesiology (study of the church), and soteriology (study of salvation) found in his epistles that form the majority of New Testament content. He was not only an extraordinary evangelist and missionary but a theologian of the first rank.

God favors an informed faith. That faith can be informed by formal learning such as advanced degrees from college and seminary; it can be from years of accumulated wisdom gleaned from experience. It can also come from mentored relationships or extended times of contemplation when the random dots on life's page slowly coalesce into a recognizable pattern. Instinctual responses may now and then save the day for an organization, but a well-informed faith (deepened and widened by the dredging of reflection and contemplation) may best provide the necessary long-term route on which to navigate that same organization.

Lines on Leadership
Taking time to become thoroughly equipped for a lifelong task goes against the adage to "strike while the iron is hot" that an opportunity recognized and not seized likely becomes an opportunity lost. A paramount quality of leadership is being able to recognize when to plunge into something or pause and gather more information or perspective on that same thing. What is the

need of the hour/day/year for you and the present task before you, plunge or pause?

_____

_____

+++

Galatians 2---Highlights: approval of Paul's gospel in Jerusalem; confrontation with Peter and visitors

The first ten verses describe a high-level meeting in Jerusalem when Paul has his version of the gospel examined by the leaders of the Jerusalem church, the "mother" church of early Christianity. The listing of names involved reads like a first-century "dream team": Paul, Barnabas, Titus, Peter, James, and John. The bulk of the NT was authored by this group (see Acts 15 entry). They were responsible for setting the parameters and directions of the early church; their contributions cannot be overestimated.

When heavyweights within any organization come together to establish policy and guidelines, it is inevitable that tensions arise. Everyone's opinions should be recognized and valued, yet everyone in the room feels deeply about their stance, their division of the organization, and their contribution to whatever issue is on the table. Paul uses language that at first suggests disparagement toward his contemporaries who lead the Jerusalem church ("reputed to be pillars"), but in reality, his disparagement is toward the false teachers who came to Antioch demanding the OT laws of circumcision be a requisite for salvation. It is not certain who called the meeting, Paul or the Jerusalem apostles. This meeting would determine whether there is one gospel or infinite variations of it, which would, in effect, nullify it (see Acts 15). They emerge at the end of the section, unified on there being no additional prerequisites to faith in Christ. This is not a product of negotiated compromise; it is the result of them sublimating their reputations to the gospel itself and making sure its proclamation rang true regardless of who did the proclaiming. A side effect of this meeting was to establish Paul's legitimacy as a fellow apostle. They examined his gospel and heard from Titus as a case study of its outcome in his life.

Paul was an outsider; he had not grown up with Jesus like Jesus' half-brother James; he had not walked and talked with Jesus during His public ministry like Peter and John. He was a "Johnny-come-lately" since he was neither part of the resurrection and ascension of Jesus nor of the birth of the church at Pentecost (Acts 2). The apostles were wrapped up with the explosive growth of the Jerusalem church; Paul had traveled all over the countryside preaching to "those" people, the Gentiles. This meeting had multiple undercurrents and could have disintegrated at multiple points. It ended with a unified approach to the gospel, and Paul was recognized as a fellow apostle.

The postscript to that meeting was a subsequent visit northward by Peter to the church at Antioch (v. 11ff). Why he came is not known, whether out of personal curiosity or as a delegate from Jerusalem to see if the church indeed practiced what Paul had described. Nonetheless, this was Peter, a rock star at any church since he had been a part of the inner circle with Jesus (Peter, James, John), had preached the very first sermon at Pentecost, and had personally seen the gospel received by Gentiles (see Acts 10). The church at Jerusalem still operated at that point as a sect of Judaism and was slowly learning how to reconcile freedom in Christ with Jewish laws. The church at Antioch had no such heritage; it had received the gospel of freedom in Christ and taken off from there. Peter saw them eating and drinking in a manner that reflected that freedom and joined in.

When men from Jerusalem showed up and started a commotion about Jewish dietary laws being disregarded, Peter started to side with them, and Paul called his hand in no uncertain terms (vs.11-14), exposing the double standard Peter was exhibiting. Paul ends the chapter with a magnificent verse that encapsulates much of the gospel ("I have been crucified with Christ; and it is no longer I who live, but Christ lives in me; and the life which I now live in the flesh I live by faith in the Son of God, who loved me, and delivered Himself up for me," v. 20). He had not been reformed or improved by gradually modifying his lifestyle; he had died to his old life, his old self, his old ways, his old understanding. He was asking Peter to put into public display that which he had already learned in Joppa (Acts 10) and what he assented to (Acts 15) concerning the freedom we have in Christ.

<u>Lines on Leadership</u>
Knowing 1) what is right and 2) undoing old habits now unprofitable in a new order of things are often at odds. Has there ever been a time when you, as a leader, deserved to be called down due to old habits or customs surfacing that were incompatible with the direction your organization was going? What was your "Peter moment" and who was the "Paul" who called your hand?

_____

_____

++

Galatians 3---Highlights: relationship of faith and law

v.28 "There is neither Jew nor Greek, there is neither slave nor free man, there is neither male nor female, for you are all one in Christ Jesus." In this one sentence, Paul addresses nationality, people group, social standing, and sexuality and tells us those obvious points of distinction that define us to the world are secondary to our identity in Christ. This verse is not about obliterating our individual identities and melding into one nameless, faceless entity; it is about us sublimating those points of distinction and elevating our relationship to Christ to that which first and foremost defines our identity. Our citizenship, our skin color, our station in life vocationally, and our gender is not what defines us <u>as much as</u> our faith relationship to Christ (vs.23-26).

This does not minimize or ignore those distinctions; indeed, the body of Christ is richer by having members from all nations, from all levels of expertise and experience in the workforce, and of course, from men's and women's perspectives on living the faith-life. If those in a group derive their primary identity from Christ, it frees them up to be less concerned about whether they are a majority or a minority within the Kingdom of God.

When a group becomes too enamored of their "favored" status as Americans, or a particular political party that might at the time be "in power", or their social class that has the most clout, or their way of life that seems threatened by the circumstances of the day, they have taken their eyes off of Christ. Col. 3.11 repeats this same thought and adds the dimension of religion. Any particular grouping of mankind will have its cyclical waxing and waning in numbers and influence. Whether I am a part of the "ins" or the "outs" does not change my relationship with Christ.

The church does a poor job of reflecting the truth of this verse, and many companies are not much farther ahead. This is not about inclusivity and diversity and denying our heritage or our standing in our country, society, or community. This is about not elevating any of those distinctions to equal or superior status to one's relationship to Christ.

Much tension and trouble in churches and companies alike could be avoided if people were not afraid of losing their "preferred" status. The state in which I currently reside is 95% Caucasian; let that sink in. When I tell them that globally speaking, they, as "white" people, are already a minority, they look at me dumbfounded. When I say the majority of the world had dark eyes, dark hair, and dark skin, they might be able to do the math and concur cognitively but go about their daily routines as if that were not true. <u>A group that is a majority or perceives itself as "favored" will naturally assume their way, their attitude, and their set of mores is the norm</u>. The day is fast approaching (if not already here) when the majority of Christians will be in the Southern Hemisphere and not the American/European axis of the last five hundred years. The majority of Christians are now more South American, African, and Asian than European descent; it will radically change theology, expressions of worship, discipleship, and evangelism[1]. The quicker the church realizes this and embraces that our unity in Christ does not mean uniformity in all things, the better off it will be.

The day is coming when another currency might replace the American dollar as the global standard; the day is coming when alternate forms of energy will supplant and eventually replace fossil fuels. Certain areas of life will experience this cycle of influence and the lack of it; we can fight it, ignore it, or learn to rest in our primary identity as being in Christ, not as part of any faction, country, or alliance.

Lines on Leadership

As a leader, what are you doing to help those belonging to your organization to establish their primary identity in Christ? How will you celebrate their distinctions yet sublimate them to their primary identity being in Him?

_____

_____

++

Galatians 4---Highlights: Sonship in Christ; children of the law and children of promise

vs. 1-2 "Now I say, as long as the heir is a child, he does not differ at all from a slave although he is owner of everything, ² but he is under guardians and managers until the date set by the father."

We talk about patron saints of this or that cause; if there is such a thing as a patron "chapter" for middle management, interns, and leaders-in-waiting, this is it. It is a continuation of a word image in chapter 3, where the Law is compared to a tutor (often translated as child-conductor), the person who accompanied the future heir to his or her instructors (Gal. 3.24-26). A child in Biblical times (v.1) had as many rights as the slaves (meaning zero). Everyone knew who the child was by name and heritage, yet he did not obtain full status as an heir until such time as set by the parent (v.2). Until then, "managers and guardians" watched over, instructed, and protected the child from having the full weight of duties and responsibilities set upon immature shoulders. When the child reached the pre-determined point set by the parent, he was officially deemed ready to assume those duties and responsibilities.

Just because one reaches official status as "heir" or a work-related title or a coveted position doesn't mean he is totally ready to handle that role. He may have gotten the notice in the mail, the courthouse document, the official handshake, or the set of keys that came with the new position, but that does not guarantee he is mentally, spiritually, or emotionally ready to tackle the new position/title. The moment of transformation must be accompanied by a period of transition.

1) In business, one may slog it out in the trenches with everyone else and one day is thrust into a leadership role. He may have acquired a title, and it may be a position he has long desired. But growing into that position will take major adjustments, and most leaders will admit privately that it takes considerable time to adjust from being under authority to having authority to perhaps one day being <u>the</u> person in authority. Acquisition of a position or title does not bestow an instant change of mindset.

2) In Christian circles, to go from being the person in the pew to the person behind the pulpit may happen when some review board stamps their application, or a church votes him in as pastor, or he clutches that new degree from seminary. It takes years, however, to truly become a shepherd who can combine compassion, conviction, and vision to lead a congregation forward.

3) In education, a person sits behind his desk through elementary through graduate schools for years until he receives the diploma. To stand up and face the class as an educator and become acknowledged as authoritative in his field may take several more years before he sees himself as the new teacher or prof and not just an imposter with credentials (see 2 Cor. 3 entry).

<u>Lines on Leadership</u>
When you were given (or obtained) your present title or position of leadership, how long did it take for you to "grow into" and become comfortable with seeing yourself as a leader?

++

Galatians 5---Highlights: relationship of living by the Spirit or the Law; the fruit of the Spirit

    The fifth chapter displays the seeds that erupt in full blossom in Romans 8 (see Rom. 8 entry). Life under the Law and life in the flesh are contrasted with a life led by the Spirit of God. Faith in the law and flesh produces bondage; faith in God's indwelling Spirit produces freedom. A twofold aspect of that freedom greatly affects how one leads in the Kingdom of God.

    The twofold nature of freedom is that we are both freed _from_ something and freed _to_ something (see Rom. 6, Col. 1 entries). Vs. 19-21 describe the life from which we are freed once we begin to follow Christ as Lord and Savior. We are freed _from_ sin and the life in the flesh (Col. 1.13). In a true sense, we are liberated, and the shackles of sin and its power over us are broken. Hallelujah. But here is where American Christians have trouble understanding the full nature of freedom. We get so caught up in "life, liberty, and the pursuit of happiness" that we begin to think freedom is the unlimited ability to do whatever I want, whenever and wherever I please, without regard to its consequences for me or others. Freedom is not only about _my_ freedom; it is about _our_ freedom. Paul calls us back to this in v. 13 when he says, "For you [plural]were called to freedom, brethren; only do not turn your freedom into an opportunity for the flesh, but through love serve one another." We are freed _from_ sin and the life of the flesh so that we are free _to_ serve others by living and walking in the Spirit.

    Later in the chapter, Paul describes what is the outcome of freedom in the Spirit: love, joy, peace, patience, kindness, goodness, faithfulness, gentleness, and self-control (vs. 22-23). All of these come from serving others and following in the footsteps of the Spirit (v. 25). I am writing this on the 4th of July, a day Americans celebrate the founding of our country. The United States declared its freedom from tyranny yet struggled after the Revolutionary War for several years before it found the balance of rights and responsibilities to each other we find in the current Constitution. American citizens, companies, and churches seem to have lost that precious balance of freedom <u>from</u> and freedom <u>to</u> in their unending demand of having personal rights recognized. Our freedom is to be used in the service of others, not declaring I can do anything I want how I want and when I want; that leads to anarchy because of the fallen nature of man that inevitably seeks destruction, degradation, and demeaning of others to elevate the individual.

<u>Lines on Leadership</u>
As a leader, I am not free to lead my group wherever I please but where I "ought to". Chapter five emphasizes that in my leadership I am never unmoored from my followship of God's Spirit. I am free to do what I have been created to do, and that is to honor God by service to Him and mankind. Is your leadership one of freedom that uses its freedom to serve others?

_____
_____

++

<u>Galatians 6</u>---Highlights: bearing one another's burdens

Vs. 7-10 "⁷Do not be deceived, God is not mocked; for whatever a man sows, this he will also reap. ⁸ For the one who sows to his own flesh shall from the flesh reap corruption, but the one who sows to the Spirit shall from the Spirit reap eternal life. ⁹ And let us not lose heart in doing good, for in due time we shall reap if we do not grow weary. ¹⁰ So then, while we have opportunity, let us do good to all men, and especially to those who are of the household of faith."

This is not about karma; this passage is about consequences, continuity, choice, and compassion. V.7 is poorly paraphrased as "garbage in, garbage out." The key phrase is "God is not mocked." The person who continually commits sins of neglect (omission) or sins of rebellion (commission) doesn't get off scot-free because God looks the other way, or is too inept to enforce His own laws. He is a God of His Word, and His Law is unassailable and incapable of being ignored. <u>Man does not break the law of God; he is broken on the law of God</u>. The <u>consequences</u> are real. If I commit an illegal act, I deserve the punishment for it, be it embezzlement, perjury, or sabotage. If I commit an immoral act, such as infidelity or cheating on documentation, I will pay either to society, God, or both. The <u>consequences</u> will come home to roost. V. 8 rephrases the same principle: if what I do is sown in the flesh, it reaps death; if I sow it in the Spirit, I receive life.

Therefore, if I, as a believer, live a life honoring the Lord and following His Spirit, I will eventually see a harvest "if I do not grow weary" (v. 9). A life of <u>continuity</u> is rewarded according to this verse. This is not about attaining or sustaining my salvation by works or about reaching some state of perfection; it is about reflecting the salvation of my soul by doing what is right regardless of who is watching or whether I see instant gratification for doing the right thing. This is long-term leadership[1].

By doing the right thing and showing <u>compassion</u> to all men, I honor the Father. Notice it is to be my initiative (v. 10, "while we have opportunity, let us do good to all men), and not me doing the right thing because my supervisor ordered it of me. Of particular interest is the phrase "especially to those of the household of faith". The term household of faith (for Christ-followers) is a euphemism for the church, for the family of believers; for the corporate world, it could be one's organization. I am to honor God by having compassion for all men, and it begins "at home" with my own group.

<u>Lines on Leadership</u>
An oft-referred-to aphorism is that 'delayed gratification is a sure sign of maturity'. Leadership over the long haul by doing the right thing does not insure success as in winning a competition, but according to this passage, it does insure there will be a harvest (v. 9). Would you describe your leadership as God-honoring, long-term oriented, or is it closer to pragmatic, get results at any cost, and make sure your organization comes out on top? If those positions are polar opposites on a spectrum, what point on that spectrum would more accurately describe your leadership in your organization?
_____
_____
++

LETTER TO THE EPHESIANS

Intro: Ephesians is the definitive epistle on how to organize a church and is best suited of all the Pauline epistles to describe how to build solid infrastructure in an organization. Ephesus was the fulcrum of Paul's ministries in Asia Minor; many of the other locations addressed in other epistles or mentioned in other NT books viewed on a map would see Ephesus as the hub of a wheel with many spokes connecting it to the outlying cities. Ephesus was especially precious to Paul because of his time teaching there (Acts 19.9), its strategic relationship to the other churches, and its location near the western coast of Asia Minor. It is one of the epistles considered the "Prison Letters", those written while Paul was confined either in Ephesus or in Rome.

++

Ephesians 1---Highlights: the present and future aspects of redemption

When I work for a company or am a church member, I want the leader(s) to care not only about my productivity but my personal welfare and development. Two remarkable images in Ephesians 1 illustrate how the two main figures of the chapter, God and Paul, cared for the readers' well-being.

1) In vs. 13-14, God places the Holy Spirit in a believer as a down payment (sealed in Him, v. 13; a pledge of our inheritance, v. 14), a form of earnest money. As I wrote this, I sat in a truck dealership waiting room where I had put down earnest money two weeks prior. That money ensured that the Toyota Tundra outside would be mine after some minor repairs were made, and it was prepared for my acceptance of it. I knew that the dealer would not show the vehicle to anyone else or take other offers on it; the earnest money was a legal deposit that reserved the truck for me and only me.

An effective leader, however, invests in a follower not only in terms of just preservation but transformation (see Lk. 6 entry). Too many emphasize the Holy Spirit's presence as insurance on the future to the detriment of its enrichment of every moment of every day (Eph. 5.18-21).

2) In vs. 15-23, Paul elaborates on what should be stirring and forming in the believer as a result of the Holy Spirit's placement in my life as God's "earnest money". This marvelous intercessory prayer focuses on three things: that the believer may experience a) the hope of His calling, b) the riches of His glory, and c) the greatness of His power.

Lines on Leadership
This book's emphasis is on the perspective of the leader. Space does not permit a full exposition of these dense verses replete with attributes of our identity in Christ as His followers. The emphasis for today is on leaders. What are you placing in the lives of followers that will not just keep them active as followers and pointed in the right direction but will also deeply enrich their lives for an entire lifetime? How are you committed to not just their preservation but their transformation?
As in most places of the NT, the word 'you' throughout this chapter refers to the plural, the collective group. This is why Paul finishes the passage describing how this transformation occurs in the church, not the individual (vs. 22-23). How are you leading your entire organization to not only stick together but grow together?

_____
_____
++

Ephesians 2---Highlights: from death to life in Christ; by grace through faith

Ephesians 2, from a Christian standpoint, describes the transformed life (vs. 8-9, "for by grace you have been saved through faith; and that not of yourselves, it is the gift of God; not a result of works, so that no one may boast") that comes by the unmerited favor of God. I acknowledge that truth with gratitude for my eternal salvation in Christ. Our attention for this chapter, however, will be on v. 10, "For we are His workmanship, created in Christ Jesus for good works, which God prepared beforehand so that we would walk in them."

The word in the original text for workmanship (handiwork, NIV; masterpiece, ISV, NLT) in Latin is *poeme,* in Greek *poiema*, from which we famously get the English word poem; yes, we are God's poetry. Each individual day is not some random word that randomly fell onto a page; the days of our lives have an Author. We were created with purpose, not as experiments or accidents ("which God prepared beforehand"); Paul uses several word images to depict how that purpose affords us both privilege and responsibility as he describes new access to the Father (vs. 13-18), new citizenship (v.19), and new roles as part of the church he compares to God's household (v. 19) and a building (vs. 20-22). Once we have been granted entrance into this new life (v.18, "through Him we both have our access in one Spirit to the Father"), we are to learn and fulfill our purpose for that life.

When you move to another country as a new citizen, you need new passports, new currency, and a new understanding of what laws are different than in your former country. The rules of engagement about everything change; your loyalty to a government, the way you seek and maintain employment, transportation, foods you eat, clothes you wear, customs you observe, and the way you interact with people of different ages and genders: it all changes. How many times do we read of those from foreign lands entering a new country as an immigrant or a refugee? In their former homeland, they were professionals such as doctors or scientists, but in their new country, they have to take menial or entry-level positions until their credentials are established, or they prove to their new employers they have expertise or value beyond their introductory pay. I may know my purpose for being there, but it takes time to discover how to live out that purpose in my newly adopted country, so it is with new life in Christ.

It is terribly exciting to learn one's true purpose in life and to walk in it; it is liberating and produces a state of well-being and completeness. It is both disconcerting and joyous to fulfill my personal purpose as part of a larger scheme of things (the building, v. 21). In terms of a household or building, perhaps a brick would think being forged at a factory would place it in a wall of distinction, but it winds up on the inside of a pizza oven, a patio barbecue station, or even the sidewalk leading up to it. The glory of a house does not go to the individual brick, the individual window pane, or the individual rafter beam; it goes to the architect or the owner of the house. (see Heb. 3.3)

Lines on Leadership
Where is your purpose in life written down so you can see it periodically? When have you last revised that statement? What is your unique purpose, and how does it fit with all the other unique purposes of other peoples' lives?
_____
_____
++

Ephesians 3---Highlights: The grounded vision

An essential task of a leader is to cast vision. The benediction in Eph. 3.20-21 explodes into a seemingly carte blanche vision where the church can become anything it wants ("Now to Him who is able to do exceeding abundantly beyond all that we ask or think, according to the power that works within us, to Him be the glory in the church and in Christ Jesus to all generations forever and ever."). It occurs at the end of the chapter, not to provide an outlet for rapturous ecstasy about unlimited possibilities but because the vision is firmly grounded in reality. Paul's desire, stated in vs. 1-19, is that the church accepts the now oft-repeated thesis that salvation and eternal life are for <u>all</u> peoples, not just the favored few. Note v. 6, "<u>Gentiles</u> are fellow heirs and fellow members of the body;" v. 8, "to preach to the <u>Gentiles</u> the unfathomable riches of Christ"; and vs. 14-15, "For this reason I bow my knees before the Father, from whom <u>every</u> family in heaven and earth derives its name."

The vision stated in vs. 20-21 is for everybody in the church, not a two-tiered vision that favors one group to the detriment of the other. Everything Paul prays in vs. 16-19 is for <u>every</u> person, not a favored group. After fifty years of ministry, I am still grieved to see the sometimes subtle, sometimes brazen differentiations of race, social class, gender, and age on display in our churches. The gospel is for all persons, and all should be given full access to its life-changing message. Some groups preach equality but practice the insidious lines near the end of Orwell's Animal Farm where "All animals are equal, but some animals are more equal than others[1]."

This is not a call for churches to gloss over the differences among people and act with a bland homogeneity as if all persons were a generic mass gathering. The differentiations between Jews and Gentiles were stark and unmistakable. The vision was grounded in this reality; the marvelous aspect of this chapter is that Paul, knowing how wide the chasm was between groups, looks toward a future when every person who has been transformed by this gospel can worship, serve, and grow together in one body because they are bound together by God Almighty.

<u>Lines on Leadership</u>
Multi-ethnic congregations are often replete with misunderstandings, missed cultural cues, and plenty of headaches around every corner for church leaders who try their best to accommodate, recognize, and honor each group's values and customs. The same headaches exist in multinational companies.

"The domain of the leader is the future . . . The most significant contribution leaders make is not to today's bottom line; it is to the long-term development of people and institutions so they can adapt, change, prosper, and grow[2]."

What is the vision you espouse for your organization? Where does it fully recognize the different groups within the whole? Where does it give everyone equal access to rewards, promotions, training, advancement, and benefits? Does it contain an element of greatness and expansion while remaining rooted in your present reality? Is the vision a shared vision infused not only with possibility but common purpose[3]?

_____

_____

++

Ephesians 4---Highlights: different faces of unity
        Chapter 4 is a classic example of the axiom <u>unity does not require uniformity</u>. Paul builds on the desire in chapter 3 for Jews

and Gentiles to come together as the body of Christ (the church) with a bridge statement that they should all "walk in a manner worthy of the calling with which you have been called" (v. 1). He then launches in two directions, the oneness of that body and the distinctiveness of different parts of that same body.

Vs. 3-6 extol the oneness of the body with phrases such as "unity of the Spirit" (v. 3), "one body, one Spirit, one hope" (v. 4), "one Lord, one faith, one baptism" (v.5), "one God and Father of all who is over all and through all and in all" (v. 6; see Rom. 11.36). Vs. 7-12 describe the distinctiveness of the body's different parts (for similar extended metaphors, see Rom. 12, 1 Cor. 12). Paul refers to the gifts of grace (v. 7), which result in different leadership functions within and for the body (v. 11, apostles, prophets, evangelists, pastors, teachers; for a fuller treatment see Alan Hirsch's 5Q[1]). Those different manifestations of grace are not given to imbue people with importance or titles that separate them from the rest of the body but rather are given to serve the entire body (vs.12-13). As Paul shows, the gifts are there to "build up the body of Christ until we all attain to the unity of the faith" (v.13) and again to glorify Christ, who is the head of the body whose parts all work together for the "building up of itself in love" (v.16).

Unity that arises out of diversity of giftedness and labor makes for a great sermon or a wonderful team pep talk, but the plain truth is that the working out of that unity is difficult. Paul acknowledges that as he describes in vs. 17-32 what the day-to-day of achieving unity looks like. Vs. 26-32 openly acknowledge the friction and disagreements that will arise from the clash of cultures and expression of those different talents to the point Paul says to get the differences out on the table and deal with them. The Greek term he uses in v. 26 for anger denotes intense passion to the point the person is beside himself, almost out of control. They are so passionate about their role, their output, and their group. I wrote this during summer preseason football camps, where emotional eruptions are commonplace on the practice field as players clash and slowly learn to channel their passion away from building up of self and more toward formation of team.

[Bonus: Punctuation can affect meaning. In v. 12, the KJV reads: "For the perfecting of the saints, for the work of the ministry"; most modern translations correctly omit the comma, which affects the meaning. In v. 11, the list of leadership functions (apostle, prophet, evangelist, pastor and teacher) without the comma conveys that leadership is to train the saints, so the <u>saints</u> do the ministry; with the comma, it conveys the leadership trains the saints, <u>and</u> the leadership does the ministry, overloading the leadership and underdeveloping the saints.]

<u>Lines on Leadership</u>
Describe as a leader how you celebrate the distinctively different elements of your workforce or church membership yet guide them into a synergistic accomplishment of a common goal and how they embrace and express their common identity.

_____
_____
++

Ephesians 5---Highlights: Light and darkness; the Christian Life; Marital Roles

The home and place of work are in some ways separate and some ways intertwined. Sociologists, psychologists, and theologians have dissected that relationship for centuries. Space does not allow a full discussion of egalitarian vs. complementarian views of marital partners, a favorite pro/con topic in churches. This chapter is a glimpse into leadership at home and work. It is often included in weddings and sermons on marriage, particularly vs. 22-33, which delineate the roles of husband and wife.

It is difficult to leave the affairs of the office and not bring them into family dynamics. A spouse engaged in a leadership role at work will often bring those modes of interaction home with him/her. It is for this reason (among others) I advocate servant leadership as a much smoother transition point from work to home than other forms of leadership. If I practice a "my-word-goes, I'm-the-boss-around-here" attitude at work and bring that home with me, it is a more drastic switch to being a spouse at home than if I have practiced servant leadership at the office (as described throughout this book), come home, and continue servant leadership.

One of the best pieces of marital advice I received from older ministers was: <u>The best gift I could give my children as a father was to be a good husband to their mother.</u> Paul admonishes husbands to love their wives and sacrificially give of themselves to the wives as Christ did for the church (vs.25-27). I wear two wedding rings, one on each ring finger. The one on my left hand signifies I am wedded in a covenant relationship with my wife; as I wrote this chapter, we celebrated our 47th anniversary. The ring on my right hand signifies I have a covenant relationship as part of the bride of Christ, His church (vs. 22-33). I have a dual role, to be 1) the servant leader in my home, ready to sacrifice for it at any time to protect and love it. I am also to 2) submit to Christ as part of His bride ("Christ is the head of the church," v. 23). If I am mindful of my dual role, I will hopefully be a better, more understanding husband, father, and leader at home and at work. I am not the lord of my manor; Christ is Lord of our home, where, as in v. 21, we are to "submit to one another out of reverence for Christ". (ESV)

<u>Bonus thought</u>: vs. 15-16 encourage me to "be careful how you walk, not as unwise men, but as wise, making the most of your time, because the days are evil". That phrase "making the most of your time" is rendered "redeem" or "buy up" in other translations; it has the connotation of cornering the market, coming into a vendor and buying out all he has of the desired commodity. It is contextually saying to live a life worthy of imitation (vs. 1-14) and to understand the implications of my actions and outlook on life. I am at all times to be under the control of His Spirit (vs. 17-20); if I do that, I will enter much easier into the complicated yet gloriously enriching relationship described in vs. 21-33. (see 1 Pet. 5 entry)

<u>Lines on Leadership</u>
Contrast and compare your leadership roles at work and home; determine if they honor Christ and if they complement each other instead of conflict.

_____
_____

++

Ephesians 6---Highlights: Spiritual Warfare

The <u>message</u> remains the same, but the <u>methods</u> must change to best communicate the message to the current generation/situation/culture. That applies to the gospel as well as a corporate mission statement. The danger is change for change's sake or to be in vogue or look cool. When cultural whims and twists in direction start to dictate the emphases of the message, and the message is subservient to the method, it becomes a dangerous imbalance. Yet how much of the gospel or corporate mission statement is lost on subsequent generations when outdated methods of transmission are used?

A case in point is the passage Eph. 6.10-20, known in Christian circles as "the armor of God". Paul describes in detail the different parts of armor for a Roman soldier and allegorizes them into a spiritual defense against the evil one (v. 11, "put on the full armor of God, that you may be able to stand firm against the schemes of the devil"). The concept is valid and paints a wonderful word image.

In today's world, however, combat is conducted with handheld RPGs (rocket-propelled grenades), nuclear weapons, intercontinental multiple-warhead missiles, and deadly drones. Paul's description of a soldier's armor as effective against such modern weapons is laughable. To relate to modern generations, the concept needs new imagery without violating the truths contained therein.

A personal illustration of this principle occurred on a Boy Scout camping and hiking trip. My son's troop trained and trained in order to tackle the Wimenuche Wilderness outside of Durango, CO. We toted sacks of deer feed up and down stadium bleachers with sweat pouring off our arms in an East Texas August to get into shape. We talked about communication and prepared (I thought) for every contingency. Apparently, I was not listening in the meetings or just decided to cheap out, but on the first day, after a nine-mile hike upward in altitude, we got near our planned campsite. We had put on our rain gear halfway on the hike. My son, another young Scout, and I had thin PVC-based rain gear that our large backpacks easily tore through during the hike. Everyone else had nylon-based rain gear that did not tear. A council of adult leaders was held, and it was determined that because the multiday hike would reach heights of 12,000ft. or higher, the dangers of doing so without intact rain gear constituted a health hazard. The two scouts and I would have to return back to the parking lot and head back to Texas. Because of the distances involved each day, there was no way to go into Durango, buy proper gear, and catch up with the troop. I cannot describe the disappointment of hiking back down the mountain those nine miles and then taking two days to drive back to East Texas. <u>We had the proper training but not the proper equipment</u>.

<u>Lines on Leadership</u>
The gospel and corporate mission statements may not need rewriting in regards to truth but in the area of relating to the current generation. What target group are you trying to reach with your message? How can you retell it in a new way to reach that target group without dilution or distortion of the original message? When was the last time you realistically did an inventory of your terminology or equipment to see if they accurately convey your desired message?

_____
_____
++

LETTER TO THE PHILIPPIANS

Intro: This is the happy epistle. Exuberance springs forth from every chapter, a remarkable achievement considering Paul wrote this while in prison in Rome. This church assisted him often with offerings sent to him during his travels (Phil. 4.16, 18; 2 Cor. 11.9). No wonder they were dear to his heart. This small book is a favorite of pastors to encourage congregations. Vs. 1.6, 1.21, 2.5, 3.10, 3.14, 4.4-8, 4.13, and 4.19 have found their way onto posters, greeting cards, and bulletin boards for many years. Rejoice, and again I say, rejoice! (4.4)

++

Philippians 1---Highlights: thanksgiving, the preaching of the gospel, to live is Christ

The message is more important than the messenger. In a world saturated with constantly moving images on television, computer screens, and phones with nonstop streaming of whatever is desired and the ability to repeat it *ad infinitum* in a looped fashion, it is all too easy for the viewer to confuse the messenger and message. At some point in the mind of the messenger, he can come to believe he IS the message. To a degree, it is understandable when a leader has spent years crafting a narrative to convey his company's culture and central message. If he has risen to prominence as the narrative's acceptance has increased, the two could easily be seen as one and the same, inseparable and indivisible.

The trouble comes when the leader erodes, implodes, is involved in scandal, loses his edge, and his ego demands more attention than the message or uses it to promote himself. Paul provides a unique perspective on this scenario in vs. 15-28 when he says, "only that in every way, whether in pretense or in truth, Christ is proclaimed; and in this I rejoice" (v.18). This hearkens back to Isaiah 40.8 which declares "the grass withers, the flower fades, but the word of our God stands forever." The Word of God is unique among all messages if it can withstand the misuse, neglect, and misrepresentation of every charlatan and huckster who has attempted to profit from it.

To be sure, Paul encourages the reader to exercise discernment (v. 9) and to be found worthy of the gospel they proclaim (v. 27). He is not oblivious to the damage a wayward messenger can do, as witnessed by his repeated warnings throughout his epistles about false teachers. But he knows how powerful the message is when the messenger is aligned with but always secondary to the main attraction. The apex of the chapter is verse 21, when Paul famously declares, "to live is Christ, and to die is gain." He is so enamored of the message of Christ he is willing to die for it (v. 21) and to suffer for it (v.29) but understands perfectly well he will never be mistaken for the One he proclaims as Messiah (see 1 Tim. 1.15). As a leader, I have to constantly balance my plea for my followers' commitment to be to the message more than the messenger.

Lines on Leadership
The German term *Lebensbotschaft* is best translated as "life message". Ruminate a bit on how similar and different your personal "life message" is from the message you are attempting to share as the leader of your organization and where the overlap or conflict lies between the two.

_____
_____

++

Philippians 2---Highlights: an ancient hymn to Christ

Chapter 2 is known as the "kenosis" passage, the most detailed and dramatic description of a servant leader in Paul's epistles. Vs. 5-11 employ poetic language suggestive of an early hymn current at the time Paul wrote this letter, or that he exchanged didactic writing for exalted prose to emphasize this side of Christ[1] (combine vs. 5-11 with Col. 1.13-20 for a more complete portrayal).

Kenosis is from the Greek verb *ekenosen,* which means "to empty", and comes from the verse 7 phrase "but [he] emptied Himself, taking the form of a bondservant", which is often misinterpreted that He gave up His nature and power as God. In Christian theology, this would be heresy as Christ was, is, and always will be God the Son. The word has more to do with the NASB's alternate reading, "laid aside His privileges", that He remained God but left the unimaginable splendors of heaven to dwell among us.

At the risk of sounding blasphemous, a TV show in the 2000s called Undercover Boss embodied this principle. The script was always the same: a CEO of a large, known company would go incognito to a local outlet or division of his/her company and usually masquerade as a new or prospective employee under the ruse of filming for HR or instructional purposes. After several scenes where the CEO found out how hard the work was, and how his employees did their jobs, the end of each episode had the two or three unsuspecting employees called up to corporate offices, usually thinking they were about to receive a reprimand. The CEOs would appear in their usual business attire and affirm or admonish as they saw fit based on their experiences, oftentimes giving the employee assistance to do a better job or help with a family situation. At no time did the CEO give up the authority of his/her position; they relinquished their surroundings and the deference of everyone in their office suite for the harsh and demanding task of collecting trash, making up hotel beds, managing a landfill, etc.

Paul started this chapter with a thesis statement that we should humbly consider the interest of others over ourselves (vs. 3-5), points to Christ as the ultimate example of that, and then ends the chapter with two examples in Timothy and Epaphroditus (vs. 19-30) as two fellow workers who will gladly sacrifice their personal interests/status for those of the Philippians. Timothy is the coauthor of several epistles (2 Cor., Col., 1 Thess., Philemon, as well as Philippians), and he could have touted his importance to this church, citing his credentials, but Paul says Timothy is not like others (v.21) looking after his own interests. Epaphroditus apparently had been sent by this church to minister to Paul (v. 25) but did not consider his position (I made it to the "inner circle," I'm in with the bigwigs now) something to be grasped and longed to be back among the Philippians.

Lines on Leadership

A pastor friend once confided he had been approached by a pastor search committee from a prominent church. Their appeal to become their pastor included words to the effect of "you can really make a name for yourself". He humbly and wisely declined to interview with them. Ambition and a rise in the ranks of your chosen profession is neither good nor bad in and of itself, but each promotion has the potential to create more and more disconnect between a leader and those whom he leads. How do you communicate your willingness to "be on the same level, walk a mile in their shoes" with your followers?

_____

_____

++

Philippians 3---Highlights: pressing on toward the upward call of Christ

vs. 13-14 "Brethren, I do not regard myself as having laid hold of it [glorified state of being eternally with Christ] yet; but one thing I do; forgetting what lies behind and reaching forward to that lies ahead, I press on toward the goal for the prize of the upward call of God in Christ Jesus."

These are perhaps the most overlapping two sentences for Christian and corporate leaders in the NT. A pursuit of a particular goal has many factors. 1) I must let go ("forgetting what lies behind") of that which had served me well to that point. 2) When I reach forward and grab hold of my goal, which is on the move, it's hang-on-for-dear-life-time since my goal is not something or somewhere but Someone (see Rom. 11 entry), a living, dynamic Person going forward. 3) The goal is indeed worthy.

When Jack Welch took the reins of General Electric in the early 1980s, it was a behemoth of a multi-faceted and multi-nation corporation with subsidiaries of subsidiaries, its tentacles spread out in all directions. He said he would divest GE of everything that couldn't be number 1 or 2 in the world in its respective field. While there are many mitigating factors then and since for GE, at the time he did this, in the course of his 20 years as CEO, the employee force shrank, profits went up, and the overall revenue of the company went from roughly 13 billion to 480 billion. While some of his hard-nosed tactics and lasting results can be debated, he displayed a singular focus on growing the company by paring down the number of enterprises in which GE was involved. He also insisted on excellence in those that remained with the goal of being the best in the business for each division or subordinate company[1].

Paul's focus is an eternal union with Christ, which is an ultimate issue, one with which no company can begin to compare. This statement hearkens back to Mt. 13 where Jesus teaches the parables of the great pearl, the treasure, and the fish in the net, all designed to show how to let go and grab hold of that which is precious beyond other things. Later in Heb. 12.1-2, the writer uses athletic language to describe the same process of shedding everything that encumbers or restricts my obtaining the prize, which here is the upward call of God in Christ Jesus. It is a life principle across social strata, time, careers, and love: to obtain that which is more valuable than all else to us demands the loss of that which is deemed secondary.

Lines on Leadership
In marriage vows, the words often include "forsaking all others". What goal have you set in your vocational or personal life, and what would it demand you forsake? How can you prevent that from becoming an obsession and using family members or colleagues as stepping stones to obtain it at their expense? The worthiness of the goal must be established; consider the counterbalance of Mt. 16.26 ("what will it profit a man if he gains the whole world and forfeits his soul?")

_____

_____

++

Philippians 4---Highlights: experiencing joy in the midst of any circumstance

You've seen it too many times. A loved one passes away, a family or church member rails against the Almighty. Someone's home succumbs to fire; a bystander judges the family as out of the will of God, deserving of this punishment. Our favorite sports team is robbed of a victory, and we curse God for abandoning us. It ranges from life/death issues to pure pettiness; we are quick to saddle God with all the blame for 'x' dreadful occurrence. Saved, born-again followers of Christ believe His death and resurrection gave them eternal life—praise the Lord. But as I read the Word He never grants us invincibility, immunity, or isolation from the woes of this world until we reach a resurrected state with Him in heaven. The Kingdom of God is a present reality and a future hope, as stated often in other chapter offerings.

At the time of writing this, I was being treated for Lyme disease, something I apparently contracted leading a Disaster Relief team months prior in Florida. I was doing the Lord's work and was bitten by some random critter that resulted in shortness of breath, stamina, and strength. The doctors thought at the time that perhaps I had done damage to my heart (it was eventually determined my thyroid had flipped from hypo to hyperthyroidism and fluctuated for over a year). At the same time, within our associational church leadership, we had men receiving shots in their eyes for macular degeneration, recovering from heart attacks, double transplant survivors, cancer, etc. Did it mean we were out of the will of God? That we were justified in berating Him for "allowing" this to happen to us?

Philippians 4.13 is very often quoted and almost as often misinterpreted. Depending on the translation, it says, in effect, 'I can do all things in/through Christ'. An infant faith expects miracles, to leap tall buildings, or show how tough or strong I can be—oh, through Christ, of course. Rule #1 in biblical interpretation: always read a verse in context. Paul is in prison, he's just said he is content in whatever circumstance he finds himself (v.11) and, in the very next verse (v.14), asks his readers to share in his affliction. I think some modern translations capture the true essence of this verse as "I can <u>endure</u> all things through Christ." Psalm 23 does not describe a detour around the valley of the shadow of death; David said God was with us <u>through</u> that dark place. Job, when his wife (delightful spouse, she) encourages him to curse God and die, replies, "Shall we indeed accept good from God and not accept adversity (Job 2.10)?" Solomon writes in Eccl. 7.14, "In the day of prosperity be happy, but in the day of adversity consider- -God has made the one as well as the other", and Jeremiah (probable author) pens in Lamentations 3.38, "Is it not from the mouth of the Most High that both good and evil come forth?" These verses don't fit in some people's theology, but a mature believer learns to grapple with the whole Word of God, not just our favorite promises. I will not praise God <u>for</u> my Lyme, nor my wife's lupus or lymphoma, nor mass killings at places of worship, nor 'x' catastrophe. I will praise Him <u>IN</u> the midst of that circumstance (see 1 Thess. 5 entry). I belong to God (1 Cor. 6.20) and am to glorify His name, period, when it feels good and also when I would rather sell the whole world for five minutes of relief or peace.

The rest of the chapter reinforces this approach. Vs. 6-8 promise the presence of God but not an answer. Verse 19 promises He will provide for my needs, not my wants. This is not a lack of faith but rather a grown grown-up, mature faith.

Thinking that God will miraculously bail me out of every situation promotes laziness and carelessness in my life. If I can fall into a gaping hole, always pray and 'poof', I'm miraculously back on the pavement without any effort, am I going to be more careful next time on my next saunter through the neighborhood? (see 2 Cor. 5 entry)

As a leader in the midst of x crisis, I need to exercise deep, quiet confidence in the Lord. If he chooses to bail our church or company out of this hole in some amazing fashion, something He is totally capable of, that is His choice as Sovereign of my life. <u>If He is sovereign, He is not subject to my expectations</u>. This is not fatalism but adult faith. I am to lead with abiding joy rooted in Him; Philippians is possibly the most joy-filled of Paul's epistles, yet he pens it shackled. If He chooses to leave our group in its dilemma, I must resist the temptation to blame God as a scapegoat, accurately assess our situation, resources, and options, and lead our people in a God-honoring plan of action.

<u>Lines on Leadership</u>
How would you describe a leadership outlook that accounts for the sovereignty of God, personal responsibility, avoidance of fatalism, and an ability to keep going in the face of adversity or unfavorable circumstance?

_____
_____
++

LETTER TO THE COLOSSIANS

The book of Colossians addresses an extraordinary spectrum of worldview, philosophy, and theology in four small chapters, all written to a few folks in a small house church in Colossae. It is breathtaking to exhibit this elevated view of Christ so few decades after His death, to go beyond Messiah and Redeemer to Creator, and the original field theory (1.17) is stunning. It is a perennial favorite for college campuses because of its breadth of subject matter. It is the companion to Ephesians as Galatians is to Romans. The majority of verses in Colossians can be found in a similar form in Ephesians. The emphasis in Ephesians is the church; in Colossians, it is undoubtedly Christ. Paul is intent on showing to Gnostics and Judaizers alike that Jesus is fully God and fully man. I will admit to preaching out of this book more times than I can remember and still continue to discover depths and varieties of true treasure.

++

Colossians 1---Highlights: Salutations, Commendations, portrait of Christ

This chapter contains a detailed description of Christ and His relationship to the church. I have preached it often; vs. 13-20 is unabashedly one of my favorite passages of Scripture. Today we confine our remarks to one verse, v. 13---"For He delivered us from the domain of darkness and transferred us to the Kingdom of His beloved Son", a verse that clearly illustrates the dual nature of salvation on a spiritual dimension and full scale of transformation on a secular dimension.

There is a two-phase (not two-stage) description of our salvation in Christ: we are saved _from_ something, and we are saved _to_ something (see Rom. 6, Gal. 5 entries). In the first phase, one is snatched from the domain where darkness reigns. To be liberated from chains, to be freed from restrictions and deprivation, is exhilarating. If one has been in a dark place long enough to where its dimness and dankness have become normal, sudden freedom of movement and the blinding light of liberty can be simultaneously joyful and fearful. Millions of slaves in the southern states were emancipated by proclamation and then by cessation of the Civil War. Chains and restrictions were removed, but opportunity to make their newfound freedom productive remained elusive. Forbearance of indebtedness and forgiveness of sin's penalties are causes of celebration, but what happens next?

The second phase is the transference to "the Kingdom of His beloved Son". As I wrote this chapter, immigration had been a controversial political topic in the U.S. for several years. The crime, corruption, and chaos of unstable countries south of the border created wave upon wave of people attempting to flee for the perceived better living conditions in the United States. Leaving their country is one phase; becoming actual citizens of another country is the second one. Without the proper documents and permission from the proper authorities, there is no legal entrance and conferment of citizenship. Spiritually Christ provides both the documents and the authority with the New Testament of His body and blood being sacrificed for our sins and His resurrection overcoming death (see the entire book of Hebrews). On a secular plane, too many activists have long sought a group's deliverance from an oppressive or inferior condition, only to have no workable environment for the group once liberated.

Whether it is poor living conditions, financial bondage, or escape from an eternal hell, once a person comes out of it, a place of safety and growth must be provided where a relapse or return to the former condition is not possible or at least difficult.

Not all Rambos make good rulers. Good leaders, in a spiritual sense, not only proclaim freedom from sin but freedom to become what God created us to be, sons and daughters of the Most High, true citizens of heaven (Phil. 3.20-21). Good leaders in society not only grant tax breaks, benefits, and bonuses to elevate persons out of poverty or abuse but help their clients/customers/citizens live productive lives.

A final note in the last phrase of today's verse regards the Son's character ("beloved"). Most sermons and reflections on this passage emphasize His power, His roles as Creator (v. 16-17, 20), as Redeemer (v.13-14), and as Head of the church (v. 18). As a minister, I want to have full confidence the Good News is not only about a God who has provided both deliverance and a divine domicile but that He is a good and loving God, that they will call Him beloved as well. The best way to convince them of His character as beloved is to emulate Him as their leader, to sacrifice, to serve, to provide, to love, to give everything I am and to greet them upon deliverance from the domain of darkness and walk alongside them in the Kingdom of the beloved Son of God, Jesus Christ, my Messiah and King.

Lines on Leadership
When have you delivered someone or a group from a "domain of darkness?" What did you provide or point out as a safe and viable alternative to that dark domain?
_____
_____
++

Colossians 2---Highlights: contrast of false (Gnosticism) and true sources of life and wisdom (Christ)

For millennia travelers were guided by the movement of the sun and stars and knowledge of certain terrain markers (when the trees vanish and the horizon is devoid of hills, they start veering westward). A few centuries ago, maps went from mythical fantasies to reliable portrayals of the lay of the land and sea. The more discoveries brave explorers like LaSalle or Lewis and Clark made, the more accurate and useful the maps became. As a child, I remember our car's glove compartment as a treasure trove of different maps from nearby states, maps that had holes and gaps in the creases from countless folding and unfolding on trips, maps that could be purchased at any roadside store.

Those maps of yesteryear located in our cars and desk drawers found their way into cyberspace during the past few decades so that I can summon them at will on my phone or mobile device from any number of sources such as Google or Apple Maps. I can print out a detailed map with towns and roads or a step-by-step list of directions. The same can be done if I will hike an area with no cell coverage or satellite links. Those maps can show elevation, rest stops, places to overnight, and anything else I want the computer program to add to it.

But the simplest and, in some ways, most satisfying way to travel/hike/canoe is with someone who knows the way. I can dispense with charts, maps, and lists; I just follow the one who knows where he is going. The trouble comes when several introduce themselves to me as a reliable guide. Then I have to choose which guide I think will have the best chance of bringing me safely to my desired destination. In this chapter, Paul patiently yet forcefully compares and contrasts the Gnostics' life map not with a competing map drawn by Christ but with Christ Himself (v.3). In a way, chapter 2 is a fuller explanation of how Christ guided us from the domain of darkness into His kingdom as described in the previous chapter. Multiple times Paul refers to "in or with Him" (vs. 9, 10, 11, 12, 20), how He plowed the ground before us to make a way (vs. 13-15), and how we are complete when we are in Him (vs. 8-10). The Gnostics offered a system, a life philosophy; Jesus offered a Savior, an invitation to not only follow Him but to share His life (Colossians 3.4).

A part of the study of leadership is to study leaders. While I have advocated my whole life that not everyone is cut out to be a leader, they can learn principles of leadership to benefit themselves and others through them by studying other proven leaders. We can talk about loyalty to an organization or program, but time and again our loyalty hinges on a person more than a precept or program.

Lines on Leadership
As you reflect on how you learned to lead, which influenced you more, precepts or persons? When you make decisions, do you think about principles or past decisions made by your former leaders?
_____
_____
++

Colossians 3--- Highlights: The nature of the new self

A book that finds its way into my backpack for repeated readings and is quoted elsewhere in this book is *Leadership is an Art* by Max DePree. He has a knack for reducing large thoughts down to succinct but profound phrases. When asked what the most difficult task of a leader was, he simply said, "intercept entropy[1]", a phrase I marvel at and quote often. "Interception of entropy" has a strong biblical basis and many applications for churches and corporations alike.

Entropy is the same basic concept in thermodynamics, communications, and astrophysics: that everything in the universe (if left alone) moves toward inaction, degeneration, dissolution, and death (if all matter ceased motion and vibration, it would all fall apart). This applies to everything from subatomic particles to star systems and from our physical bodies to the body of Christ. We find it as a concept when Paul describes the effect of sin on the cosmos and in our lives in Romans. We find it spelled out in 2 Cor. 4.16a, where Paul describes our outer man as decaying. From the moment we are birthed, our bodies age, weaken, stiffen, and break down. Thank God Paul goes on to describe the "interception" of entropy in 2 Cor. 4.16b, where he says, "yet our inner man is being renewed day by day". In the chapter at hand, Colossians 3.10 says, "put on the new self who is being renewed to a true knowledge according to the image of the One who created him." Entropy can be intercepted.

Notice the passive voice, "being renewed". I knew from pre-back surgery MRIs what the problem was: herniated disc at L3. But I had tried therapy, drugs, and exercise, and nothing was helping that had helped in the past; I needed a more drastic course of action and expertise I couldn't provide myself. The neurosurgeon expertly plied his trade, and I mended nicely. There is an element here of self-help, a more likely element of partnership in the renewal of myself and an outside entity (the Lord), and an acknowledgment that without Him, any effort on my part would be futile.

So on a physical level, disease, friction, and age eventually lead to breakdowns; we must find ways to deliberately arrest them. On a spiritually personal level, we can know for years that we have a sin problem and be headed downhill toward an inevitable end, but we cannot pull ourselves out of it. Salvation is not a grand self-help program; it is a glorious "interception of entropy" when Christ arrests our plunge into eternal death and infuses us with His life (Rom. 6.23; see Col. 1 entry). We need to apply this phrase, "interception of entropy", to the life of a church/organization as well. On a corporate level, it may be time to ask some tough questions: have we taken stock of our situation honestly? Is there some area of church/company life where erosion (i.e., entropy) is taking place, and we won't admit it? Are we using any kind of accountability or metrics to measure that entropy? Is it time to change directions? Should we change a methodology, shuffle personnel, infuse our group with something or someone new? Must we redefine what it means to be a church? On a denominational basis, I am hearing this conversation broaden to include declining baptisms, church closings, or an overall direction for the entire body of Christ. The natural state of creation and man is for entropy to kick in and take over unless there is a deliberate intervention by Christ and/or His followers to effect change.

But wait, there's more. The last half of that verse says we are being renewed more and more in the image of Christ (obvious from the wider chapter context). The context of chapter 3 is not about the acquisition of godlike powers but the character of Christ. Taken to its logical conclusion, it means I will resemble less of my old self and become, as the verse says, a new self. This is not a modification or improvement on the old version; it is a new self. <u>This is part of the fear of change: I'm not sure who I'll be on the other side of it</u>. It makes an individual uneasy and a group even more so. Homeostasis implies everything has reached an equilibrium, equal temperatures, equal levels, and equal status. It may look great in a painting, but life is not a still-life watercolor; it is a never-ending video. Entropy is nature's way of easing everything toward homeostasis; it may work for psychological or biological systems, but for me, as a leader, I am determined not to let my charges, my corporation, and my church slide into entropy. I must intercept entropy. Ever onward, ever upward.

Lines on Leadership
What are you doing in your company, your church, and your life to intercept entropy?

_____

_____

++

Colossians 4---Highlights: Evangelism and an annotated list of fellow workers

Some scriptures yield a general concept of living. Others take on flesh as you see them lived out in detail before your eyes; this story is the latter.

Most spring breaks of my college campus ministry days were spent on mission trips with college students. Sometimes the trip was direct servant evangelism on beaches at Padre Island with free breakfasts, providing free rides around town, especially at night, and witnessing along the way. Other times we would partner with a local Habitat for Humanity chapter on a house build. I tried to give a variety of opportunities each year. After several years of doing this, I decided to return to our previous routine of going to the same location each year to build familiarity and momentum for our efforts from year to year.

We chose Chicago, which was a sixteen-hour drive over two days each way from our college group in Marshall, TX. In years past, our college had ministered alongside Uptown Baptist Church in the Uptown neighborhood, a ten-square-block area with over 40 languages spoken. Uptown BC was a large sprawling building where ten different language congregations met and was a great lab for our TX students to do cross-cultural missions in one location. Through this church we learned of a fledgling church restart in the Lakeview area a few blocks from Wrigley Field. The former church had lost its vision for its neighborhood, dwindled to a few older members, and given the property over to the association.

When we arrived that cold March, we found an older building in need of a major overhaul. We were warm bodies, not experts at plumbing, carpentry, or masonry. So we did what we could the first days there to paint, caulk, and restore it enough to launch a new work, the Chicagoland Community Church, or C3. The church planter/pastor, Jon Pennington, wanted us to go into the neighborhood and knock on doors to share about the new work with the residents, <u>and he wanted us to go at night</u>. I more than mildly protested I wouldn't do that at home in a strange neighborhood out of safety considerations, much less here in the city. The pastor replied, "God will make a way like in Colossians 4.2 ("pray that God may open a door for the word")." He was supposed to say that, of course, but I was not convinced.

Somehow the local ABC TV affiliate got wind of our presence there that day and decided to come film us with a novel angle (here was a group of college students opting out of the beach and getting smashed during spring break in order to help "our Windy City"). They took videos of us painting and cleaning up the street outside the church and interviewed our students and me. I had about thirty minutes advance notice before their arrival and gathered the students to say that they would have a chance to say maybe one or two sentences, and when they ask a question, make it count, citing Colossians 4.6, "let your speech always be with grace, seasoned with salt, so that you may know how you should respond to each person." The TV crew came, filmed, and I thought that was the end of it.

That evening, when we ventured forth to knock on doors, instead of being told 'scram' or worse, as soon as the people heard the TX drawl (howdy, y'all), they remarked, "You must be the group I just saw on the evening news. Come on in." We couldn't believe it! Sometimes, Bible verses need explanation, background study, and reflection; sometimes, they just need to be simply worn like a jacket, to venture forth clothed in the Word. As a leader who had lived overseas and ministered in another culture, I knew I had to trust the person living in that culture more than my casual knowledge of it; I also had to trust he knew how to apply the Word to the needs in that culture better than I, and that faith and the Word would inform each other. I am not sure who learned more that night, the students or their leader.

Lines on Leadership
When has a door unexpectedly opened for you as a leader to share a message? How did it come about?

_____

_____

++

1ST LETTER TO THE THESSALONIANS

Intro: 1 Thessalonians is one of, if not the earliest, of the Pauline epistles. Because he spent little time there before being forced to exit the city (see Acts 17), he wondered about their well-being and stability. Timothy brought a report, and this letter is the result. Paul addresses specific issues in the church, one being uncertainty about the Lord Jesus' return. Each of the five chapters ends with a reference to Christ's return (*Parousia*, His appearing).

++

1st Thessalonians 1---Highlights: affirmation of the Thessalonians for their example, zeal, and faith

When a person starts out in his ministry or career, he has no idea which disciples or colleagues will go by the wayside and which ones will flourish. Prognostication is not my realm of expertise. Some I had felt sure would have meteoric rises faded quickly; others excelled so greatly that I thought would slide to the back of the pack. The Thessalonians were a part of Paul's earliest missionary efforts, and he left them hastily before he could teach there extensively (Acts 17). How relieved he must have been to receive the reports from Timothy that the Thessalonicans had continued in the faith. Timothy gave a balanced report with both advances and detours this young church had taken (Acts 18.5). The letters of 1st and 2nd Thessalonians are Paul's responses to that report.

In this chapter, Paul lauds their consistency and adherence to the standards he introduced in his short tenure among them. Verses 5-7 recount how he and his coauthors (Silvanus and Timothy) provided an incarnational example of the gospel; the Thessalonicans imitated what they saw in him, his associates, and the Lord (meaning they acknowledged the alignment of Paul's, Silvanus', and Timothy's life with the Lord and His gospel); and they, in turn, became "an example to all the believers in Macedonia." (v.7b)

A pastoral colleague recounted to me how his extended family's business had succeeded for decades by providing a consistent product and not cutting corners to increase profits. They had stuck to their principles and standards even though some of their customers had left them seeking better deals and cheaper prices. After discovering their "better deals" were due to inferior products that didn't hold up, those customers eventually returned to his extended family's business acknowledging the quality, durability, and reliability of their products. I added how disappointed I had been with a guitar acquisition of mine made by a renowned company. They had started using some elements in their production that looked the same as before but did not hold up to years of use. The tone and the appearance of the guitar remained the same, but the durability and reliability of the product suffered from cutting corners either to increase profits or perhaps to cover for their inability to find the best components. After that purchase, every subsequent guitar purchase has been preceded by research into how, when, and where it was made.

<u>Lines of Leadership</u>
The true test of how well we have discipled/trained/equipped our followers is to follow the progress or regress of succeeding generations. First of all, did they even produce a succeeding generation? Secondly, did they cut corners and lower standards to produce the next generation? Thirdly, is the gospel (or brand in a corporate sense) recognizable in every succeeding generation?

Quality control in some groups is a given; for others, an elective. What measures in your church or organization ensure your message or product remains consistent from generation to generation?

_____

_____

++

1st Thessalonians 2—Highlights: Paul's ministry to Thessalonica was more personal than professional

In this chapter, Paul reveals his pastoral and parental relationship with this local church. From the opening verses, where he describes the church as his children (v.7), to the last verses, where he describes the Thessalonians as his "crown of exultation" (v.19), there is no mention of "professional distance" and muted affection. Paul openly affirms and adores this fledgling congregation. He often speaks in other epistles about the tenacity needed to proclaim the gospel amid hardships and adversity, but here he shows the tenderness needed to let a church know his heart was knit with theirs, and when he taught them, it was always undergirded with genuine love.

Pictured with me is Steve Alberts, a terrific minister who came to me while in college with many questions, open ears, a desire to learn, and a heart to serve Christ. He passed me up long ago in effectiveness (3 John 4) with youth. It has been my honor to train him as a college student, preside at his wedding, officiate the funeral of his second-born child, and preach

 his ordination sermon. He is a great husband and dad, and he and his devoted wife Shannon have three great children, Hannah, Marshall, and Wesley Allan (my namesake). They have done a remarkable job of parenting. One year I received an invitation to teach at a retreat near Tyler, TX, for Chinese graduate students studying abroad. God orchestrated it so that same spring, the Alberts moved from AR to a new church staff position in Tyler, and at the same time, Wesley and Marshall made professions of faith. I was invited to share in the baptisms of both boys that weekend of the retreat. What a thrill: a rare moment baptizing disciples of a disciple, and one who bore my name. What a joy many years ago to write a letter of blessing to the yet unborn Wesley Allan; what a greater joy to see him fulfill it before my eyes. A discipling relationship today can (over the years) yield many generations of believers (see 2 Tim. 2 entry). Pray today for God to reveal your next son or daughter in the faith.

My prayer for business leaders reading this is that at some point, some of their employees will go from being someone to pay in exchange for their work to loving them and investing in them, as Paul describes in v. 8 ("Having thus a fond affection for you, we were well pleased to impart to you not only the gospel of God but also our own lives, because you had become very dear to us.") (see Philemon entry). Paul finishes the chapter practically gushing about the Thessalonicans, that "you are our glory and joy" (v.20). This is one of the earliest letters Paul wrote, so one could think, sure, he started out this way, personable, intimate, but when he became the famous apostle, he likely forgot all the "little people" along the way. Organizations are made up of people, and whether a church is that small extended family in the holler or a megachurch, whether a company is a Ma and Pa operation or a multinational behemoth, there is a way to scale this type of affirmation for associates.

To be sure, this approach will not come naturally for some folks who see affection as a sign of weakness and vulnerability. And to be honest, some congregations or companies would not respond well to such an approach. In some cultures, affection is only for a family or loved ones; in others, everyone hugs and kisses everyone else. But everyone, regardless of culture, appreciates affirmation and knowing someone appreciates not only their contribution to the group but them as persons. Who is your "hope or joy or crown of exultation?" (v.19)

Lines on Leadership
(also see Rom. 16 entry). Who among your work associates do you need to affirm today? Not just compliment but look in the eye and tell them, 'I believe in you?'

_____
_____
++

1st Thessalonians 3---Highlights: encouragement resulting from Timothy's visit and report

A fiduciary is "a person to whom property or power is entrusted for the benefit of another[1]." Most businesses start out with noble aspirations of bettering the lives of the customers, giving outstanding customer service, and wowing clients by exceeding their expectations. If they are successful, the temptation is to become self-important, to start thinking the customer is fortunate to have found my business because, after all, they benefit by using *our* product, and they should thank us for existing. They cease to think of themselves as fiduciaries.

Employees and employers should not be faulted for having pride in their work, but when that pride sees the customer as a vehicle to the company's success instead of vice versa (the company existing to benefit others), this violates the spirit of servant leadership so strongly espoused in scripture and in this book. Paul distills this in verse 8 as he says, "for now we really live if you stand firm in the Lord." In this chapter, he continues to praise the good news Timothy has brought him of the Thessalonicans' progress in living out the gospel.

A cynical person could point out that Paul writes 1. and 2. Thessalonians early in his ministry, and that he has yet to become an esteemed and sought-out missionary and theologian of his later years; perhaps he is gushing over early success as we often do when that first big batch of orders comes in or for a church the first wave of people become members of our new church plant. 'Give him time', the cynic thinks, and Paul eventually will start thinking how lucky these folks are to have sat under my teaching. Thankfully, in some of his later writings, such as the Pastoral Epistles to the very same Timothy and to Titus, we see that the development of Paul into a leading voice within "the Way" (Acts 9.9, 23; 24.14) has not puffed up his self-worth, but rather he displays an enduring gratitude for what God has done in his life (1 Tim. 1.15) and through Paul in the lives of Timothy and Titus.

A church that thinks people should flock to their services just because of their name and reputation has drifted away from a fiduciary stance. Every pastor, every senior manager, every CEO needs to retain the fiduciary mindset that I will do better when my folks, my customers, my employees, and my church members are doing well.

Lines on Leadership
When was the last time you communicated to your church, your company, or your downline that much of your joy in life comes largely from them flourishing? (v.8, "for now we live if you are standing fast in the Lord." (ESV)

_____

_____

++

1st Thessalonians 4---Highlights: Sanctification and the Second Coming of Christ

Paul makes reference in each chapter of 1 Thessalonians to the return of Jesus Christ (1.10; 2.19; 3.13; 4.13-18; 5.3-6). The longest reference is in chapter 4, known by some as "the Rapture chapter". The theological area called *eschatology* means the study of last things. Unfortunately, Christians have argued for over 2000 years over the finer points of eschatology, and almost every camp reads its version of how the world will end and Christ will return into this passage (4.13-18). Basically, the differing camps argue about the sequencing of events: will there be a period of tribulation; does Christ come before, in the middle of it, or at the end of it; and why will He return?

Why did Paul feel compelled to write about this in one of his earliest epistles? Because believers commonly understood that Christ had ascended (Acts 1.9) into heaven, and it was predicted two verses later by a heavenly being that "this Jesus, who has been taken up from you into heaven, will come in just the same way as you have watched Him go into heaven" (Acts 1.11). By the time Paul began his missionary journeys, believers were dying natural deaths, and those remaining had begun to wonder: If His return is imminent, why has He not returned?

What will happen to those who have died waiting for His reentry into this world?

According to Christian understandings of the Old Testament, the Jewish people (not the writers of the OT, but its readers and interpreters) missed the Messiah's coming as twofold. The Hebrew people still await a conquering Messiah, and Christians say His coming is in two parts: first as a Suffering Servant (Isaiah 53) and later as a King of Kings (Rev. 19). Christians believe Jesus, as portrayed in the four Gospels, was the Messiah Isaiah predicted and that this same Christ will return this time as the King of Kings. As a Christ follower, I agree with this interpretation of Scripture, but in the back of my mind, I often wonder: the Jews felt so sure they could read the Word and correctly predict His coming, and I believe they missed it. What if we as Christians do the same thing and read the Word but wrongly predict the when's, the how's, and the where's of His second coming just like the Jews did about His first coming? The more one reads the eschatological explanations, the more confusing they can become.

So Paul attempts here to give the Thessalonians and anyone else reading this letter peace ("therefore comfort one another with these words," v. 18): regardless of whether the believer was dead or alive, it is not a factor in "missing out" on the when, where, and how He comes again. The emphasis here is not on the details but on assuring increasingly anxious readers. Of more importance to Paul is that whenever, wherever, and however He comes, the reader is ready to be received by Him. <u>Being prepared is more important that being on target with a prediction as to the particulars</u>.

Reference was made in an earlier entry (Acts 16) to Reggie McNeal's tough questions for the church. When I interviewed for my present position, I told the committee if they wanted to know my priorities to read *The Present Future* by McNeal. One of the prime shifts he advocates for both churches and businesses is away from prediction and toward preparation. The increasing complexities, twists, pandemics, political shifts, and acceleration of information flow—all of these and more contribute to the futility of projections with any detail or accuracy. I am not a fan of a total lack of planning and flying by the seat of your pants: planning and preparation are not mutually exclusive or antiphonal. This chapter teaches me to prepare for the future because I will have a hard time predicting it. It is not either/or, but both/and with the weight on preparation instead of prediction.

Lines on Leadership
As a believer, I firmly believe Christ is coming again. I cannot with certainty predict when He will come, but I can prepare for it. If he comes before any tribulation, a time of pressure and persecution, a time of separating wheat and chaff, I am gone before it "gets bad". If He comes during or after a tribulation, I have to ask myself, am I prepared to weather persecution and pay a higher price for being a believer? How is your church or company positioned in terms of faith and flexibility as you look toward the future?

_____
_____
++

1ˢᵗ Thessalonians 5---Highlights: end times remarks; everyday conduct

Verses 16-18 offer a framework for prayer and outlook on life that at first glance seems rather frothy and Pollyanish: "rejoice always, pray without ceasing, and in everything give thanks, for this is God's will for you in Christ Jesus." You can almost imagine someone skipping across a field of flowers to some chorus of insipid ditties about sunshine and rainbows. In reality, it is part of a multilayered and adult approach to life modeled by Paul and appropriate for the complexities of everyday contemporary life. Alert: this chapter conjures some disturbing images.

Paul remains consistent before and after his imprisonments, beatings, shipwrecks, and setbacks in admonishing believers to remain thankful and display unwavering gratitude to the Father regardless of one's lot in life (Eph. 5.20, Phil. 4.6, Col. 3.16). The word multilayered is used because gratitude has multiple levels. The first is a one-size-fits-all, lifelong attitude of thanks being an automatic response whenever a person or thing or event is recalled or comes across the horizon. In that case, one is thankful _for_ (Eph. 5.20) x person, thing, or event and is glad to recount to the Father why the thanks-giver is grateful. This works wonderfully when the person, thing, or event is positive.

The second level is when the person, thing, or event is horrific, and you cannot thank God _for_ it: the horrors of war, a deadly auto accident, the toll of a pandemic, a messy divorce. This is where the small preposition _in_ comes into play. I cannot at that moment give thanks _for_ that loss; grief, anger, and frustration must be acknowledged and given an outlet for expression. I can give thanks _in_ the midst of, _in_ spite of, because I know God has not abandoned me. He promises to walk through the valley of the shadow of death with me, not help me skirt that valley (Ps. 23. 4) (see Phil. 4 entry).

Salvation, or success in business, or the love of another precious soul all have their worth, and at times are incalculable and invaluable. But it makes us neither impervious nor invincible; it does not shield us from injury. Holiness and hurt are not opposite spectrum ends of human existence. For the joy set before Him, Christ endured the cross (Heb.12.2), and before the power of the resurrection comes the sufferings and conformity to His death (Phil. 3.10). The third level of gratitude occurs when you leave the firm footing of the joy of everyday life to plunge into currents of tragedy, give thanks in the midst and in spite of the loss, and emerge on the far banks to continue to thank the Father for His deliverance and companionship in every moment, the good and the wretched. It is a deep, abiding, forged-by-trials kind of joy.

Lines on Leadership
When I daily enter my office, I see a bronze wall hanging with the German poem written by Dietrich Bohhoeffer shortly before his execution in a German concentration camp: "von guten Mächten wunderbar geboren, erwarten wir was kommen mag; Gott ist mit uns am Abend und am Morgen und ganz gewiß am jeden neuen Tag (we are surrounded by the good power of our Lord and we can await whatever befalls us; God is with us in the light and the coming darkness, and most assuredly in every new day)."
The victories in life often exact a heavy price (Rom. 8.35-39). What setback or loss have you recently experienced? How will you give thanks now, in its aftermath, and in the days afterward?
_____
_____

++

2ND LETTER TO THE THESSALONIANS

Intro: This letter was written shortly after 1 Thessalonians and addressed a different issue than the first letter. In the previous letter, Paul addressed the concerns about the second coming of Christ. Some of the Thessalonians decided if He was coming back, why bother working? Why not put down my tools and just sit or stand around gazing into the sky for His imminent return? The suddenness of His return (1 Thess. 5.2, like a thief in the night) was being confused with the immediacy of His return.[1]

++

2nd Thessalonians 1---Highlights: the faith and perseverance of the Thessalonians

The same authorial trio (Paul, Silvanus, & Timothy) pens this short epistle as well as 1 Thessalonians. It begins much like its predecessor with obligatory salutations and affirmations. It quickly describes two facets of excellence that are pertinent to both churches and other organizations.

The first facet (v. 4, "your perseverance and faith in the midst of all your persecutions and afflictions which you endure") is that if you excel in a particular area, it garners notoriety and then the inevitable pushback or resistance. It is a sobering thought when Paul tells them suffering was to be expected if they engaged in Kingdom work. They don't suffer to enter the Kingdom of God, but they suffer because of their identification with the Kingdom. This can range from naysayers to detractors to saboteurs. In former times just as it took a while to form a reputation, it took a while to organize resistance to it. As this book is written, social media allows for instant negative feedback and attacks on whatever products, opinions, or ideology is presented by anyone. If you espouse something or promote an event, most web platforms have ways to "boost" or expand your audience by a range of fees. Every expansion brings new waves of criticism and attempts to "shout" down your position, idea, or product. To take a stand today for anything invites instant attacks, definitely not for the faint of heart or those with thin skin.

The second facet occurs as we encounter suffering for the sake of the Kingdom (v.5) and God declares us "worthy of our calling" (v.11). Friedrich Nietzsche's writings are not overly friendly to the Christian faith, but one of his more quoted lines that has made its way into the general vernacular is appropriate here: *aus der Kriegschule des Lebens* (out of life's school of war or of hard knocks), *was mich nicht umbringt, macht mich stärker* (what does not kill me will make me stronger[1]). The creation of a diamond itself involves great heat and pressure over many years, but no diamond emerges from the mines dazzling and faceted; that takes a skilled jeweler who rather violently (as far as the diamond goes) chips and carves away parts of what is valuable (the carved pieces are, after all, also diamond) to create something of even greater worth.

It is my prayer that American believers realize they are not the Kingdom standard on following Christ; for many of them, persecution occurs "over there somewhere"; their churches have largely become complacent and soft. Persecution purifies and strengthens. I have often been humbled to visit believers in persecuted countries and realize while they may not have all the resources of the American church, they are better representatives of this chapter as they pay the price to live out their calling.

Lines on Leadership
How, if ever, has your group suffered for its mission? Was the resistance to your group debilitating or a springboard from which to go forward?

_____
_____

+++

2nd Thessalonians 2---Highlights: the man of lawlessness, the son of perdition/destruction

Those wanting some juicy tidbit of secret inside information on the identity of the "man of lawlessness" (v.8), the Antichrist, or any other allusion to these figures might as well skip this chapter.

Paul's message in this chapter is not meant to reveal identities but recognize our primary duty when sensationalism overtakes the moment, which is to keep the main thing the main thing. It's not very catchy, but it is biblical. For Paul, the proclamation of the gospel was paramount, even in the face of sensational news, not to "be quickly shaken from your composure or be disturbed by a spirit or a message or a letter as if from us to the effect that the day of the Lord has come" (v. 2). This book was written during a time when social media and news outlets are everywhere 24/7; when a story breaks, it is instantly on every channel, streaming network, and social platform. Every breaking story takes on a breathless importance and feels like it will "change the world". In the year of this writing, the world was wrestling with a global pandemic (coronavirus or COVID-19), increasing worldwide climate calamities, and much political unrest from mass movements of refugees to unstable governments. Internet vehicles such as Twitter, Instagram, Facebook, and others have allowed the average citizen to leverage their opinion as larger and more seemingly valid ("wow, they have thousands of followers, what they say MUST be true") than ever before.

This leads to rampant speculation and unfounded hysteria. Word inflation occurs when normal declarative sentences take on ominous meanings and rack up exclamation points, emojis, stars, and... This chapter reminds me to take a deep breath, understand when the true world-ending events start to unravel, it will be apparent, and get back to doing what is truly important, the main mission of the church or organization. Leaders find a way not to be distracted by every swell and ebb of public opinion and keep the message on task, headed in the right direction.

<u>Lines on Leadership</u>
As a leader, what voices and sources do you consider reliable for the data you use in decision-making? In an era of conspiracy theories, faked videos, and computer-generated narratives, how do you determine what is reliable information?

_____

_____

++

2<u>nd</u> Thessalonians 3---Highlights: get to work

The larger context of both Thessalonian epistles is the growing uncertainty of the believers there about the predicted return of Christ. In earlier chapters, Paul addresses the believers' concerns about what will happen to loved ones who die before the *Parousia* (appearing) of their Lord Jesus. Here in 2 Thessalonians 3, Paul confronts yet another aspect of faulty understanding about Jesus' second coming.

The admonitions in vs. 6-13 are summed up in one simple phrase: if you don't work, you don't eat. Most in contemporary Western society would read that in terms of their solitary personal output and thinking, 'Well, of course, if I don't work and earn a salary or work in my own fields to produce crops, naturally, I won't get paid or won't have a harvest'. In English, the word 'you' is the same for 2nd person singular and 2nd person plural, and Western readers' default understanding of 'you' is singular. The verses are written to the congregation in Thessalonica as a whole. After Pentecost, the believers in Jerusalem worshipped together, ate meals together, and pooled their resources together (Acts 2.44-47). This became a pattern for new works in new locations, and most, if not all, of the new local churches met in homes.

Some were leading "undisciplined lives" (v. 11) and not working because they thought: why should we engage in menial tasks when Jesus is about to come back and lead us to a heavenly existence? Others may have figured out that since the group was pooling both food and financial resources if we slacked off, there would still be plenty for us because most except us would work hard. Paul makes it clear we owe it both to our fellow believers and to the Lord to work in a disciplined and honest fashion until He comes.

A small but pivotal book in my ministry has been Brother Lawrence's *The Practice* of *the Presence of God*. It is public domain and can be found easily online and read in one sitting[1]. Lawrence was a 17th-century monk working in a monastery kitchen doing basic, unseen tasks considered demeaning, unimportant, and trivial to those in charge of more "important" tasks. My first reading of the book had me shaking my head at such a "small" work. It didn't have the sweeping power of Augustine or the insight of Machiavelli's treatise on political acumen. It took a second reading to humble me and see Lawrence's pure joy came from his work because it was unto the Lord; he worshipped through his work, and his prayer and potato peeling merged into a labor of love. The Lord can come when He deems it time; I am to honor Him with hard work up until that time He does return.

<u>Lines on Leadership</u>
What tasks are you putting off, thinking something cataclysmic is about to occur? Do you see your hard work like the Thessalonicans, something to be avoided, or like Brother Lawrence, something with which to honor the Father?
_____
_____
++

1ST LETTER TO TIMOTHY

Intro: 1 and 2 Timothy plus Titus form the Pastoral Epistles, a veritable manual for pastoral duties written by the veteran missionary to his trusted apprentices and eventual successors. The two epistles to Timothy have been my guidebook for decades in discipling generations of "Timothys" to continue in their ministry and to go deeper, farther, higher, and faster than I ever thought possible. These epistles also constitute the last ones written by Paul, so there is a poignancy to them that makes the reader pause and think: what would I say if I knew this was the last communication with a dear follower and/or likely successor?

++

1 Timothy 1---Highlights: Warnings of false teachers, the goal of our ministry, keeping the distinctiveness of our ministry

V.5 "The goal of our instruction is love from a pure heart, a good conscience, & a sincere faith." (NASB) This chapter sets the pattern for 1 Timothy, 2 Timothy, and Titus. Paul displays all three life phases of leadership: learning, leading, and leaving a legacy[1] in this chapter and every chapter of the three epistles. V. 5 is not just a bumper sticker slogan; it is the culmination of a life of leadership.

The bulk of the chapter reminds Timothy that Paul's years of learning, teaching, missionary work, and experiences are boiled down into this verse. Paul doesn't recommend a style of leadership or a method of instruction; he says the sum of your leadership should result in these three things (pure heart, good conscience, and sincere faith), which in turn result in love. V.17 ("Now to the King eternal, immortal, invisible, the only God . . .") is not a sideline detour in this discourse; it is the goal of the goal. Paul never gets over the impact of his conversion (vs. 12-16) and how his deliverance leads to worship in v. 17. Your leadership,

Timothy, should point yourself and every disciple of yours towards Jesus (as the Christ, vs. 14, 15, 16; as King, v. 17). And it must be done honorably, not with deceit or ulterior motives: Paul deliberately used adjectival modifiers to keep everything on track; <u>pure</u> heart, <u>good</u> conscience, <u>sincere</u> faith. He contrasts the wrong way to lead in the listing of men gone astray (vs. 9-10) with the life changed by the "glorious gospel" (v.11), which he describes in vs. 12-16, showing how he himself at one time was leading (as a defender of the Jewish faith he was active in rounding up Christians for imprisonment) but leading astray. He uses another example at the end of the chapter (v. 20) of those whose hearts, conscience, and faith are devoid of purity, goodness, and sincerity. The sum of your efforts must be measured by this goal in v. 5.

Joseph Rost's definition of leadership relates well to 1 Timothy 1: "Leadership is an influence relationship among leaders and followers who intend real changes that reflect their mutual purposes[2]." It is obvious from the beginning lines ("to Timothy, my true child in the faith") Paul is speaking out of an "influence relationship" about a transformative love that has as its goal the Savior common to them both. Paul is at the "leaving a legacy" phase and wishes to direct Timothy to a life trajectory where he one day can do the same for others (see 2 Tim. 2 entry). Timothy's leadership is to result in changed lives that will, in turn, change the lives of others, all to the glory and honor of Jesus Christ (their "mutual purposes").

<u>Lines on Leadership</u>
How many of us have as our goal to build a bigger organization, a bigger church, a bigger ministry? While a part of that is commendable, it is easy to lose sight of our goal being

transformed lives, either by the product or service we offer or the message we proclaim. What is the true goal of your instruction?

_____

_____

++

1ˢᵗ Timothy 2---Highlights: intercessory prayer for authorities; instructions for women

Over the years, we all acquire a "hat collection". In v. 7, Paul states, "for this I was appointed a preacher and an apostle as a teacher of the Gentiles in faith and truth." Every person who has worked or led has been asked at some point in their career to wear multiple hats. Sometimes this can be frustrating and burdensome if the hats denote conflicting duties; other times, it can be enriching if the different "hats" reinforce each other's functions.

The three terms Paul uses are related but not synonymous. The term preacher (*kerux*) in the CSB, LEB, and NIV is translated as "herald", one who openly proclaims the message of the day issued by the king. Of and by himself, the herald is of little importance; his position is made important by the message or the authority of the message's Author. The term apostle (*apostolos*) is a transliterated word that means 'one who is sent' and is often described as the nearest thing in the NT to what we today would call a missionary, one sent from his/her "home base" to cross barriers such as geography, language, social class, or ethnicities. The term teacher (*didaskalos*) here has more to do with Paul's audience (the Gentiles) than the actual function. All three terms are bound to the main verb in the verse, that Paul was 'appointed', and from many other passages we can safely deduce the appointment was by none other than God himself (see Acts 9, 22, 26; also Gal. 1.1). 'Preacher' deals with the message; 'apostle' deals with the relationship to God (that he has the same status as the twelve Jesus deemed His apostles); and 'teacher' deals with the audience to which God has sent him with God's gospel message.

When a leader allows ever-increasing responsibilities to pile up in a random manner, they can easily overwhelm and scream for one's time and attention to the point of doing a mediocre to an unsatisfactory job at all of them. The different roles a leader undertakes or 'hats' a leader wears should be complementary and synergistic in nature. From a secular standpoint, a leader should choose carefully which roles he/she takes on over the course of one's leadership development, so they amplify and build upon each other to produce not only a multi-talented but a multi-pronged approach to one's leadership, making a person more adaptable to more situations (and usually more valuable). From a Christian standpoint, a leader must trust the Father that He will chart the leader's path so he can be most effective for the Kingdom of God.

I have been in ministry positions as a youth, pastor, college campus minister, and missionary. Educationally I have degrees in music education, religious education, and leadership. In my present position as an associational mission strategist, I work with multiple churches in ten counties in Appalachia. In the course of one week with our pastors, I can be a counselor, a cheerleader, a consultant, an arbitrator, a worship leader, a preacher, a teacher, an administrator, a long-range planner, a researcher, and a confidant.

The work is often exhausting but rewarding. I learned a long time ago (early in my ministry) I do a poor job when I have to play dual roles simultaneously of husband and minister. Also, I can translate pretty well from German to English or vice versa as long as the direction remains the same, but when I must freely switch back and forth between the two languages in a mediating fashion, my tongue and brain both get hopelessly tangled up. I have had to learn to wear as few hats at one time as possible, so I can concentrate on the task at hand and plan out my 'wardrobe' so I know in advance which hat(s) I'm to wear during the course of that day.

Lines on Leadership
How many hats do you wear in your chosen calling/vocation? Which ones conflict, which ones complement? Do you have one particular hat that is suitable for "wearing" in every situation? If so, which one is it?
_____
_____
++

1st Timothy 3---Highlights: Qualifications for overseers, deacons, women; early confession or hymn

I have worked with many churches in the pastoral succession process, and this chapter contains the list of NT characteristics most quoted by church constitutions, bylaws, and search committees concerning the role and nature of pastors and deacons. It emphasizes character more than competence or calling (see 1 Tim. 4 entry). It is not a job description *per se* but significant guidelines for Timothy and Titus (see Titus 1.5) to search for and appoint leaders in the churches they started or oversaw. Many church leaders describe the difference to me concerning elders and deacons by saying elders lead or are responsible for the spiritual direction of the church body, and deacons serve the church body. Those descriptions are not mutually exclusive but will often overlap.

An initial reading of the qualifications yields several differences that stand out as unique to each function of overseer or deacon (there are more than listed here):

<u>Overseers</u> are to:

<u>Be able to teach</u>, v.2 (They are responsible for the Word of God's main proclamation, instruction, and dissemination within the body; it is a primary, not an exclusive trait, as all are instructed to be able to teach 2 Tim. 2.24)

<u>Be hospitable</u>, v.2 (no national chain of hotels existed then, and most inns were not reputable; to open one's home to others of the Way was crucial to the strengthening and expansion of the fledgling movement of Christianity);

<u>Not be a new convert</u>, v.6 (literally 'newly planted[1] or shallow roots); most commentators speak of the danger of vanity and pride, but also, if the person is a new convert, he still has residual concepts of sin, salvation, personal atonement, and other beliefs he might bring from his former religion that are contrary to the Word and need correction);

<u>Have a good reputation outside of the church</u>, v.7 (this doesn't mean he has to join every civic organization in town, but it does mean his integrity should extend into his business dealings and reputation with everyone in the community, not just those of the local flock who may be enamored of his pulpit or other pastoral skills).

<u>Deacons</u> are uniquely described as: men of dignity (v. 8); not double-tongued (v.8); free of sordid gain (v.8); holding to the mystery of faith (v. 9); and in need of testing before becoming a deacon (v.10).

This is not a description of a first-class or second-class arrangement but rather the selection of men with these characteristics for certain functions within the church. Too often, I see elders and deacons spar with one another over power and control issues instead of being on the same team. In football, it is a rare person who plays on both sides of the ball, but both offense and defense players speak of being on the same team. To carry that analogy further, it is admittedly true the highest-paid players on a team's football roster are usually the high-profile positions of quarterback, running back, and receivers, but wise stars of the game are quick to give praise to their teammates, knowing they deserve the "high standing and great confidence in the faith" listed in v. 13 for deacons, not overseers. For too long we have seen overseers, elders, pastors, bishops, and deacons as a corporate hierarchy of sorts; the ground at the foot of the cross is level, and we all serve out our calling and our responsibilities for the sake of the Kingdom and the glory of our Lord. It is not about higher or lower standards but characteristics commensurate to the task at hand. The unifiers in the lists in both I Tim. 3 and Titus are faithfulness to one's wife and the family being grounded in the faith.

If people cannot be found who exemplify these traits, then discipleship is employed to train and equip until the traits emerge in some of the disciples who eventually aspire to fulfill the functions of overseer and deacon.

<u>Lines on Leadership</u>
For people already in leadership, these qualities serve as a diagnostic in a corrective and affirming manner. A periodic review of one's life using 1 Timothy 3 is recommended. As you stand now, would Timothy or Titus have considered you for designation as an overseer or deacon in the early church or as a worthy leader in your organization?

_____

_____

++

1st Timothy 4---Highlights: false and true teachings; a young minister's balanced approach to leadership

A stool is a useful piece of furniture. You can sit on it, support your leg playing a guitar, or stand on it to retrieve something from a high shelf. Stools come with three or more legs. You never see a one or a two-legged stool because it would be comically unstable (perhaps not for an expert unicyclist). Also, a stool with three or more legs would be unstable and basically useless if one leg was rusty or riddled with termites to the point of not supporting weight. So to be useful and stable, the stool needs three (or more) solid, sturdy legs. In verses 6-16, Paul outlines the "legs" of the stool for a balanced leader. The three legs are: 1) competence, 2) character, and 3) calling; the "bonus" legs are chemistry and culture.

1) In verse 6, Paul tells Timothy to be (constantly) nourished on words of faith and of sound doctrine. Vs. 1-5 warn of fanciful, harmful teachings, and, to insure Timothy does not fall into such practices; he should be trained to discern true from counterfeit. An informed faith in some circles is equated with a diluted or neutered faith because they believe education, by default, neutralizes passion for God. Degrees are no guarantee of spiritual effectiveness, but they are not automatic disqualifiers for a person to lead a flock of God's people. Learning can lead to a simple acquisition of knowledge instead of forging one's faith and the faith of others (see 2 Tim. 3 entry). Whether the person seeks formal schooling, self-taught skills from extensive reading, trial by fire, or training from a mentor (or the best, all the above), competence is necessary for a leader to face the countless challenges of ministry or a career.

2) In v. 12, the young leader is wisely told to concentrate on character qualities. Paul knows some will question a younger leader's usefulness. Character connects better with some folks

than competence (hence the old saw, people don't care how much you know until they know how much you care). Most church members can't tell you the specifics of sermons preached, but like layers and layers of paper mache` that make up a recognizable figure. The sermons preached and seen in the preacher's life over the years reinforce the <u>character</u> of the man, which is what most church members remember.

3) In verse 14, Paul admonishes Timothy to be mindful of the collective affirmation of his elders by "the laying on of hands by the presbytery." In some Christian circles, this is thought to confer spiritual authority; in others, it is a prayerful ceremony denoting endorsement and recognition by fellow brothers in Christ of one's <u>calling</u>.

Competence without character may produce a technically accurate sermon but not the life that backs it up. Character without competence may result in a genuinely nice person everyone respects and likes, but it does not guarantee the skills needed to face formidable challenges. Competence and character without calling are one of the scariest incomplete combinations. The minister who does not operate out of a clear and abiding sense of <u>calling</u> wilts and crumbles over the long haul when competence and character are questioned or prove ineffective. <u>Sometimes the only thing that keeps a leader on task when his competency and character are questioned is the surety of his calling</u>.

The bonus "legs" for the stool image are <u>chemistry</u> and <u>culture</u>. <u>Chemistry</u> is an alliterative substitute for the simple word 'fit.' A person may be more than adequately qualified for a ministry or career position, but if it is not a good 'fit' (which could be for a <u>lot</u> of reasons), all the competence, character, and even calling won't necessarily make the partnership between pastor and parishioners or leader and organization mesh. <u>Culture</u> is a part of that 'fit.' If the minister is from another country, or another region, doesn't speak the dialect, doesn't know all the cultural 'cues,' or doesn't understand the unwritten values and taboos of his chosen field, it contributes to an initial and sometimes enduring awkwardness.

The Saturn V booster stage was the large rocket that launched the Apollo program. The five engines belched fire as they lifted the entire payload off the ground into space, producing 750,000 pounds of thrust. If those five boosters did not fire in a balanced manner, they could all be firing, but with one dominant or one weaker than the others, the whole rocket went off course. Competence, character, calling, chemistry, and culture must work together in a balanced blend to create an effective leader and leadership environment and propel him/her forward.

Lines on Leadership

Do you consider yourself a balanced leader in the areas of competence, character, calling, chemistry, and culture? How would you describe your strengths/weaknesses as a leader in each area?

_____

_____

++

1ˢᵗ Timothy 5---Highlights: support of widows; interaction with leaders of the church

This chapter is a primer for those older than Timothy within the congregation, which at his age was the majority of the members. This age-old balance of <u>affirming</u> those under one's charge while still claiming the right to <u>analyze</u> their position, their

403

performance, or their decisions is a difficult yet necessary duty of a leader.

Paul reminds Timothy the church is, in essence, a family (v. 1-2). His default starting point for all members within the church is to honor them as his fathers, mothers, sisters, and brothers. He then gives definite guidelines for the treatment of widows within the congregation as to material assistance and does not mince words about how to exclude some from that assistance (vs. 9-16). The latter half of the chapter turns the spotlight on the elders of the church and will garner the majority of our attention.

Evaluation of a subordinate by superiors is a standard operating procedure for most organizations, with ever higher levels of senior management evaluating the level below them until the top rung of the ladder is reached and a procedure is devised to evaluate those in charge or who hold the greatest responsibility. In corporations, this usually takes the form of a review board of peers or a board of directors, people who are not employees of the corporation. Unfortunately, for many organizations, such a group's members are people chosen more for their large pocketbooks or undying loyalty to the institution or to the organization's leader. The transgressions of many a football coach, corporate CEO, university president, or church pastor are ignored or excused as long as the shareholders are amply rewarded with dividends or as long as the organization grows and is deemed successful. Poor behavior and poor decisions by the leader, overlooked by those charged with observing and accounting for them, usually lead to long-term negative consequences. As one who works with the leadership of churches across our state, I see this over and over: a pastor coaxes the church into a building project that is more a memorial to him than a vehicle to advance the Kingdom; a secretary cooks the books to cover embezzlement; or raises are given by an adoring group of deacons or elders to the church staff when in reality the church is in deficit spending.

A system of accountability should be in place from the beginning of a leader's tenure in an organization, parameters of expected behavior spelled out and judgment rendered without partiality (v. 21).

Respect/Affirmation: Paul repeats here what is quoted elsewhere in his writings (1 Cor. 9.14) and in the Gospels (Luke 10.7); the laborer is worthy of his wages and double honor (vs. 17-18). If a person leads with any distinction and excellence, the inevitable howling and opposition will arise. Every decision and every policy enacted will have its detractors and doubters. Paul's admonition in v. 19 not to receive an accusation against an elder except when multiple witnesses come forth is timelier today than ever. The leader deserves to be accorded respect and affirmation as the default mode, but that should never translate into a free ride or a carte blanche allowance to do whatever he pleases. It must be balanced with review and accountability.

Review/Accountability: If, after a thorough review of the leader, a pattern of indiscretion, improper decisions, or abuse of authority has been established, the elder should be rebuked "in the presence of all" (v.20), which shows the congregation/organization the leader is accountable to his people and to God. Paul uses very strong language in v. 21 to remain steadfast and impartial in applying the standards of scripture and the sacred covenant between members of the church/organization to the leader's life.

He closes the chapter repeating this balance: don't be too hasty to endorse a leader until you've vetted him and watched him carefully (v.22); if the church/organization will not hold the leader accountable, the Lord will. Make no mistake: the sins and the righteousness of a leader's life and his accomplishments will come to light in the current or succeeding generations (vs. 24-25).

Final word to leaders: we have no right to demand accountability of others if we are not willing to undergo scrutiny. If we only accept adulation and not the honest feedback needed to make us a better leader, yet demand that of others, we are weak, insecure, and lead by fear rather than faith. Leaders need both respect and review, affirmation and accountability.

Lines on Leadership
Does your organization have a mechanism in place to evaluate your performance as a leader? If so, does it have the necessary authority and resources to properly carry out its duty? If not, why not?

_____
_____

++

1st Timothy 6---Highlights: various final instructions and review of principles stated in chapters 1-5

v.19, ". . . that they may take hold of that which is life indeed." What really matters is a summation statement. Paul has talked twice about the love of money being the root of all evil (v. 10) and not to fix one's hopes on the "uncertainty" of riches but on God, "who richly supplies us with all things to enjoy".

Much of my thinking and teaching involves a spectrum. Countless times I have drawn a line on a marker board, written opposing terms at the respective ends (Imagine simple contrasts like short/long, fast/slow, safe/dangerous), and asked the group to imagine it as a conveyor belt that can move in either direction simultaneously.

X < _____ > Y

One disturbing spectrum is when the poles are: virtue/vice, good/evil, or capacity to serve God/capacity to sin against Him.

It is disturbing because it seems the spectrum is widening. Each technological advance seems to expand our ability to engage in ministry or engage in sin. In olden times (i.e., pre-smartphones), the farther away someone lived, the more expensive the call, and I could only hear their voice. Now with fiber optics, calling someone anywhere in the world is inexpensive ('free' with some phone apps such as Skype or Signal). Now I can not only hear them, but I can also see them. Concepts of distance and intimacy are being totally restructured. In the near future, I anticipate further advances in virtual and augmented reality will expand those sensory connections from sound and sight to touch, smell, and even taste. My ability to enter the world of another locale, another situation, and the sphere of another life is rapidly growing. Which direction on that spectrum I head, whether to share the truth of God's Word or share in a destructive activity, is my choice, and I can go farther down my chosen trajectory than ever before.

Some of Paul's last instructions to his younger protégé Timothy were to "flee from youthful lusts (passions, ESV) and pursue righteousness, faith, love, and peace, along with those who call on the Lord from a pure heart." (2 Tim. 2.22, NASB). Earlier, he told Timothy, "the goal of our instruction is love from a pure heart, a good conscience, and a sincere faith." (see 1 Tim. 1 entry) Life is a dynamic enterprise; it moves in one direction or the other, honoring the Father or dishonoring Him.

Assigning some imaginary line of demarcation on that spectrum is arbitrary and foolish. I cannot count the times a young person has asked when discussing dating or relating to the sexes, "where is the line, how far it too far, when does it become wrong to . . .?" Unfortunately, many a believer never outgrows this adolescent attitude; as an adult, they are more concerned with how close they can dangle themselves over a precipice without falling rather than their lives actively tracking toward Christ (Phil. 3.10-21). The above admonition says to pursue God "with those who call on the Lord from a pure heart". This is why we all need members of a covenant community of faith (i.e., a local church) to help us see where we are on the spectrum. This is where accountability comes to bear, and one reason why the "one another's" are is in Scripture.

In the management of time, leisure, technology, possessions, and resources, I need to periodically engage in spectrum thinking and have the vulnerability to ask others to show me if I am/am not headed in the right direction. Worshipping and ministering alongside other believers are surely the first steps. Seek first the Kingdom of God—direction counts as well as devotion.

Lines on Leadership
Do I see myself as straddling some imaginary fence on some arbitrary line of demarcation between forbidden and permissible behavior in x area of my life? What prevents me from taking a direction and decidedly walking that way? (for a fuller treatment of this idea, see Eugene Peterson's *Long Obedience in the Same Direction*[1])

_____

_____

++

2ND LETTER TO TIMOTHY

Intro: There is an air of finality to 2 Timothy. These are some of the last words Paul knows he will share with his young protégé. It is a spelled-out succession plan for the work at Ephesus, and in a wider sense, it is the passing of a generational torch. Paul makes it plain he does not expect to be released from prison, his fate is sealed, and soon Timothy will assume greater mantles of leadership.

++

2nd Timothy 1---Highlights: it's all about the Gospel, Timothy

This epistle opens much like countless scenes in novels and movies. Greetings are given, and pleasantries about the work and the family. As soon as Paul and Timothy are out of earshot of others, the mood (and, of course, the film's musical score) turns somber and somewhat furtive as Paul issues four quick imperatives: 1) to kindle afresh (the gift of God within Timothy, v. 6); to not be ashamed (of the gospel nor those who preach it, v. 8); to retain (the standard of sound words he received from Paul, v. 13); and to guard (the treasure entrusted to him, v. 14).

In verse 7, Paul reminded Timothy that God does not give us a spirit of fear (which Timothy likely exhibited as he slowly realized the gravity of the scene) but a spirit of power and love and a sound mind (discipline, NASB). The treasure (of the gospel) must be kept pure from corruption, addition, revision, dilution, and distortion (which is explained throughout both Timothy epistles as Paul warned about the various wiles of false teachers). In literature and film, this treasure takes many forms: a disk with code names of spies, a damning dossier, a doomsday device, precious jewels, a baby, the Arkenstone of the Hobbit, great wealth, a magic incantation, forbidden technology, a video expose, or a dark secret.

In 2 Timothy 1, the treasure is the Gospel. This is the first of several mentions in 2 Timothy that represents the passing of the torch onto the next generation. Paul commands Timothy to guard this treasure with his life and that the Holy Spirit will help you protect it. He also declares Timothy worthy to receive it as he uses the word 'entrust'. Most commentaries describe Paul making a deposit, in essence treating Timothy as a steward to whom Paul could give the treasure, knowing it was in good hands.

But Timothy is not only to guard the Gospel with his life; he is to let the Gospel become his life. The Gospel is not a set of principles. The Gospel is at its core incarnational: the truth of God became Truth in the life of Christ (Jn. 14.6); He is called the Wisdom of God (1 Cor. 1.30) and the Word of God (Jn. 1.1, 14); the Will of God is expressed through the death, burial, and resurrection of Christ (1 Cor. 15.3ff); and He was prophesied as Immanuel, God with us (Isaiah 7.14; Mt. 1.23). Timothy is to embody the Gospel.

When a pastor approaches the pulpit to preach, his heart should always be broken for his people; his eyes should dance because he is about to impart a wondrous message of hope and change; his knees should buckle slightly under the claim he is about to make, that the Gospel can transform your life because it has transformed him. Timothy was entrusted with the gospel of Paul's message and the gospel of Paul, the man. When the two entrusted gospels of message and man align well, they will not remain hidden, and they will transform lives.

Lines on Leadership

Just like the parable of the talents (see Mt. 25.14ff), this treasure is not to be hoarded and forgotten; it is to be openly displayed (2.2, in the presence of many witnesses). With what treasure of faith or fortune have you been entrusted? How are you using it to lead in your ministry or career?

_____

_____

++

2<u>nd</u> Timothy 2—Highlights: discipleship; selected instructions on ministry

This will be one of the longest entries in this book because I have preached the first seven verses more often than any others in Scripture. It is the signature passage for discipleship, which should be at the heart of any ministry or business, teaching others to teach others to teach others. These verses are the biblical distillation of the centuries-old practice of *training* (showing how to do something) and *equipping* (giving the person the tools to instill the training) exemplified by the parent to child, teacher to pupil, master to apprentice, supervisor to subordinate, and here with Paul to Timothy.

Verse 1 singles out Timothy: No matter what happens to others, Paul talks straight to Timothy and no one else. No matter what anyone else does, stay strong in the grace of Christ. The rest of the three seemingly disparate word images (soldier, athlete, and farmer) are all about professions that require effort and discipline, so there is to be a balance of God's grace and personal discipline in Timothy's ministry. Verse 7 is the bookend summation of this same idea, of the partnership between Timothy's efforts being fueled by and bathed in the Lord's wisdom.

Verse 2 is the fulcrum of the teaching as there are four generations of men listed: Paul, Timothy, reliable or faithful men, and others also. Timothy is not to be a <u>disciple</u> of Paul only but a <u>discipler</u> of succeeding generations of believers, a <u>disciplemaker</u>—the minister who is only interested in his own followers' or disciples' practices addition. To make disciples who will make other disciples, all with the mindset to see at least two generations beyond themselves, is to practice Kingdom multiplication (see Mt. 28 entry). One of the key words in the verse is the adjective describing the men Timothy was to disciple, usually translated as 'faithful' (NASB, ESV, CSB, KJV) or 'reliable' (NIV). This may sound crass, but to be both effective and efficient within the Kingdom, one has to consider the rate of investment in relationship to time. Ministers and senior leaders of organizations have mounting pressure on their time from more and more sources, and to take time to invest in others' training means those trained must be committed to the same standard and multi-generational training. Our cheap-grace/easy-believism approach to gaining converts produces decisions, not disciples. Churches have dispensed with counting the costs up front of discipleship (Lk. 14) and sold new members on the privileges of salvation without telling them the responsibilities of a Kingdom citizen and that the mandate from the Master is to make disciples. Jesus taught the multitudes, He had many followers, He chose twelve, and He gave His prime time to three. We should walk in His steps (Jn. 12.26, 1 Pet. 2.21).

Paul starts the three-word images off with empathy and identification as he says suffer <u>with me</u> the hardships of soldiering (v.3). Timothy must be willing to endure the rigors of combat and the prep for it. That which is good and proper has to be shed in order to accomplish the best; the soldier/minister must be able to take a command from the Master and fulfill it regardless of the cost (v.4).

The second image is simple: you don't win if you don't play according to the rules (v.5). <u>There is no shortcut to spiritual maturity. Period</u>. You want to win? Train, push, and stay disciplined. When I am a professor, I tell the students on the first day that grace is a theological concept, not an educational one. If they want the grade, they will earn it according to the syllabus. If you want the medal at the Olympics, it is not given for participation; it is given to the person who beats out all the others for that spot on the podium. Too many believers want the magic sermon, the magic song, the magic revival service that will instantly transform them into a solid disciple of Christ. Those things can inspire and truly change the direction of one's life, but the primary vehicle for growth is when the true disciple practices the spiritual disciplines to become the man or woman of God he/she needs to be.

The third image is one of a farmer being rewarded because of his hard work. What do they all have in common? Seven is a heavenly number, so here are seven commonalities and a few foundational insights for discipleship. For the sake of brevity, I have not made the obvious parallels to ministry and church life for each commonality and encourage the reader to take time to reflect on them to that end:

1) <u>A well-defined foe</u>---The soldier knows who to shoot, the athlete knows who to beat (an opponent, a team, a time), and the farmer knows which weevil, which weather, which water conditions are all harmful to his seedlings and does what is needed to protect them.

2) <u>A well-defined objective</u>---The soldier knows where he is headed when the maneuver commences and what he is to take

or destroy; the athlete knows where the goal line/home base/net is and how to be rewarded for reaching it.

3) <u>The need for superior equipment</u>---The soldier cannot function with a jammed gun or broken down jeep; the athlete needs the best glove/helmet/cleats/racket/bicycle or anything else that can legally give him an edge; the farmer of today cannot produce the needed yield per acre with a hand scythe and a hoe and outdated fertilizers, so he goes heavily into debt to purchase and maintain the large combines and other machinery needed to harvest.

4) <u>The community is intense</u>---there is no deeper bond between men than a band of brothers in combat; listen to athletes after a contest extol the bond between teammates and how often the team inspired them to excel; just sit in an informal fraternity of farmers and listen not only to the lingo but to the love of the land and each other's farm as a family's livelihood. (suggested reading[1], *Life Together* by Dietrich Bonhoeffer about the secret seminary and its extraordinary fellowship during WWII)

5) <u>The goal is never met</u>---There will always be the next battle, the next season, the next crop.

6) <u>The mundane is the norm</u>---The soldier drills and drills to ingrain the commands and obedience necessary on the battlefield; the athlete reps and reps to ingrain the muscle memory and plays called from the bench so when the situation is grave, emotions are subdued, and training rises to the occasion; the life of a farmer is preparing, planting, nurturing, harvesting, selling, repeating, most of it alone.

7) <u>The isolation of excellence</u>---If the soldier is separated by sound, darkness, and death from his comrades, he is to persevere and fulfill the last command given with whatever resources are at hand; the athlete who excels in competition is

the one who has put in the gym time, the film time, the practice of fundamentals time, the alone time; the farmer spends the majority of his time alone out in the barn or the field. The farther up the scale of excellence a person goes, the fewer folks who are there with them. To take sports as an example, at the club level or public school level, one can easily stand out with talent. At the collegiate scholarship level, everyone there was good at HS, and the level of excellence was raised, the same exponentially at the pro level. <u>That which separates the winner from the loser becomes smaller and smaller, yet it requires more and more effort</u>.

Two Additional Insights:

1) <u>All three of the word images require a mentor</u>---The soldier has a drill instructor, then a sergeant, always a higher-up teaching him the hows, whys, whats, whens, and wheres of the next level; the athlete needs a coach to take his talent and merge it with a commitment to achieve the next level; the farmer has someone show him how and when to fertilize, how deep, and when to plow when the right time to harvest to achieve the maximum yield.

2) <u>All three of the word images must eventually stand on their own two feet</u>---A soldier learns to lead from his superiors and knows through promotion, attrition, or death, he may one day take his commanding officer's place; once the athlete steps across the yard lines or the base paths, the coach cannot go with him; the coach cannot throw the pass or make the free throw for the athlete; the farmer eventually is the only one on that tractor making the decisions for hundreds of acres and thousands of people's nutrition.

Discipleship should be the heart of the church's and the pastor's ministry, not peripheral; it is not extra-curricular. It is not tossing a handbook and Bible at someone and saying, see you in six weeks. Discipleship is a life-transforming process that occurs best in the overall context of life itself, not just a scheduled time over coffee or a classroom at the church building. Jesus taught His disciples by living with them, eating with them, and teaching along the way as they passed wheat fields, fig-trees, seashores, and temples.

Lines on Leadership
It is one of the greatest joys of my life to see hundreds of disciples spread around the globe in Kingdom work, teaching others to teach others to teach others to the glory of God. Who are your spiritual grandchildren and great-grandchildren?

_____
_____
++

2nd Timothy 3---Highlights: signs of last days; warns about false teachers; the value of the Scriptures

The price for speaking and living the truth has risen steadily in the 21st-century world. Paul warns Timothy in this chapter about two consequences when people abandon truth: first, people generate their own version of it that produces a substitute 'godliness' so they can divorce it from any demands made by a Creator God (v. 5); and secondly, when they continually learn falsehoods, it fills the mind but never results in "a knowledge of the truth" (v. 7) much like empty calories consumed produce a full stomach but ultimately poor nutrition.

The unmooring of society from a concept of absolute truth and the ability for anyone to publish their thoughts online for the world to view have paired to produce an ungodly amount of ungodly 'wisdom.' Anyone's opinion becomes (in their own mind) their manufactured 'truth' because it is in print on some post (as if this bestows a degree of legitimacy simply by existing), some blog, or some article. <u>If everyone's opinion is valid, then in reality, none of them are since they have no standard of truth by which to measure them.</u> The flood of information, be it misinformation or disinformation or just a conglomeration of words, pours over us without ceasing and increases exponentially by the year. In centuries past, people took time to ponder, discuss, and reflect on someone's postulate or discovery. No more; we don't have time to compare and contrast anything with an objective standard of truth because as soon as I read something, hear something, or come in contact with information, here comes the next wave of info. So we just accept it all, suspend judgment, and let it wash over us. Every idea, product, fashion, renaming of societal sectors, or loony legislation attains instant validity if there is no standard against which it is to be measured.

If you use some other external source such as the Bible, the Koran, the Bhagavad Gita, a company code of ethics, or the American Bill of Rights in today's society as your standard for truth, you join me as part of a minority in society. The majority have chosen their own internal, tailor-made, custom-fitted set of rules by which they will live life and measure their progress. If I get to set the rules, I will always win or make it to the finish line first, something I learned on the grade school recess playground. If a person helps make the rules, that person will make sure they are personally beneficial or even give him a distinct advantage (think how parties in power in Congress work). We either make our set of life principles conform to our wishes, or we conform to them. It all depends on how much authority you accede to that set of life principles over your own life.

Paul declares in v. 16 that the Scripture is inspired, or as the NIV translates it, "God-breathed". As a Christ follower, I agree with Paul that not only is the Bible God speaking truth into my life, but also His truth is transformative. All of the "teaching, reproof, correction, and training in righteousness" (v.16) is not just about Christlike calisthenics; it is preparation for the work of the Kingdom, as he states in the next verse. The one persistent question that still rings in my ears from professors in graduate studies is the simple two-word retort, "<u>So what</u>?" I spend time in the Word to be transformed <u>so that</u> I am adequate (NASB,) complete (CSB, ESV), capable (NET), thoroughly equipped (NIV) "for every good work" (v.17). In an earlier epistle Paul describes these good works as God ordained and "prepared beforehand that we should walk in them". (Eph. 2.10) The training and chipping away at the raw and rough patches of my life is not meant to just get me in great shape or look better; it is to better serve my King in His kingdom for His honor and glory. Leadership doesn't get easier if done by principle more than profit or shifting policies; if anything, it becomes harder because you will be in the minority in a world obsessed with bottom lines more than justice, fairness, love, and honor. God honors the man who honors Him (Isaiah 58.12-14).

<u>Lines on Leadership</u>
By what set of life principles do I measure my life and lead? Do I order my day and the plans of my organization according to that set of life principles?

_____
_____

++

2nd Timothy 4---Highlights: a final charge to Paul's young charge; an exit soliloquy; and final remarks about coworkers

Vs. 6-8 "For I am already being poured out as a drink offering, and the time of my departure has come. I have fought the good fight, I have finished the course, I have kept the faith; in the future there is laid up for me the crown of righteousness, which the Lord, the righteous Judge, will award to me on that day; and not only to me, but also to all who have loved His appearing."

Throughout my ministry, I have practiced something I learned from this chapter. I have always read ten years ahead of where I was in terms of life development. If I was thirty, I read about physiological, psychological, spiritual, and vocational changes that occur when one turns forty and so forth. It has helped me anticipate so many things internally and externally. I knew ahead of time about muscles atrophying, loss of concentration, and the recovery time becoming longer and longer after a major event/trip. I knew my advancing age would alter the relationships I had with the college students during my campus ministry days because they always stayed (for the most part) 18-22 years of age. My choice of recreation, hobbies, reading material, topics of conversation, choice of friends—pretty much every facet of living changed with each decade. Instead of denying my fate, I needed to face it and deal with it; better to be proactive than procrastinate till something forced my hand.

Paul knows in these verses that his earthly existence is about to conclude, likely in the form of execution or death in a Roman prison. But there are no remorseful tones in the parting words that approach poetry; indeed, there is a sense of victory because he will receive an awarded crown for a life honoring God. The phrase "loved His appearing" refers to the 2nd coming of Christ. I have always prayed I can say the same when I see the end approaching. In 2023 I reached a major <u>transition</u> in my ministry: I laid down my full-time ministry and <u>transitioned</u> (I refuse to say retirement) to a new life chapter where I teach adjunct for one or more institutions, do intentional interim pastorates (help churches address their dysfunctions with a diagnostic approach to the period between pastors), travel, and write, all at a pace commensurate with my physical health, mental clarity, and spiritual vitality. Paul knew he would no longer roam the Roman world as a missionary, and by asking for his cloak, books, and parchments (v.13), he acknowledged the transition to another role within the emerging church, to write and codify all of his thoughts for succeeding generations.

There is no regret, no remorse in Paul's words---and no fear; he is realistic about his earthly existence. It will soon cease, and he is not afraid to use words like 'finish the course'. But his realistic depiction of terrestrial life melts into an expectancy of a triumphant celestial one as he focuses on an eternal future and a longing to be with his Lord. The previous verses of chapter 4 describe the passing of the ministry baton to Timothy, a solemn charge to preach the Word "in and out of season" when it gives him joy and when it is difficult, and a reminder to "fulfill your ministry" (v.5). Paul was not hesitant to let the younger generation replace him; he prepared his young protégé well and knew he would succeed.

Ideally, Paul would have walked alongside Timothy for many years, slowly retreating into the shadows but always reachable and available for counsel and encouragement. Prison and distance have altered that. Too many senior executives, senior pastors, and senior managers have treated the younger generation as usurpers, callow competitors who need to wait their turn until they depart the scene under their own terms. How much better to follow Paul's example on three levels:

1) to realistically face my next stage of life and prepare for it instead of denying it;

2) to take time while I have it to prepare the next generation of servant leaders who will admittedly take my place (we are all interim, see Jn. 1 and Acts 20 entries);

3) realize the death of my career and death of my physical body are not ultimate retirements but rather transitions to something Steven Curtis Chapman called the "glorious unknown".

Chorus: *"Saddle up your horses, we've got a trail to blaze; Through the wild blue yonder of God's Amazing Grace; Let's follow our leader into the Glorious Unknown, This is the life like no other, this is the Great Adventure[1]."*

Lines on Leadership
_____
_____
++

LETTER TO TITUS

Intro: While the Paul-Timothy relationship is more celebrated and known in Christian circles than the one between Paul and Titus, Titus was, in actuality, an important part of the pastoral and missionary work throughout the Middle East (likely from Antioch, Gal. 2.3) and the Mediterranean world. Titus was probably older and more prepared than Timothy to take charge of projects in Paul's absence/stead (told to appoint elders in each church, Titus 1.5)

++

Titus 1---Highlights: Salutation; qualifications for elders given who are to be appointed in every city

      Timothy is not the only "true child" of Paul (1 Cor. 4.17; Phil. 2.22; 2 Tim. 1.2, 2.1). He says similar things about Onesimus (Philemon 10) and here in this chapter about Titus (v.4), and what binds them all together is their connection to Paul and their "common faith." Paul shows tremendous confidence in each of them (Timothy, Onesimus, and Titus) because he has seen in them the very things he describes in this epistle. Before Paul and Barnabas departed the newly constituted churches in Lystra, Iconium, and Antioch in Acts 14.23, they selected men to lead them. In this epistle, Paul saddles his associate with the same yet more formidable task: to complete the unfinished task of organizing the local churches (v.5), to appoint elders in every city, and to make sure they adhere to and lead out of this "common faith (v.3)". Paul did this in partnership with Barnabas; he now shows strong faith in Titus by sending him to do the same thing alone.

      I currently live in a state losing population; our region lies in the heart of Appalachia. The main north/south interstate is locally known as "Hillbilly Highway" because so many of our folks leave on it for more lucrative jobs southward in more prosperous states. This underscores the emphasis of this epistle: local leadership development. I often tell our churches few people are rushing to our area saying, 'please let me lead your congregations;' (if they do, they are often running from others or their past). If there is to be a "next" generation of leadership for our churches, it should develop from within. Titus did not have a bus full of elders; he could simply drop them off in each city for each local church. He had to oversee the selection of leaders in each town who were of sufficient character (Titus 1), loyal to the doctrines of grace outlined in chapters 1 & 2, and who would grow into their positions in these young churches.

In a corporate sense, some franchises have steep entry fees or buy-ins; find sufficient funds, and you can be an owner of a local x franchise. One reason for the success of Chick-fil-A is how senior owners/operators are chosen. The "buy-in" is $10,000, a modest sum when stacked up against comparable franchise opportunities requiring $1,000,000+. But instead of buy to own, Chick-fil-A operators/owners are sifted through a rigorous process to ensure the success of both the business and the operator. In their own words, "competitive candidates will show evidence of personal financial integrity and stewardship, proven business leadership-and business acumen, an entrepreneurial spirit, a growth mindset, and strong character[1]." They practically mirror this epistle and Titus' mandate to find people who reflect this portrait of a leader.

Lines on Leadership
Leadership succession or transfer of leadership is a hit-and-miss proposition for continued excellence if by bloodline, purchase, or

seniority only. What criteria are used by your organization to promote from within?

_____

_____

++

Titus 2---Highlights: How to deal with doctrinal instruction to various ages within the group

As a leader, I should read this chapter from two perspectives: how I lead others and how I lead myself.

<u>Leading others</u>: The emphasis of this chapter is how to impart sound doctrine throughout the church among the different age groupings. Every verse underscores each age group has different characteristics and different outcomes of this teaching. On a small group basis, it is possible to tailor my instruction to the individual needs of my students; on a larger scale, I become a leader of leaders, so this customization of instruction can continue. We are to "deny ungodliness and worldly desires and to live sensibly, righteously and godly in this present age" (v. 12). That means a world of different things for a young man or an old one, a single female entering college or grappling with recent widowhood. When I preach, when I teach, when I write curriculum, and when I train in an organization, I need to take into consideration all the different backgrounds, ages, and learning styles of those in our group and how best to meet their needs, so the material taught is effectively received.

<u>Self-leadership</u>: If I lead others, and can't lead myself, hypocrisy and hollow words of instruction are not far off and become inevitable; if I do not lead myself, I cannot "speak and exhort with all authority" as Paul instructs (v. 15). (see 2 Tim. 4 entry) In teaching a 'leadership in ministry' course for a Texas seminary for several years, I always made the first module of the

class a look inward. A leader needs to know his strengths and weaknesses, his affinities and his aversions, and his abilities to instruct and to relate. There is no way one person can be adept at meeting the needs of all the various ages and life stages mentioned in this chapter. Operate from my strengths <u>and</u> operate on my deficiencies. Authority comes from different sources, but the surest one is from within, confident in who I am. From a Christian perspective, this provides an interesting balance: I should be confident in my abilities yet always cognizant that all I have and am come from the Lord.

    The chapter ends with admonitions reminiscent of the one to Timothy (1 Tim. 4.12), "Let no one disregard you" (v. 15), yet without the emphasis on youth. Titus may have been older than Timothy, or perhaps Paul was reminding Titus how many times he had seen Paul's teachings arouse mobs and resistance on their travels together. Although consideration should be given to the different groups taught (vs. 1-10), no compromise should be shown on the actual content, which here is the gospel of Christ's grace and certainty of His return (vs. 11-14). This short statement connects Titus 1 & 2 as Titus is exhorted to appoint elders in every city (1.5) and given criteria by which to measure them. He can only lead others if he has confidently led himself. Compassion toward my audience, conviction in regard to my message (see Mt. 25 entry).

<u>Lines on Leadership</u>
What concessions should you make in regard to the age/gender/ethnicity/education/experience in the transmission of your message to your target group? What convictions should you shore up in the message you are transmitting?

++

Titus 3---Highlights: relationship to all types of people as a pastor, the nature of salvation

For a pastor, the sequence of this chapter is of interest as well as the content. Paul reminds Titus in the first verses how far they have both come from their former lives (v.3) and how graciously and gloriously God has saved them (vs. 4-8). Because Titus has been delivered from that life, he needs to be both patient and prudent; patient with those still in such situations and in need of the gospel's message; and prudent in how he deals with what various translations call a "factious man (v.10, NASB)," a "divisive person (CSB, NIV, NET)," or in the KJV, a "heretick".

I personally speak fast, think fast, and am prone to make provocative statements as a part of my teaching style, all magnets for those who like to contest any and all things said by anyone in authority. My natural tendency is to not back down but dig in my heels and let the contest begin, the blood flow, and see who has the most points accrued and limbs intact at the end of it all. I am so glad that early in my ministry, my wife loaned me a book I've never returned. It was by Joyce Landorf and called *Irregular People*. Landorf described how perfectly normal it was that some people just do not "click" with others, and no matter if I tried to appease, open meaningful dialogue, or show kindness, that particular "irregular person" and I would never be on the same page[1]. There are many biblical reasons for the plurality of elders as leadership for a church, and this deserves to be on that list. In a larger church or corporation, other staff members, elders, or deacons can be brought to bear on the situation that can either relate to or at least communicate with the person in question better than I can and hopefully diffuse a potentially explosive situation.

Where this borders on intractable is when a small church or business has but one staff member, the pastor/CEO, and everyone in the church/business is related. If the "factious man" is uncle, father, brother, cousin, and nephew to everyone else in the church, this can be a conundrum for the pastor. For a small business owner, it may be a fellow employee or worse, a customer who makes the owner's blood boil simply by setting foot in the store. The state in which I reside as I write requires no concealed weapon permit to conceal or open carry. So I always assume the person making trouble is "packing" and try not to rile them by retaliation. The news media are full of stories of disgruntled employees, church members, and family disruptors who blow their stack, whip out the gun, and start firing randomly in fury. With the emotional nets of support provided by the community and extended family slowly vanishing from our social networks, this type of person will likely be seen more frequently.

In the era of online social media, a divisive person revels in his newfound leverage to spew hatred, lies, personal attacks, play the victim, and countless other tactics that are multiplied by shares, going viral, etc. The wise, mature leader does not retaliate but understands he is to reject the person, walk away, and leave it for others to handle. Paul amplifies this process in 2 Tim. 2. 21-26 as he admonishes Timothy to flee (not just reject, flee), concentrate on a pure heart, and lean on the company of those who call upon the Lord (2 Tim. 2.22). He also tells Timothy to "refuse foolish speculations (v.23) but holds out hope perhaps the person can "come to their senses from the snare of the devil" (v. 26).

One of the few things I still remember from seminary lectures decades ago was Professor Marsh often saying, "Every man is my superior in at least one way." If the room or town is small and the factious man cannot be avoided, sometimes adopting a learner's posture reveals the hurt or fear that compels the person to be so antagonistic. As much as I want to think of myself as mature or spiritual, I must realize that I am also that "irregular person" Landorf spoke of for a select few in my life. I agree with Paul's advice to Titus not to allow one's blood pressure to rise or ulcers to form on account of this troublemaker. If I walk away or refer the person elsewhere, I can always pray for the person that he will come to his senses, as Paul hopes in 2 Tim 2. I can also pray that the person will rant or spew long enough that his stance alienates enough people so that he eventually stands alone, self-condemned by his own words and actions (Titus 3.11).

<u>Lines on Leadership</u>
Who is the irregular person in my professional life? Personal life? To whom can I refer this person for help? How can I constructively work around this or make this a win/win scenario?
_____
_____
++

LETTER TO PHILEMON

This smallest of Paul's epistles at first seems insignificant, yet it addresses the weighty subjects of redemption, forgiveness, restoration, and the upheaval of foundational social structures. This letter is a master class on how to appeal on behalf of someone who has failed at life.

In most universities and organizations, an office exists to secure large amounts of donated funds to enable the institution to function (tuition or profits alone rarely suffice in and of themselves). In the world of fundraising, patience, timing, and relationship are crucial to secure the support of major donors for a respective institution/cause. Paul begins with an Affirmation, moves to an Ask, and awaits an Answer. The first verses are sincere and flow from an ongoing relationship Paul has with Philemon, a wealthy believer in whose house a church meets. He compliments Philemon and how God has used him to bless others. He affirms all that God has done for and through him. Instead of leaning on his position and title as an already recognized apostle and ordering Philemon, Paul appeals for a runaway slave to be restored to right standing with Philemon. Considering all that the slave has done to offend Philemon, the request is considerable. Development officers spend weeks, months, and sometimes even years of developing relationships with donors, drinking countless cups of coffee, learning about the family members and needs, celebrating anniversaries and birthdays, and attending marriages and funerals of the donors' loved ones. The relationship must be sincere and abiding if a significant Ask will be made. What if I ask for $10,000 when the donor might be capable of getting $10 million? Have I matched the donor's interests and the needs of my institution precisely? Is this the right time to ask, knowing I may have one shot at it?

Paul's expert handling of this situation may have arisen from his prior association with Barnabas (see Acts 13ff, especially Acts 15.36-41). At that time, Paul and Barnabas had won a hard-fought victory to extend the gospel to Gentiles as well as Jews. Paul wanted to embark on a victory lap missionary journey to revisit cities where they had preached. Barnabas wanted to take John Mark with them, who had not lived up to his obligations on the initial trip. It resulted in the fissure of one of the greatest missionary duos ever, yet later in Paul's writings, we see John Mark described as 'useful' to the ministry (2 Tim. 4.11), meaning he eventually came to see the wisdom of a second chance for the young man. Apparently, Mark had made good on his additional opportunity. Paul desired a second chance for a young man named Onesimus.

Paul deliberately uses the very same Greek word (useful) to describe the man at the center of tension in Philemon (v.11, Onesimus) and deftly makes a wordplay on his name. What a risk-and-reward situation! The slave who stole from Philemon and ran away now stands on Philemon's doorstep with a letter from Paul containing this request. The restoration of Onesimus to his former standing in the household would be dramatic enough, but Paul asks for even more: accept this slave, not only as regained property, but as a person (v.15); not only as a person, but a brother in Christ (v.16); and not only as a fellow believer, but as a true partner in the Kingdom of God (v.17). Paul cashes in all his chips, and the ace up his sleeve is the fact that Philemon owes his life to Paul (v.19). With this simple but profound act Paul advocates for quantum leaps in societal norms. Although the abolition of slavery is not overtly mentioned in the NT, this is an unmistakable blow to it as Paul desires for Onesimus to be granted more rights and privileges than he had <u>before</u> he transgressed against his owner.

Sometimes leaders must decide if an employee or associate is worthy of their "all-in" investment of trust. Paul went beyond allowing his name to be used as a reference on a resume; indeed, OT law allowed Paul to keep Onesimus as a runaway slave, and he was in no way obligated to send him back to Philemon (Deuteronomy 23.15-16). This was a personal sacrifice for Paul to give up what was rightfully his, not only from a legal sense but relational, as Onesimus had become like a son to him (v.10-13).

At the end of the 1993 film *Schindler's List,* Oskar Schindler, an industrialist and Nazi sympathizer who saved over 1100 Jews from extermination in WWII, is about to go into hiding as the "Schindler Jews" are liberated at the end of the war. As a gift, the grateful Jews hand him a ring with the inscription, "Whoever saves one life saves the world entire[1]." It is a powerful reminder that for all our concentration on theory, training, grand visions, theology, or strategy, it always comes down to one sale, one transaction, one conversation, one conversion, one life at a time. In Acts 9, the a) courage of an ordinary citizen of Damascus named Ananias and b) the initiative of Barnabas to obey the Lord and help a man known to jail and kill believers (pre-conversion Saul/Paul) turn the course of history. Here Paul returns the favor, and the letter ends with the reader not knowing the eventual Answer.

(Spoiler alert: this one turned out well; we see Onesimus mentioned as a partner in Kingdom work in another Pauline letter (Col. 4.9)). I will admit not everyone in whom I have invested time, effort, reputation, and money produced a positive rate of return on that investment. But this short letter compels me to try and try again. One of my former students in my college ministry years came to our campus with a police record; he found his calling when we gave him a leadership position as he coordinated Kids Clubs at various area apartment complexes. That grew into a life of missions overseas. The story doesn't end there; he made some major, costly mistakes that ended his overseas mission career and could have cost him his family and marriage. Through other Paul's in his life, who sacrificed far more than I ever did, he underwent extensive counseling and restoration and now heads up an ever-growing ministry that does the same for others. So who will be your "Onesimus"?

<u>Lines on Leadership</u>
Who in your organization or church is a potential Onesimus? Are you withholding redemption or forgiveness from him/her and thereby hindering his/her development or the progress of your organization/church? Who is the person in whom you are willing to invest personal capital, who can go from 'useless' to 'useful?'

_____
_____
++

LETTER TO THE HEBREWS

Intro: Hebrews is the mystery epistle. No one knows with certainty who wrote it. Paul is generally mentioned, as well as Luke, Barnabas, Apollos, or even Priscilla. More important is the major theme of Hebrews, which is to systematically show why Jesus is not just a way but _the_ Way. It is directed at a Jewish audience and is laced with OT references to show how Jesus was a fulfillment of the OT prophecies and is their Messiah, their King, and their High Priest. It is worthy of much more comprehensive treatment than it can be given in this book.

++

Hebrews 1---Highlights: God has spoken to us through His Son

In its current iteration, the Internet makes it easy to stumble upon the following type of video: A person purported to be a leading authority in his/her field has discovered something so revolutionary, so remarkable, so beyond anything anyone has ever presented before now that you will not believe how good it is. Usually, the narrator speaks breathlessly and without pause, as if they can breathe and talk at the same time, not a nanosecond of silence between sentences. The images cut back and forth in sync with the narrator's voice to create an aura of inevitability; you know where this is headed. Eventually, a product appears without which you simply cannot live. How have you existed without this product or program? Today (and today only), you can have it for 20/30/40; oh, why not act now in the next hour and get 50% off that price. Its appeal overshadows its lack of merit, and the lure of finding such a great "deal" is overpowering.

If verses 1-4 are read in a style of a sideshow carny ("step right up and see what's behind the curtain, it is so colossal, so stupendous, it will rattle your brain and buckle your knees"),

Jesus (not actually named until Heb. 2.9) could be dismissed as the latest Barnum and Bailey concoction. But when seen as truth, the passage does indeed rattle the brain and buckle the knees---if it is true, then inconceivably God has entered our world as foretold by the prophets (v.1). Can a being so powerful and majestic actually have been "among us" (Immanuel)?

The writer of Hebrews proceeds to strengthen his claim (that the Son of God has been in our midst) by quoting Psalm after Psalm after Psalm (Ps. 2; 45; 102; 103; 104; 110) the Messiah would fulfill. The Son of God has been "appointed heir of all things <u>through whom also He made the world</u>. He is the <u>radiance of His glory</u> and the <u>exact representation of His nature</u>, and <u>upholds all things by the word of His power</u>." The one sought for centuries—He has come—and you missed Him.

Hebrews 1, in a way, restates John 1; the Son of God, the Creator/Redeemer, came to dwell among us. We read so long in the scriptures about the coming Messiah, yet when He came, it was in an unexpected way and was not the person for whom we had built up a specific image (a recurrent theme in the four gospels). The letter is written specifically to a Jewish audience (The Epistle to the <u>HEBREWS</u>) and acknowledges they were fairly accurate concerning the <u>concept</u> of the Messiah (the numerous OT references) but missed His <u>identity</u>.

<u>Lines on Leadership</u>
Has there been a solution, a life-changing event, an expected person that you had spoken of so much and led people to anticipate—and yet missed it when it/he/she came? What signs were missed which were so obvious in hindsight? What can you do to prevent missing it/him/her in the future?

++

Hebrews 2---Highlights: Jesus as Son of God and Son of Man (one of us)

vs. 17-18, "He had to be made like His brethren in all things, that He might become a merciful and faithful high priest in things pertaining to God, to make propitiation for the sins of the people. For since He Himself was tempted in that which He has suffered, He is able to come to the aid of those who are tempted." (Also Heb. 4.15 "For we do not have a high priest who cannot sympathize with our weaknesses, but One who has been tempted in all things as we are, yet without sin.")

An aphorism sure to be familiar is this time-worn statement: "People don't care how much you know until they know how much you care." It sounds like something an elderly aunt says to nieces and nephews gathered around the fireplace. Empathy is neither an equivalent to knowledge or experience nor a substitute for them, but it can certainly enhance knowledge or experience.

Identification with humanity is a large portion of the attraction to Jesus as a Savior. He was not some lofty Messiah issuing edicts from afar; He came and dwelt among us (Jn. 1.14); He was tempted like us; He encountered the same challenges every other person does. This endears Jesus to us and gives comfort; whatever I'm going through, He has experienced and overcome or endured (no, He never drove in rush hour, but He had to handle anger, frustration, and other people's foolishness). In 2022 one of the most expansive and expensive ad campaigns for quiet evangelism was online and seen by millions in video ads as "He Gets Us. Jesus[1]." It was centered entirely on this concept of Christ connecting through empathy before the edict. One of our pastors who worked for years in a rough Bronx neighborhood summarized this in a simple but profound way: you can feed people, or you can eat with them. It is one thing to provide <u>for</u> someone; it is the next level to engage <u>with</u> someone. Empathy should precede edict.

<u>Lines on Leadership</u>
This chapter is replete with references to Christ's identification with us (v. 11, "He is not ashamed to call them brethren.") The author often refers to Christ's role as our heavenly high priest. He is a priest well acquainted with our humanity through commonly shared experiences. While it is possible to lead from a distant post or out of a professionally distant relationship, leading a group is made so much easier when the followers are convinced our leader is "one of us" and that "he understands what I'm going through because he's been there, done that." In today's parlance, he would be seen as having a high EQ, Emotional Quotient, or Emotional Intelligence.

In what ways do you identify with the members of your group? If they were interviewed by an outside source, what would the answer be when asked: what are the <u>initial</u> connecting points between you and your leader? What are his/her <u>strongest</u> connection points?

_____

_____

++

Hebrews 3---Highlights: Jesus as High Priest and the Cost of Unbelief

Hebrews 3 is one of the tougher chapters for me to read as a pastor and as a leader. Jesus and Moses sacrificed their lives for the sake of their followers. Moses gave his last forty years to direct the Exodus through the wilderness; Jesus led the Way to eternal salvation through His death, burial, and resurrection and to an eternal relationship with the Father through His example and teaching.

They poured themselves into their followers, yet the majority of this chapter describes and warns of the consequences of their unbelief when they refuse to believe in the leader and the direction he wants to take them. You can feel the frustration and depth of sorrow when reading the intercessory prayer of Moses as he repeatedly stands in the gap and advocates for his people to God (Deut. 9.25-29); when Jesus pleads for the city of Jerusalem (Mt. 23.37); when Jesus watches the disciples walk away from His teaching (Jn. 6.59-66); and when Jesus prays what many consider the true Lord's Prayer (Jn. 17).

The centuries-old debate between the sovereignty of God and the free will of man will be mentioned here but not resolved. On the human level, every leader at some point will experience the pain and sorrow of knowing a way is good and true and having the people look you straight in the eye and tick off the reasons they refuse to look at facts, refuse to consider logic, refuse to realize the benefits they can have if they go in this or that direction. If almighty God in His sovereignty allows for some to "walk away" from the Promised Land of Moses or the Promised Land of Christ's Kingdom, I have to understand my leadership might be effective, but it is not absolute. There will be some who simply walk away regardless of what is offered to them.

The most chilling verse here is v. 19, "And so we see that they were not able to enter because of unbelief." Moses did not plead with God to lower His standards or look the other way and let Moses' people slide by. Jesus, when people walked away from

Him (see Jn. 6 entry), did not run after them and say, 'Wait, we can find a common ground solution, please don't go; hey, name your terms, I'll try to meet them.' (Jn. 6.65) Both Moses and Jesus stood by their original statements. When I have to tell a church it is living on the memory of what used to be and not living in the reality of its present situation, I am often told we no longer need your services. It grieves me to see them walk away from counsel born out of fifty years of dealing with churches. I admire Moses and Jesus for laying out reality and sticking to it. It still was extremely painful for Moses to look out among the thousands under his care and know many of those thousands would not enter into the Promised Land, and for Jesus to share the truth as the Son of God and see people walk away in rejection of Him and His truth.

Lines on Leadership
The balance between the completion of a purpose and the welfare and followship of the people is difficult to attain and impossible to maintain. What are your non-negotiables concerning your group's mission or reason for existence? How do you reconcile this with Hebrews 2 and the example of empathy for one's flock (see also Jn. 10 entry)?

_____

_____

++

Hebrews 4---Highlights: entering into the believer's 'rest'.
    vs. 10-11 "For the one who has entered His <u>rest</u> has himself also <u>rested</u> from his works, as God did from His. Let us therefore, be diligent to enter that <u>rest</u>, lest anyone fall through following the same example of disobedience."

The word "rest" appears seven times in chapter 4. (vs. 1, 3, 5, 8, 9, 10, & 11). This is not about a nap (English), a *siesta* (Spanish), or *ein Mittagsschlaf* (German). It is not about a recovery period from a busy schedule (although, as a traveling pastor, at my house Sunday afternoon is called "the holy hour" for a specific reason and is observed religiously). <u>It is less about the cessation of activity and more about the security of identity</u>. The modern paraphrase The Message sheds some light on this verse: "For as long, then, as that promise of resting in him pulls us on to God's goal for us, we need to be careful that we're not disqualified." (v. 11, MSG) There is a dialectical tension in this verse of being paused (or, more accurately, 'resting <u>in</u> him') and being in motion ('on to God's goal for us'). God is not a static being who just sits around in eternity, basking in the eternal praises of people. God is always on the move. The key here is the point of reference. The reference point is not my life, not within me, but God. It is not about entering my rest but entering the rest of God. If I hurtled through the air by myself at 600 mph, it would rip off my clothes, and my body would try to shed my skin as well in the howling wind. If I do the same in a modern plane, I hardly raise an eyebrow because I am safely inside the plane. It is about being in Him, which is one reason among many we see the phrase "in Christ" over 50x in the NT.

In the Beatitudes (see Mt. 5.1-12), there is a similar dialectical tension with some verses ending in "for theirs <u>is</u> the kingdom" and some in "they <u>shall be</u> filled, they <u>shall</u> receive mercy, and they <u>shall</u> inherit the earth". As said earlier, the kingdom of God is not a location; it is a relationship with Jesus Christ. There is both a present and a future element to the Kingdom of God. I can experience it now as a quality of life; I will one day experience it in its fullness with the added element of quantity (as in eternally). I can rest <u>in</u> Him now; I will one day enter into an eternal rest in His eternal Presence. Placing my faith in Christ means I place my life in His hands, and I rest in them.

Lines on Leadership

In the modern world, there is a growing sense that any finish line promised at the beginning of a business quarter, company campaign, or church's budget meeting is a constantly moving, impossible-to-hit target. How will you, as a leader, provide "rest" both in the present and in the future for your respective group? In what will they "rest" as they stay on the move?

_____

_____

++

Hebrews 5---Highlights: Jesus' role as High Priest of the order of Melchizedek

v.12 "For though you should in fact be teachers by this time, you need someone to teach you the beginning elements of God's utterances. You have gone back to needing milk, not solid food." (NET) The context of this statement is not competence and understanding; it is one of courage and resolve. When confronted with the claims made in previous chapters about the superiority of Jesus (and combined with the ones to come later in Hebrews), the persons in question had retreated back into what is comfortable, which in this case is life before Jesus entered the equation.

This book was written during and on the back side of the initial wave of COVID-19, a virus that changed society in every way imaginable in the third decade of the 21st century. Whole industries, governments, societal structures (including the church), and educational practices were first shut down and then confronted with what has been called the "New Normal", a phrase some are loathe to utter or recognize. Something in our human nature draws us back to a prior default position, even when the default position is no longer defensible or no longer exists.

Someone who learns a manufacturing skill for a product that is no longer made or desired is futility personified; a seminary that graduates students to pastor churches that no longer exist in forms as taught is lunacy. I wrote this chapter while at a trustee meeting for a major seminary. We discussed new educational trends, including this new reality: online education long ago moved from an option to a necessity and is evolving at rapid speeds. The seminary's location is unique and is a large part of its identity; online theological education greatly reduces that distinction. It affects budgets for the physical campus, dorm space, the type of faculty, investments in technology, and recruitment. Millions of dollars have to be committed years in advance, and our decisions demand not only the correct information and projections but courage and resolve.

Lines on Leadership
The gospel story throughout the NT speaks about a New Normal. Jesus' first sermon (Lk. 4) spoke of a global reach of God's grace instead of a provincial one. His Sermon on the Mount repeatedly contains the phrase, "You have heard it said, but I say unto you . . ." (Mt. 5-7). The Pentecost event (Acts 2) gave evidence a New Normal was in their midst.

In what New Normal does your group find itself? As the leader, how are you handling the New Normal? What are you doing to not only help others tolerate it but embrace it? "New Normal" does not automatically imply a movement away from a traditional to a progressive mindset; it means all the rules, values, and outcomes of actions have changed. How do you articulate the difference between the New Normal and a traditional/progressive spectrum for your group?

Bonus thought----Marshall McLuhan on Edgar Allan Poe's short story "Descent into the Maelstrom": "Pattern recognition in the midst of a huge, overwhelming, destructive force is the way out of the maelstrom. They had two choices: Learn to make the leap, or die paralyzed by the whirl[1]."

_____
_____

++

Hebrews 6---Highlights: Falling Away, a Better Way

vs.1-2---"Therefore leaving the elementary teaching about the Christ, let us press on to maturity, not laying again a foundation of repentance from dead works and of faith toward God, of instruction about washings and laying on of hands, and the resurrection of the dead and eternal judgment."

Fundamentals are foundational. To neglect or fail to acknowledge the fundamentals (values, history, or skills) is usually detrimental to an organization. The issue at hand in these verses above is when the fundamentals lose sight of their original purpose and become an end unto themselves, when nothing beyond the fundamentals can be envisioned. When a structure's foundation is laid, there is great anticipation of what is to come because while the foundation is essential to the erection of a building, it is not where the occupants of the building live or work. The foundation is that upon which the rest of the building rests and depends.

In church circles (I'm certain I'll lose several readers after this entry), fundamentals are essential to the faith but retardant to growth when maturity in the faith is viewed as suspicious and inherently liberal. To grow beyond the fundamentals is not to abandon them but to build upon them. As an evangelical Christian, I am dedicated to evangelism and missions, to proclaim the gospel, and call men to salvation. But in too many instances, that call to salvation is repeated over and over to the same crowd. The leadership cannot see beyond that clarion call to salvation to maturity in Christ. As mentioned before, discipleship is not an optional extracurricular activity for super saints; it should be a natural progression from infancy in Christ to maturity in Him. Evangelism without discipleship produces breadth but little depth, and the church built with those ratios buckles in challenging or adverse times.

Pastors often complain about their flock's lack of Biblical knowledge, the willingness of anyone in the congregation to step up and be involved, or avoidance of leadership roles. My usual response is: you nurtured this situation by preaching and teaching the basics yet never equipped the flock to become mature believers. You ingrained the fundamentals of their theology in them but not their responsibilities as maturing members of the body of Christ (which are natural outcomes of the fundamentals).

This is a church member issue as well as a pastoral one. So many want to know the bare essentials, what will squeak me into heaven, and that's as far as I want to know or do anything spiritual. 'Give me a ritual, a mantra, a checklist, and I'll click those off my daily to-do chart so I can go on with life.' Others live in fear of wandering from or diluting their faith if they think or do anything that looks like coloring outside the lines or is not specifically spelled out in a literal fashion what I am to do or am allowed to do. They remain mired in the fundamentals and cannot envision them as a foundation upon which to build.

Lines on Leadership
The process of parenting is costly, seems to last forever, and has mountains of frustration attached; but when done properly, when the instilled values are there to insure the children's ability to act maturely when the occasion calls for it—it is so worth all the costs, time, and love poured into our progeny. What are you doing to bring your group beyond the elementary bedrock foundations of your group to maturity in their decision-making, maturity in their application of values, and maturity in their representation of your group to the outside world?

_____

_____

++

Hebrews 7---Highlights: further comparison of Melchizedek and Christ's priesthoods

The significance of this chapter depends on understanding the relative positions of the central characters (Abraham, Melchizedek, and Jesus) to one another. Abraham is the universally recognized progenitor of Jews (through Isaac, the son of promise) and of Arabs (through Ishmael). Yet he submits to and willingly gives a tenth of his recent battle spoils to Melchizedek, a "priest of the most High God" (v.1), a man we know little about, save the Genesis account (Gen. 24), which is recounted in Heb. 7. He is a king and priest, and the Hebrews author concludes that Melchizedek is the greater of the two (v.7) by the logic of Abraham receiving a blessing from Melchizedek.

If $b > a$, and $c > b$, then $c > a$. If b is greater than a, and c is greater than b, then c, by logic, is also greater than a.

Vs. 4-10 speak of the greatness of Melchizedek in relation to Abraham ($b > a$). Vs. 11-25 show the superiority of Jesus to Melchizedek ($c > b$), making Him greater than both

Melchizedek and Abraham (c > b or a). Jesus is the "guarantee of a better covenant" (v. 22). Since His superiority is established, and He is resurrected and will never die, Jesus becomes superior for the present and the future (v.24).

Lines on Leadership

The Founding Fathers in American history were truly extraordinary. Biographies of George Washington, Benjamin Franklin, Samuel Adams, and others describe their uncanny wisdom and courage to face and defeat tyranny. Yet, in all their wisdom and courage, they avoided dealing decisively with the issue of slavery. The language referring to slavery in the Constitution was designed to placate everyone politically but satisfy no one. Eighty years later, a president (Abraham Lincoln) showed both wisdom and courage to address the issue that had formally split the states and to try to heal a fractured nation. A hundred years later, Lyndon Johnson signed the Civil Rights Act that codified rights for African American citizens promised decades earlier. Forty-three years later, an African American was elected president of the United States, Barack Obama.

This is not an attempt to make a close parallel to the character or stature of the individual men depicted in Heb. 7 with those referenced from American history. The thought for today is repeated and fleshed out in more detail in Heb. 11: Standing on the shoulders of giants allows us to see further down the road and to go places where they could not. Melchizedek had no clue he would provide an archetype for the Savior as he received battle booty in a Middle Eastern wilderness. John Wycliffe had no clue in the 14th century when he translated the Bible into the vernacular that he would provide the spark for the Reformation that began a century later and that organizations such as the

Wycliffe Bible Translators would span the globe translating the Bible into hundreds of languages.

On which giant's shoulders do you stand? How are you advancing their stances, their actions, and their visions?

_____

_____

++

Hebrews 8---Highlights: a new covenant

v. 13 "When He said, 'A new covenant,' He has made the first obsolete. But whatever is becoming obsolete and growing old is ready to disappear."

At a trustee meeting of New Orleans Baptist Theological Seminary, I was a bit frustrated. I could not connect to the internet anywhere on campus with my laptop computer. I had tried in the lodging, library, and conference room where our meetings were held. It had connected flawlessly in years past. I motioned for the campus tech guru who attends our meetings to come and help. She explained the campus internet had operated on a 2.4 gigahertz system, and the new one operated on a 5.0 gigahertz system. Older model computers (mine was then approaching seven years of usage) simply cannot connect to the newer signal. I asked if there was any way to upgrade this computer to accept the new signal. She said there was any number of wireless adapters I could buy and simply insert into a USB port on the computer that would allow me to operate on both 2.4 and 5.0 gigahertz.

I should have stopped there, but I went ahead and asked where I could purchase such a device. She motioned and said the Walmart about a ¼ mile down the road should have them. It dawned (embarrassingly so) on me like a déjà vu moment we had had this same conversation at the last meeting a few months ago.

When she saw the 'oh, oh, you caught me' look in my eyes, she smiled wryly and walked away.

I am in the sunset years of my ministry. There are changes occurring in Christian ministry I have predicted for some time but am ill-equipped at my age to address. It is appropriate for another more suited to the needs of the times to come and take my place in this corner of His Kingdom. The computer upon which I have composed this book is still as capable as ever for that which I have always used it: typing text, sending emails, and researching cyberspace entries. But in its present state of existence, it is increasingly ineffective overall as more industries switch to new frequencies.

I am still capable of many things I've done for five decades: preaching, teaching, giving counsel, and analyzing situations (but from the story above, it appears the memory is fading!). Adding new skills at this age is increasingly difficult or impossible, and adding RAM to my memory is (not yet, at least) possible. It is simply time for someone more attuned to and familiar with the times in which we live to supersede me, who can do a better job of taking the timeless truths of the Word and addressing these current times in a more effective manner.

Lines on Leadership

The book of Hebrews is, in some ways, a one-point treatise with thirteen sub-points. Each chapter is a facet of the main thought that the new supersedes the old, accept it, and lives within the new. In what new systems are you, as a leader, being forced to operate? What would it take to work within that new system: new skills, new software, new resources—or a new leader?

++

Hebrews 9---Highlights: the old and new covenants

Vs. 16-17 "For where a covenant [testament] is, there must of necessity be the death of the one who made it. For a covenant is valid only when men are dead, for it is never in force while the one who made it lives."

Hebrews 9 is a favorite landing spot for preachers. It describes in detail the difference between the Old Covenant (Testament) and the New Covenant (Testament). For the uninitiated reader, the chapter reads as a barbaric, bloody ritual that sounds repulsive---that blood sacrifice is necessary to cleanse a person or a people from sin. It has been called the scarlet thread, that blood ties together the Old and New Testaments. From the first book (Genesis) to the final book (Revelation), blood shed for the remission of sin is a common theme. As a Christian, I rejoice in what Christ has done for me, combining the roles of priest (v.11), temple (v.11), and sacrificial Lamb (v.14). The theological ramifications of this chapter are deep and precious to me, yet the focus of this book is leadership. Let us turn our attention to the two verses above.

In October of the last year, my wife and I reworked and rewrote our wills. We wrote wills as young marrieds over forty years ago before we began in international missions as a precaution, not knowing what would happen "over there". Over the decades the circumstances changed: persons named as guardians for our (then) children were now superfluous as our boys became adults; our fortunes and stages of life changed considerably. After dealing over the last few years with our deceased parents' estates, irrevocable trusts, and wills, we knew it was time to update our own wills. Once our signatures were affixed to those documents in 2022, they rendered the previous wills null and void.

One reason many people avoid having wills made is the resultant acknowledgment of their own impending mortality. Another reason is the uncertainty about or unwillingness to name heirs and their shares of the estate. Lawyers and funeral directors have relayed horror stories to me about the knockdown, dragged-out struggles among family members over the particulars of wills when read to the extended family.

We have informed our beneficiaries about all life insurance policies, investments, locations of documents, and wills. The simple but profound truth is that none of these will go into effect until we die. We have tried to invest and place our assets in such a way that they will take care of our last years and provide a foundation for continued prosperity for our beneficiaries.

<u>Lines on Leadership</u>
What steps have you taken to insure the value and results of your leadership live on in the lives of succeeding generations? What plans have you made to benefit others after you have departed the scene, either in retirement, relocation, or death?

_____
_____
++

Hebrews 10---Highlights: a once-and-for-all sacrifice

Vs. 24-25 "Let us hold fast the confession of our hope without wavering, for He who promised is faithful; and let us consider how to stimulate one another to love and good deeds, not forsaking the assembling together, as is the habit of some, but encouraging one another; and all the more as you see the day drawing near."

<u>Before there was Creation, there was Community</u>. Christianity espouses what is called a Triune God (God the Father, God the Son, and God the Holy Spirit). From the early Church Fathers to today's theologians, the debate has raged as to whether or not within the Trinity there is one consciousness or three, one will or three in perfect unity, and basically how to adequately describe what is colloquially called the "three in one" approach to understanding the Trinity. For the theologians reading this entry, the statement 'before there was Creation, there was Community) is neither an endorsement of nor a rejection of social trinitarianism.

At some level within the Godhead, there has always existed before creation through eternity a harmonious relationship between the Father, Son, and Holy Spirit. If humans were created in the image of God (Gen. 1.27), and God has always existed as a Trinity, then at some level within human existence, <u>we are to reflect the nature of God and live in harmony and community</u>. Some theologians describe what is called a tripartite being (body, soul, spirit) as the Trinitarian imprint on man. If viewed on a societal level, we are created to relate to each other in a vital, organic fashion. Depending on the NT translation used, there are 40-50+ instances of the phrase "one another". I believe the multiple "one another's" are not coincidences but a deliberate attempt of the biblical authors (through divine inspiration) to emphasize this communal existence of believers. Kingdom living is not just about a relationship of the individual to God, but a relationship lived out within a body we call the church.

Neuroscience says that roughly 20% of our nerve connections are called "mirror neurons." When a person sits still in a movie theater, these specialized neurons enable the entire body to experience the sensation of a roller coaster, of flying in space or swimming through water. When people engage in deep conversation, the neurons are firing on all cylinders to help us 'rejoice when others rejoice and weep when they weep[1]' (Rom. 12.15). We were created in His image to relate to one another, to stimulate one another to love and do good deeds, and to encourage one another when times are good and when times are tough (our feature verse).

Lines on Leadership

How do you gauge if the members of your group connect with one another, and at what level? (For the leader or preacher: <u>if the only time you gauge this connection level is when you are speaking to the group as a whole, you are mainly gauging their connection to you, not to each other</u>.) What environment have you created that promotes the "stimulation" or "provocation" of one another to "love and good deeds," to edification, to creating a mutually positive work environment?

_____

_____

+++

Hebrews 11---Highlights: the roll call of faith

v. 1 "Now faith is the assurance of things hoped for, the conviction of things not seen."

v. 6 "And without faith is it impossible to please Him, for he who comes to God must believe that He is, and that He is a rewarder of those who seek Him."

v. 13 "All these died in faith, without receiving the promises, but having seen them and having welcomed them from a distance." vs. 39-40 "And all these, having gained approval through their faith, did not receive what was promised, because God had provided something [Jesus]better for us, so that apart from us they should not be made perfect."

Hebrews 11 is famously labeled the "roll call of faith". Faith is defined at the beginning, a long list of biblical characters who exemplified faith spanning centuries, sexes, roles, and outcomes is given, and the declaration is made twice that even though they all exhibited faith (and often paid a high price for it, vs. 33-38), they did not receive what was promised.

The word translated "assurance" in v. 1 appears in other translations as "reality" (CSB), "substance" (KJV), "confidence" (NIV), and "being sure" (NET). The original Greek word is *hypostasis*, a word that has been transliterated into the English language and is used in philosophy as foundation and essence, that which supports from below or within, and in Christian theology as that which describes the perfect union of Christ as God and man. The faith of those listed in this chapter was not wishful thinking, 'gee, I-hope-it-all-turns-out-okay' type of faith. It is solid, unshakeable, and the basis of their accomplishments and feats. Their faith was rooted in the past (the track record of God's dealings with man) and looked toward the future (the coming Messiah and His kingdom, vs. 14-16).

<u>Lines on Leadership</u>
The object of one's faith is more important than the amount of faith; this truism is repeated throughout this book. Many venerable ideas and institutions have fallen by the wayside in my lifetime, things in which previous generations placed faith. As a leader, I have to be careful about that in which I place my faith because it is never just a personal choice; it affects all those who look to me for leadership. I want the object of my faith to be one in which I have full confidence, enough to recommend to

succeeding generations. Money, government, and financial institutions have all failed in years past; in what have you placed your faith, and in what have you staked the future of your organization?

_____

_____

++

Hebrews 12---Highlights: fatherly discipline, the kingdom will never fade

v. 8 "But if you are without discipline, of which all have become partakers, then you are illegitimate children and not sons." v. 11 "All discipline for the moment seems not to be joyful, but sorrowful; yet to those who have been trained by it, afterwards, it yields the peaceful fruit of righteousness."

The writer of Hebrews details an analogy of how a father disciplines his children, and the very fact that he has administered discipline is in itself evidence that the child is his. The KJV is much blunter in v. 8 compared to today's language and uses the term 'bastard'. Discipline is seen as a sign of belonging to a family. Either the writer of Hebrews was Paul or had read Paul's writings because in 2 Cor. 7.9-10, Paul speaks directly to the Corinthians about the very same topic:

> I now rejoice, not that you were made sorrowful, but that you were made sorrowful to the point of repentance; for you were made sorrowful according to the will of God, in order that you might not suffer loss in anything through us. For the sorrow that is according to the will of God produces a repentance without regret, leading to salvation; but the sorrow of the world produces death."

Godly discipline is never meant to be punitive alone; rather, it has a goal of repentance that leads to redemption, restoration, reconciliation, and righteousness (see 2 Cor. 7 entry). To NOT experience divine discipline may sound on the surface much more desirable (God just needs to stay out of my life and leave me alone), but according to this chapter, it indicates I am not part of the family of God, <u>a position that may have temporary comfort but eternal separation</u>. As quoted in the Phil. 4 entry, Job (Job 2.10) wisely replied to his wife, "Shall we accept good from God and not accept adversity?" I weary at the prospect of yet another round of carving, pruning, being broken and put back together, but I know the Lord wants me to conform to the image of His Son (Rom. 8.29). There is no shortcut to spiritual maturity. Discipline prepares me for future assignments.

<u>Lines on Leadership</u>
Discipline within an organization is a difficult topic most leaders want to either avoid or lean on to keep order within the ranks. Policies that spell out consequences are understandable, but they should periodically be reviewed to ensure the end goal is redemption, progress, and the collective advancement of all, and not just designed to keep someone "in line". As a leader, what is your outlook on discipline within your group? Do your people have known clear paths to the restoration of their rank/standing in your group?

_____

_____

++

Hebrews 13---Highlights: the immutability of Christ, parting words
      vs. 2-3 "Do not neglect to show hospitality to strangers, for by this some have entertained angels without knowing it. Remember the prisoners, as though in prison with them, and

those who are ill-treated, since you yourselves also are in the body." vs. 7, 17 "⁷Remember those who led you, who spoke the word of God to you; and considering the result of their conduct, imitate their faith. ¹⁷ Obey your leaders, and submit to them; for they keep watch over your souls, as those who will give an account. Let them do this with joy and not with grief, for this would be unprofitable for you."

Biblically speaking, v. 2 is an obvious reference to numerous appearances in the OT, such as when Abraham encounters three men on their way to destroy Sodom (Gen. 18-19) and Gideon meets an angel who commissions him to form an army (Judges 6). Practically speaking, this hearkens back to Heb. 2 and treating every man as my superior in at least one way. Verses 2 and 3 are directed at leaders, and verse 17 at followers. Every person I come in contact with is a potential diamond in the rough, a mother lode of information, or the missing piece of the puzzle for my group. How many times have you met someone who you thought obviously had no merit or place in your organization, yet you gave them the benefit of the doubt and a second chance to prove themselves? If the person proves to be worthless and bereft of potential, I would rather err on the side of initially granting him respect and graciousness.

One of the most powerful chapels I have ever attended was at the seminary where I am a trustee. Two gentlemen, plus the seminary president, conducted an extended interview. The two related their pilgrimage from violent offenders to believers in Christ to ordained pastors who now go back into that prison system (Angola, once one of the most notorious prisons in America) to not only preach and teach but organize churches within the prison system. They personified the phrase in v. 3, "Remember the prisoners, <u>as though in prison with them</u>." (see Heb. 2 entry)

Leaders who show that level of respect, courage, and empathy are more prone to receive the obedience encouraged by followers in vs. 7 and 17.

Lines on Leadership
Southwest Airlines, since its inception and at the time of this writing, has had one of the highest rates of job applications per job in its industry. Instead of the pyramid of importance being shareholders, customers, and employees, they have always put employees on the pinnacle of priorities, then customers, then shareholders. They discovered when the employees are treated with respect and empathy, they become a formidable force that generates a high level of customer satisfaction, which in turn creates smiling faces of shareholders because of the generated profits. Happy employees produce happy customers who, in turn, make for repeat customers and, thus, happy shareholders[1]. How do you show respect, hospitality, and empathy for all who come into your sphere of influence?

_____

_____

++

LETTER FROM JAMES

Intro: Although two different men named James were counted among the twelve apostles of Christ, the author of this letter was neither of them. James was also the name of Jesus' half-brother (Mt. 13.55). He became one of the prominent leaders in the early church at Jerusalem, as evidenced by several references in Acts. This epistle has been called "the most Jewish book of the NT[1]" and has more in common with the gospel of Matthew than any other NT book. He showed great wisdom and leadership in how he handled the watershed moments, such as the council of Jerusalem in Acts 15. This epistle bearing his name reflects that same practical wisdom in how his faith translated to everyday occurrences.

++

James 1---Highlights: facing trials and temptations, pure and undefiled religion

Vs. 18,22 "In the exercise of His will He brought us forth by the word of truth; . . . prove yourselves doers of the word, and not merely hearers who delude themselves." The author of James is widely thought to be the half-brother of Jesus and was the first pastor of the Jerusalem church. This epistle exhibits great wisdom gleaned from years of dealing with various factions and cultures within the nascent movement that transformed from a sect within Judaism into the global, technicolor body of Christ (see Acts 2, 6, 15). How thrilling and terrifying it must have been to pastor such an instant multicultural megachurch (Acts 2.41).

As a leader, the various admonitions of chapter 1 revolve around verse 18 ("in the exercise of His will He brought us forth by the <u>word of truth</u>") and the *Auswirkung* of that truth in our lives. Taking a stand on what I believe to be truth will bring me "various trials" (v. 2), it will prevent me being double-minded (v. 5-8), it will result in blessedness and a crown of life (v. 12), it will help me recognize the temptations of evil (vs. 13-15), and I will become a practitioner of the truth instead of just a believer (v. 22).

Great ideas and great visions must be resourced; otherwise, they remain good intentions but never morph into reality. The wisdom from God (v. 5, 17) comes from reading His Word, encountering the living Word of God, and seeing the Word mesh and clash with everyday life. I am to be persecuted for being a promoter of, a profiteer from, and a personification of the truth. James is not interested in philosophical diatribes or the skills of a sophist, he wants the reader to act because the truth has been made evident to him, and the reader is compelled to act after receiving both the knowledge of and the transformation by the truth (v.21, "in humility receive the word implanted, which is able to save your souls"). This is why pure and undefiled religion is defined simply in v. 27 as visiting orphans and widows in distress; no multisyllabic phrases of great eloquence; if you've been changed, then go in His name. Army leadership training boils this down to three one-syllable words: Be/Know/Do. Become the truth, know the truth by experiencing it, and act out of that truth[1]. Verse 22 ("be doers of the word") is the natural outgrowth of v. 18; if we have been born by the word of truth, let us become doers of it and "handle accurately ("rightly divide", KJV) the word of truth." (2 Tim. 2.15) Incarnate it, know it, exemplify it.

Lines on Leadership
What is the foundational truth upon which your leadership is based? Is it a Person, a Principle, or a set of sub-truths? Are all of

your actions and decisions the results of your standing on that truth? Are you willing to stake your reputation, future, investments, position, and standing in your organization on it---or sacrifice them for it? (see Rom. 4, 9, 10 entries)

_____

_____

++

James 2---Highlights: addressing partiality and favoritism; a relationship of faith and works

The grade school recess playground is a fascinating sociological laboratory and microcosmos of human existence. It is an initial experience in establishing laws that govern behavior. Trees or rocks are designated as bases or out of bounds, exceptions are spelled out, and the basis for winning and losing is determined. Many of the games played deal with winnowing out those who didn't make it over a line, grab the last chair, or score enough points. We learn to be simultaneously adamant about fairness and advantages for our team/side, which invariably creates tensions and clashes.

Self-preservation is not just an individual concept but can extend to a corporate entity as well. If we feel threatened, or someone is about to take advantage of us using lawful means, we instinctively dig in, collect our own gaggle of law experts, and the loophole search is on to find ways to gain the upper hand in whatever tussle is afoot.

This chapter is about achieving a mature and delicate balance as a leader. Yes, I am bound by love and loyalty to look out for "my own" organization and make sure it is fairly treated. But I must be ready to apply the same standards and expectations to others as well, not just reserve the right to be treated fairly for my own group only. Favoritism is strongly admonished in vs. 1-13; it gives a temporary feeling of superiority and "winning" an edge, but, in the end, it is destructive to all involved.

The pivot point is vs. 12-16; a servant leader seeks ways to make the law of liberty active for all, wants mercy to triumph over judgment for all, and orders his interaction with others to benefit all, especially those who are less fortunate (vs. 2, 5, 8, 15-16). From the Torah (Lev. 19.18) to the Gospels (Matt. 7.12) to James' royal law (v. 12, love your neighbor as yourself), the message is consistent: I received grace from God and should extend it to others.

As theologues, people are often caught up in the nonexistent argument about whether salvation is from faith or from works (vs. 14-26). These verses are a natural progression of living by the royal law (v.8) and the law of liberty (v. 12), not a false dichotomy. I have been shown mercy by the Lord Jesus Christ, resulting in liberation from sin. Out of gratitude to Him I show mercy, compassion, and fairness to others. (Matt. 5.7)

Lines on Leadership
Each day in my journal, I reflect on the interactions of the previous day and pray over the ones coming up today. I circle every name and ask myself: did I serve, shun, or unduly favor that person? Did my actions bring him/her closer to Christ or further away?

_____

_____
++

James 3---Highlights: Higher standards; the power of the tongue; the contrast of earthly/heavenly wisdom

"Let not many of you become teachers, my brethren, knowing that as such we shall incur a stricter judgment" (v.1). Leaders are held to higher standards. It does not seem fair and never will; if a person desires to lead, he/she will be singled out, used as a measuring stick for others, and has a large, prominent target placed figuratively on his/her back. James acknowledges in v. 2 that we all stumble (because we are flawed humans, including leaders), and the part of our anatomy and leadership that betrays us most often is the tongue (vs.3-12).

The more prominent the leader/teacher, the more his/her words impact other lives. The more prominent the leader/teacher, the fewer decisions and pronouncements they usually make, but the ones they do make carry far more weight than those made by subordinates. Their decisions are analyzed, parsed, reproduced, touted, shouted, etched in stone, and become company policy, then company culture, and then *company-speak*.

I think quickly and, for the most part, out loud, meaning I talk out my thought process. This can be constructive in a small discussion group, especially during a brainstorming formation of ideas or possibilities, but counterproductive when addressing a larger crowd as their leader. Those words need to be measured and weighed for their potential effectiveness or damage. It is why I developed a habit of journaling, so the sharp edges of my thoughts could be seen as insightful or inciting. I review whether I honored the Father of light (James 1.17) or the father of lies (Jn. 8.44).

I used to pride myself on the ability to speak extemporaneously, but in my latter years, I have seen the need to commit my words to paper or computer screens so I can evaluate their negative and positive potential. Something may sound great rattling around in my brain but it rapidly loses its logic when it appears on my computer screen.

I do not always get to choose which words I speak will be deemed "important". If a person is a prominent leader, every chance encounter can possibly create a lifelong memory for the other person. What seemed (to me) to be a casual aside may be recounted multiple times by that person when he says to friends, "Do you know what our leader told me? He said, '... '"

Heaven-originated wisdom is described in v. 17 as "Pure, peaceable, gentle, and full of mercy and good fruit." A Kingdom leader does not have to be exciting, charismatic, or an Elmer Gantry clone to inspire his group. According to James 1.19, he should be quick to listen and slow to speak. Solomon wrote in a similar fashion when he penned Proverbs 18.21, saying that death and life were in the power of the tongue and they that love it shall eat of its fruit. A brief reflective pause can prevent major faux pas.

Lines on Leadership
A leader has a target on his back and can use that target to his advantage if he speaks well-chosen words. Earlier in 1 Tim. 3 Paul spoke of those who aspire to lead. What words have you spoken recently that would make others aspire to lead or avoid leadership opportunities?

_____

_____
++

James 4---Highlights: warnings against worldliness, for reliance on God, about the fleetingness of life

Faith is not an exclusively spiritual concept. People exercise faith on a daily basis whether they are Christ-followers or not. Every time I step on a ladder rung, I show faith in the ladder to keep me from falling. Every time I drive on a highway, I show faith that the other vehicles in both directions will respect the lanes. Every time I open a can of beans to cook for dinner, I show faith that the product was safely produced and delivered to me as the consumer. I "faith" my way through each day all day long.

Faith requires an object (see Lk. 17 entry). I cannot just have faith, hope, or love (1 Cor. 13.13); they must have an object. I love someone or something; I hope <u>for</u> something; I have faith <u>in</u> something or someone. Here James exhorts us not to place our ultimate faith in worldly things and worldly behavior. At first glance, the actions mentioned (lust, murder, envy, fighting, adultery, vs. 2-3) can be dismissed by saying, 'I obviously don't operate in that realm.' But when I reflect on how I leverage my position at work to my advantage, they become all too familiar in my thoughts, words, and deeds toward others. My faith winds up being in worldly tactics for advancement, and ultimately my faith becomes anchored in self (v.3) because my prayers/desires become focused on my own pleasures/happiness/advancement. James contrasts this with the remarkable statement in v. 10, "Humble yourselves in the presence of the Lord, and He will exalt you. The sequence is both important and ancient, as Solomon long ago noted that humility comes before honor (Prov. 15.33; see 1 Pet. 5 entry). We foolishly think that because we are leaders, we are in charge of our own lives. We make all these wonderful plans for ourselves, for others, and for our organizations, but James points out (vs. 12-16) there's only one Person in charge of our very life. If I trust Him with my life, why not trust Him with my leadership?

Lines on Leadership
If I, as a Christian leader, am totally honest, there are times I am not above the use of my relationship with God to gain an inside track, to ask Him to favor me over others, and to "arrange" things so I can get that promotion, that contract, that title (see James 2 entry). It is not fatalism to learn reliance on the Father, to patiently rely on His timing and His way. In the end, it is about His glory, not mine.

_____

_____

++

James 5---Highlights: Discipline in the Christian Life, prayer, avoiding being sidetracked

v. 16 "Therefore, confess your sins to one another, and pray for one another so that you may be healed. The effective prayer of a righteous man can accomplish much."

Prayer is a neglected and powerful leadership tool; too often, it is relegated to a last resort ("all we can do now is pray") when it should be a primary catalyst for decision-making. When this verse is coupled with other concepts in this chapter, prayer becomes a powerful "positioner" to place us where God can use us and bless us.

Prayer is not a business transaction where I offer certain currency, and the proprietor is bound to sell or deliver to me a desired product on demand. The farmer in v. 7 shows us that seeds are planted, and then a necessary time must elapse before the harvest is possible. In our hurry-up, instantaneous society, we tend to think since information can be obtained quickly, results should be just as forthcoming. The admonition in v. 12 (do not swear by heaven or earth, let your yes be yes, your no be no) shows me prayer is not a showcase for my emotions or oratorical ability; my requests are to be simple, restrained, and unadorned. Prayer is not a simple arithmetical equation; I pray, and God is bound by my prayer to do x thing.

Prayer is not primarily about arithmetic but rather alignment: I need to align my heart with His heart, my will with His will, and my thoughts with His thoughts. God is not wringing His hands in heaven about how to make all of our prayers mix and match properly so that everyone gets what he thinks he needs or wants; He is not a Santa Claus figure frantically trying to fulfill the wish lists of His children. He is singularly focused on His will and His Kingdom. That does not mean He is immune to our cries or broken hearts; it means His will is pure, good, holy, and perfect, and I best serve the Kingdom, my organization, and my personal situation when I spend less time trying to bend God's ear or negotiate with Him, and more time getting in line with His plan for my life. (see 1 Jn. 5 entry).

<u>Lines on Leadership</u>
Leaders want to make bold decisions and take bold action. Reflection seems to be counter to that image, but taking the proper time to reflect and align my decisions with the Word and Spirit of God reassures me I am making a wise decision. What do you need to incorporate into your decision-making process to properly align it with God's will so you can "accomplish much (v.16)?"

_____

_____

++

1ST LETTER FROM PETER

Intro: Peter's influence on the early church is large. He may not have written as many epistles as Paul, but his place in the leadership among the twelve apostles, preaching the Pentecost sermon (Acts 2), and representing the Jerusalem church often in various other locations cements his place in the panoply of early saints.

The brash, impetuous Peter of the gospels is tempered by the infusion of the Holy Spirit in Acts 2 in his life. After that point, he listens first and talks later. His first epistle is a general one sent to various locations as a cyclical letter (1 Pet. 1.1). It is a primer in preparation for an increase in the persecution that came several decades after its composition.

++

1st Peter 1---Highlights: Nature of salvation and the relation of the believer to God and fellow believers

For years I had a poster in the book closet of my campus ministry office where students could not see it. It was a simple drawing with Charlie Brown of Peanuts fame standing on the pitcher's mound saying, "I love mankind, it's people I can't stand." It was my secret refuge when someone came in with yet another inane idea or insane scheme that invited my involvement.

Verse 16 has a practical side as well as a theological one: "You shall be holy because I am holy." (God speaking, Lev. 11.44). The corollary comes in v. 22 when Peter admonishes, "Since you have in obedience to the truth purified your souls for a sincere love of the brethren, fervently love one another from the heart." Life would be a lot simpler if we could just exist in the vertical relationship of man to God. But if we say we have been transformed by His love, then we as channels of that love need to have an outlet, lest it fester and stagnate in us by not flowing outward (like the Jordan River feeding into the Dead Sea). I wish we could keep the scope of our attention generic and global and not have to live that out daily on a local level, but my world is made up of colleagues, church members, family, and neighbors. Peter goes beyond a "sincere" love of the brethren to a "fervent" love of them. This goes beyond tolerance and coexistence. In biblical Greek, the word translated "sincere" meant not hypocritical, to not wear a theatrical mask. So I have to be genuine about my love for the brethren. If that weren't enough, I am urged to love them "fervently". The word translated "fervently" has roots in stretching, unceasingly so, striving and straining as in athletics to gain an edge.

Here is where the difficulty lies. Those who wear passion on their sleeves can be frighteningly intimidating to some. It can be interpreted from "he's mad at me" because his eyes are always bulging, and he gets all worked up about things to "he's hitting on me" because he looks at me intently and puts his arm on a shoulder. Those whose passion runs deep and silent run the risk of people mistaking their calm veneer as passive or apathetic. I lean toward the former excess; I tend to stare someone down and say, "I believe in you", to the point it can make someone uncomfortable. I've had to learn to distinguish emotion from passion and find ways that are not threatening to express it. Servant leadership is the best way to exhibit a "fervent love of the brethren" to channel that emotion into sacrifice and service.

<u>Lines on Leadership</u>
Advanced telecommunications and pandemics combined in the early 2020s to create both accessibility to and distance from one another. Churches and companies will have to find new ways to create what in churches we call a covenant bond and, in

corporations, a true esprit d' corps. How will you express your effective and "fervent" love for the members of your group in today's society?

_____

_____

++

1st Peter 2---Highlights: Our identity in Christ, Christ as role model, honoring authority

What is your primary identity? From what or from whom do you derive your primary identity? The stock Sunday School answer to any teacher's question (God, Jesus, or the Bible) in this case would be a correct response. The world, your family, and your work associates can call you whatever they want, but our primary identity must be what God says we are. How our heavenly Father describes us is infinitely more important than any labels attached to us by others. The Psalms declare us to be "fearfully and wonderfully made" (Ps. 139). Paul calls believers God's own possession (Gal. 3.29) and the bride of Christ (Eph. 5). John said our faith in Jesus has made us children of God (John 1.12), and Jesus Himself calls us His friends (John 15.12-15).

Peter uses multiple word images in chapter two to describe our identity as: newborn babes (v. 2); living stones making up the house of God (v. 5); a chosen race (v. 9); a royal priesthood (v. 9); a holy nation (v. 9); and a people belonging to God (v. 9). Each of those terms deserves fuller treatment than allowed in this format. The common denominator for other NT writers and Peter's references is this: all identity is wrapped up in relationships[1].

If I was the only entity in the universe and had nothing to which I could compare myself, it would be impossible to define who I was or what my identity was. My worldview is derived from relationships. My mind is, in large part, memories established through countless interactions with others and my surroundings. My heritage and very humanity are determined and confirmed by my similarity to those around me and a common consensus on what to call ourselves as a race, a species, or a citizenry.

So my identity is wrapped up with my relationships, and to a Christian, none is more important than the one to God. What He says about me matters more than any person or organization, or family member. That preaches well but is difficult to live out. I love my family, my church, my favorite teams, my favorite avocations, my job, and my colleagues in our association—but my primary identity can never be derived from them, as people often disappoint us, abandon us, or change their relationships with us. Christ, on the other hand, remains constant (Heb. 13.5), and God's love for us endures forever (Psalms 100-107).

Many years ago, when Robert McGee was in the process of writing *Search for Significance,* he came to our church to teach its basic principles. I still have the pre-publication manuscript copy he gave me. It became a book, a workbook, and a seminar used in and beyond our denomination. The basic truth I remember from those sessions was: no matter what I do, <u>God will never love me less or more than He does right now, that my identity was not wrapped up in my performance but rather in His promises</u>[2].

We have multiple identities: parent, child, sibling, employee, member of organizations, neighbor, citizen, team member, or significant other for someone else. This chapter reminds me I remain all those identities, but I operate my daily life and lead from my primary or operative identity. Vs. 1-12 describe those word images, vs. 13-20 describe my relationship to authority and superiors, and vs. 21-25 remind me that everything is secondary to my relationship to Christ, in whose steps I follow (v.21).

Lines on Leadership
Not everything will turn up roses and sunshine just because I lead from my primary identity in Christ. Vs. 13-20 challenge us to work for reasonable <u>and</u> unreasonable masters and to expect suffering, the context of what it means to follow "in His steps" in v. 21. How would you describe your primary identity?

_____

_____

++

1st Peter 3---Highlights: husband/wife relations; persecution and a Christian response; meaning of baptism

I am indebted to Kevin Belcher, pastor of Burke Memorial Baptist Church in Princeton, WV, at the time of writing this book, for some of the thoughts below concerning 1 Peter 3.15.

V.15, "Sanctify Christ as Lord in your hearts, always being ready to make a defense to everyone who asks you to give an account for the hope that is in you, yet with gentleness and reverence," is a classic proof text for what Christians call "apologetics". It is from a particular definition of the word *apology*, meaning a word spoken in favor of or in defense of a certain stance or belief. Apologetics is the rational defense of one's faith using all known knowledge and logic to create a strong narrative based on evidence more than emotion, on facts more than feeling.

This is valuable in and of itself, but when read in context v. 15, it takes on a sharpness born of pressure. Verses 14 and 17 speak of the blessedness that comes from being persecuted as one suffers for righteousness' sake. It is in line with Christ's words when He admonishes His disciples (Mt. 10.16-23) that, when the time comes, the words to speak will be given to us by the Holy

Spirit. Jesus does not speak of deliverance out of a situation but the defense of the truth and then take whatever consequences come (usually persecution). When He says not to worry about what to say when hauled in front of government authorities, He is not speaking against preparation but about the courage of the moment. The Holy Spirit will not only give you the words but the boldness to speak them, as demonstrated time and time again in the book of Acts.

In the Old Testament, those thrown into the fiery furnace of Daniel 3 declared their faith in God to deliver them (Shadrach, Meshach, and Abednego). They also were willing to suffer loss of life for their belief (Daniel 3.18, "But even if He does not [deliver us], let it be known to you, O king, that we are not going to serve your gods or worship the golden image that you have set up"). A word in defense of one's faith takes preparation, reflection, weighing the consequences of speaking out or not speaking out, timing, courage, and will. If one's faith is not worth defending and the effort/costs it takes to do so, then it likely is not worth holding onto it at all.

Lines on Leadership

How deeply embedded is your conviction about that to which you have dedicated your life? Can you articulate the reasons why you are bent on its completion or its defense? Is your reasoning solid enough to withstand resistance and open hostility (vs. 16-17)? Which price is greater, speaking the truth and taking the consequences, or speaking what is expedient to save one's job/reputation/life?

_____

_____

++

1st Peter 4---Highlights: Suffering for the faith; love by hospitality and spiritual gifts; suffering for the faith

1 Cor. 12 and Rom. 12 (see respective entries) list spiritual gifts and how they are to be used. The unique aspect of Peter's contribution to spiritual gifts is that the gift is bookended by suffering. <u>In the midst of promised suffering to come, exercise your spiritual gift</u>. Verse 1 speaks of the suffering of Christ, verse 7, the nearness of the end of all things, and verses 12-19, the certainty of suffering as we walk in His steps and share in His suffering. In the midst of this, we are commanded to love through the exercise of our spiritual gift (here, it is singular or primary). This passage reinforces my definition of a spiritual gift found in the 1 Cor. 12 entry: a spiritual gift is the path of least resistance by which the grace of God flows through me into the lives of others. The NIV translates the verse as "Each of you should use whatever gift you have received to serve others as faithful stewards of God's grace in its various forms." The NASB calls the gift "special" to be "employed in serving one another as good stewards of the manifold grace of God." In my humble opinion, the use of the singular 'gift' here does not denote an exclusive, solitary gift but a primary one.

The German word used for the term "steward" is *Haushalter* (LUT), the one in charge of the house affairs of another person. A spiritual gift is not intended to be a cause of bragging or puffing up one's chest as if a person "owns" the gift. We are stewards of the grace of God that is meant to flow through us to others; our blessings from exercising the gift are a secondary byproduct. Peter further explains our speaking and serving have one goal, the exaltation of God (v. 11, "so that in all things God may be praised through Jesus Christ"), not the edification of the individual. Times of suffering are when the gifts are needed most within the body of Christ. In dark times, the light shines from the candle to light the way for others. Exercising the gift will not be without consequences; just as living the Christian life outlined in the Beatitudes (see Matt. 5 entry) brings inevitable persecution, a spiritual gift displayed in the life of the believer brings pressure and resistance.

Lines on Leadership
In v. 10, the gift is received, not earned, bought, or seized, so I have no right to boast about its presence in my life. It is a gift to be poured out on others more than a skill to be honed. What is your primary spiritual gift? How do you employ it: mainly to advance your career, burnish your reputation, or serve others?

_____

_____
+++

1st Peter 5---Highlights: characteristics of a church elder; warnings of persecution to come

Verses 1-7 constitute one of the strongest NT descriptions of servant leadership. Peter echoes Pauline thinking (Ephesians 5. 21ff) about the man in marriage being dually cognizant of his responsibility for his bride yet simultaneously being part of the submissive bride (the church) to Christ. I am to exercise leadership of the "flock" as a shepherd (v. 2), always mindful that I do so as an *undershepherd* to the Chief Shepherd (Christ, v. 4). I had never heard that word until we started our mission work in Germany and several pastors referred to themselves as *Unterhirten* (in German, *Hirte* means shepherd) as a deferential sign to God; they understood their place in His Kingdom. The term itself does not appear in most translations, but the concept is clear in this passage and Eph. 5.

Peter continues the thought when he exhorts the younger men in the congregation to follow the examples of their elders as undershepherds as he uses the word 'likewise' and to even "dress" like them as they "clothe themselves in humility (v.5)." Gene Wilkes' book *Jesus on Leadership* takes this principle and expands it in its first three chapters under the headings "Humble Your Heart", "First Be a Follower", and "Find Greatness in Service[1]." This sequence is illustrative of v. 6, to "humble oneself under the mighty hand of God, <u>that He may exalt you at the proper time</u>." In our get-ahead-at-all-costs world, the norm is breakneck/cutthroat competition. This is definitely a countercultural approach: to be faithful in humble service and wait on the Lord to exalt (i.e., promote) you at the time, place, and manner of His choosing. This is not a Christian version of the Cinderella tale, where she is forced to serve her stepmother and stepsisters until the prince elevates her to his side. There is room in Peter's model for excellence and distinguishing one's work, room to be an effective leader within your chosen or allotted realm. As Wilkes points out in his fourth chapter, 1 Peter 5 begins and ends with the leader's complete trust being placed in Christ. Christ does the placement (v.6), sees us through the persecution (v.1, 9), and accompanies us all the way to perfect peace (v.10) and glory with Him in eternity. My trust in Christ enables me to take risks within the confines of my service[2].

As a seminary student in the 1970s, my part-time job was to drive a Sears parts truck to outlying mechanics on a 150-mile nightly loop from Fort Worth, TX, to Azle to Weatherford and back. My supervisor was from the old school of "show them who's boss". His threats of intimidation and physical harm were intended to spur productivity but succeeded in me avoiding him at all costs and complicating communication about problems out on the field. The first pastor I worked under as a youth pastor while at seminary (he likely shows up in other chapters of this book as an example of how NOT to the pastor) would bluster his way in and out of the halls, shake his fist in my face on two separate occasions, and try to lead by bullying his congregation. I knew there had to be a better way; thank God I found 1 Peter 5.1-7.

<u>Lines on Leadership</u>
Every leader teaches me what to do or what NOT to do. Who has been an example/antithesis of 1 Peter 5.1-7 to you? If your subordinates read this passage, would they think of you?
_____
_____

++

2ND LETTER FROM PETER

Intro: Over the centuries, there have been endless arguments about whether or not Peter wrote this second epistle bearing his name. 'Peter' in the early Christian world was a rock star, and many manuscripts emerged in the first three centuries of Christendom bearing that name as the authors tried to cash in posterity-wise on his fame.

It bears much resemblance in sections to Jude and also to 1 Peter. It is a rich and incisive concentration of biblical truth and prophecy in three short chapters.

++

<u>2 Peter 1</u>—Highlights: character development, being eyewitnesses, no private interpretations

The sequence of character development listed in vs. 5-11 reveals several aspects of Peter's spiritual growth. As an evangelical, I believe salvation is full and free when a person accepts the incredible offer of Christ's sacrifice on the cross and the abolishment of spiritual death through His resurrection. <u>Salvation is granted, but sanctification is grown in partnership with His Holy Spirit</u>. Character is developed as the Lord chisels, carves, shapes, prunes, and molds us into His likeness (Rom. 8.29). Peter is a rough and tumble fisherman who repeatedly spoke before he thought, often without consideration of the consequences; now he writes about conforming his life to the image of His "Lord and Savior Jesus Christ" (v. 11). What was it like to walk the hills and shores of Galilee in what you thought would be a temporary stint with an itinerant rabbi to gain a few tips on life, only to have your life unalterably changed by a man who goes from friend to mentor to Messiah—to God incarnate? To see Jesus walk on water, to touch His empty garments in an empty tomb, to be granted the privilege of preaching the 1st post-Pentecost sermon, and to be shown in Acts 10, the gospel is not just for Jews (his people) but for everyone? How many conversations and Q&A sessions did it take Peter, how many cocks crowing, and how many times did Jesus have to correct him throughout the gospels? Yet here is Peter saying it was all worth it to gain entrance into "the eternal kingdom" of his friend, now viewed as his King (v.11).

Transformation in a person can be both point and process. <u>A quick turnaround as external evidence of change may provide drama but not necessarily depth</u>. Sustainability of trajectory, which Eugene Peterson describes as a "long obedience in the same direction" in his book of the same title, is more desirable in a mentoree, trainee, or junior partner than spikes and plunges in a person's growth and usually a better indicator of long term success (see 1 Tim. 6 entry). Peter had his detours and setbacks, but he persevered in following his Christ and slowly saw transformation along the way. I have stood in several of the locales mentioned in Scripture (Capernaum, Migdal, Tabgha) surrounding the Sea of Galilee, where many of those 'aha' moments occurred in Peter's life. What a marvel to think the brash fisherman of Luke 5 becomes the Bishop of Rome and (for Catholics) their first pope.

It doesn't happen overnight. I have kept a journal for 40+ years averaging 2-3 volumes per year. When I think nothing has happened, and all is stagnant and static, I review the journals to see how far I have come—and how far I have to go. I see the people, the places, the events, and the decisions that have shaped my life and how, from my perspective, the Lord wove and sculpted me into the person I am today.

Peter speaks honestly about his death being imminent (v. 14), and I realize I have many more years behind me than in front of me. I want, with my last breath, to be developing the character and trajectory of individual lives on a human level for the betterment of society and on a spiritual level for the Kingdom of God. I pray my family, my colleagues, and the folks I train will have considered the time spent walking, working, and living with me as steps closer to conformity to the character and person of Christ.

<u>Lines on Leadership</u>
Does the sequence of character development in vs. 5-8 remotely resemble my leadership? Am I demanding that of myself as well as others in our organization?
_____
_____
++

2 Peter 2---Highlights: description of false prophets, emphasis on the providence of God toward faithful

As a leader, this chapter is one of the most painful to read as one recognizes past friends who have become foes. 2 Peter 2 contains one of the most complete and searing condemnations of false prophets in the NT. Here is a partial compilation of their traits:

V. 1: They arise from within your group; they secretly introduce destructive heresies and forsake the entrance into the group provided by the Master.
V. 2: They distort the truth.
V. 3: Willing to lie in order to exploit their fellow members/workers.
V. 10: Willing to use the sensual to entice the unsuspecting; despise authority; have lost reverential deference to their God

V. 12: Instead of trying to learn what they don't understand, they attack it.

V. 13: When they feel their deception is sufficient and durable enough they become open and brazen in its practice   V. 14: The insatiability of sin; sin begets and feeds on sin

V. 15: Having once known the way of righteousness they have forsaken it and learned to love unrighteousness

V. 17: "Springs without water, mists driven by a storm"

V. 18: Reminiscent of drug dealers hooking others into their circle of users, they "promise freedom while they themselves are slaves of corruption".

V. 20-21: To have rejected the light in favor of darkness causes their hearts to harden beyond what they were before they were exposed to the light   V. 22

"A sow, after washing, returns to wallowing in the mire"

This is one of the more unpleasant facets of leadership. You came on a church staff with large expectations of how great it was going to be working alongside like-minded servants. You started in the office with guys who pledged their friendship and alliance with you to make this company soar. The professional ties grew stronger to the point they became personal, and you thought you had made lifelong ties to partners in ministry or business. You were in this together. It rarely happens overnight; you are promoted, or someone else in the organization shines, and a myriad of factors (jealousy, they "done me wrong", being left behind, not getting due credit) converge in the mind of your associate to where he becomes less and less ally and more and more adversary.

Once the person's true intent has been exposed, if you have the authority or duty to handle that person, the pain begins and rarely disappears altogether, regardless of how many years pass. You must find the proper blend of punitive and redemptive as you deal with the individual. The pain is doubled if it is a trusted associate or personal friend. There will be two sets of scars: one from the damage inflicted on you and your organization by the rogue partner; and one when your relationship with them is permanently altered. Your efforts and emotions have to be diverted from the goal at hand to deal with the subversion and damage. Fighting for the truth is a costly battle, not only in terms of expended effort but deep bonds that have now been betrayed. This is amplified further if family is involved. Peter does not give detailed tools and procedures to use to ferret out false prophets; those must be gleaned from other NT passages (see 2 Tim. 3 entry).

Lines on Leadership
When have you had to deal with associates gone awry? What was the tipping point for you? How did you handle the sense of loss both for your organization and for you personally?

_____
_____
++

2 Peter 3---Highlights: The Coming of Christ, the New Heaven and Earth, Paul as writer of scripture

Various authors, speakers, and political figures have used variants on the following statement to describe not being on the same plane or page as another person: "They are playing checkers when the game at hand is chess." The rules and pace of the game of checkers are light years from chess in terms of simplicity and speed. The number of opening moves for checkers is limited by the few black or red checkers able to move at all; by the third move of chess for each side, the possibilities of sequences numbers in the trillions. Both games have elements of offense and defense, but the strategy for chess is infinitely more complex.

Peter reminds us that the Lord's timing (v.8), the Lord's ability to bring His will to fruition (v. 9), and the Lord's end goal (our salvation, v.15) are not like ours (nor are His thoughts, Isaiah 55.8). Instead of wasting time devising eschatological scenarios (speculation on end times has occupied many a pastor's waking hours), a person should spend his time discerning the past patterns and current intent of the Father.

2 Peter 3 is the flip side of 2 Peter 2 in terms of trust. The previous chapter was a sober warning to be on constant guard against those who arise from within the midst of one's organization to bring ruin upon it (2 Pet. 2.1). Here we are to trust the person in charge even when we don't understand His strategy or His total plan. Twice in these two chapters (vs. 2.7; 3.17), Peter calls the false prophets and heretics "unprincipled" (NASB-1995), unscrupulous (NASB), lawless, and guilty of "unrestrained behavior of the immoral" (HCSB). The Lord's will is an extension of His character, His patience, and pace of history inscrutable to fallen man (v. 9, 15). The character of God is not assailable or attainable by mortal man. His character is so pure and strong all truth and laws by which the universe operates emanate from the character of God (see Colossians 1.13-20). (See 1 Timothy 4 entry for a fuller explanation of the relationship between character, competency, and calling)

Lines on Leadership
I trust the revealed character of God. Translating this to a human plane and looking at a human organization of any kind is more difficult. Most leadership in terms of quantity occurs in the middle of organizations: middle management, foremen, directors, and department heads. They have both subordinates

and superiors. How to balance trust, accountability, integrity, adherence to company policy, and loyalty to relationships is a challenging issue. Who do you need to watch within your organization as to their ability to subvert it? Who do you need to trust even though you are not sure of their intent? How do you distinguish between them?

_____

_____

++

1ST LETTER FROM JOHN

Intro: 1 John uses the word "know" over 30 times in most translations. By this or that, you will <u>know</u> God, <u>know</u> your salvation is sure. John could have pointed at certain facts or faith assertions or built some airtight argument constructed on logic. A closer look at those five chapters reveals it is not in reasoning or revelation alone that we know we have eternal life in Him, but rather <u>through our obedience</u> (2.3-6; 3.14-18; 4.8) and submission to the Spirit (3.24; 4.13). <u>Obedience clarifies our faith</u>. In our modern society and its corresponding smugness, we assert a need to 'understand in order to obey', so we sit and peruse the situation, negotiate what we want to call fact or non-fact, and say I'll obey when I have 'all the facts', which is never achievable (there's always more to discover about a truth). An old Jewish saying reverses this: "Obey to understand." When the Psalmist wrote, "Be still & <u>know</u> that I am God" (Ps. 46.10), it was not to just contemplate His existence. It should buckle my knees in submission, in holy fear and trembling. The mind can play tricks; the heart can be deceived; it is with the will we decide to obey our Father, follow our Christ, and submit to His Spirit.

++

<u>1 John 1</u>---Highlights: Intro, Jesus as Incarnate Word; God is Light

v. 7, "...If we walk in the light as He Himself is in the light, we have fellowship with one another, and the blood of Jesus His Son cleanses us from all sin." v. 9 "If we confess our sins, He is faithful and righteous to forgive our sins and to cleanse us from all unrighteousness." These are not contradictory or parallel statements. Christians say I have been saved (regeneration, born again of Christ), I am being saved (sanctification, the process of striving toward Christlikeness), and I will be saved (glorification, the transformation to a glorified resurrected body in an eternal life with Christ). While this is wonderful to contemplate in the sense of salvation, what does this have to do with leadership?

A key word for leaders in this passage is "confess". The compound word means simply "to agree with". As often mentioned, the first duty of a leader is to define reality. As a leader, I should take full stock of what I am and what I am not before I try to lead others. There is a positive confession and a negative one. Positive confession agrees when my Christ says I am His child (Jn. 1.12). Negative confession agrees with Christ when He says, "no man comes to the Father but by Me" (Jn. 14.6), when He says, "everyone who commits sin is a slave to sin" (Jn. 8.34), and when He says we deceive ourselves if we say we have no sin (1 Jn. 1.8, 10). Sin loves the wrong things or the right things in the wrong way.

On a corporate or secular plane, this is not just admitting shortcomings such as lack of talent or skill or lack of height or heft. This is learning to not only admit but agree with the fact that I crossed the line here, offended there, mucked up the process yesterday, or cost the company a contract because of my negligence. A servant leader will not cover up his mistakes but freely own up to them and learn from them. On a spiritual plane, these verses are a great comfort: as I walk (euphemism for live) in His light, He exposes more and more of how I fall short of His expectations for my life. Both on a secular and spiritual level, I need to avoid dwelling on my sins, denying them, minimizing them, rationalizing them, or pretending they don't exist and have no consequences. Restoring fellowship with those around me and with my Lord is more important than my pride and saving face. Simple to say, hard to do, this is the downfall of many a leader when he refuses to acknowledge his transgressions and attempts to shift blame. It doesn't take long in the forum of public affairs to see this played out over and over with public figures in politics, business, and the church.

My confession of sin to my Lord and my followers means I agree that I have stumbled, I openly acknowledge it, and we go on with restored fellowship when forgiveness is extended. That forgiveness from Christ is assured in this passage; gaining it from colleagues can sometimes be painful and meted out gradually. Confession is not only "good for the soul," it's good for business, good for the church, and good for the country when its leaders will admit they are flawed like the rest of us.

Lines on Leadership
Prominence and power don't require perfection. Sin should be confessed in its proper sphere of influence, meaning if I have affected a private or close circle of colleagues, I don't need to shout it to the general public or share it on social media. What sins, private or public, ancient or recent, need to be dealt with in order to restore your fellowship with God and with man?

_____
_____
++

1 John 2---Highlights: Christ as our Advocate; stay separate from the world; eternal life as our promise

The first rule of hermeneutics (bible interpretation) mentioned several times in this book is: always read a passage in context. A cursory look at this chapter seems to depict spiritual life as a transaction instead of a transformation. Get in line, obey, and you get *X* for doing *Y*, which sounds like countless other religions. However, two of the most repeated terms in 1 John are 'know' and 'abide' (in other translations, remain, reside, or live). Christianity is, at its heart, not a religion but a relationship. A reading of the entire five chapters of 1 John reveals repeated usages of 'know' (30-40x) and 'abide' (10-15x), depending on the translation. Our obedience is not to be a cold tit for tat out of duty but born out of a personal relationship with our Master and Messiah. Vs. 5-6 are pivotal, "By this we know that we are in Him; the one who says he abides in Him ought himself to walk in the same manner as He walked."

In John's gospel (see Jn.15 entry), we defined abide as "in living, vital connection". Throughout the NT, various images are used to describe this symbiotic coupling of our life with Christ: a common yoke (Mt. 11.28), the vines and branches of Jn. 15, and parts of the body connected to the body's Head (Col. 1.18). Paul uses the same words about walking as He walked in Col. 2.6-7; Peter in 1 Pet. 2.21, and Luke in quoting Jesus in Lk. 9.23. I can study all the commandments I want and try to obey as many as I can remember, but trying to do that can be paralyzing and overwhelming. There is definitely a time and place to break down a golfer's swing, a basketballer's jump shot, or an executive's decision-making regimen. <u>But the far superior way to learn from a leader is found in the latter phrase of v. 6 ("in the same manner as He walked."), to follow him long enough to where the gait, the voice inflections, the body language, the timing of gestures, and the pace of his step are not carefully measured but unconsciously imitated</u>. A casual afternoon in a public park watching children with their parents reinforces this: watch their gestures, body language, or how they amble down a path together.

That is but the beginning as one starts to resemble a leader's motions and speech. Then comes the character and values; finally, the thoughts overlap to the point that it becomes hard to distinguish the two. I did not have the free choice of selecting my parents, but I now can decide whom I will imitate and follow in terms of my leadership. Some will be in my organization, especially when I begin employment or membership. Others throughout my year might be an author in my field, someone who excels at our common craft, an historical figure, or a pioneer who broke ground for those who followed in his/her path (examine the different models of mentors in *Connecting* by Stanley and Clinton[1]).

Lines on Leadership

For those who are believers: are you honest about how in sync or out of sync your daily walk is with your Master? Is part of your private devotional time given to an examination of walking in the manner He walked? For those who are in a corporate setting: of which company figure do your colleagues say you remind them? Is that instructional or aspirational?

_____

_____

++

1 John 3---Highlights: the relationship between identity, love, obedience, and action

v. 18, "Little children, let us not love with word or with tongue, but in deed and truth." After multiple illustrations of how our love of others reflects on our Father, this admonition serves as a summation of the simple yet profound principle that love is more verb than noun, an action more than a concept.

Love has been bestowed on us by the Father as an inheritance (v. 1), and we are declared His children in the present, not future tense ("and such we *are*"). So love is our identity; it is in the spiritual DNA if we are born again, sired by the Holy Spirit of God. We act out of our identity (vs.1-9). Our deeds of love reinforce our identity; they don't create it (v. 10) and confirm that we possess eternal life as we "love the brethren" (v. 14).

The interesting pairing is in the second phrase of the main verse; we love "in deed and truth". If love is more verb than noun, then truth is revealed more in action than abstract thought. Too often, we relegate truth to philosophical musings or spiritualize it by saying Jesus is the embodiment of truth (John 14.6). I prefer to view the three I AM statements in John 14.6 as dynamic (I am the Way, the Truth, and the Life), that Jesus as Life is movement and power more than a shining luminescence to admire (more flow than glow), that Jesus as the Way is more a vehicle in which I am conveyed than a path I walk, and that Jesus as Truth is not something to be studied as much as Someone to follow. Here, John repeats in simpler language his previous ideas in his gospel that when we are in living vital connection with God's Word and fulfilling it, then the revealed truth sets us free (John 8.31-32).

How does this relate to leadership in the church and corporate worlds? Today our society is enraptured with image over substance, with branding being the secret to success. If we project the proper image online, the proper tagline on our advertising, and the proper logo that encapsulates our values, people will be drawn to our organization. That may be effective initially, but who we are is ultimately wrapped up much more in our actions than our image. At the root of the word 'obey' is to hear, to understand. It is why Jesus and the OT prophets often said read and heed; to the modern mind, those are two separate options; in biblical terms, to understand and obey are two sides of the same coin (for a negative comparison, see 2 Tim. 3.7).
This isn't flashy or glamorous and is not about ad campaigns, pep talks, or strategy sessions. Those have their place in training and decision-making, but effective day-to-day leadership and

resultant "followship" (see Mt. 8 & 11 entries) are more likely to be learned in the hard work of incarnating and fulfilling what we already know to be true. I can only implore and beseech my group with "ought to'" for so long; sooner or later, my followers need the "how to's" in order to develop from followers into leaders, and there is no better method to show the way than to lead the way by becoming the way. "Let us not love [lead] with word or tongue, but in deed and truth."

Lines on Leadership
If your organization's members were asked to give a description of you as a leader, would they concentrate more on your policies or your personification of them?

_____

_____

++

1 John 4---Highlights: the relationship between God's love and our ability to love

This chapter on love rivals 1 Corinthians 13. While it may lack the poetic qualities of Paul's paean to godly love, John offers powerful insights into how to live life out of and through God's love.

Verse 19 is an absolutely pivotal biblical statement: "We love, because He first loved us." In seven short words, John delivers a stunning foundational concept: our love is always a reaction to the initiatory love of God. The Father initiated the chain of love between Creator and creation: He (out of His nature and volition) took upon Himself the role of Redeemer and loved us through Jesus Christ. He did not wait around for the creatures to beg and bargain for His love. In the wider scope of the chapter, John declares that the love of God is not one of impulse, one that waxes and wanes, or a love dependent on our response. It is relentless and without end, never tapering off.

I can apprehend (think about) but never comprehend (wrap my head and hands around) such a love. I have always desired to treat students, church members, and, lately, the churches in my association with impartiality and equality. However, as a human, I know I inevitably show favoritism to those who respond well to my teaching or with whom I just "hit it off". Loving a church (or, more specifically, loving a pastor) who has ignored me or openly opposed me is admittedly difficult. Yet I am to do exactly that according to v. 7 and following: love one another because the origin of love is God. Love is rooted in and a manifestation of His Person. Verse 8 and again v. 16 contain a statement that in English can be grossly misinterpreted, that "God is love." This is not an example of the commutative equation (if a=b then b=a). <u>Nowhere</u> in scripture is love elevated to the status of a deity, and every commentary written on this passage speaks to this. All that love is can be found in God, but love is not a god or the God. I worship the God who is love, but not love itself.

We can love without thought of reward or rejection because of v. 18 ("perfect love casts out fear"). The word perfect is unfortunate because, in most readers' minds, the word perfect conjures up "unblemished", "total perfection", or "without fault". The Greek word used here has more of the connotation of completeness, maturity; in German, *völlig* or *vollkommend*, meaning it has come into fullness or fruition. If I love as God loves, it will be without reservation, without end, and mature in the sense of "in spite of"; childlike love is innocent and pure but can be directed or diverted easily. Mature, "vollkommend" love continues even when I realize the object of that love has proven itself unworthy or unresponsive. It is why John, in his gospel, has

Jesus compare Himself to a shepherd (John 10) who will lay down His life for His sheep. His love is a sacrificial one, and one that can be given with confidence because "greater is he that is in you than he who is in the world" (v.4). The indwelling love of God does not mean I will always conquer, but it does empower me to continue loving when circumstances do not remain favorable. We love because He first loved us.

<u>Lines on Leadership</u>
To love on an institutional basis (to love my organization) means I must love the individuals who together are that organization. The Great Shepherd (Heb. 13.20) not only loves the herd but each of the sheep. How can I, as a leader, do a better job today of loving my organization and those who comprise it with a 1 John 4 love?

_____

_____

++

1 John 5---Highlights: different ways we can know we have eternal life

Vs. 13-15--"These things I have written to you who believe in the name of the Son of God, in order that you may <u>know</u> that you have eternal life. And this is the confidence which we have before Him, that, if we ask anything according to His will, He hears us. And if we <u>know</u> that He hears us in whatever we ask, we <u>know</u> that we have the requests which we have asked from Him." [emphasis mine]

At first, hearing this passage sounds like classic double talk. The key phrase is "according to His will". Where do I find His will? If I can know what His will is, I can couch my request in His words and His intent. Where do I find both? For evangelicals, the primary source is the Word of God, the Bible; contained in those 66 books are the expressed nature, will, and recorded actions of God toward His creation and those who would be His children. For charismatics, the primary source is often personal revelation, what God has revealed to me through His Holy Spirit. So we have to strike a balance between interpretation of God's word and illumination by the Spirit. Searching the scriptures and sensitivity to the Spirit of God will yield a broad and deep understanding of who God is and how He operates.

On a corporate level, the more time I listen to a superior speak his/her heart, share dreams for the company, and chronicle his decision-making, and couple that with his written articles, memos, policy papers, emails, and other communications, the better I can anticipate how a personal request of mine will be received. On both a corporate and church level, this is not about an attempt to negotiate with or circumvent the will of my boss or Lord, but rather to get aligned with it. In John's gospel, Jesus says it this way: "And whatever you ask in My name, that will I do, that the Father may be glorified in the Son" (Jn. 14.13) and "If you abide in Me, and My words abide in you, ask whatever you wish, and it shall be done for you."(Jn. 15.7) Notice this is not a carte blanche approach to ask for whatever I can dream up; it has parameters and given boundaries. "In My name" means "I would endorse it", and I can know better what He would endorse by abiding in Him and knowing His words, again, the balance of His presence and His precepts. (see Js. 5 entry)

Lines on Leadership

As a follower, how well do I know the heart and intent of my superior or my Lord? As a leader, how well do I disclose to my colleagues/employees/church members my heart and my

intent? How well have I provided an environment where my vision and their desires can mesh into a seamless whole?
_____
_____

++

JOHN'S 2ND LETTER

2nd John---Highlights: walk according to the commandments and guard against heresy

At first glance, this short letter looks like personal correspondence to a "chosen lady". Such language was used euphemistically of a local congregation in case the epistle fell into unfriendly or government hands[1]. At second glance, the letter embraces two seemingly contradictory admonitions. The congregation is commanded, as in every Johannine epistle, to love one another (v. 5), yet in verses 10-11, the same congregation is told to withhold hospitality. The solution is found in v. 7. Because Christ has come in the flesh (Jn. 1.14) as Immanuel (God with us), believers have salvation, the essence of the Good News. It also means those who deny Jesus is God come in the flesh are both "deceivers" and "antichrists". The denial of hospitality is not arbitrary but defined carefully, and the litmus test is the deity of Christ, something Gnostics and other groups continued in the early decades of the church to deny or dilute.

One of the hardest conundrums for any organization is how to balance inclusivity and exclusivity. To err on the side of exclusivity is to be perceived as fundamental, closeminded, paranoid, or worse. To err on the side of inclusivity is to take a chance of inviting those inherently opposed to the organization's goals or identity into the fold. Once inside the organization, they can neutralize or weaken it from within for the sake of appearing tolerant or accommodating or generous.

Tolerance, accommodation, and generosity have their limits. When they result in the destruction of the organization from within, nothing is left to be tolerant, accommodating, or generous. Loving service can be rendered to any person in the form of ministry or outreach, but to take in those bent on diluting or denying the basic tenets of the organization is not a good way to exhibit that loving service. The command to not open the door to such persons was not issued to individuals but to the church. John was relentless to declare the deity of Christ and have Jesus proclaim it Himself repeatedly in John's gospel and his revelation. This was not a peripheral issue but a core doctrine for John and a definite line in the sand.

<u>Lines of Leadership</u>

What tenets of your organization/church/leadership circle are non-negotiable? How are they used in determining who is allowed in your leadership team?

_____
_____

++

JOHN'S 3RD LETTER

3rd John---Highlights: written to a real person, Gaius; refusal of John's authority by Diotrephes

The fourth verse ("I have no greater joy than this, to hear of my children walking in the truth") has been a favorite in my correspondence for years when writing a former student or disciple. What does it mean to "walk in the truth"? One thing it does not mean is pew-sitting. When did attendance become the primary criterion for spiritual maturity? I am for attending church functions, but just "showing up" in and of itself is not a reliable indication of a true disciple. "Disciple" (*mathetes*) means "follower". We have allowed "following" to mean assent to a set of truths instead of actively following after a leader who Himself is dynamic, a Messiah on the move. Jesus said, "If anyone serves Me, let him follow Me; and where I am, there shall My servant also be" (Jn. 12.26). I go where He goes and walk where He walks (1 Pet. 2.22; Col. 2.6-7). A true disciple of Jesus is also a disciplemaker, one who instructs others how to follow Christ (see the 2 Tim 2 entry).

To better understand what "walking in the truth" means, I offer this briefly annotated list of older and newer resources (most can be obtained or found online; some are mentioned elsewhere in this work); please share your favorites for later editions:

Books

1)The Master Plan of Evangelism by R. Coleman—If I had five books left in my library, this would be one of them. This is the classic of classics on equipping people to be disciples/disciplemakers like our Lord.

2) MasterLife by A. Willis—I am indebted to Avery for this diagnostic/instructional tool to show me how to become a disciple. It can be found in a workbook and book form.

3) *Multiplying Disciples: the New Testament Method of Church Growth* by Waylon Moore—Waylon has been a proponent of discipleship for decades. It is the simplest no-nonsense approach to discipleship I know.

4) *The Cost of Discipleship* by Dietrich Bonhoeffer—A German Lutheran pastor killed in a WWII concentration camp, the classic narrative on counting the costs (Lk. 14.25ff) to be a disciple.

Real-Life Discipleship and *DiscipleShift* by Jim Putnam—Pastor of a humongous church in ID that practices small group discipleship; this is practical, attainable, and replicable.

5) *Mentoring* by Tim Elmore—Positive, practical, biblically-based guide on how to mentor 1-1. Tim has many great offerings on his website www.growingleaders.com.

6) *Connecting* by P. Stanley and J. Clinton—This is written by dedicated Christians for a secular audience; outstanding in describing the various roles in which one can mentor others.

Transformation: How Glocal Churches Transform Lives and the World by Bob Roberts, Jr.—Bob's church north of FW, TX, has planted scores of churches and sees itself as a local body connected to a global purpose (hence the mash-up word 'glocal').

Websites:

http://www.discipleshiplibrary.com/—100's of speakers on classic discipleship topics; Dr. Howard Hendricks alone has over 20 sessions on it; he impacted me in my college days. http://gregogden.com/—Terrific approach to small group discipleship, book *Discipleship Essentials,* Discipleship.org—an online community of disciples and disciplemakers' resources

Lines on Leadership

There are too many free and affordable resources available to anyone to use the excuse, "My church doesn't emphasize discipleship" or "I don't get anything out of our church services."

Whether or not you grow in Christ is ultimately your choice. Start following and show others how to do it. When do you start?
_____
_____
++

LETTER FROM JUDE

JUDE---Highlights: contending for the faith and Christ

The movies are constructed to evoke a powerful emotional response within the viewer. The size of the screen, the swelling of the music score, the artful use of the camera angles, the expert editing, and the mixture of light and darkness are all designed to identify with the struggles of the characters and draw you into identification with one or more of them. Through that character, you vicariously grieve, rejoice, love and lose, win and die. The new phenomenon of readily available videos of real-life events provided by everything from personal smartphones to police body cams provides those same struggles we view on the silver screen but without editing, musical themes, or plot development.

Jude is not grand cinema but rather the TikTok/Google headline of the NT, as it distills many of its great narratives and didactic passages into less than a minute of reading material. It revolves around these simple questions: do I know for what or for whom I am living? And am I willing to engage in the struggle to maintain it?

Jude makes it clear we are in a struggle. We are admonished in v. 3 to "contend earnestly", a word in Greek (*epagonizomai*, to contend for) from which we transliterate the English word *agonize*. This is not a description of some polite diplomatic exchange but rather a conflict of cosmic proportions as the ensuing verses describe the Exodus from Egypt to the Promised Land, angelic rebellions, and archangels squaring off against the devil himself. This is not about the daily hassle of schedule glitches, unruly children, or car breakdowns but rather about the prime battle of life between good and evil, truth and untruth, and right and wrong.

The key is to contend **for**, but what am I contending **for**? Jude points out two things: I contend for the faith (v.3) and the Lord Jesus Christ (vs. 1, 4, 21). The word faith here is a stand-in for the sum of all Christian doctrine, and Jesus is both source and subject of all those doctrinal truths. All the examples of contention for the faith seen in Pauline references (boxing, competition, soldiers, legal proceedings) come to bear in this short epistle as the Christian life is seen not as one of ease and peaceful bliss but a daily battle. The battle here is not for my survival, my honor, or my position in life, but rather for the Giver of life, the One who makes me worthy (v. 24), and the grantor of eternal life (v.21).

A leader in the midst of these daily battles can often make the mistake of concentrating on what he contends <u>against</u> instead of what/whom he contends <u>for</u>. Yes, I need to identify the adversary, but I always focus on and never forget what I am fighting <u>for</u>. Yes, the tactics of enemies are varied and effective, as outlined in vs. 4, 8, 10, 12, 13, 16, & 19. A leader should be knowledgeable of them but should not stoop to their level to "fight fire with fire"; even Michael the archangel demonstrated we should contend not in a tit-for-tat mode nor stoop to their nefarious ways but maintain our integrity and remember the "battle is the Lord's" (Ps. 20.7; Prov. 21.31).

<u>Lines on Leadership</u>
Can I clearly define the cause of my struggles? Is that "cause" something I rail <u>against</u> or something/someone <u>for</u> which I contend?

_____

_____
++

JOHN'S REVELATION

Intro: All of the other 26 NT books lend themselves to cross-referencing Christian and marketplace leadership. *Reflectional Leadership* will concentrate on overtly Christian themes in the Revelation because of the subject matter. It will deal less with *eschatology* (the study of last things) and more with everyday leadership. I invite you to walk through Revelation's chapters and discover why this book ignites the spirit 2000 years later, why it provides some of the purest images we have of Christ and His Kingdom, and how Revelation propels us into renewed servant leadership.

This book's approach to Revelation is not comprehensive and does not go into detail on each symbol or any possible connection to present-day society. It follows the grand narrative as the book was written primarily (though not exclusively) for the first-century Christians undergoing open persecution. The Revelation of John tells the reader to hold on, the risen Christ will triumph. His return may not be swift, but it is sure. Amen. Come, Lord Jesus. (Rev. 22.20b)

++

Revelation 1---Highlights: message to the 7 churches, The Vision on Patmos

Rev. 1.15b "His voice was like the sound of many waters." Rev. 14.2 "And I heard a voice from heaven like the sound of many waters and like the sound of loud thunder, and the voice which I heard was like the sound of harpists playing on their harps."

Most of us have known someone who showed promise as a peer during our formative years: they excelled at math, track, oratory, innovation, etc. Years later, your paths crossed, and the difference was striking in how you recognized the person. It was not so much the adulations or accomplishments that garnered your attention as it was the bearing, the eyes; above all, it was...the voice.

The acclaimed actor Daniel Day-Lewis once said, "The voice is the fingerprint of the soul[1]." It is unique to each person. The voice can acquire culture through education; the phrases gain additional heft through crafted use of imagery and vocabulary. Certain rhythms and cadences emerge to produce a distinctive speaking style. It acquires confidence through repeated usage. The voice can also acquire gravitas through trauma that triggers resolve. This might be a great victory or defeat, an injury, a grave loss, or in the case of Jesus Christ in Rev. 1, a death, burial, and resurrection.

The verses above speak of Christ's voice as many waters, loud thunder, and harp tones. In West Texas, where you see not just for miles but days, you can stand on a high mesa and see the dark, distant thunderheads hurl lightning bolts. The thunder rolls like an invisible tsunami across those plains uninterrupted for what seems like hours until it washes over you. Here in West Virginia, I often hear the "many waters" when I encounter waterfalls on my customary hikes. Fascination is fueled not only by the sound and the infinite patterns of the splash but the power of the rushing torrent as it plummets into the pool below. Both the thunder and the waterfalls can take on musical qualities like notes from a harp. The beauty and immensity of creation overcome the eye and the ear and compel me to motionlessly reflect on its Author; all of creation is but the faint echo of His voice (Ps. 33.6, 9).

There is a difference in volume and sonority. Volume is measured in decibels, sonority in depth. When one violin plays a note, there is a unique way it wafts through a hall. When five violins play the same note, it is not necessarily louder, but it acquires a depth of tone and goes deeper into the spirit as it vibrates through space. When an entire string orchestra sounds the same note, it acquires yet more depth, expanse, timbre, and size. Sonority is a primary appeal for choral or orchestral works.

I cannot imagine the sonority of the voice coming from the risen Lord. This is the same voice that created the universe (Ps. 33.6, 9; Col. 1.16). John writes that "He fell at His feet as a dead man (v. 17)." To hear the risen Jesus say, "I am the Alpha and the Omega who is and who was and who is to come, the Almighty (v.8)," would have shaken me out of my boots and onto my knees. Later in the chapter, He expands on this by saying, "Do not be afraid; I am the first and the last, and the living One; and I was dead, and behold, I am alive forevermore, and I have the keys of death and of Hades (vs. 17-18)." What I hear in my spirit during worship and prayer is, again, a faint echo of His voice; one day, I shall hear it unfiltered, undiluted, unrestrained by my insufficient human ears and sinful nature (1 Thess. 4.16). That voice can raise the dead to resurrected life, and I will hear it for an eternity. Speak, O Lord, speak to us the Word of God (Heb. 1.1-3a).

<u>Lines on Leadership</u>
As a follower, how do I respond to the voices of those who exercise authority over me? As a leader, how do I consciously or unconsciously use my voice to convey my heart and intent? How well do I choose my words in the presence of those who desire to fulfill them?

_____

_____

++

Revelation 2---Highlights: Messages to the churches at Ephesus, Smyrna, Pergamum, Thyatira

Revelation 2 and 3 contain what are referred to as the "seven letters to seven churches." Each letter to each church has a recognizable framework: a commendation, an admonition, and the imperative "He who has an ear, let him hear what the Spirit says to the churches." When seen on a map, six of the seven churches form a rough circle around Ephesus, a community pastored at different times by Paul, Timothy, and John, the author of Revelation. In today's parlance, those surrounding churches may have been daughter or satellite churches of the mother church in Ephesus.

Therefore in Rev. 2, we will give attention to the charge given to the church in Ephesus. It is simple yet pierces the heart 2000 years later. v. 4, "<u>But I have this against you, that you have left your first love.</u>" Countless sermons have been preached using this text as a fulcrum. The trouble comes because it is difficult to pinpoint what the "first love" is. Commentators are split among the first love being Christ, the church, the lost, or love for one another.

This is more confession than equivocation. As a minister of the gospel for five decades, I wish I could say I had been true to my first love, whether that was Christ, the church, the lost, or one another. But my heart has strayed or been distracted on many occasions, some for long stretches of time. How easy it is to get bogged down in details, to let the mission overshadow the Master, to hone in on some goal and leave God out of the picture. There have been times I persevered not because of my devotion to the Lord but pride in getting something accomplished. Times when I was more concerned with my career trajectory than the Lord Jesus I represented. There were times when I cared more about staying busy than staying devoted. Whether we are in church work or the corporate world, losing sight of our first love is a danger we must always monitor. In light of chapter 1, I have sometimes lost sight of my first love because I got out of earshot of that first love's voice.

Lines on Leadership
As a hard worker and mostly unrepentant workaholic, I have no problem filling up a workday, a workweek, or a career with activity and, to a degree, with accomplishments. That kind of drive makes me oblivious at times to how off base and far away from my first love I've strayed. This is why, regardless of my position in my organization, I need a designated person who has the freedom, without fear of retaliation, to speak truth into my life and call me back to my first love. King David had Nathan (2 Sam. 12); who in your life has the right to speak directly to you about straying from your first love?

_____

_____

++

Revelation 3---Highlights: Messages to the churches at Sardis, Philadelphia, Laodecia

Vs. 15-17 "I know your works: you are neither cold nor hot. Would that you were either cold or hot! [16] So, because you are lukewarm, and neither hot nor cold, I will spit you out of my mouth. [17] For you say, I am rich, I have prospered, and I need nothing, not realizing that you are wretched, pitiable, poor, blind, and naked." (ESV)

The last three of the seven churches, Sardis, Philadelphia, and Laodecia, are addressed in chapter 3; Laodecia was saved for last, with the letter 'L' being forever (in English) associated with lukewarm. The word translated 'spit' is actually violent in meaning and more literally translated as 'vomit'. Mediocre, lukewarm devotion to the Lord is especially abhorrent to Him. It is self-deluding: v. 17 explains that it deceives the person into thinking all is well or at least acceptable when it is much direr than self-evaluated.

This chapter is most famous for v. 20, which is somewhat lifted from the context for evangelistic appeals; when viewed as a whole narrative, v. 18 shows the utter futility of trying to heal myself by my tepid efforts; only God can provide the riches, the raiment, and the remedy necessary. V.19 shows He will reprove and discipline me before He equips me. In v. 20, Jesus knocking on the door of one's life is not a plea for entrance like some traveling salesman with a product to push. He stands and knocks as one with authority; if I want my life changed for the better, the only way to do so is to let Him enter <u>and take over</u>. When I let Him in, and live in His strength, His light, and His presence, then in Him and only in Him will I succeed.

Mediocre, half-hearted devotion, as in vs. 15-16, is like me trying to fire-cure a clay pot with a match and a single candle instead of a full-fledged kiln; I can muddle along like that and stay active but never achieve. In each of the seven churches, the phrase "he who overcomes" is applied conditionally (Ephesus, 2.7; Smyrna, 2.11; Pergamum, 2.17; Thyatira, 2.26; Sardis, 3.5; Philadelphia, 3.12; Laodecia, 3.21). It is in Him I triumph; I only win if I let Him in.

<u>Lines on Leadership</u>
Where have you let the years, the defeats, and the inertia numb you into neutral instead of overcoming in Him? On a scale from A to Z, is Christ parenthetical, peripheral, prominent, or preeminent in your life?

++

Revelation 4---Highlights: the throne of God, the Holy, Holy, Holy and Worthy Art Thou

This chapter is not meant to be understood but rather to be absorbed. As soon as one reads in v. 2 that John was "in the Spirit" and "behold, a throne was standing in heaven", all earthly references fail to convey the impact of the remainder of this chapter.

Our eyes respond to a limited range of light (think infrared, ultraviolet). Our ears respond to a limited range of sound (think ultrasonic dog whistles or bat-generated sonar). Any language has its own limitations of descriptive prowess. John describes a scene in heaven, yet he can only use earthbound terminology because he has never been to heaven before. English has one of the largest vocabularies of any language, partly due to its proclivity for assimilation, yet it cannot adequately depict the majesty of a setting that has no equal here on earth. The stones that embellish the throne, the creatures and elders before the throne, and the sea in front of it are all couched in "the appearance of" or connected in simile fashion "it is like" and use earthly points of reference. Our eyes, ears, and language fail to do justice to the scene John is commanded to convey.

Computer-generated imagery (CGI), especially in storylines of superheroes and supervillains, has dominated cinema and television in recent years. It has dazzled the eyes yet dulled the spirit in terms of apprehending truth. Imagery has become an inferior substitute for substance.

Chapter 4 is not about visual spectacle but rather spiritual supremacy. To try to mentally visualize literal creatures, literal lamps, and literal elders falling down to worship as a total scene is not the aim of the chapter. It is centered on the confessional worship of v. 11:

> "Worthy are you, our Lord and God, to receive glory and honor and power, for you created all things, and by your will they existed and were created." (ESV)

Lines on Leadership
I can become inured to suffering, success, intimidation, and any other thing designed to motivate me toward achievement. Jaw-dropping is less the point of this chapter than the dropping of one's guard, the dropping to a position of submission, a dropping of my resistance to the Lordship of Christ. My confidence in my abilities and my assets should always take a back seat to my connection to a risen, seated-on-the-throne, totally in charge of this or any other universe Lord Jesus Christ. In all honesty, what is the primary motivation for you to lead and serve?

_____

_____

++

Revelation 5---Highlights: the book of seven seals, angelic exaltation of the Lamb worthy to open it

The chapter opens with a sense of dread and despair because no one can be found worthy to open a particular book. The book's contents are not specifically described, but the fact it is written "written inside and on the back (v.1)" is an indication it is unusual for parchment or scroll, and most commentators identify the book with various Biblical references such as the book of woes (Rev. 10.8-11), events of the end times (Dan. 8.26), a last will or testament (Roman ones traditionally had seven seals[1]), or the book of life (Rev. 3.5; 17.8; 20.12).

The despair turns to delight and surprise: delight because an elder declares there is one worthy; and surprise, because two polar opposite images are assigned to the One, found worthy. The first image in v. 5 is the "Lion, from the tribe of Judah." The second in v. 6 is a "Lamb, standing as if slain". The further surprise is the repeated use of not the Lion but the Lamb as the creatures and elders fall down before it (v.8), 1000's proclaim the Lamb as worthy (v. 12), and the chorus expands to "every created thing which is in heaven and on the earth and under the earth and on the sea, and all things in them, I heard saying, 'To Him who sits on the throne, and to the Lamb be blessing and honor and glory and dominion forever and ever' (v.13)."

If most companies or leaders are left to their own choices, most would choose the more powerful, the more dynamic of the two images as the company logo. A lion is synonymous with strength as the "King of the Jungle"; a lamb is seen as docile, dumb, and directionless. This is no ordinary lamb; this Lamb is allowed to approach God's throne (v.7) and takes the special book from the very hand of God.

As in the previous chapter, the emphasis is not on descriptions of visual images that border on the bizarre (horns, eyes, harps, golden bowls) to the uninitiated unacquainted with their symbolism. Nor should the emphasis be on the side issue of men becoming a kingdom and priests who will reign upon the earth (vs. 9-10). They would commit the same faux pas as Jesus' disciples (Mt. 20.20ff), focusing on a possible sharing of power instead of the One who made the power-sharing possible through His blood purchase of their souls (v.9). This Lamb was destined to be slain for us before the foundation of the world (Eph. 1.4) and is destined for praise long after that world has vanished into eternity.

Lines on Leadership

As a kingdom leader, I find it heady that I might one day "reign on earth" (v.10). As a kingdom leader, however, I can never lose sight of this: if it is indeed a kingdom, there is but one King and His name is King Jesus. The rapid expansion of praise for Him from elders to thousands to the entire created order is breathtaking. I can either grouse about being left in His shadow or join the chorus. Christian leadership derives its legitimacy not from one's accomplishments but from acknowledgment of Him as our Redeemer. I choose the risen Lamb.

_____

_____

++

Revelation 6---Highlights: six of seven seals: false Christ, War, Famine, Death, Martyrdom, Terror

No NT chapter screams to be read in context like Rev. 6. By itself, it is a terrifying passage of scripture with scenes of increasing disaster and destruction unfolding on every side. It comes immediately after two chapters of exalted worship (Rev. 4, 5) and plunges the reader into heart-stopping, paralyzing terror.

Rev. 6 is a global scale of Jesus' sequence in the Beatitudes of finding God, following God, and the consequences of identification with Him (see Mt. 5 entry). Another similarity with the Beatitudes is the tension in this chapter (and throughout the Revelation) of the present and future manifestations of the Kingdom. Some commentaries tie Revelation to a primarily 1st-century audience as encouragement during the early church's ongoing persecution. Others see it primarily as a prophecy of things yet to occur. Within those same Beatitudes, one finds tension when some verses speak in the present (for theirs is the kingdom of heaven), and other verses use a future tense (<u>shall</u> be comforted, <u>shall</u> receive mercy, <u>shall</u> see God). I agree with those who see Revelation as addressing <u>both</u> the present and the future; it is written <u>to</u> a first-century audience but also <u>for</u> future generations.

John the Revelator began the book with the term *tribulation* (1.9) to describe what was to come in his unfolding narrative. Tribulation can be translated as 'pressure' with a mental image of x number of objects in decreasing space, like walls closing in from all sides, crushing everything within the walls. The pressure is such that some will not escape it and will suffer martyrdom (vs. 9-11). Notice in Rev. 1.9 that John describes himself as "your brother and fellow partaker in the tribulation and kingdom and perseverance which are in Jesus." Tribulation and the kingdom are linked to identification with Jesus in the Sermon on the Mount and the Revelation. The promises of a false Christ (that to become "more than conquerors" in Christ (Rom. 8.37) means I will be healthy, wealthy, and safe from harm) have softened present-day Christendom into a deceived state of ill-preparedness for the hostility and open disdain coming its way. If the writer of Hebrews can say that Jesus "for the joy set before Him endured the cross" (Heb. 12.2), and Paul can say our goal is to "know Him, and the power of His resurrection and the fellowship of His sufferings, being conformed to His death" (Phil. 3.10), as a leader in His kingdom I must expect to follow in His steps (Jn. 15.18) and be ready to experience the seals of Revelation 6 and whatever else our Lord allows to intersect with my life until He is ready to take me home.

Lines on Leadership
If and when tribulation/pressure of the magnitude described in Rev. 6 was to befall you, upon what would you lean to survive? Could you claim the promises of scripture concerning the presence of God (Phil. 4.7) and his steadfastness toward us (Heb. 13.5-6) in the face of such calamity?

_____

_____

++

Revelation 7---Highlights: interlude, the 144,000 remnant, the nations before the throne

There are several memorials to the Holocaust around the world. None grips the soul more than *Yad Vashem,* the World Holocaust Remembrance Center in Jerusalem. When one enters the main building, it is visually compressing; it is one long, tall, narrow 3D triangle of metal that threatens to close in on the entrant. The person wanders from side room to side room to be confronted with the horrors and cost of being a Jew in WWII Europe, always crossing back into the stark metallic triangle. After several hours of gut-wrenching exhibits, a person emerges into the fresh air and panorama of the Israeli countryside below.

A short walk through a peaceful garden scene (which is lined with trees planted to honor The Righteous among the Nations, those non-Jews who aided and supported Jews during the Holocaust) brings a person into one of the more haunting yet inspiring experiences of a trip to the Holy Land. The building is a memorial to the two million children numbered among the six million Jews Holocaust victims. The haunting aspect is hearing the nonstop reading of the two million children's names and country of origin, one after another after another. The inspiring aspect, after one's eyes grow accustomed to the disorientation, is what appears to be an infinite hall of candles and their reflections in every direction.

I could not help but see a correlation in my mind between these two buildings to Revelation 7. Yad Vashem drew me to vs. 4-8, where the symbolic number of 144,000 represents the remnants from the tribes of Israel. The children's memorial drew me to vs. 9-17 as those "from every nation and all tribes and peoples and tongues". In one large room within Yad Vashem is a collection available to researchers of photos, audio and video recordings, and other records of Holocaust victims. It especially reminded me of v. 14, "These are the ones who come out of the great tribulation, and they have washed their robes and made them white in the blood of the Lamb."

Lines on Leadership
The point here is not the crossing of theological lines to compare things Jewish and Christian. For today, it is to see the deep cost of singling out any particular group and objectifying, ostracizing, and eliminating them (see Acts 8 entry). Most leaders have a strong resolve to protect and defend what they perceive as their own territory, their own possessions, or their own people. But to defend the defenseless, especially when they are not "my" kind and of no advantage to me personally, takes extraordinary courage and devotion. What ethnic, social, or religious groups that look, speak, and act differently than you are you willing to defend? Which ones are you honestly not willing to defend? Would you have been counted among those in v. 14?
In v. 17 ("for the Lamb in the center of the throne shall be their shepherd, and shall guide them to springs of life"), the word translated 'guide' or 'lead' has connotations of shepherding, yet it is the Lamb who has become the shepherd. Are you willing to

sometimes reverse roles to lead? For those who are pastors, do you need to be reminded to Whom your flock belongs?

_____

_____

++

Revelation 8---Highlights: the seventh Seal, Trumpets 1-4 of seven, hail and fire; mountain burning with fire; star named Wormwood; 1/3 of the heavenly lights were extinguished

  The interval at the beginning (v.1) is significant. My Baptist background tells me that when there is complete silence, that means the pastor dropped his bulletin and doesn't know what should come next. Last month I was in a worship service that showed the maturation of a congregation. It is a small country church that just happens to be inside city limits. They have the normal undercurrent of movement, whispers, and mothers chiding children to stop squirming. I had visited that church many times over the years. The pastor has brought a new sense of reverence and awareness of God's presence in the service. When he asked the fifty or so in attendance to quietly pray before the elements of the Lord's Supper (Eucharist) were dispensed, the silence became noticeable, then deafening. It was not just a lull in the service; it was a new expectancy of God to speak during this reflection on and identification with the death and resurrection of Jesus through a time-honored rite.

  God does speak in Revelation 8 but not in a way most would welcome. The opening of the seventh seal results in four of seven trumpets being sounded in vs. 7-12 (which, to a younger generation, has the appearance of ushering in a new video game level). The horror and terror of the seven seals have been raised to a global scale as each trumpet heralds yet more dire and unthinkable tragedies. An eagle appears in v. 13 to basically say,

'If you think these four have been bad, wait until you see the next three.'

Lines on Leadership

The two bookend interludes (vs. 1, 13) offer an opportunity for mankind to repent and cry out to God for mercy and deliverance (the next chapter shows mankind's response). Take a moment to adopt different roles in the chapter. The angels show no emotion one way or the other, showing neither remorse nor glee at announcing the coming of these plagues upon mankind. If you were the angel, the eagle, or one of many who "dwell on the earth", what would be your reaction to this overwhelming series of judgments?

When you are thrust into a role of announcing doom, failure, or major setbacks, what is your tendency: to overstate the problem to soften the blow of impending reality? Or to tell the unvarnished truth? To tell your followers the bad news in one fell swoop or piecemeal it in a palatable sequence?

_____

_____

++

Revelation 9---Highlights: Fifth and sixth trumpets

v.17a, "and this is how I saw the vision" v. 20, 21, "and the rest of mankind did not repent of the works of their hands." Although a reader would consider the entire Revelation an attempt by John to describe a vision, verse 17 is the only direct reference in the book to it being a vision. In some ways, a vision is meant for a specific audience, and John was writing to a first-century one. In other ways, a vision can be so overwhelming, so awe-inspiring, the beholder is compelled to record it whether or not others will ever read it or comprehend it. If it was for a first-century audience of believers increasingly persecuted for their faith, the imagery is understandable both from OT references to a (to them) present-day Roman military presence. If it is for a future audience, the extended imagery of locusts armed with mighty weapons to oppress the faithful becomes plausible. Commentators agree on one point: that John is describing a gospel that stirs up opposition and one that, even after the destruction and plagues reminiscent of Moses' and Pharaoh's struggle in Egypt, results in a stubborn refusal to repent.

The term 'vision', as used in contemporary leadership literature, usually has the receiver of the vision as the primary implementer of that vision. Church and corporate leaders alike usually share a vision that benefits the institution but also has that leader at the center of the vision or possessing some degree of indispensability for that vision. A contemporary vision is usually connected to the comparative mode for the current situation: stronger, deeper, faster, longer, etc. John delivers a vision that is confusing and frightening, one that doesn't result in a better situation but a worse one where resistance to the gospel seems to stiffen in the face of so much might and destruction. John is not a central figure for this vision; he is merely the messenger, the conveyor of that which he himself does not likely understand.

Lines on Leadership

Reflect on a time when you felt the necessity to share a disturbing scenario or even something on the scale of a vision but were not yet sure of its implications. If that had never happened to you, how would you likely handle such a situation? Would you seek additional reflection time, consult with trusted advisors (think the book of Daniel), sit on it, or crowdsource it?

++

Revelation 10---Highlights: the strong angel, seven claps of thunder, the little scroll (book)

v. 4 "And when the seven peals of thunder had spoken, I was about to write; and I heard a voice from heaven saying, 'Seal up the things which the seven peals of thunder have spoken, and do not write them.'"

The rapid-fire disclosure of image after image to this point in Revelation has been equally dazzling and dizzying. It comes to an abrupt halt when the angel bestriding land and sea (v.2) orders John to put down his quill, roll up the scroll, and keep what he has heard (the seven peals of thunder) to himself. Thunder is often used before and after this verse in Revelation to depict the majesty and gravity of the impending edict or action. Yet the meaning of or the reason for these seven particular peals of thunder is never revealed. It was for John's ears and eyes only. This is one of the most difficult lessons for a leader. There are times when sitting on information can cost a company its competitive or inventive edge. This is not one of them. The angel, a formidable figure, orders John to bury what he has experienced in the inner recesses of his mind. To others, an experience can be so harrowing or dark (hand-to-hand combat, life and death moment, or personal trauma) the deeper one can bury it, the better. Many of those experiences go to the grave unrevealed. We will never know the 'what' or the 'why' as to the eternal silence on these seven peals of thunder because John obeyed the angel.

The hardest aspect of such a command is that a person can never come to complete inner peace with certainty that he/she has done the right thing. What if this information could have saved a life, averted a catastrophe, or altered the course of events? How would one ever know unless they talk about the information to another, but to do so would betray the holy command of an angel speaking on behalf of the Almighty? Who decides who has the "right to know"?

Lines on Leadership
Confidentiality is foundational to the counselor or client relationship, be it legal or therapeutic. In my work with churches and countless disciples, it repeatedly comes into play. This is one reason among many I journal extensively, to transfer the weight of information or decisions (that must remain hidden) from my heart to the journal page. John was not allowed even that outlet. How do you deal with confidential information? What is your level of integrity when sworn to secrecy? What mitigating circumstances would alter your initial decision concerning confidential information?

_____

_____

++

Revelation 11---Highlights: the two witnesses, the seventh trumpet

Vs. 3-4 "And I will grant authority to my two witnesses, and they will prophesy for 1,260 days, clothed in sackcloth. 4 These are the two olive trees and the two lampstands that stand before the Lord of the earth."

The identity of the two witnesses has fascinated and frustrated theologians for centuries. Speculation runs from Moses and Elijah (to represent the Law and the Prophets, see Mt. 17) to Peter and Paul as pillars of the nascent NT church. They are given considerable latitude and powers to proclaim the word of the Lord for 3.5 years. The beast from the bottomless pit (v.7) then kills them and leaves them dead in the street for 3.5 days. The world views their bodies (now possible with constant 24/7 news cycles and satellites), but no one buries them (a huge insult to Middle Eastern customs). Then they experience a resurrection and ascension to heaven.

One author describes the various scenes in Revelation as a diorama, as if John is spinning in circles, seeing a constant barrage of exhibits where the characters, in a looped fashion, continue to act out their appointed scene. The unifying aspect of Revelation is the eventual triumph of the Lamb of God, Jesus Christ, and the perseverance of His bride, the church, in the midst of increasing persecution and pressure. The temptation is to bog down in determining the times, manners, and details of His predicted consummation of history, such as the identity of the witnesses.

The story of the two witnesses sounds like a recurring nightmare that defies explanation. Their identity is not as important as their function, to proclaim the gospel even to the point of giving their lives for it. The leadership principle is not wrapped up in their identity but in their connection to the OT. "What are the two branches of the olive trees . . . Do you not know what these are? I said, 'No, my lord.' Then he said, 'These are the two anointed ones who stand by the Lord of the whole earth (Zech. 4.12-13).'"

Lines on Leadership

A vision is rarely so unique, so new that it defies any connection to the past. As a leader, I need to acknowledge those who came before me and those who laid the foundation for my vision.

Sometimes it is a germ of an idea that I am able to figure out, flesh out, or add more clarity. Zechariah's vision reappears with more detail and focus in Rev. 11. Sometimes, what the previous visionary started finds its full embodiment in the newer vision.

Because you, as a reader, are in your own "present", you automatically identify with being in the "Revelation" position instead of the "Zechariah" position. I write this shortly before I retire from full-time ministry, most of those years preparing the next generation of servant leaders for the Kingdom. I've always considered myself as a forward-thinking person, standing on the shoulders of my predecessors. Now I find myself ready to switch "positions". Others will come and either build upon or discard the vision(s) I set out. I pray I gave a good example of one willing to switch roles and that I will be gracious when others treat my visions as worthy or not. Who has built up on your visions of yesteryear? Whose visions did you use to formulate your own?

_____

_____

+++

Revelation 12---Highlights: the woman, Israel/church; The Angel, Michael

The book of Revelation is not a simple linear narrative of the sequence of events leading up to the consummation of history. It is a series of images that tell and retell the struggle of forces far beyond the realm of human mastery, forces both good and evil at scales that defy imagination. In Rev. 12, John invokes several Middle Eastern retellings from many different traditions about this cosmic struggle personified by the woman, her offspring, and the evil dragon[1]. The church (some would say Israel) is pictured here in Rev. 12 as a woman with a child pursued by a giant red dragon eventually named as Satan (v.9). The woman is given refuge by God (v. 6), has Michael the angel fight on her defense (v.7), two wings of an eagle (v.14) and the entire earth (v.16) join in concert to protect and preserve her. She is loved and cared for by all the forces of good.

That does not make her offspring (vs. 11, 17) impervious to harm or difficulty. They are persecuted by the dragon Satan (vs. 12-13, 17), and some give their lives to overcome Satan "because of the blood of the Lamb and because of the word of their testimony; they did not love their life even to death." (v.11). His offspring not only persevere, they sacrifice at great cost. Unfortunately, the church of today is more interested in appeasement of evil than the advancement of the gospel, in pulling up the drawbridge and hurling invectives at the crowd a safe distance below rather than going toe to toe with the forces of evil.

<u>Lines on Leadership</u>
This is one of the shorter entries in the book. The struggle is never over until our Creator/Redeemer God declares it so. The "rest" I am promised in Christ (Heb. 4) is internal within my spirit during this life; I shall not know the eternal rest of God, His Shalom, Seine Ruhe until He declares the struggles over. I sometimes balk at having to re-enter the fray over and over, and I chafe at what looks to me as unfair, unprovoked attacks simply because I belong to Christ.

What is one area of your leadership that is constantly attacked from without and from within? If it is unjust, are you willing to strive against it even to (v.11) forsaking one's very life for the honor of your Lord? If the Lord calls you into guerrilla warfare (a constant poke and prod and run and hide to fight another day) or to a full frontal all-out assault (think D-Day invasion), are you ready to engage and to persevere? Are you prepared to do so in the manner and length of time (the number 1260 days in v.5 is repeated throughout Revelation and other biblical references; it denotes a long but measured time of adversity or danger) He dictates?

_____

_____

++

Revelation 13---Highlights: the Beast from the Sea, the Beast from the Earth

    vs. 16-17 "and he causes all the small and the great, and the rich and the poor, and the free men and the slaves, to be given a mark on their right hand or on their forehead, [17] and he provides that no one should be able to buy or to sell, except the one who has the mark, either the name of the beast or the number of his name." (666, v.18)

    Eph. 1.13-14 "In Him, you also, after listening to the message of truth, the gospel of your salvation---having also believed, you were sealed in Him with the Holy Spirit of promise, [14] who is given as a pledge of our inheritance, with a view to the redemption of God's own possession, to the praise of His glory." Throughout scripture from Genesis to Revelation, the evil one attempts to deceive mankind by imitating the Savior. Throughout Revelation, he tries to represent himself as a false Trinity (beast, dragon, false prophet); he has a "fatal" wound and recovers from it (v.3, 12) to imitate the death, burial, and resurrection of Christ, he performs great signs (v.13) to mock the miracles of Christ, and at the end of the chapter he creates a mark that will identify the bearer as belonging to him (famously called the mark of the beast). The Lord gives the believer the Holy Spirit as a pledge or a down payment to show the believer is an heir of the Kingdom (Eph. quote above).

The difference between the beast in Rev. 13 and God is consistent. The beast wants to enslave us, the Lord enables us to become what He created us to be. It has always been frighteningly fascinating to see across the centuries how many people will gladly give up freedom and loyalty for showy displays of power instead of discerning whether or not there is substance behind the glitz (v.4, 13-15). Rhetoric and flashy gestures tend to beguile and bewitch when they should make a person beware. Politicians and religious figures have a special propensity and commensurate resources to lure the masses to their side. When they combine forces, it produces an especially potent pair capable of seducing whole societies.

Lines on Leadership
Discernment can result in a hefty price tag. Those who are aware of the beast's real intentions pay a heavy price (v. 7, 15, & 17). Every eventual leader starts out as a follower; a wise choice must be made as to whether the leader followed is worthy of one's faith. Many potential leaders have deep-sixed their careers by following someone with outsized claims or credentials. What criteria do you use to establish a leader is worthy of your attention, loyalty, and trust?

_____
_____
++

Revelation 14---Highlights: the 144,000; the angel and the Gospel; the reapers

The most remarkable part of Revelation 14 is not the 144,000, symbolic of all believers (vs. 1-5); it is not the reapers (vs. 14-19) whose sickles harvest the entire earth; it is not the amount of blood (v. 20) flowing from the wine press of God's wrath. The most remarkable part is that in the midst of all this, the proclamation of the Gospel continues (vs. 6-8). It is an "eternal" gospel, and it is a global gospel in that it is for "every nation, and tribe and tongue and people" (v.6)

This gospel is not preached in some hidden corner of some village church tucked away in the woods. It is spoken directly to the terror of the beast's temporary upper hand. I get distracted preaching when a lone baby starts crying, or there is undue commotion within the pews. What would I do if the entire crowd was waving guns and threatening bodily harm unless I ceased preaching? Would I continue if the brazen forces of evil personified threatened to storm the stage?

Lines on Leadership
The stakes are high in this chapter. The blessings in v. 13 are the first direct words from the Spirit of God speaking in Revelation (v. 13, "Blessed are the dead who die in the Lord from now on!" "Yes," says the Spirit, "that they may rest from their labors"). This is an open acknowledgment that those who respond to the gospel will pay dearly for it. This is not a deviation from the four gospels, the book of Acts, or any of the epistles; it is consistent with all NT writers who warn that the Gospel will evince retaliation and counteroffensives. The difference is the scale. Would the gospel I now preach and teach wither in the face of such opposition? Would I soften its edges and try to fit in an increasingly hostile environment? Would I be willing to take up the title 'martyr'?
Anyone who stands in the pulpit in front of the "sacred desk" and dares to speak on behalf of God to God's people needs to be aware of the spiritual warfare surrounding his sermon. While the scene in Rev. 14 is indeed frightening, it is a matter of scale, not a matter of uniqueness. Every time a person begins to speak the

gospel and proclaim the need for repentance, the need for submission, the need to lay down one's life in exchange for the truth and life found in Christ, he should realize the forces of evil lurk about, attempting to distract and neutralize the congregation's focus on the Father and His Gospel. (v.7)

_____

_____

++

Revelation 15---Highlights: a heavenly scene but not idyllic

One of the most famous "anticlimaxes" in literature is the "Scouring of the Shire" in *Return of the King*, the third in the *Lord of the Rings* trilogy by J.R.R. Tolkien. After monumental ordeals, challenges, impossible odds, and setbacks, Frodo and Samwise Gamgee take the one Ring up Mount Doom and destroy it, thereby destroying the realm of Sauron. The release of the lands and their peoples from Sauron's evil power is dramatic and inspiring. Yet in Tolkien's masterpiece, once the four Hobbits (Frodo, Samwise, Merry, and Pippin) return to the Shire, instead of the blissful ending depicted in the Peter Jackson film trilogy (the scouring of the Shire is briefly alluded to in the extended version of *The Return of the King*), they find they must once again muster up the courage and fight yet another battle to reclaim the Shire from the minions of the deposed yet still troublesome ex-wizard Saruman.

Rev. 15.2-4 pours onto the page in a rush of joyful song. The reader is tempted to join the chorus singing the "Song of Moses the bond-servant of God and the song of the Lamb." It sounds and appears as if this is the closing curtain, the finale of this multiple-act opera. Yet once again, there is no finality to the song; there is no respite for the victors and martyrs.

V. 5 "⁵After these things I looked, and the temple of the tabernacle was opened, ⁶and the seven angels who had the seven plagues came out of the temple . . . And one of the four living creatures gave to the seven angels seven golden bowls full of the wrath of God, who lives forever and ever." Here we go yet again.

Lines on Leadership
In any military chain of command, there is always a higher-up who gives the orders and sets the parameters, times, and tactics for battle. No matter where I stand in the order of the Kingdom of God, there is always the King of Kings, the Lord of Lords. He alone decides when everything is finished. I may flag and falter, I may pray this last battle was the final one, but the war is not over until a foe is totally vanquished, concedes, or is eliminated. In the case of ultimate things, I can hold on because I know the outcome of this struggle (Rev. 19-22). I write this in the last year of full-time ministry. I would choose personally to quietly glide into retirement; that has not happened as one scenario after another pops up in our churches, demanding my time and effort.

Battle-tested and battle-weary can coexist in the same person. The song in vs. 3-4 does not promise refuge, only the presence of a Redeemer. As long as I am with Him, I can persevere, put on the well-worn armor, and head out to the battlefront one more time. What promise or image do you hold onto in the midst of conflict or battles, an image that promises one day this too shall pass?

_____

_____

++

Revelation 16---Highlights: Six bowls of wrath, Armageddon, a seventh bowl of wrath

Vs. 9, 11 "⁹And men were scorched with fierce heat; and they blasphemed the name of God who has the power over these plagues; and they did not repent, so as to give Him glory." "¹¹and they blasphemed the God of heaven because of their pains and their sores; and they did not repent of their deeds."

The bowls of wrath are poured out in rapid succession, each one terrible in its own right. They are poured out in judgment, not as a show of power or retribution. This is not a wrathful God delighting in each sore (v. 2), each scorching (v. 9), or each throbbing pain (v. 10). The permanence or the passing of each sore, scorched body, or pain is dependent on the response of man in this chapter. A refusal to bend the knee or bow one's spirit in submission to the Father is preceded each time by the cursing of His name and His purpose for mankind (vs. 9-11).

These are times for which there are no adequate words. Vs. 13-16 describe the lead-up to the battle name that strikes fear in the heart of believers and unbelievers alike---Har-Magedon or Armageddon. The plain of Megiddo where this will be fought is today peaceful farmland, easily seen from atop Mt. Carmel or Tel Megiddo; it is hard to imagine such a bucolic scene embroiled in fierce fighting with blood covering the ground (Rev. 14.20). Yet the battle of all battles is actually a side issue in the chapter.

The refusal of men to cry out to God for mercy and deliverance is the main subject. The desire of the Lord is "not wishing for any to perish but for all to come to repentance" (1 Pet. 3.9). My mind is oriented towards pain, as in, whatever I can do to avoid it, I will. The same thing goes for loss; I will do whatever I have to in order to avoid the loss. So it is difficult for me to conceive a God who orders bowls like these to be poured out unless there is an element of redemption.

Repeatedly (see Jn. 6 and Heb. 3 entries), I have to suspend identification with that person in darkness, pain, or illness and understand this is the end result of sin and man's rebellion against God. On a miniscule scale, I can vividly remember our oldest child as a strong-willed toddler who had been told the consequences of his behavior. I remember his insistence I couldn't budge him or make him behave. I can still see him standing defiantly in the hallway of our townhome in Trier, Germany, waiting to see if I would back down from my stated consequences or carry them out. Multiply that by millions upon countless millions of souls defiantly shaking their fists in the face of the Father, temporarily flush with assurances of the unclean spirits' signs (v.13) that they could continue to defy the Almighty. It is a terrible sight to see pride in its last stages, self-deceived; it sees itself as stronger than God.

Lines on Leadership
If God backs down and does not carry out His consequences (repeatedly postponed not out of weakness but out of longsuffering divine forbearance), He is a feckless Father and allows man to ascend the throne of his life instead of its rightful Resident. Every leader has to determine in the day-to-day battles if he/she is fighting for God or fighting God. Every leader will one day be in a position to administer justice that will be personally painful. That is simple to write but difficult to recognize. How do you know you fight for a just cause, for the right side, for truth? How resolutely can you administer proper justice?

_____

_____

++

Revelation 17---Highlights: Babylon, mother of harlots, the victory of the Lamb

Counterfeiting is as old as the Garden of Eden. The serpent tried to present deception as wisdom and revelation, that Eve was getting the "inside track on truth" when, in reality, it was phony. It had the appearance of genuineness; the decision to accept the counterfeit as truth had disastrous effects then and has done so ever since.

The best-known form of contemporary counterfeiting is that of money. The Federal government undertakes great lengths to ensure our country's paper currency is distinguishable from fake denominations. It incorporates numerous layers of colored inks, watermarks, micro-printing, specially blended paper (25% linen, 75% cotton), color-shifting ink, and intricate engraving. Special tools, from UV light to pens to elaborate machines, are needed to detect real bills from expertly manufactured fake ones[1]. The cost to the American economy is staggering, estimated by some agencies as hundreds of billions yearly. And this is just counterfeit money; counterfeit goods, counterfeit medications, and counterfeit online services all conspire to cost the economy hundreds of billions more.

The beast and company are contrasted with the Messiah in Rev. 17 to show their counterfeit ways. John makes sure to contrast the fake with the genuine with the repeated phrase "who was and is not" (vs. 8, 11) as opposed to the Christ, "who is and who was, and who is to come," the eternal I AM (Rev. 1.8). The royal trappings and self-proclaimed titles of the great "mother of harlots" (vs. 4-5) are contrasted with the Lamb's titles of Lord of Lords and King of Kings (v. 14).

<u>Lines on Leadership</u>
If the only thing a person has seen in a given category is counterfeit, how can that person distinguish it from the genuine? "All the ways of a man are pure in his own eyes, but

the Lord weighs the spirit." (Prov. 16.2, ESV) People unfamiliar with the Word of God have a difficult time distinguishing whether the leaders of state or the leaders of our souls are grounded in truth.

The government uses elaborate means to separate counterfeit currency from legal tender; as in Revelation 13, how do you determine whether or not the message and platform of those you follow are genuine or counterfeit?

_____

_____

++

Revelation 18---Highlights: Babylon's demise

John begins to tie up the enormity of Rev. 1-17 as Rev. 18 rushes toward a final climax of history to then usher in a new order of creation. Before a new order can be instituted, the old one must be deposed and disposed of. Rev. 18 is a monumental collapse of whatever ruling power one can imagine: Rome, a corrupt religious system, communism, oligarchy, dictatorship---all are rolled into this image of a fallen institution.

Rev. 18 is representative of the inevitable death of individual civilizations and collectively all human civilizations[1,2]. Every great civilization or institution sees itself as unstoppable, invincible, and incapable of collapse or decline. History says otherwise, with the seeds of its demise usually internal more than external.

Power and self-delusion often reinforce one another to produce a faux assurance of one's destiny. This phenomenon is detailed in Eric Metaxas' bio of Martin Luther as he describes the undoing of Luther's former friend turned foe, Thomas Münster. Münster took Luther's ideas of reform from essence to excess and thought he could bring about revolution and the overthrow of both papacy and royalty by establishing (through violence) a new societal order. He fought nobles, churches, Luther, and anything else that stood in his way, inflamed the longstanding frustrations of peasants into a conflagration of revolt, and became convinced of his lone ability to divine the Almighty's will. He was genuinely surprised when everything fell apart in short order[3].

"'After annihilating all rulers,' Pfeiffer said, 'he intended to carry out a Christian reformation.' But instead, eighty thousand peasants had died, and the Reformation of Luther had been so mixed up with the sprawling blood-soaked tragedy that in the eyes of any inclined against that Reformation, it was further discredited. On May 27 [1525], Münster and fifty-three others---including Pfeiffer among them---were beheaded[4]."

John's personification of this fallen kingdom utters these defiant words in 18.7, "For she says in her heart, 'I sit as a queen and I am not a widow, and will never see mourning.'" His deliberate linkage to Isaiah 47.7ff, Zephaniah 2.15, and Ezekiel 28.2ff is not plagiarism but rather an underscore of his Revelation belonging to the grand tradition of prophecies about the fall of evil and the triumph of good.

Lines on Leadership
Many a ruler or CEO starts off with noble aspirations that eventually transform into manifestations of evil. The transformation is least noticeable to the leader himself. It can occur through the accumulation of power or wealth, adulation, etc. Expedience begins to replace conviction as one's driving force. As a follower of Christ, I rejoice in the overall story of Revelation that the glory and victory belong to the Lord; but as a leader, this chapter and all others in John's Revelation humble me and remind me I need periodic outside evaluations of my

image, intent, and outcomes. This has been asked before, but who or what helps you to examine your motives, whether or not entropy has set in, or if you have developed a fatal flaw in your leadership?

_____

_____

++

Revelation 19---Highlights: 4x hallelujah, marriage of the Lamb, Christ's coming, Beast and False Prophet

    Most great museums do not merely display great artifacts; each visitor is engaged by exhibits, informed by plaques or videos, and enveloped with multi-sensory experiences. The Art Institute of Chicago fascinates and frustrates. Each room is a feast for the senses and the spirit, with countless statues, armor, paintings, jewelry, tapestries, and everything that celebrates human creativity. I have been multiple times and never scratched the surface of its total offerings. Entrance to the Smithsonian Air and Space Museum is an immediate visual overload as biplanes to space vehicles hover overhead, ready to sweep the visitor into realms unknown. The British Museum in London seems to have something from every ten minutes of human history; my favorite spot there is to stand in front of the Rosetta Stone and tell myself repeatedly, "I am standing in front of THE Rosetta Stone."

    The book of Revelation is roughly analogous to those museums. There is the route suggested by the brochure a visitor receives with his ticket on which rooms to see first, which would correspond to reading Revelation straight through by chapters. Upon multiple visits, one may want to spend more time in one "room/chapter" than the others. Special programs staged periodically by the museum offer a grander metanarrative of the centuries.

Rev. 19 is that special room where all of the museum hallways converge. The grand themes are all on display at once, the visitor's head spinning from one image to another. One scene is a new yet familiar iteration of heavenly throngs from previous chapters singing hallelujahs to the victorious God. Another scene is the marriage supper of Christ the Lamb. Yet another has a conquering army with Christ leading the way on a white horse. That scene's action leads the visitor's eyes to the fourth scene as the beast and the false prophet are thrown alive into the lake of fire. Every battle, every sacrifice, and every loss comes crashing together in an exultant, eternal shout of victory. Let the celebrations commence.

Lines on Leadership

Every museum displays an average of less than 10% of its cumulative holdings at any one time[1]. At the end of John's gospel, he writes: "And there are also many other things which Jesus did, which if they were written in detail, I suppose that even the world itself would not contain the books which were written." (John 21.25) As spectacular in scope and grandeur as Rev. 19 is, I suspect it is but the proverbial tip of the iceberg of what God desires to show us. Rather than a still mural on a large wall, each scene is more like a holographic entry point where the person can step into it as it occurs and be in the middle as it unfolds. It is where time and eternity intersect.

A leader must draw wisely from life experiences and the accumulated cultural trappings of his/her institution if the leader wants to construct a narrative for others that accurately portrays its heritage and future. What led to your group's greatest triumph? What points the way to your group's future that you would want to display in that special room where all hallways converged?

++

Revelation 20---Highlights: binding, brief freedom, and eventual doom of Satan; God's judgment throne

The meaning of the millennium (mentioned in vs. 2, 3, 4, 5, 6, & 7) has never found a clear consensus. Its repeated mentions have spawned several sub-branches of *eschatology* (the study of last things) using the prefixes **a**-millennial (using the Greek prefix meaning none, so no such thing as a special or literal millennium); **pre**-millennial (certain things have to occur before the millennium is ushered in); **post**-millennial (certain things have to wait until the millennium has passed; for some this includes the 2nd coming of Christ); and the very bad preacher joke, **pan**-millennial (meaning everything will pan out). Much of the confusion comes from whether the millennium is a literal 1000 years, symbolic of an unspecified long time, or another unknown period.

Satan, who has caused untold and immeasurable misery among mankind, is inexplicably loosed for a short time in v. 7 to once more wreak havoc and then three verses later is cast into the lake of fire to join his hirelings, the beast and the false prophet forever. If the millennium is a literal 1000 years, and this is sequential, it makes little sense to bind Satan (v.2) and "store" him in "the abyss" for 1000 years only to let him for some fresh air, gather together a large army and wage war. If the scene is viewed as yet another perspective/facet on the events already described in previous chapters (16.13-17.8), the emphasis is not on the details but the conclusion: the forces of evil that have plagued mankind since the fall (Gen. 3) are once and for all eliminated from ever plaguing humanity again. The accuser who constantly brings up our shortcomings, sins, and failures in the heavenly courts will be absent during the great white throne judgment of God (vs. 11-15)

Lines on Leadership
Regardless of the sequence of events, the outcome is sure: God wins, and Satan loses (vs. 12-15). In war, sport, business, and church, if one senses the end is near, that is not the time to let up or let down one's guard; finish strong and finish well must remain the mindset of a successful leader. What is your tendency as you lead and sense you are coming to the end of the struggle/battle? Do you take the foot off the gas pedal? Do you maintain course? What signal are you waiting on to tell you it is time to lay down your arms and cease fighting?

_____
_____
++

Revelation 21---Highlights: The New Heaven and Earth, the New Jerusalem

Few things in Revelation generate more discussion than the nature of the New Heaven and the New Earth. Are the new Heaven and Earth literal and permanent or temporary replacements for the old Heaven and Earth? Are they symbolic of a new existence in the afterlife? For some theologians, heaven is reserved for God and angelic beings, and man was made for the earth; on the earth will he always live. Others believe the new Heaven and Earth are earth-bound corollaries for indescribable eternal places of abode.

Whether or not the new Jerusalem is a stand-in for the church, an enormous giant jewel bedecked apartment complex, the ultimate in urban renewal (v. 16, 1500 mi. width x 1500 mi.

length x 1500 mi. height= 3,375,000,000 cubic miles), or designed to be a poetic expression of a place befitting a deity's dwelling place (vs. 22-23), we will not know until we see it. It is easy to degenerate into meaningless arguments and speculations (would some sides of the city be more desirable than others, like mountain or seaside views? Would there ever be apartment swapping, a penthouse reserved for special saints, or apartments on the inside of the structure like the more affordable rooms on a cruise ship)?

The emphasis of chapter 21 is not <u>where</u> we will live eternally but with <u>Whom</u>. As in John's gospel, the emphasis is not on our living quarters but on the Person with whom we will spend eternity (Jn. 14.3, "I go to prepare a place for you. I will come again, and receive you to Myself; <u>that where I am, there you may be also</u>." Jn. 12.26, "If anyone serves Me, let him follow Me; and <u>where I am there shall my servant also be;</u> if anyone serves Me, the Father will honor him." [emphasis mine])

v.3, "And I heard a loud voice from the throne saying, 'Behold, the tabernacle of God is among men, and He shall dwell among them, and they shall be His people, and God Himself shall be among them.'" v. 5, "He who sits on the throne said, 'Behold, I am making all things new." v. 23, "And the city has no need of the sun or of the moon to shine upon it, for the glory of God has illumined it, and its lamp is the Lamb."

Throughout the Revelation, the throne of God is emphasized (4.5, 7.17, 20.11, 21.3, 22.1), partly to portray God's majesty but also to show God's desire to be in the midst of His people.

<u>Lines on Leadership</u>
Leadership has always debated the proper distance to maintain with group members. From the beginning of creation, God has

desired to be not only accessible to but in the midst of His people. From the Garden of Eden to the Tabernacle in the Wilderness to His temple in Jerusalem to His Holy Spirit indwelling His church, the redeemed, to the very name Immanuel, meaning God with us---it has been His aim and desire for us to dwell with Him. How do you demonstrate to the group you lead that you not only appreciate what they do for you but that you are fiercely devoted to them?

_____

_____

++

Revelation 22---Highlights: The River of Life, Tree of Life, Final Messages

Revelation contains over 500 allusions to the OT; the majority of its verses contain references to an OT text[1]. It is firmly rooted in the biblical promises and grand story of creation, redemption, and reunion.

The Bible begins with the Garden of Eden and ends with a spectacular orchard with the tree of life on either side of a river that flows from the throne of God (vs. 1-2). It begins with the fall of man and expulsion from that garden (Gen. 3); it ends with a final judgment of mankind and God living again among His people[2] (Rev. 20-22). In the Bible's initial chapters, we find the first promise of a Messiah (Gen. 3.15); in the gospels, we find Jesus Christ as the manifestation of that promise; and in its last chapter, we receive the promise that He will rule forever and ever (Rev. 22.1-5). The first words of God in Genesis are the declaration, "Let there be light" (Gen. 1.3); in John's gospel, Jesus is declared the light of the world (Jn. 1.4-9, 8.12); and in Rev. 22 He who sits upon the throne of God and the Lamb will Himself illumine the people of God forever (v.5).

Time will not be the dominant factor in eternity. We speak of forever and a day, forever and ever, eternal life consisting of an endless string of events because a passage of time is the only existence we know on earth. We think in terms of eternity as length without limits, going on and on; perhaps eternity is an eternal present, an eternity bound up in each moment, like multiverses within multiverses or an as-yet unimagined existence. Time is simultaneous of no concern and of deep concern in Rev. 22. On one hand, Rev. 22.5 tells us there will be no passage of day into night, and no sun will appear and disappear again because God Himself will be our constant light. Yet the chapter mentions twice that Christ is coming quickly (vs. 7, 20).

John's vision is firmly connected to the past and the future as he concludes Revelation. He moves between timely occurrences in tight sequences and timeless messages of triumph and overcoming sin, death, and evil. He honors the prophecies of his people (Jews) yet speaks of the gathered nations of every tribe and tongue. This all-encompassing series of dioramas called Revelation ends with a double Amen (vs. 20-21) and a reminder that the grace of the Lord Jesus is ours today and the presence of the Lord Jesus will one day be ours forever. It is a fitting end to Revelation and the NT. Amen, Come, Lord Jesus.

Lines on Leadership

What God started, He will finish. Every time I visit the land of Israel, I become more and more convinced of the inevitability of Christ's return. Personally, I hope it occurs in my lifetime, as has every believer since Christ promised 3x in John 14 (vs. 3, 18, 28) He would return for us. Whatever scales Christ uses to equate "quickly" (Rev. 22.12, 20) with 2000 years and counting is for Him to decide. Because of everything I have read in the NT and decades of watching Christ at work in my life, I have no doubt that what He starts, He will finish.

As a leader, I pray I can stay true to my mission in life until I finish it or pass it on to the next generation for fulfillment. I pray my life has been in line with 22.17, where the Spirit, the church, and the one seeking eternal life all agree: even so, come Lord Jesus. Is that your prayer as well?

_____
_____

++

FINAL THOUGHTS

Each of the 260 chapter entries was designed to let its truth emerge through the lens of leadership. If you have begun to read the Word of God through "leadership eyes", I pray it is a habit you find beneficial and will pass on to others. After decades of teaching others to teach others to teach others, I have great confidence in the succeeding generations to take the reins and servant towels (see John 13 entry) of leadership within our churches, corporations, and communities. If you consider yourself part of the "next" generation of Kingdom leadership, I pray you will serve, adapt, and transform as you lead, always to His glory and for His honor. To dialogue with the author about any of the ideas contained in this book (or any other subject), please write to: reflectionalleadershipat@gmail.com.

FOOTNOTES

<u>Matthew 2</u>—[1]may-ji, a caste of wise men specializing in astrology, medicine, and natural science; from liner notes, Hebrew-Greek Key Study Bible, ed. Spiros Zodhiates, 1990, AMG Publishers, Chattanooga, TN. p. 1260.

[2] accounts of Muslims encountering Christ in dreams, https://www.ifoundthetruth.com, accessed 12-20-22.

<u>Matthew 8</u>— [1] James Lovell, poem The Present Crisis, accessed 12-20-22, https://poets.org/poem/present-crisis.

[2] Leonard Sweet, *Rings of Fire: Walking in Faith Through a Volcanic Future* (Colorado Springs, CO: NavPress, 2019), p. x.

<u>Matthew 10</u>---[1] Max DePree, *Leadership is an Art (*New York, NY: Doubleday, 1989), p. 9.

[2] William Cohen, *Drucker on Leadership: New Lessons from the Father of Modern Management* (San Francisco CA: Jossey-Bass, 2010), p. 4.

<u>Matthew 11</u>—[1]*CSB Study Bible* Nashville, TN: Holman Bible Publishers, 2017), p. 1519.

<u>Matthew 13</u>—[1] for an explanation of tares' origin and growing habits, see https://www.biblestudytools.com/dictionary/tares, accessed 12-20-22.

<u>Matthew 15</u>—[1] Dr. Bob Utley took several years to compile the Free Bible Commentary, an excellent resource for NT studies. It is free to all at www.freebiblecommentary.org and also a part of Logos Bible Software. This specific reference is found at http://www.freebiblecommentary.org/new_testament_studies/VOL01/VOL01_15.html

<u>Matthew 18</u>---[1] C.S. Lewis, *Mere Christianity* (New York: Touchstone, 1996), pp 74-75.

<u>Matthew 20</u>—[1]ESV Study Bible, English Standard Version, Crossway Bibles, Wheaton, IL, 2008. P.1862.

Matthew 21—[1] Bob Utley, accessed 2-20-22, http://www.freebiblecommentary.org/new_testament_studies/VOL01/VOL01_21.html.

Matthew 22-[1] Avery Willis and Kay Moore, *The Disciple's Cross: MasterLife, Book 1* (Nashville, TN: Lifeway Press, 1996).

Matthew 25—[1] D.T. Niles quote on evangelism, https://www.goodreads.com/quotes/9696369-evangelism-is-just-one-beggar-telling-another-where-to-find, accessed Dec. 23, 2022.

================================

Mark 3—[1] Jim Collins, *Good to Great: Why Some Companies Make the Leap…and Others Don't* (New York, NY: HarperCollins, 2001), p. 41.

Mark 7 --- [1] The Expositor's Bible Commentary, Frank Gaebelein, general editor, Zondervan, Grand Rapids, MI, 1984, vol. 8, p. 678.

Mark 11---[1] Collins, *Good to Great*, pp. 17-40.

Mark 15---[1] ESV Study Bible, p. 1931 and p. 2184

Mark 16---[1] Wayne C. Booth, Gregory G. Colomb, Joseph M. Williams, *The Craft of Research*, 2nd ed. (Chicago IL: University of Chicago Press, 2003), p.84.

==

Luke 3---[1] Gaebelein, Expositor's, vol. 8, pp. 854-855. Also, based on the author's personal visits to Qumran in 2016 and 2019.

Luke 6---[1] Jim Putnam, *DiscipleShift: Five Steps That Help Your Church to Make Disciples Who Make Disciples* (Grand Rapids MI: Zondervan, 2013).

[2] Reggie McNeal, *The Present Future: Six Tough Questions for the Church* (San Francisco, CA: Jossey-Bass, 2003), p. 144.

Luke 14—[1] Hans Rosling, *Factfulness: Ten Reasons We're Wrong About the World—and Why Things Are Better Than You Think* (New York, NY: Flatiron Books, 2018).

[2] Stephen Covey, *The 7 Habits of Highly Effective People: Restoring the Character Ethic* (New York, NY: Simon & Schuster, 2004).

Luke 16—[1] Adm. William McRaven, *Make Your Bed: Little Things That Can Change Your Life...and Maybe the World* (New York, NY: Grand Central Publishing, 2017).

Luke 19—[1] CSB, p. 1643.

[2] ESV, p. 1997.

Luke 20—[1] https://www.dictionary.com/browse/diplomacy, see definition #3, accessed 12-20-22.

Luke 21—[1] https://www.biblegateway.com/resources/encyclopedia-of-the-bible/Treasury-Temple, accessed 12-20-22.

Luke 22—[1] Jeanne Damoff, *Parting the Waters: Finding Beauty in Brokenness.* (WinePress Publishing. BookBaby. 2008).

==

John 3---[1] DePree, p. 9.

John 4---[1] CSB, p. 1673.

[2] Kenneth Bailey, *Jesus Through Middle Eastern Eyes: Cultural Studies in the Gospels* (Downers Grove IL: IVP Academic, 2008), p. 203.

[3] HLN news broadcast, Robin Meade, anchor, Friday, Feb. 19, 2021. HLN ceased broadcasting as a subsidiary of CNN in Dec. 2022.

John 5---Ron Heifetz is the author of several excellent books on adaptive leadership. The two I personally recommend are:

[1] Ronald A. Heifetz and Marty Linsky, *Leadership on the Line* (Boston, MA: Harvard Business School Press, 2002) also

[2] Ronald A. Heifetz, Ronald, Alexander Grashow, and Marty Linksy, *The Practice of Adaptive Leadership* (Boston, MA: Harvard Business School Press, 2009).

John 9—[1] ESV, p. 2042.

John 12—[1]YouTube video interview on Acoustic Letter with Tony Polecastro and Bob Taylor, 2016. https://www.youtube.com/watch?v=r2nxIf4uMQo.

John 13---[1]to view the Max Greinke sculpture of Jesus washing the disciples feet, see http://www.divineservantart.com/ also see https://artoffaith.net/collections/divine-servant/products/divine-servant-life-size-bronze, accessed 12-24-22.

[2] Oscar Thompson, *Concentric Circles of Concern* (Nashville TN: Broadman Press, 1981), pp. 84-101.

[3] Gene Wilkes, *Jesus on Leadership: Timeless Wisdom on Servant Leadership* (Carol Stream IL: Tyndale House Publishers, 1998), p.21.

[4] Henri Nouwen, *In the Name of Jesus: Reflections on Christian Leadership* (New York NY: Crossroad Publishing, 1989), pp. 82-84.

[5] James M. Kouzes, and Barry Z. Posner, *The Leadership Challenge: How to Make Extraordinary Things Happen in Organizations*, 6th ed. (Hoboken NJ: Wiley and Sons, 2017).

[6] The Leadership Challenge (TLC), pp. 71-72.

John 16---[1] Arthur F. Holmes, *The Idea of a Christian College* (Grand Rapids MI: Eerdmans, 1975), p. 47.

[2] http://www.understandchristianity.com/basic-teachings-of-christianity/the-trinity/, accessed 12-20-22.

John 18--[1]James K. Dew Jr. and Mark W. Foreman, *How Do We Know: An Introduction to Epistemology* (Downers Grove IL: Intervarsity Press, 2020), p. ix.

==

Acts 1---[1]McNeal, p. 92.

Acts 2---[1] Eric Metaxas, *Martin Luther: The Man Who Rediscovered God and Changed the World* (New York NY: Viking Penguin Random House, 2017), p. 21.

² to introduce the reader to the subject of AI and its implications for society, the author suggests:

Joshua K. Smith, *Robotic Persons: Our Future with Social Robots* (Bloomington IN: Westbow Press, 2021).

James Barrat, *Our Final Invention: Artificial Intelligence and the End of the Human Era* (New York NY: Thomas Dunne Books, 2013).

Acts 6—The author suggests a good short intro to the impact of culture on ministry is: ¹ Sherwood G. Lingenfelter and Marvin K. Mayers, *Ministering Cross Culturally: an Incarnational Model for Personal Relationships* (Grand Rapids MI: Baker Book House, 1986).

Acts 8—For an account of the Buffalo NY mass shooting incident see: ¹https://www.nbcnews.com/news/us-news/buffalo-supermarket-shooting-suspect-posted-apparent-manifesto-repeate-rcna28889.

Acts 10---¹ Jim Collins and Jerry I. Porras, *Built to Last: Successful Habits of Visionary Companies* (New York NY: Harper Business, HarperCollins, 2002). The author suggests reading chapter 4 (Preserve the Core/Stimulate Progress) and chapter 5 (Big Hairy Audacious Goals).

Acts 11—¹ Gaebelein, *Expositor*, vol. 9, p. 399.

² https://www.biblegateway.com/resources/encyclopedia-of-the-bible/Cyrene, accessed 12-20-22.

Acts12---¹ see: https://my.clevelandclinic.org/health/articles/22229-cephalohematoma, accessed 12-21-22.

² Christian hymn It Is Well With My Soul, Horatio McSpafford, verse 1, accessed 12-20-22 at https://hymnary.org/text/when_peace_like_a_river_attendeth_my_way.

³ Gaebelein, *Expositor*, vol. 9, p. 413.

Acts 16---[1] Henry Blackaby and Claude King. *Experiencing God* (Nashville TN: Lifeway Press, 1990), p. 107.

==

Romans, intro---[1] Specimens of the Table Talk of the late Samuel Taylor Coleridge, vol. II. 1835. John Murray, London, p. 193.

Romans 5—[1] Tod Bolsinger, *Canoeing the Mountains: Christian Leadership in Uncharted Territory* (Downers Grove IL: Intervarsity Press, 2018), p.21.

I recommend this book very highly among recent entries in leadership literature. Bolsinger takes a similar approach to mine of emphasizing servant, adaptive, and transformational leadership and brilliantly uses the historic Lewis and Clark expedition as the book's framework.

[2] Bolsinger, ibid.

Romans 6---[1] Dylan, Bob. *Slow Train Coming*, "Gotta Serve Somebody," multiple labels over the years, first released on August 20, 1979.

Romans 8---[1] The Mission was a motion picture released in 1986, directed by Roland Joffe, starring Jeremy Irons, Robert Di Niro, and Liam Neeson. The basic information on the film can be found at: imbd.com or URL link https://www.imdb.com/title/tt0091530/?ref_=fn_al_tt_1, accessed 12-22-22.

The particular scene of Mendoza's attempt at repentance can be viewed at: https://www.youtube.com/watch?v=xoJKszzC7L0, accessed on 12-22-22.

Romans 11—[1] Os Guinness, *The Call: Finding and Fulfilling the Central Purpose of Your Life* (Nashville TN: Word Publishing, 1998), p. 31.

[2] Guinness, p. 46.

Romans 13—[1] website for archbishops remarks as Queen Elizabeth's funeral, Sept. 19, 2022 https://www.archbishopofcanterbury.org/speaking-writing/sermons/archbishop-canterburys-sermon-state-funeral-her-majesty-queen-elizabeth-ii

² Ibid.

Romans 15---¹ https://www.sciencedaily.com/releases/2007/05/070525000642.htm. see also https://www.usnews.com/news/cities/articles/2018-10-02/the-urbanization-of-the-globe-what-it-means-for-our-growing-cities, both accessed 12-20-22.

² Nouwen, pp. 81-82.

Romans 16---¹ James Taylor, recorded album *Hourglass*. "Line 'Em All Up," released May 20, 1997.

² Kouzes & Posner, pp. 245-294.

===

1 Corinthians 2---¹ Michael Pollan, *In Defense of Food: An Eater's Manifesto* (New York NY: The Penguin Press, 2008), pp. 148-150.

² Pollan, p. 1, 10.

1 Cor. 3---¹ Prayer of St. Francis accessed 12-25-22 at https://www.ewtn.com/catholicism/devotions/prayer-of-st-francis-837

1 Cor. 4---¹ From a sermon preached by Dr. Jeff Iorg, then president of Gateway Seminary, CA, at the Shepherding the Shepherds conference at Canaan Valley, WV, July 13, 2021, author in attendance.

² Wilkes, p. 121ff.

³ *Lincoln*, a 2012 film by Steven Spielberg, main actor Daniel Day-Lewis, the scene is Lincoln pressing for the passage of the 13th amendment, https://www.youtube.com/watch?v=1qjtugr2618, accessed on 12-25-22.

1 Cor. 10---¹ Nouwen, p. 77.

² George Orwell, *Nineteen Eighty-four: Oxford's World Classics,* ed. John Bowen (Oxford UK: Oxford University Press, 2021), p.205.

1 Cor. 15---¹ https://www.dictionary.com/browse/axiom, accessed 12-25-22.

1 Cor. 16---¹ Heifetz, *Leadership on the Line*, p.223. Kouzes & Posner, p. 313 as two examples among many.

===

2 Cor. 2—¹Ron Dunn sermon on Chained to the Chariot, http://rondunn.com/chained-to-the-chariot/, accessed 12-23-22.

² Gabelein, vol. 10, p. 332.

³Philip E. Hughes, The Second Epistle to the Corinthians: TNICNT (Grand Rapids MI: Eerdmans, 1962), pp. 76-84.

2 Cor. 3—¹ Full-length movie "The Matrix," released 1999, directed by L. and L. Wachowski, main actors Keanu Reeves, Laurence Fishburne, Carrie Moss: https://www.imdb.com/title/tt0133093/?ref_=fn_al_tt_1, accessed 12-30-22.

2 Cor. 6—¹ Gordon T. Smith, *Wisdom from Babylon: Leadership for the Church in a Secular Age* (Downers Grove IL: IVP Academic-Intervarsity Press, 2020), p. 93-94.

² Lesslie Newbigin, *Foolishness to the Greeks: The Gospel and Western Culture* (Grand Rapids MI: Eerdmans, 1986).

2 Cor. 7—¹ Blackaby and King, pp. 83-107.

2 Cor. 10---¹ Walter Isaacson, *The Code Breaker: Jennifer Doudna, Gene Editing, and the Future of the Human Race* (New York NY: Simon & Schuster, 2021).

² https://leadergrow.com/wp-content/uploads/2019/09/Trust-but-Verify.pdf downloaded 11-22-2022.

[3] Stephen Covey, *Smart Trust: The Defining Skill that Transforms Managers into Leaders* (New York NY: Free Press, Simon & Schuster, 2012).

===

Galatians 3---[1] Phillip Jenkins, *The Next Christendom: The Coming of Global Christianity* (Oxford UK: Oxford University Press, 2002), p.2.

Galatians 6---[1] Roger Parrott, *The Longview: Lasting Strategies for Rising Leaders* (Colorado Springs CO: David Cook), 2009.

===

Ephesians 3—[1] Orwell, George, *Animal Farm* (first pub. 1944. Current web edition public domain by eBooks@Adelaide, 2014), p. 103.

[2] Kouzes & Posner, p. xiv.

[3] Kouzes & Posner, p. 97.

Ephesians 4---[1] Alan Hirsch, *5Q: Reactivating the Original Intelligence and Capacity of the Body of Christ* (Colombia: 100movements.com, 2017).

===

Philippians 2—[1] Gaebelein, vol. 11., p.123.

Philippians 3—[1] https://www.casestudyinc.com/ge-turnaround-and-jack-welch-leadership/, accessed 12-20-22.

===

Colossians 3---[1] DePree, p. 98.

===

1 Thess. 3---[1] https://www.dictionary.com/browse/fiduciary, accessed 12-20-22.

===

2 Thessalonians intro ----[1] Zodhiates, p. 1592.

2 Thessalonians 1---[1] https://www.litcharts.com/lit/twilight-of-the-idols/maxims-and-arrows, accessed 12-20-22.

2 Thessalonians 3--[1] https://churchleaders.com/pastors/free-resources-pastors/145403-brother-lawrence-free-ebook-the-practice-of-the-presence-of-god.html, accessed 12-19-22.

==

1 Timothy 1---[1] Jeff Iorg, *Seasons of a Leader's Life: Learning, Leading, and Leaving Your Legacy* (Nashville TN: B&H Publishing Group, 2013). Anything Dr. Iorg writes is well grounded in scripture and everyday life. I highly recommend anything he has written.

[2] Jeff Iorg, *Leading Major Change in Your Ministry* (Nashville TN: B&H Publishing Group, 2018), p. 7.

1 Timothy 3---[1] Gaebelein, *Expositor*, v. 11, p. 365.

1 Timothy 6---[1] Eugene Peterson, *A Long Obedience in the Same Direction: Discipleship in an Instant Society*, 2nd ed. (Downers Grove IL: Intervarsity Press, 2000).

==

2 Timothy 2---[1] Dietrich Bonhoeffer, *Life Together: The Classic Exploration of Faith in Community* (San Francisco CA: Harper & Row Publishers, 1954).

2 Timothy 4--[1] Steven Curtis Chapman, artist; song, The Great Adventure; lyrics. https://www.azlyrics.com/lyrics/stevencurtischapman/thegreatadventure.html accessed at 12-19-22.

==

Titus 1---[1] https://www.chick-fil-a.com/franchise, accessed 11-20-21.

Titus 3---[1] Joyce Landorf, *Irregular People* (Waco TX: Word Books, 1982).

==

Philemon—[1] Full-length movie Schindler's List, released 1993, directed by Steven Spielberg, main actors Liam Neeson, Ralph Fiennes, Ben Kingsley. The scene mentioned is at the end of the film when Schindler is leaving the workers he has saved from the Nazis: https://www.youtube.com/watch?v=3g4LxLHoIag, accessed 12-26-22.

===

Hebrews 1---[1] In 2022, an unknown group funded and broadcast in print, video, and streaming platforms an advertising campaign known as He Gets Us designed to show Jesus as an empathetic Savior: https://hegetsus.com/en, accessed 12-20-22.

Hebrews 5---[1] WIRED magazine, Oct. 2022 issue, p. 36, quote of Marshall McLuhan's on a short story by Edgar Allan Poe. Story written by Anthony Lydgate and was entitled "Abandon Ship."

Hebrews 10---[1] Daniel Goleman, *Social Intelligence: The New Science of Human Relationships* (New York NY: Bantam Books, 2006), p.43.

Hebrews 13---[1] Online article describing the inverted pyramid of priorities for Southwest Airlines: https://leaderchat.org/2011/01/10/customers-employees-and-shareholders%E2%80%94who-comes-first-in-your-organization/, accessed 11-20-22.

===

James, intro---[1] Zodhiates, p. 1636.

James 1---[1] Frances Hesselbein and Eric K. Shinseki, *Be/Know/Do: Leadership the Army Way* (San Francisco CA: Jossey-Bass, 2004).

===

1 Peter 2---[1] Psychology Today article, 5 Keys About Identity Theory, posted Jan. 25, 2019: https://www.psychologytoday.com/us/blog/science-choice/201901/5-key-ideas-about-identity-theory, accessed 12-18-22.

[2] Robert S. McGee, *The Search for Significance* (Nashville TN: Thomas Nelson, 2003), chapter on Performance Trap, p. 29ff.

1 Peter 5---[1] Wilkes, pp. 31, 59, 85.

[2] Wilkes, p. 131.

===

1 John 2---[1] Paul D. Stanley and Robert J. Clinton, *Connecting: The Mentoring Relationships You Need in Life* (Colorado Springs CO: NavPress, 1992), p 35-46.

===

2 John----[1] Zodhiates, p. 1666.

===

Revelation 1--- [1] YouTube video, Oprah's Next Chapter, OWN network, Oprah Winfrey interview with Daniel Day-Lewis on developing the voice he used for Spielberg's biopic Lincoln, https://www.youtube.com/watch?v=5g9v8y5FvSo, accessed 12-21-22.

Revelation 5---[1] Utley, http://www.freebiblecommentary.org/new_testament_studies/VOL12/VOL12_03.html

Revelation 12---[1] Utley, http://www.freebiblecommentary.org/new_testament_studies/VOL12/VOL12_07.html

Revelation 17---[1] Fit Small Business online article, How to Detect Counterfeit Money: 8 Ways to Tell if a Bill is Fake, https://fitsmallbusiness.com/how-to-detect-counterfeit-money/, accessed 12-30-22.

Revelation 18---[1] G.B. Caird, *A Commentary on the Revelation of St. John the Divine* (New York NY: Harper & Row, 1966), p. 223.

[2] Leon Morris, *The Revelation of St. John: An Introduction and Commentary* (Grand Rapids MI: Eerdmans, 1976), p. 214.

[3] Metaxas, Eric. *Martin Luther: The Man Who Rediscovered God and Changed the World* (New York NY: Viking Penguin Random House, 2017), pp. 315-337.

[4] Metaxas, p. 337.

<u>Revelation 19</u>---[1]   Online article on storage versus display percentages of large museums, https://qz.com/583354/why-is-so-much-of-the-worlds-great-art-in-storage, accessed 12-23-22.

<u>Revelation 22</u>--- [1] Douglas Ezell, *Revelations on Revelation: New Sounds from Old Symbols* (Waco TX: Word Books, 1977), p. 20.

[2] ESV, p. 2945.

BIBLIOGRAPHY

Bailey, Kenneth. *Jesus Through Middle Eastern Eyes: Cultural Studies in the Gospels*. Downers Grove IL: IVP Academic, 2008.

Barrat, James. *Our Final Invention: Artificial Intelligence and the End of the Human Era*. New York NY: Thomas Dunne Books, 2013.

Blackaby, Henry, and King, Claude. *Experiencing God*. Nashville, TN: LifeWay Press, 1990.

Bolsinger, Tod. *Canoeing the Mountains: Christian Leadership in Uncharted Territory*. Downers Grove IL: Intervarsity Press, 2018.

Bonhoeffer, Dietrich. *Life Together: The Classic Exploration of Faith in Community*. San Francisco CA: Harper & Row Publishers, 1954.

Booth, Wayne C., Colomb, Gregory G., Williams, Joseph M. *The Craft of Research*. 2nd ed. Chicago IL: University of Chicago Press, 2003.

Cohen, William. *Drucker on Leadership: New Lessons from the Father of Modern Management*. San Francisco CA: Jossey-Bass, 2010.

Caird, G.B. *A Commentary on the Revelation of St. John the Divine*. New York NY: Harper & Row, 1966.

Collins, Jim. *Good to Great: Why Some Companies Make the Leap...and Others Don't*. New York, NY: HarperCollins, 2001.

Collins, Jim and Porras, Jerry I. *Built to Last: Successful Habits of Visionary Companies*. New York NY: Harper Business, HarperCollins, 2002.

Covey, Stephen. *The 7 Habits of Highly Effective People: Restoring the Character Ethic*. New York, NY: Simon & Schuster, 2004.

Covey, Stephen. *Smart Trust: The Defining Skill that Transforms Managers into Leaders.* New York NY: Free Press, Simon & Schuster, 2012.

Damoff, Jeanne. Parting the Waters: Finding Beauty in Brokenness. WinePress Publishing. BookBaby, 2008.

DePree, Max. *Leadership is an Art.* New York, NY: Doubleday, 1989.

Dew Jr., James K. and Foreman, Mark W. *How Do We Know?: An Introduction to Epistemology.* Downers Grove IL IVP Press, 2020.

Ezell, Douglas. *Revelations on Revelation: New Sounds from Old Symbols.* Waco TX: Word Books, 1977.

Gaebelein, Frank, gen. ed. *The Expositor's Bible Commentary.* Zondervan, Grand Rapids, MI, 1984.

Goleman, Daniel. *Social Intelligence: The New Science of Human Relationships.* New York NY: Bantam Books, 2006.

Guinness, Os. *The Call: Finding and Fulfilling the Central Purpose of Your Life.* Nashville TN: Word Publishing, 1998.

Heifetz, Ronald A. and Linsky, Marty. *Leadership on the Line.* Boston, MA: Harvard Business School Press, 2002.

Heifetz, Ronald A., Grashow, Alexander, and Linksy, Marty. *The Practice of Adaptive Leadership.* Boston, MA: Harvard Business School Press, 2009.

Hesselbein, Frances and Shinseki, Eric K. *Be/Know/Do: Leadership the Army Way.* San Francisco CA: Jossey-Bass, 2004.

Hirsch, Alan. *5Q: Reactivating the Original Intelligence and Capacity of the Body of Christ.* Colombia: 100movements.com, 2017.

Holmes, Arthur F. *The Idea of a Christian College.* Grand Rapids MI: Eerdmans, 1975.

Hughes, Philip E. *The Second Epistle to the Corinthians: The New*

International Commentary on the New Testament. Grand Rapids MI: Eerdmans, 1962.

Iorg, Jeff. *Leading Major Change in Your Ministry*. Nashville TN: B&H Publishing Group, 2018.

Iorg, Jeff. *Seasons of a Leader's Life: Learning, Leading, and Leaving Your Legacy*. Nashville TN: B&H Publishing Group, 2013.

Isaacson, Walter. *The Code Breaker: Jennifer Doudna, Gene Editing, and the Future of the Human Race*. New York NY: Simon & Schuster, 2021.

Jenkins, Phillip. *The Next Christendom: The Coming of Global Christianity*. Oxford UK: Oxford University Press, 2002.

Kouzes, James M., and Posner, Barry Z. *The Leadership Challenge: How to Make Extraordinary Things Happen in Organizations*, 6th ed. Hoboken NJ: Wiley and Sons, 2017.

Landorf, Joyce. *Irregular People*. Waco TX: Word Books, 1982.

Lingenfelter, Sherwood G. and Mayers, Marvin K. *Ministering Cross Culturally: an Incarnational Model for Personal Relationships*. Grand Rapids MI: Baker Book House, 1986.

McGee, Robert S. *The Search for Significance*. Nashville TN: Thomas Nelson, 2003.

McNeal, Reggie. *The Present Future: Six Tough Questions for the Church*. San Francisco, CA: Jossey-Bass, 2003.

McRaven, Adm. William. *Make Your Bed: Little Things that Can Change Your Life...and Maybe the World*. New York, NY: Grand Central Publishing, 2017.

Metaxas, Eric. *Martin Luther: The Man Who Rediscovered God and Changed the World*. New York NY: Viking Penguin Random House, 2017.

Morris, Leon. *The Revelation of St. John: An Introduction and Commentary*. Grand Rapids MI: Eerdmans, 1976.

Newbigin, Lesslie. *Foolishness to the Greeks: The Gospel and

Western Culture. Grand Rapids MI: Eerdmans, 1986.

Nouwen, Henri. *In the Name of Jesus: Reflections on Christian Leadership.* New York NY: Crossroad Publishing, 1989.

Orwell, George. *Nineteen Eighty-four: Oxford's World Classics,* ed. John Bowen. Oxford UK: Oxford University Press, 2021.

Parrott, Roger. *The Longview: Lasting Strategies for Rising Leaders.* Colorado Springs CO: David Cook, 2009.

Peterson, Eugene. *A Long Obedience in the Same Direction: Discipleship in an Instant Society*, 2nd ed. Downers Grove IL: Intervarsity Press, 2000.

Pollan, Michael. *In Defense of Food: An Eater's Manifesto.* New York NY: The Penguin Press, 2008.

Putnam, Jim. *DiscipleShift: Five Steps That Help Your Church to Make Disciples Who Make Disciples.* Grand Rapids MI: Zondervan, 2013.

Rosling, Hans. *Factfulness: Ten Reasons We're Wrong about the World—and Why Things Are Better Than You Think.* New York, NY: Flatiron Books, 2018.

Smith, Gordon T. *Wisdom from Babylon: Leadership for the Church in a Secular Age.* Downers Grove IL: VP Academic-Intervarsity Press, 2020.

Smith, Joshua K. *Robotic Persons: Our Future with Social Robots.* Bloomington IN: Westbow Press, 2021.

Stanley, Paul D. and Clinton, Robert J. *Connecting: The Mentoring Relationships You Need in Life.* Colorado Springs CO: NavPress, 1992.

Sweet, Leonard. *Rings of Fire: Walking in Faith Through a Volcanic Future.* Colorado Springs, CO: NavPress, 2019.

Thompson, Oscar. *Concentric Circles of Concern.* Nashville TN: Broadman Press, 1981.

Wilkes, Gene. *Jesus on Leadership: Timeless Wisdom on Servant*

Leadership. Carol Stream IL: Tyndale House Publishers, 1998.

Willis, Avery, and Moore, Kay. *The Disciple's Cross: MasterLife, Book 1*. Nashville, TN: Lifeway Press, 1996.